The Search for Galina

the search for GALINA

Thomas Shapcott

Chatto & Windus
LONDON

Published in 1989 by
Chatto & Windus Limited
30 Bedford Square
London WC1B 3RP

A CIP catalogue record for this book is available from the
British Library.

ISBN 0 7011 3320 1

The author gratefully acknowledges the following
books which contributed greatly to his research on
historical details for this novel: Harrison E. Salisbury,
The 900 Days: The Siege of Leningrad (Macmillan, London);
Sergei Varshavsky and Boris Rest, *The Ordeal of the Hermitage:
The Siege of Leningrad 1941–1944* (Aurora Art Publishers,
Leningrad/Harry M. Abrams Inc. New York); John Erickson,
The Road to Stalingrad (Weidenfeld & Nicolson, London);
John Vader, *Red Cedar* (Reed Books Pty Ltd, Sydney).
Judith Wright's poem, 'The Precipice' is
reproduced by permission of Angus & Robertson, Sydney.

Photoset by Rowland Phototypesetting Limited
Bury St Edmunds, Suffolk
Printed in Great Britain by
Mackays of Chatham plc, Chatham, Kent

For Rodney Hall and Göran Tunström

'A question to you,' said Columcille, to his strange visitor from another realm. 'What used this loch we are looking at to be in the old time?' 'I know that,' said the young man. 'It was yellow. It was blossoming, it was green. It was hilly. It was a place of drinking. It had silver in it and chariots. I went through it when I was a deer. When I was a salmon. When I was a wild dog. When I was a man I bathed in it. I carried a yellow sail and a green sail . . . I know not father nor mother. I speak with the living and the dead.'

John Sharkey, *Celtic Mysteries*

ONE

MORETON BAY

The Big Scrub: 1600 square kilometres of rainforest in Northern New South Wales, the greatest natural reservoir of ecological wealth in Australia, dense with the richest stands of timber, such as Australian red cedar (Toona australis), *the 'red gold' of legends; or with whole civilisations of birds of the forest, birds of the canopies, birds that nested in the mid-point hollows of the lower branches, in the crow's-nest ferns, the staghorn or elkhorn ferns and orchids far above the moist composting forest floor. There were forest animals, aerial or ground shuffling, and reptiles or insects stranger than any dream or legend.*

The big scrub was cleared; it was burned to the ground.

Today, there are no pockets of rainforest larger than a handkerchief.

Moist-eyed cattle graze and look up slowly from the grasslands that were once cathedrals of quiet and shade.

As Louise Tiffany Daley wrote in her book Men and a River: *'Rare trees – rosewood, tulip, sandalwood, and white beech, all prized by the cabinet-makers – were burnt in the great conflagrations which could be seen for miles. The smoke hung like a pall over the hills as the whole face of the country slowly changed, and the land which Captain Cook had praised in its "pure state of nature" was turned to other uses.'*

The red cedars were among the largest and greatest of Australian trees: in the Big Scrub they were excelling – over a thousand years old, often with bases ten foot thick, their great buttresses were indeed

3

cathedral-like and inspiring. 'The dreadful beauty and unreality of the forest was a subconscious fear they tried to subdue in wild, drunken sprees. Existence was always close to the knife-edge of disaster from a falling tree or in the raging creeks at floodtime,' wrote Louise Tiffany Daley.

Red cedar: red gold. It is a paradox in itself. The lust for the tree led to the destruction not only of the tree but of its entire habitat. There will be no more cedar industry. They have destroyed the forests. And yet, what we admire firstly and with a curious reverence, is the polished inner heartwood, the timber itself. That is its own magic. I have seen surly faces open with vulnerability and wonder as they uncovered the red cedar dining table inherited from grandparents and kept always under a blanket; I have seen the rough-fingered sons of farmers stroke a cabinet piece polished with their own hands as if they fondled more than wood. Indeed, in parts of Australia to mention the words 'red cedar' is to generate a sort of spirit of myth that exists hardly at all in our currency. Perhaps only the name 'Ned Kelly' is similar in its capacity to evoke some quickening of the spirit, some outreach to origins and ancestors still wild among us.

Red cedar is to be my theme. My subject is to be the history of the Big Scrub.

David Cumberland: *The Big Scrub: A History*
(Bullion Press, 1985)

4

I

David paused. There were only two cars on the island. There was only one sandy strip of road, from the jetty to the beach huts on the other side. Parked by the wooden butt of the structure he noticed a different car, battered enough to have the island look, but definitely a stranger. David examined it closely, opened a door, sniffed. Apart from a yellowish newspaper on the back seat it was anonymous enough. He shrugged, he refused to allow himself to feel crowded.

Reaching his own track to the little cottage he paused. Something caught his eye where the mangrove swamp was now drowning in risen mist. Trespass. He shoved forward. Someone in a sort of cloak, or was it a blanket thrown over the shoulders?

'Looking for me?' His own voice sounded hoarse, unused; aggressive enough.

The figure turned. It raised a hand, then shambled towards him.

'Ask me a question?'

'Who the hell are you and what are you doing here?' Before he realised it, David responded to the stranger's request, twice over.

'Fair enough. Thank you.'

Now he was closer, David could see it was indeed an old grey army blanket. Out of its shroud poked a round face with carroty hair in a wad of loose curls. A boyish face that could be forty-five or twenty-four.

'The name's Clyde. Clyde the Carter, that's what I get called. Clydesdale carter, daggy garter, dog and cat eater. Only joking,' he added, curling his milky face into hillocks and buckles. 'I'm over here because it's the full moon,' he added. He snorted and coughed, spat phlegm, then broke into giggles, almost losing his blanket to reveal a pallid shoulder. 'Night fishing.'

'This is my end.'

David's shoulders hunched, his face darkened. He was wearing only ragged khaki shorts. His dark skin had become tight, his nipples were buttons. This had always been unchallenged territory. Last year at this time he and Deirdre had gone spearing mudcrabs, squelching in gumboots. This was personal territory, only nominally public.

'This is nobody's property,' the other said simply. 'You feel threatened?'

'I'm telling you to clear out.'

'Look at the sea. Y'know it's teeming with fish. Do you think what I take from the sea matters? Can you eat all of it? If you can, then you're a bloody marvel. I dips me lid. But if you're that special, son, then Clyde the Carter's no big threat. Crumbs from your table, feller, crumbs.'

The mist seemed to smother the trees now. It was moving fast, with that strange silence about it, like a white cloak. Friendliness or mockery? David found himself unwillingly intrigued. He last spoke to another human four weeks ago, when he came over to the island. His limbs had a strange stiffness. Had he slept for days on end? When did he last swim? Once he had been an otter, a fish. With his gleaming swarthy skin he once had been the first to begin training in the swimming season, the first to have a magnificent tan.

This other's skin was so pallid; against David's it looked disturbingly unnatural.

'How did you get here? When did you come? When did they let you out?'

'A triad of questions now? You owning or asking?'

'Me? No, mate,' David's voice was gravel. 'I don't want anything, not a thing. Except peace and quiet. And to have the privacy of my own bit of mangrove and beach.'

'Yours, is it? And the mist here: that yours? Or the mangroves – did your own ancestors name them? And the crabs, boy, the mudcrabs, eh? That's what you're thinking, go on, admit it. I see through you:

down to trap mudcrabs, I hear you thinking, the jennies that the law would impound, down to trap them and sell them in the pub over at Cleveland. That what you're thinking? Could be right.'

But it was clear he was not equipped for crab-hunting. He sat down on a fallen trunk of banksia that had re-rooted itself. He had a crooked grin. Bad teeth. Or were they, too, only crooked?

'So what's your moniker? Or do you keep secrets?'

'Yes, I keep secrets.'

David rubbed the bristles on his chin. His thick fingers absently explored eyes, nose, ears. He licked dry lips and tasted salt. When had he last eaten? But the other's question still hung with its terrible goodwill over him. When had he last heard someone use the expression 'moniker'? When had David, himself, been so transparently innocent? 'I'm David Cumberland. I live here.' He jerked his shoulder in the direction of the red cliff, now sullen in moonlight. 'Up on the hill.' But he had to explain. The silence demanded. 'At least, in the school holidays.' Snared again. 'I'm a school teacher.'

Clyde the Carter slapped his thighs with disbelief and laughter. 'And I'm the Lord of the Moonshine! No, but seriously,' he grabbed David with a cold fist, 'there'd be stranger things. A school teacher; well and why not? A big black devil like you: I can see you keeping the little devils in their place fair enough. Shove you in a shirt and tie – it'd be a white shirt too. Am I right in that?'

'I'm on leave.' David felt the need to reassert his command of territory. He slouched down beside the other in ostentatious informality. 'And if it's any interest to you, I'm a bloody good teacher: history, geography, English. But you shed all that like a second skin, when you cross the bay to this island. Least, I do.'

'That's the island speaking in you. That's how it gets you in. Welcome aboard.' Clyde shook his hand formally, with a disturbing proprietorship.

'Welcome to you too,' David spluttered, surprised into a grin. 'You've got to be new here. What brings you over? Got relatives? Friends? You didn't get taken with the ads they put out when they subdivided the big swamp?'

'I've been here seven years.'

David stood up. 'Don't believe you!' Only a dozen houses and David's was the newest. Impossible. He looked hard at this Clyde the Carter. The stranger's small eyes were squinting, but they were blue as ice-splinters. No, impossible. He leaned against the tree – his tree – and contemplated the stranger who remained seated as though he were safely ensconced in a favourite chair.

II

The red cedar forests are forgotten, but not forgotten. Early descriptions of initial European contact with the stands of giant cedar still resonate and fill us with a sense, not of our loss and deprivation, but of something marvellous, so that we dream of discovering the lost paradise in some far reach of a National Park, some gully neglected or inaccessible to timber getters, some yet to be discovered Eden of virgin territory.

This is how Alexander Harris, in the 1840s, described the cedar territory and his responses: 'The costly and fragrant cedar was at this time a common forest tree in the shady recesses and beside the cool stony creeks of this vast old mountain . . . Some of these trees were noble-looking objects, with their great spurs running out at the butt like the buttresses of a castle; and when one of them fell before the axe, what a body of timber it crushed down before it, and what an opening it made in the brush! . . . The wood of the trees generally where we were cutting was very flowery and variegated, and the colour very good: when first cut, nothing could exceed the splendid crimson of some of the planks. There is a very fragrant scent from it, of which, however, a person working among it soon ceases to be sensible. Another singular and beautiful peculiarity is, the flame it yields in burning. Laying on the fire of a night sometimes a heavy outside slab in its green state, I used to observe it, as it were, melt gradually away in an almost imperceptible flame of indescribably beautiful pink; the flame

itself looking more like mere light than fire . . . If any man can without
exaggeration at night say he is as tired as a dog after a hard day's run, it
is the cedar-sawyer. A striking peculiarity of the class is their colour, or
rather deficiency of all colour. A few months' residence and hard work
in the brush leaves most men as pallid as corpses . . . These logs being
freighted to Sydney and on to England are cut up in timber-yards as
they are wanted. It is far from unlikely, reader, that the very table thou
art now reading on is a part of the thews and sinews of one of these
stately gallants of my old mountain woods.'

David Cumberland: *The Big Scrub: A History* (ibid)

*

David's history of the Big River country and the great logging sagas
had received dutiful reviews in the Northern Rivers newspapers and
one brief mention in the *Sydney Morning Herald*, but not much more.
Four years' enterprise. But he had told himself that acclaim was the
least part. The job was done. It was out. And there had been at least
one enjoyable and surprising spin-off. David had been asked to
arrange a segment of the itinerary for a small group of visiting Soviet
writers. It was part of some official cultural exchange and he had been
released for the week from his new desk job in Adult Education.
Someone remembered David and his book when Vladimir Smolich,
one of the visiting poets, insisted on seeing Australian rainforests and
the red cedar. Vladimir Smolich was, it turned out, famous in his own
language for his great epic poem about reafforestation, which had
been likened to the paintings of Isaac Levitan; it was, the local
organisers were instructed, a masterpiece. Smolich, in requesting this
segment of the itinerary, was making a significant gesture in cultural
relationships. He had researched in Leningrad as much as he could on
Australian trees, so different from the birch and pine forests of the
Baltic plains; his interest was genuine. David had leapt at the assign-
ment. He had even memorised some words and phrases of Russian,
though there would be, he was assured, an interpreter.

For David the project in itself was an adventure. To be used,
stretched: he enjoyed nothing better. Most of the time these things
remained bottled up, almost out of reach. Sometimes he wondered if
Deirdre, his wife, knew that this inside, locked part of him was the
most real. She never confessed to having finished his book.

When David first met the visiting party of three, he was greeted as an
author himself. It was the most enjoyable flattery. They were pretty

much what he had been warned to expect: large, pale and pasty from a direct flight out of arctic Moscow to summer Australia. The interpreter Gregor Volkovich from the outset did all the talking. It was only when Volkovich dozed off in the front seat beside David that Vladimir Smolich briefly addressed him, though David had noticed, through the rear view mirror, the way Smolich's restless eyes absorbed the swift passing landscape with a look, David thought, of magnetic intensity, as if mentally photographing everything.

They stopped for the night in Byron Bay and after a rather uncomfortable meal in the restaurant of the Poinsiana Motel David was relieved when Gregor Volkovich announced that travel fatigue had taken its toll; he would retire and look at Australian television. He had been told the commercial advertisements were technically quite sophisticated. His voice was doubtful. As Gregor rose the other two Russians also made to retire, but Vladimir Smolich paused, then returned to David. In his interpreter's hearing he said, 'One moment. I am sure that Gregor will not mind if I stay a while with Mr Cumberland. Mr Cumberland is a tree man, a writer, an expert on the rainforests of this area. I have read Mr Cumberland's little book. I have read it with attention.'

'Have you? Have you really?' He was surprised that Smolich was in command of such fluent English. 'I'm no real expert,' he added, 'though I have taken an interest in rainforest plant life. It began with my admiration for the local red cedar. There are so many fabulous yarns and stories, going right back to convict days.'

'Yes?' the interpreter Gregor stifled a yawn.

'My new friend Mr Cumberland will be full of instructive stories ...' Vladimir Smolich grinned warmly, intrigued by the glint of enthusiasm.

'David. Please, call me David.'

The two men smiled together. Gregor opened his arms so that David hurried on with his anecdote.

'And did you know that the last big stand of cedar forest to be logged was way up in the Atherton Tableland, behind Cairns? It was auctioned in London, long distance, and sold by Burns Philp for some amazing price. Only problem was: how to get it out. 1912 I think this was. Finally they decided to float the logs down the Barron River when it was in flood. Down they all went until they came to the Barron Falls. That's some waterfall. When these thousand-year-old giant logs got to the bottom, the newspapers of the day reported, there was no piece of timber larger than a matchstick.'

'Fascinating!' Vladimir Smolich sat down again across from him.

'Certainly Vladimir must stay to discuss these matters.' Gregor Volkovich beamed. 'We are anticipating from Vladimir Smolich another great poem of the forests. Although I do not yet see how he will make an Australian rainforest appealing to readers in his own country. That,' Gregor thumped the other on the shoulder, 'is where the genius and talent are called in.'

'There may be in Mr Cumberland's stories and tales some clue, some parallel that can be used to illuminate the universal laws of peace and brotherhood.' Vladimir smiled. 'My listeners will learn of an exotic world certainly, but I hope one where our understanding joins hands, where we recreate the mysteries.'

'Vladimir's poem,' Gregor explained, 'speaks much of the arboreal mysteries, of the triumph of man in reafforestation making a pact with the future conjoined with the past. Very eloquent, very famous.'

It was when they were alone, after Gregor Volkovich and the other, silent third member of the party retired, that Vladimir Smolich gripped David.

'You must tell me, quite quickly, this one thing: how far from this village, Byron Bay, is another town, Mullumbimby. Such a strange name, is it Aboriginal? I checked the road map you so kindly passed over. I have located it. Mullumbimby is a place of great importance for me.'

'You must be kidding!' Mullumbimby, to David's memory, was a sleepy hamlet just off the main road a few miles north. 'Why Mullumbimby?'

In Mullumbimby, explained Gregor in a whisper, lived one of the most famous poets of the Leningrad siege during the Great Patriotic War that began in 1941. Her name was Galina Darovskaya and she lived now in this remote village. He must see her, he wanted to kneel at her feet and pay homage. Though she had been expelled from the Writers' Union in the secret purges of the late 1940s when Stalin vented his fear and hatred of Leningrad, Moscow's rival city, Galina Darovskaya was revered by all who had known her; those remaining. They believed that if she returned she would be reinstated with honour. The Stalinist days were long over, though the path to reinstatement was difficult, and many believed her dead. Only Galina's return would open the possibility of her rehabilitation. It was something her old friends wished for her. There had been many rumours; these must be squashed.

Gregor Volkovich, a Moscow apparatchik, was not one of Galina Darovskaya's supporters; Vladimir Smolich himself had always written of her as of someone now dead. In truth, she was in danger of passing from living memory. Her words were long out of print. Only a few treasured copies and some typescripts were passed round among friends and admirers. He had been lucky, his mother had known her. He had obtained her present address, in remote Australia, from his mother some five years earlier. Though he had never written to her, he had begun his manoeuvres to be included in this rather insignificant cultural exchange. He was desperate to meet her.

The other writer in their party, Misha Pirogov, was not from Leningrad. Smolich shrugged: he was a man of no importance, this trip was merely some sort of reward.

It was eighteen kilometres north to Mullumbimby. The time was only 8 p.m. No problem; David offered.

When they turned off the Pacific Highway they drove the last six kilometres through narrow ranges and trees like white pillars. In the car lights all was mysterious and full of wooded depths. They seemed to twist into a rich and remote countryside, a place the Highway gave no hint of.

'Mr Cumberland is welcome. You are from here? You live in this district?' Galina Darovskaya surveyed David from the centre of her small crowded room.

David shook his head. Her accent was thick, almost impossible to understand. She was tiny, birdlike, but her back was straight and her thin face pointed up high cheekbones, beaked nose and black eyes. The eyes were so large in the face with its pallor and rogue streak of lipstick that David at first thought her much taller than in fact she was.

'You have the look,' she said. 'You are in part aboriginal?'

'Me?' David was prickly. 'That's Cornish. Black Cornish. My father was from Cornwall. There's no aborigine.'

'You are angry? Why should you be angry? My only friend in this town, she is aborigine, part aborigine. She has taught me much.'

'I'm not knocking them. It's just that they've nothing to do with me. Nothing.'

'You are perhaps uncertain. Many people in this country are uncerain. You would not be the first.'

Vladimir Smolich stood all this time, both hands clasping Galina's one, thin as paper. Twice he stooped to kiss it. In the pause he spoke to her rapidly and quietly in Russian. She motioned them both to sit down. There were two over-large chesterfields, draped with shawls and fringed black velvet and antimacassars. She insisted they sit. They sank back into the embrace of the wide arms and she hurried out to the kitchen annexe and returned bearing wafers and chocolate, with sweet tea in silver-handled glasses.

David had time to examine the room properly. In one corner was a large porcelain stove; it had pale tiles of a floral, stylised motif. He had not seen one like it. There was a samovar. A wooden chair – a throne, rather, with high, ornate back and brown leather padding, affixed with brass pins. Several small side tables, cluttered with objects: shells, dried leaves, photographs in silver frames, two small ikons. The wall had been painted dark blue, with a stencil design of green leaves. It was covered with paintings. They seemed amateurish to David: slightly Byzantine faces with huge eyes, portraits, some perhaps of saints.

There was a large, full-size portrait, clearly by another hand, behind the door, half obscured. Vladimir pointed to it.

'Galina. She was twenty. It is by Boris Ugarov. When I was a student I fell in love with Galina because of a reproduction of that painting. Now I am honoured to see the very work. To see the very woman.'

A girl of twenty, delicate featured, unsmiling, one gloved hand drawn up to drag a large kerchief around her chin. The eyes stared out of the canvas, as if the dark background (a wall? somewhere bleak and unprotected) forced the interior fires to a greater heat and intensity. Between the glove and heavy sleeves of the coat, pale skin was exposed, a wrist of porcelain fragility.

David looked at Galina Darovskaya more closely. Vladimir could not constrain himself. Although he once or twice turned to David, half apologetically as if to include him, the conversation burst and flowed in Russian, excited, sometimes full of laughter from both Vladimir and Galina, sometimes almost halting, query, answer, pause. The fate of some mutual acquaintance, David thought: dead, dead. It was a litany. And then, again, laughter, leaves rippling, exploding in updraught.

Suddenly Galina rose from the arm of the chesterfield and picked up a large shell. She pressed this upon David in her low, halting English, urged him to keep it.

'I cannot give you my poems. There is no English. A friend here once, she tried to make English, I was very grateful, I was very moved. But the English: it has no sound, it has no music. My poetry, it has music, it *is* music. That cannot be moved across language. This shell. Listen to the sound of the music in this shell. That is the sound of my poetry in my language.'

'And you still write poetry?' David, teacher of English, amateur chronicler in love with the impassioned histories of Manning Clark, heard his own voice as a stranger – its dryness, its inhibition.

She shook her head. 'Here there is no poetry. There is poetry, but not in my language. But Vladimir Smolich tells me he is to make such poetry. The young writers, they are so talented, they have such belief. He has told me his plans for the poem. They are exciting, they are impressive, he will write his poem and it will be wonderful. But me, my poetry is Leningrad, the streets and canals, the people of Leningrad, it is all Leningrad. That was my mistake. But the poems are still Leningrad. I have offered Vladimir Smolich the last poems. They were written twenty years ago. They are not published. Vladimir tells me someone will publish them. I do not know. I will keep my own copies. My Leningrad died forty years back.'

Gregor stepped in. 'Galina Darovskaya helped make that Leningrad transcendental. Now she has the opportunity – if she will take it – of renewing her sources. And her talents, which she will forgive me for saying are exalted. You see, friend David, we are about major business.'

Galina smiled, almost coquettish, then looked downwards.

'For Gregor, business and pleasure are duty and idolatry. He forgets I am an old woman.'

'You are an Immortal!'

'Our friend here does not understand such language.' She reached out her hand for David's, almost protectively. 'And neither, I think, do I.'

Gregor continued to look hard at her. Though her fingers still rested on his, David knew he was excluded.

That whole encounter now flooded back. In the dark of his small island retreat, David brushed salt from his eyes. He scraped a twig across sand-ripples. He had accepted this man who called himself Clyde the Carter into his own meditative silences. Clyde, wrapped in an incongruous grey blanket, seemed similarly abstracted. How long had they sat in this gathering dusk? And did it matter?

He would have to invite this new beach friend up to their shack on the hill.

'Come on,' he said, rising.

III

The island retreat had taken two years to build, mainly weekends and school holidays, Deirdre and the two boys helped; every plank, nail and fitting had to be brought across in the little motorboat that served as the island's ferry. They camped in tents on the site. Each stage of building was an achievement. *I can do it*, David kept telling himself. And he had. Those days were the best ones. Their no-grog agreement had been an easy triumph: truly, he had not needed a drop. He slapped nails through timber and sawed. It was all his own. Deirdre was supportive – they had been together in this.

Once the shack was built their urge to return to the island had, it is true, diminished. Christmas last year they remained in Sydney; it was such a long drive, the kids were older now and had a whole string of friends, Deirdre had things to catch up on. David had his big promotion. Despite that one terrible two-day bender – 'pigged out on Hogmanay' Deirdre had called it – they had not missed the island. The boys mastered the Sydney public transport system from Palm Beach to the Blue Mountains that holiday, they did not once whinge of boredom. The island shack remained unpainted.

These last two years drink had not seemed a problem at first, perhaps there were really no problems; Deirdre so supportive, always so supportive. All their friends remarked to David just how understanding and wonderful Deirdre was. Her concern tightened and choked, perhaps that was the start. She would do anything if she felt it helped. Even to the point of self-humiliation. If he took one beer bottle from the fridge, he could feel her tension behind him, though she never once reprimanded. Of course it made him brazen. Deirdre failed each test. She had not read his book.

David knew he was being unfair; the very consciousness of this unfairness increased the burden. He spat out into the night. He was standing on the edge of the wooden planking that formed the verandah. His new friend had gone to relieve himself in the outdoor toilet, a septic tank that seemed a natural home for spiders and often quite large lizards. Perhaps David should have warned Clyde. The sudden thought of that pale man bolting out with a black snake at his heels filled David with mirth. He gave a chuckle. It submerged the old nagging tensions. There was more to life than tensions. That was the island.

'Your verandah is the half-way place.'

Clyde the Carter dumped himself down on the edge, his bare feet trailing in the red dust, his blanketed body relaxing on the floorboards. There was no rail. The verandah, like the rest of the house, was built of bits and pieces, demolition timber, recycled planks. But it was solid, on low concrete stumps. The verandah was one of the main living spaces in summer.

'It is neither inside nor out, yet here you've got the best of both worlds all right.' Clyde's leisurely drawl was like a nudge. 'It's what I like about houses this part of the world. Open and airy, neither the one thing nor the other. Bring the outside in and the inside out.'

'Well, it's the sub-tropics impose that.'

David was standing, beer bottle in hand. The silvery mist on the mangrove flats shone below them. David had found his old lumber jacket. He had produced the beer.

Clyde the Carter, who had lived on the island for seven years, laughed at David's wonder. 'There you go; I've always been sensible,' he explained. 'Moment the sun sets, then I'm out and about. Not that there's far on this island to be up or about in.' He leaned back proprietorially. 'But the island has its ins and outs. My skin cannot tolerate the sun.'

He had bared his shoulder again. David noted his chest covered with blue tattoo marks. But the shoulders, freckled and pale, almost glowed in the wan light; unhealthy pallor, like the underbelly of a lizard.

'So I learned early not to fight the old man. Stayed inside till he cleared off, as he was bound to do.'

'You mean the sunlight?'

'You got it, the old man. He's in his savage mood this part of the globe all right. That's his right, but there are many more hours to play in, to be awake in. Daylight's only half the time.'

'A night owl, then?' David suggested.

'Now wouldn't you know it, this man's got insight.' But Clyde curbed his mockery. 'By the dark of your skin I'd say you're a day fowl, friend. A sunshine boy, a tanned wonder, and good health to you and the cancers.'

'I've got olive skin,' David admitted, 'and I can't remember a touch of sunburn in my life. It's the black Cornish in me. When I was younger I just about lived on the beach.'

'Aha, so you've the Celt hidden there? It will out, me boy, it will out when you least expect it – one of the night parties, one of the ceremonial evenings that get beyond themselves and into you.'

David laughed. 'Not me, mate. Though I've had a share of good parties. Get me started, I'll sing like a shower. With a bit of lubrication. Used to have some good parties,' he said ruminatively. He took another swig. 'Well. We all like to remember the good times. In my first year of teaching, that was the great year. I made the state rugby team, I was down the coast each weekend – I lived for the life-saving club – and the sheilas. It's youth itself is a kind of drunkenness – didn't actually drink all that much grog back then. Too busy keeping in training. Later though; well, lately.'

He paused. David was conscious he was now thirty-four.

Clyde the Carter lifted his bottle from the boards. Where it had been standing there was a damp circle. The first dew was beginning to settle around them. Did the man feel nothing? He raised the drink to David. Tolerance? Encouragement? Mockery? David was no easy target.

'Here. Come inside,' he suggested. 'Come and have a bite to eat. If there's anything.'

This would be their first visitor. It would be like dining with a ghost. Not really: there was something undeniably substantial indeed about this Clyde. He took up all the space around himself. How could this island have hidden him from David for so long? 'You're so vulnerable, David,' Deirdre had once laughed. It was when he was absorbed in his forest history book. 'You just don't see; you block out everything.' He had thought at the time it was not a claim or a protest; rather, her maternal protectiveness. It had its compensations. He had understood that his book, his research, was a private sort of thing, he had even insisted it be so – Deirdre or the boys would not dare go into his little study. And when the book was out, he had presented her with the first copy. 'No, I can't read it now – it is too close to all the strain of it,' she had said at the time. He said he understood.

Clyde shared a house, one of the seafront ones round the other side of the island. His cousin was Jim, the owner of the one ferry boat and mailman for the seven inhabited islands in this part of the large bay. Clyde often used Jim's boat for night fishing, or else there was the dinghy. His profession, he said, was net mender.

David laughed. 'Not much money in that,' he chuckled.

'That and the fish: I'm not a shadow yet,' Clyde squinted, 'and yourself?'

'As I said, I'm in the teaching game. Adult Education, actually. They transferred me upward, as they say. Class room to office. I saw it as a way to try out new ideas. You get tired; it burns you out, year after year. I'm not a conformist, you see. There was a whole rat-pack . . . when my book came out, one of them slammed it hard in the *Herald* – even my wife thought I was paranoid. Well, that's all in the past. The changeover was harder than I thought. Six months of hell, if you'd like to know. Anyway, right now I'm on this bit of long service leave. Seeing I'd finished building the main part of our shack, this seemed the logical spot.'

'Just you alone?'

'Deirdre has her job. She's the steady one – no, not whinging. Wonder you haven't seen Deirdre, every time she and the kids come up, they have long walks after dinner. Dusk. Perhaps you have seen them? Of course it's months since . . .'

'Aha, yes, the lady of the fair braids with the dark puppies.'

'Deirdre always plaits her hair on the island, it's the only time she does. She keeps me in place. Actually, she's terrific. Well, so you have seen her.'

'I remember her. No, not to be jealous. We've not spoken.' Clyde might have added more, but he pulled one side of his face in a grin, and gave a small shrug.

'That's unusual, she didn't speak to you. Dee's a friendly soul, chats to everyone.'

'You may not believe me now, Davey my new friend, but it's me: I never talk to people. You see, you've brought out something. One gets used to not speaking. Then it can rush out in a torrent.'

'You right for another bottle?'

David, too, after this month-long silence, found himself as garrulous as strangers beside each other on a long bus trip. Whatever may have tumbled out, it seemed a fair enough bet that Clyde the Carter would have no reason to hoard it.

'What's this about a book? You said you had a book come out?'

'It was torn to shreds in the *Sydney Morning Herald* review pages. I put too much into that book. Now I don't talk about it.'

They got on to fishing, and the best spots. They speculated on nearby Garden Island, which had once been a plant quarantine, and was now reputed to be overgrown with tropical fruit trees: jackfruit, durian, rambutan, carambola. It was unapproachable, guarded by an elderly caretaker, another loner. They had talked brands of beer, of ale, they discussed the plant life on the island. David rekindled an old ardour.

'I think I have a sort of affinity with this place,' he admitted. 'The very first time we came over, just off chance – damned awkward to arrange transport but someone said it was special. It was. We both loved the joint. Then we saw the FOR SALE sign.'

'Trees. Place. It's not everyone who says they feel an affinity. Most people laugh . . .'

'We looked at it. We both said *wham!*'

'No, don't retreat. Don't shut the book. You got a copy of that book of yours? Course you got a copy. What's its subject?'

David traced paths in the beer slop. He kept his eyes averted, as if expecting to blow.

'It's a sort of history – the old cedar days. They said it was too biased against the historical facts! Too passionate. I'm a greenie,' he announced.

'Don't feed me opinions. Give me the book,' Clyde commanded.

David knew there was a copy – two copies – in the other room.

'And don't apologise.'

David knew this reader would be sympathetic. When he handed over the book Clyde nodded. 'What a man! To have achieved this thing! All the research – I'll bet! You know, lad, it's not the point to pit yourself against perfection. But to have the resistance and the research. I dips me lid.'

A calm settled upon them. They ate the brown bread David had uncovered in the kitchen (how did it get there?); he opened a tin of sardines. They sat on two chairs at the wobbly table. They were no longer drinking, even the second bottle seemed too much. There had been quiet weekends in his lifesaving days, when it was wet, or end of season: a similar calm, a companionable silence when no one suggested grog. Coffee perhaps. Or tea, David remembered tea with its grandparent calm and placidity. And words, words were no longer imperative. In the small glow of the kerosene lamp the figure of Clyde the Carter was no longer curious, he just was. Of course he had been here seven years, he could have been here forever.

Sometime after midnight he got up. 'See you tomorrow,' he said as he jerked his grey blanket more firmly around his shoulders, grabbing the book to his chest.

David did not question the proposition.

He slept that night like a top, but he woke spinning, disoriented.

IV

The Forestry Commission of New South Wales published a bulletin for students on the Australian red cedar. It states: 'It is one of the few native deciduous trees, losing its leaves during the winter. Unlike many of the overseas deciduous trees, red cedar does not take on brilliant autumn colours before it sheds its leaves. However, when the new leaves appear in the spring, they are for a while a bright and distinctive copper-red. At this time the cedar trees can be easily spotted from a distance – a feature which helped the early cedar getters locate new trees and groves. The heartwood from old trees is a deep red, though in young trees it is often pinkish. It has a distinct and pleasant 'cedary' smell; it is usually straight grained with marked annual growth rings, giving it a distinctive and beautiful figure; it is light in weight (it is one of the few native trees whose logs will float in water); it is very durable and resistant to decay; is soft and easy to work; takes an excellent polish; and has a fine and natural lustre. Its major defect as a timber is its softness, and it can be easily dented.'

One could add that red cedar is also resistant to insect pests such as white-ant infestation or borers. It is a tree like any other, but unlike any other it carries in its heart a rich secret. You would not know, from the grey and scaly bark with a red outer and whitish inner layer, that this is the timber of most astonishing and perfect beauty, resembling rich marble that inspires us to perfection. It would have been better, and more clear, had early botanists or even timber getters given it one *of its Aboriginal names:* woolia, *or* woota; mumin *or* mugurpul. *As it is, the common name, red cedar, is easily confused with the so-called 'Western red cedar' coming into the country from North America, and that timber is grossly inferior.*

David Cumberland: *The Big Scrub: A History* (ibid)

*

David made a point of being around when Jim the ferryman pulled into the jetty at 11 a.m. with the island mail and four sacks of potatoes and other assorted groceries.

'Oho? Y'r up and battlin', Davey, me boy!' He gave David a sideways squint. 'Six loaves of bread all up I left on tick but either the possums got 'em or you're a lousy eater.' He threw the rope and David scrabbled up for it, then tied it deftly. 'Got ya the beer and rum on tick too. And all that milk and eggs. Gotta get some protein, some vitamins, some carbohydrates into y' and that's one way. Keep the pecker up.'

'What rum?'

'Y' didn't find the bottle of Bundaberg? Well strike me dead, maybe it wasn't possums, though whoever goes across to your antbed headland? Sure you didn't drink it? Course ya drunk it. Flat like a fish, on the camp stretcher, each time I come; though I hollered and hollered.'

'I've been here one month. A full moon last night. A full moon the night I came over. And, you know, it's pretty much a blank. Really wiped myself out this time . . .'

'Don't know about wiping yourself out. Revved yourself up that first week. That time you walked in when we were over at Hazel's; staggering like a loonie with that case of champagne. Bloody champagne! Must be the first case of champagne to go on this island. Come to think of it, maybe Jan the Jenny could be a secret champagne sozzler. Never seen no empties, but.'

'That what happened to the champagne? Thanks for reminding me about the champagne. I remember now. It was given to me the arvo I left work, threw it in the boot. Christ, I'd forgotten even taking it out . . .'

'I took it out, buster. Over at Cleveland. You bailed me up at the pub there, druv straight up from Sydney, you said. You were dead set on getting across, like you were jack of the mainland; like you had a real set to escape. Got you over round midnight. *And* unloaded you, grog, tucker and everything down to the last snotrag. You were pissed as a newt before you ever reached Cleveland. Don't know how you ever slipped through the booze-bus networks the cops set up down the turnoff. Friday night! That's their regular cash banking night with the booze-bus.'

'I drove like an angel. Always do when I'm pissed. Mind goes into overdrive, reflexes take over. Superb conditioning.'

'Lots of practice.'

'Smile when you say that, Jim. No, I'm not aggro. Can't understand people who have no road sense – you know, scan the next mile ahead, side roads and rear vision mirror, flow of the traffic, any small anomalies, never slip out of the radar tracking gear in your mind . . . driving at night's easiest, you see cars coming miles ahead. Nine hundred kilometres.'

'Y'r a great drinker, Davey boy.'

'You know what that champagne was? It was special, a gift. It was Russian. Georgian champagne.'

'So you told us. You told us and told us.'

'I did? Well, if I did then that's all right. Did I say where it came from, who it came from?'

'You don't really remember, David, do you? All the great mystery, the hassle? Not even the fight in the kitchen?'

'Give us some clues.'

'About that fight?'

'No. What I said.'

'Well you did yatter on about your Russians. How you took them out to the red cedar stands around Lismore and up Murwillumbah. Out into the rainforest. Freaked them out, thought they wuz in Tarzan country, that's what you said. Then you went on about one of 'em, Ivan, or Vladimir or something. That's when we started into "Ivan Skavinsky Skavar".'

'No Galina?'

The other shook his head.

'I hope that the stuff – the Georgian champagne – tasted all it's cracked up to be. That's the trouble when you're shickered, might as well drink metho.'

'You ended up drinking sweet sherry, that night. Over at Tim's place.'

'Makes me want to vomit.'

'That too. You were a treat that night, boyo. Opened me eyes, I can tell you. Here we all sized you and the missus up years back, time you first came over: nice quiet school teachers, into the self-improvement, into the herbal tea and lettuces, back to nature and self-reliance, boy scout stuff. We respected you for it, don't get me wrong. Tell the truth, even had a sneaking admiration of your short-cuts with the construction. You've got a knack, boy, give you that. Gave you five more years, meself, five at the maximum. The kids will get bored, turn into teenagers overnight. Wife will get tired of the sandflies and mozzies. Hubby will curse that there's no corner shop, no pub, no new company. Once a year check-over from now on, I said. Then a last minute spick-and-span, a paint job, and they'll sell it. They'll have discovered Pacific Cruises, or Bali, or Europe by Package. Mark my word, I said. That's how it goes with lots of 'em.'

'And instead I turned up, pissed and permanent.'

'Permanent? You don't mean it. You're not the type.'

'Well, I'm here. And I'm on long service leave.'

David laughed. They had reached his shack now.

'So I've clearly disproved your convictions. Where's that rum you talked about?'

They recovered the empty bottle. It was under the tankstand, among litter and rubble. Too many bottles. Jim the ferryman kept scratching his head, but this island had many burnt-out cases.

David finally worked out the gist of his four-week sojourn – the midnight arrival, over-tensed, over-drunk, over-anxious at the decision itself (something barely admitted) and the last scene with Deirdre. Then the champagne party and another blank out.

He had turned up at most of the dozen houses over by the beach, in the succeeding days, talkative and hearty, explaining whatever non-sensical thing flowed through his head, being fed and talked to, being looked after. Getting everything out of his system. That's how he must think of it: sluicing out all the storage, all the corrosion and muck. Even Jan the Jenny, notoriously reclusive, threw a party, Jim reminded him; she even found a new red wig to put on, long Clara Bow ringlets. Surely David could remember that? Yes, he did remember something about that.

No, some things it's best not to remember.

He didn't ask himself. What's the point? Somewhere, deep, he knew he had been through a necessary purging. It was instinctive: almost impersonal. He was an instrument, a chalice. He had often felt that, an impersonality. After the ritual purging, he had come through.

It was only after Jim left that David remembered he had not even asked the immediate question: who was Clyde the Carter? How come Clyde had not been encountered?

After all, in retrospect, he realised, Jim had been describing just about everyone in the island community and David's almost ritual visit to each shack and bungalow. Had Clyde been there at one of the booze-ups?

No. Even through sludge and horror and self-absorption, David knew Clyde would be recorded. He knew his own retrieval system. That was why he was a perfect drunk-driver. That's why he could coast a whole month in some psychic overdrive. Clyde, yesterday, was clear and specific. Almost, indeed, the key, the pivot to this new clarity, this new self-determination. Clyde was not the sort of presence that fades out of memory; not at all. There was something unexplainable in him.

Not even the hint of that anaesthetising thirst. Only the old, persistent fuzzy tongue. What was his breath like? This had been the worst, the most continuous. And the build-up: long, slow and inexorable, not at all like any previous time when it had been a sudden switch-off, a sudden wipe-out. Perhaps Deirdre was, as ever, the key? How far could you run? How deep could you tunnel? That last afternoon, with the kids sitting there in front of the TV set with the drama all round them, louder than *Homicide*; Deirdre herself, those panic eyes behind her anger, her 'please be sensible, David, just be sensible'; and all the while there was this ratchet force inside, urging him, almost tugging his body; *up to the island, the island, it's the only place*. And beyond that was the plan already formulated – he had even known the drive-in bottle shop where he intended to stock up (forgetting the champagne stacked in the boot). And at first it had been so clear, so simple; a calm announcement (rehearsed for a week): 'Well, I've decided to take two months of my long service leave. Let them stew in that Department, let them transfer me back to classrooms . . .' Deirdre at first had been bewildered. How could she arrange a similar leave break? at such short notice? No, he had said, it's just me. Me alone. Saying it, how could he realise the earthquake danger, the seismic upheaval? Deirdre and the two boys still clawed at his conscience. And in the end, there had been their silence. Of course it was not sullenness. At the time he had only an immediate self-justifying anger. Their silence, though, had won out. It lasts longer than noise, and will not be smothered.

He was not yet out of danger. The island, though, had been moving into a different perspective. It was now Clyde's territory.

V

Of course he did find out. David made a point of checking with Jim later in the afternoon when the three MacKenzie kids were brought across in the boat from Russell Island, where the small school was located.

Clyde the Carter was genuine. He was a distant cousin of Jim's, turned up out of the blue ('Seven years ago? Yairs, guess time flies over here.') saying 'not a peep, not a peep out of me'. Jim, tell the truth, hardly noticed him. Every morning, there'd be fish fresh in the refrigerator. Jim had his own power generator; there was no electricity on the island, most people used Portagas. Clyde would have gone to bed at the crack of light in his sleep-out, no matter how hot the day got. Occasionally they sat together in the evening. Jim often took the pool players across to the pub at Cleveland, or to the drive-in. Clyde was never one of the group.

So Clyde was a cousin. Someone who became truly alive only when the sun was down. Three years ago he went out and bought his own dinghy with outboard motor. Jim had been impressed at his saving power, made him realise Clyde had a whole hidden world that included sales contacts, fishing connections. He was a great fisherman, had a real instinct for locating schools of mullet, mackerel, tailor, squire. Sniffed them out as if they were brothers, Jim added.

That was his dinghy, down by the three creeks, it was usually tied to one of the paperbarks, had David seen it? Sometimes he used Jim's big boat; Jim reckoned that was fair trade for the fish.

Jim was at most mildly surprised that David had only just run into Clyde.

'Had to happen sometime,' was all he said, as if David had been always the tourist, negligent and self-absorbed, or as if Clyde had his own part in this, determining who should or should not be a party to his nocturnal existence.

'Clyde's okay. Don't misunderstand me. Actually I really should get to pick his brains more often,' Jim admitted. 'But you know how it is. Sort of bullies you, if you like.' Jim sneezed and thumped himself. 'Yes, bless me, well Clyde's half my size, but he does have this – what is it? – energy. Hah! Seeing he sleeps half his life, and the best time of day – *all* the day – guess that's not a surprise neither.' Jim could not offer much more, except his implicit fear and admiration and a generous puzzlement. Family.

Clyde turned up again, just after sunset. This time he was more conventionally garbed: a dark green windcheater and matching corded trousers. The pale features lost colour against the sharp moss colours. But his prominent features – lips, ear tips, eyebrows and the cold climate cheeks and the ice-blue eyes – these had become over-sharp and emphatic.

'Davo, grab a greatcoat and a rod, this moon's magical.'

He threw down on the kitchen table fresh fish – a squire, a snapper. 'Hoe into this when you're peckish, mate. But come and have a feast with your eyes on the moon.'

David rose up grinning, slightly incredulous. He himself had stood, on occasion, just to gaze at the moon. But you don't say it. You don't invite others. You hoard it.

'There. There, now. Whadda you think of that!'

There was no mist. Clear moonlight and shadows down on the flats among mangroves reflected the strange silver where at day everything would be dense green, dark, or blue water. Only the sand strip seemed untransformed: duller but substantial. The balance of space had turned skywards.

'That's what we're made of, just as much as of sunlight!'

Clyde chuckled. Then he led David back onto his own verandah like a guest. He sat down.

'It's not everyone I take out to make prayers to the moonlight,' he noted. 'Jim me cousin, now. Fine man, but not a moonlight man. Not even a proper fishing person, though he's spent half his life on the water. Fish see Jim and turn somersaults, play skipping-rope with his line, make a breakfast of his bait and nibble round the hook like it were chicken bone.'

'Fish see you and come running into your hand. That's what I'm told.'

'You been asking? They say fishing's a knack. I don't know. Had it since I was a kid. Y'see why I ended up here, on this island? In the old days it must have been paradise.'

'It's a big stretch of water, all right,' said David, warming up, 'and it's got a lot going for it, I'll say that. The big sand islands – Stradbroke and Moreton – nothing like that down in the Hawkesbury or Sydney harbour areas. Somehow it seems more open up here. You know the first time I was ever up here, in Queensland? My uncle – Dad's brother – took me on a camping trip, I must have been twelve or thirteen. We went up to a place called the Bunya Mountains, in from the coast back up there,' he nodded vaguely in a westerly direction. 'And we camped by a little creek, with sandy reaches, in this great tall forest up in the mountain. Full of bunya pines – araucaria – like the monkey puzzles. They have these great clusters of nuts in a cone like a beehive or those paper-wasp nests, only as large as a giant's head.' David's eyes glistened with the recollection.

'Well, we were lucky. They only bear fruit every seven years, and this was the time. The place was full of them, littering the ground. My uncle told me how the aboriginal tribes used to have great feasts and ceremonies at those times; call other tribes from a hundred miles away and tribal wars and fights would be forgotten. They just hoed into the nuts. What they could not eat – raw or roasted – after three or four days, they'd bury in the shallow sand of the creek, then go off hunting wallabies and kangaroos. When they came back after a day or two, whoosh to the fires and meat's on the menu. Accompanied by tasty seedling bunya sprouts. And the whites thought they were dumb, unskilled in agricultural know-how. My uncle taught me a lot that trip. But best of all, he taught me to look around, and to enjoy the bush and then the beaches. Needed no second call to get me surfing and splashing; I was a fish all right.'

'And your uncle was the big event in your life?'

'He wasn't like Dad. Dad was the silent one. Uncle Clem was like me

31

a bit, though he was nuggety and real out-of-doors type. Never shaved. Always had stubble. And his skin was as rough as an ironbark. Brown as a berry.'

'And he taught you native lore?'

'Too right he did. Knew everything about bushcraft. Guess I worshipped him in a teenage sort of way. Made it hard on Dad. Used to call me 'Nig'. Somehow, from him, it seemed affectionate. I never let anyone else use the term. Absolutely.'

'They say the local natives were great men, great sturdy fellows here. Gentle as wallabies, brave as a sea eagle.' Clyde stroked his own gingery chin. 'Jim says I go crazy with similes. Doesn't know what a simile is but that's what he means. I always believed that we're roped into nature, why not bring it indoors in our talk, in our name making. You're a school teacher, I'm not such a challenge with words. You don't run scared from words. I read your book. Good on you.'

David found himself uncomfortable, his mind promptly sat on the edge of its desk and took the initiative. Clyde, for instance. Clyde really was transparent, quite transparent – one of those word-drunk kids in the front row who cannot shut up; they never get things right but are full of sudden insights just at the moment you give up on them. Too impatient to concentrate, too top-of-the-head to learn discipline.

David had learned discipline. He was choked with discipline. His western suburbs accent still surfaced occasionally, and the grudging speech; but he had also been determined. He had enjoyed discovering for his pupils recent Australian poetry – Dawe, Beaver, Murray.

'That book is water under the bridge. I stopped working on that subject two years back.'

'Isn't there a drop to offer?'

'Sorry.' David clambered up for two beer bottles. As he sat down again he rubbed his chin. 'I better watch out. I'll be losing my reputation.'

No. Sometimes he hated the false heartiness, the mirror of his speech patterns reflecting back. Sometimes he despised his bright defensiveness.

'Your reputation, Dave boy? Think I can place that. Here, let me give you a riddle: what's dark as a shadow, light as a fire and drunk as a late harvest? It's you. It's you, the school teacher who lives up on red antheap. That's what we call this place. You know that? Red Antheap.'

'Ha ha. Funny. Not much of a riddle, though. And what's this all about, Red Antheap?'

'Don't get shirty. Here, let me tell you another riddle.'

'No, thanks.'

'You schoolteachers hear them all. Dingo riddles. Irish riddles. You haven't stopped working on that cedar subject at all. You don't fool me. Know what's interesting? It's a book about *you*. It's about you, not some bloody rainforest native.'

'You're a bit of a mystery, Clyde. I think it was dangerous to give you that book. Nobody else had noticed.' David rose and stretched, then went down on his hunkers, closer to Clyde. 'No, I'm not flattered – and you're not flattering me. Good. We'll leave it at that. I like someone who is different. Full of surprises. I like that.'

'I'm one step further than you, friend David Cumberland. I like *myself*. I enjoy liking myself. You're rubbed raw, like that pitsawn timber. So I'll forgive you your patronising tone at this moment.' Clyde caught David by the shoulder, then released his grip. 'Guess I've taken a shine to you. You're one person on this island that knows what I'm getting at. You make good conversation. And a pretty good, muddled slanging match with history. And you make good silences.'

'You're a strange one.'

'Good. So we're partners, then?'

With the truthfulness of mock formality, they shook on it. Then each turned to his beer and sipped thoughtfully. Clyde tossed his dregs out into the darkness.

'Man. This is the night you must out on the water. Fishing, we'll now go fishing.'

Why not? And what did it matter that there were already two large fish stacked in the Portagas refrigerator? Something had begun.

'I'll come with you.'

VI

'I wanted you out on the water so we could talk. I can say things here.' Clyde's voice seemed strange in the small space of the boat. The moonlight filled the ripples around them with shadows and phosphoresence.

'Let me tell you something. Nothing to do with anything at all. Or perhaps it's to do with everything. You with me?'

David caught the challenge and the hesitation.

'I look at you, and I look at me,' Clyde continued. 'We are utterly different. More than that: we are polarities. Me, fair as a salmon-splash in moonlight. You, dark as bushfire stumps in the sun.' Clyde laughed at his own verbal invention. 'Yes, you and me, from the moment we stepped out and became ourselves – which is around the time hair sprouted in our armpits and our mothers grew wary of our voices – each of us, Dave, had to make some sort of pact with ourselves. We're the special ones. Your book tells me that. There are rules that we set – or maybe they're set for us. I'm not splitting hairs. But each one individually. There are private rules that we break at our own risk.'

'The social contract?'

'Never that. That's outside these rules. These are our personal rules. We are the special ones.'

'What are you getting at?'

'If we break these rules, we know. You've surely seen the sort of thing happen. In your book you describe the hunger for cedar. Those early timber getters were following quite individual rules, their own *geis*. Or just take a local, suburban example – you and a friend drive home from the pub. Two separate cars. You get home feeling supreme because the drive boosted your ego and your wits. You were in your own rules. He gets booked only three blocks from the pub.'

'How did you know?'

'He has broken his personal rule. He's gone into his death-zone. You've stayed in your sphere because your zone does not have the same danger signs. Your death-zone could be something quite different. When you break your rules, you'll know.'

'And *your* danger zone?'

'You never ask another man that. You can guess it if you like, but to know the secret sanctions is to gain power.' Clyde's face was a dim mask in the moonlight. 'I've become aware of my own death-zones. Sunshine. There, that's one. The only sunshine I can bear is like the way a fish sees the sunshine, through deep layers of water.'

'Does it help to know?' David dragged his fingers in the water.

'Perhaps not. We're ruled by passions, not awareness, matey.'

David eased his neck. The stars mocked his small tension symptoms.

'Your theory has a logic,' he conceded. 'Let's see, what I like best is its idea of a personal morality. That's what you're on about, isn't it? A personal set of good marks and bad marks – not a socially imposed one.'

'Yes. In the old Celtic beliefs, once you broke your *geis*, the aura that surrounded yourself and protected you, then you were open to attack. I like to see it as a sort of natural protective body fluid. Once it's broken the cancers can get in, or the external antibodies. Or your enemies.'

'Aha! So you *are* a prisoner of the Gaelic!'

'Not a prisoner. I had to try to explain myself to myself. Once you've found what works for *you*, you're in a position of power. Until I accepted the terms of my *geis* I got sunburnt like everybody else.'

'Not me.'

'Davey, why defensive? Your burns and scalds and suffering need not be the sun, but they're certain. You're rubbed raw.'

'You wouldn't know a thing. I can take care of myself.'

'Nobody says that unless they're uncertain.'

David tossed in another line. The sinker plopped in the darkness. A tug. His bait was instantly stolen.

35

'Protective auras! The only person I've known with a protective aura was Galina Darovskaya . . .'

The small ripples against the side of the boat echoed David's secure enunciation of the name – *Galina Darovskaya, Galina Darovskaya*. But it was a conspiratorial whisper. Clyde seemed almost deliberately inattentive.

'You think on the implications of the personal *geis*,' he said. 'There are boundaries, and we don't always know till we have to face them. For instance, do you think you could live with yourself if you had murdered a man?'

Clyde the Carter picked up the oars and rowed further. David snatched back his line. They reached the shadow of Garden Island. Dark high cliffs loomed. After the bright moonlight this crowded them in. Clyde let down the anchor.

'Well, there are obvious circumstances – starvation, for instance. Terminal cancer. Do you think you could kill a man? Have you actually asked yourself? Is that a forbidden thing? Or a possible one?'

David had curbed the temptation to laugh.

'These "rules" you spoke about. Some things, Clyde, are taboo for everyone.'

'You're already beginning to doubt that. You're already beginning to ask yourself.'

'Damn you. There was a woman I met once, not so long back, she went through the Siege of Leningrad. An incredible period. But she survived. At least in the same body. Leningrad was a city of three million before Hitler invaded. They were roped off, isolated, pilferers were shot on sight. Would you call that murder under such conditions? Well, I wonder.'

'Many would have found such rigorous acts disastrous for their personal life-zone. Many would. Others would take great satisfaction.'

'We can't imagine those times in those conditions, Clyde.'

'Starvation doesn't make plump bodies. There would even be some discovered they could become cannibals and still keep their life-zone intact.'

'But not Galina. Though she's obsessed by those times, that's certain. She said they made gruel by tearing off wallpaper and soaking it to get the old paste behind. It had been made from a sort of potato flour. They made jelly by boiling old boots, she swore it. Damn it; there is a natural repugnance, you bastard. You could tell the cannibals, Galina said. Why do you drag these things out of my memory? She said you could pick them. Full cheeks, sparkling eyes. A sort of greasiness. It was such a contrast to the dry pallor of starvation, she told me, or the bloated up dystrophy of those who tried to stave off things with water.'

'And who's to say . . . ?'

'Of course you're right. Who's to say what each of us might have done. But that's desperation, that's panic and fear and starvation. Ritual eating of human flesh is an utterly different matter, if you want to bring that subject up. Headhunters who ate the brains and kidneys and liver of their enemies did it for formal, ritual purposes. To appropriate the strength of their enemies. Or some of the aboriginal tribes here, where their witch-doctors gained spiritual strength and purity from certain ritual eating of flesh. To pass on the wisdom of the deceased elders. And that is quite different again from your little gothic theories of individual moralities, personal whatsis.'

'*Geis.*'

'Gaelic garlic.'

'Be careful, you're catching my tongue.'

Clyde was holding his thin line between the sensitive forefinger and thumb of his left hand. All the time in the world. They had been speaking out into the darkness, not towards each other.

'There's some strange parallels in magic,' he continued, 'some appropriations that crop up in whole different cultures. I'm not saying there's no large patterns. I'm saying that inside them there's individual rules and barriers. Me and you again. Our life-zone, our death-zone, quite different. My choice is still my choice and there's some things I do with impunity and to hell with all artificial rules that say different. It's what I mean when I say I'm my own man.'

'Lucky you.' David leant down, dissatisfied, and tossed out some bait with a scatter. Group movement under the water.

In the darkness under Garden Island the small dinghy bobbed gently. Clyde threw out another line. David remained crouched on his plank. He had not intended to mention Galina, he had promised not to betray her confessions. Here he had more than betrayed her, he had been forced into displaying her. He had believed her when she had begged for his silence.

'But we started with the personal limits, and the obvious criminality of murder, not of cannibalism,' David heard his own voice slap out across water. 'Were you thinking something specific? You weren't warming up for some confession, yourself, were you, Clyde?'

'Now there's the romantic imagination,' the other voice boomed back at him. 'There's no one I've had a mind to kill, Davey, and no one on this island I've got hooked into. Something I read, something I brooded a bit over. I read a lot, y'know. You can think aloud in a small boat, this dinghy. This is me favourite place for night fishing. And for thinking.'

'Gloomy.'

'Only a sun person says that. And you saying it is a betrayal of your own instincts. You see, I know you better than you know yourself, now, having learned you through your own writings. This place is like a well – the darkest place draws the sweetest water. Here, it's the darkest place draws in the sweetest creature. Don't get me wrong, Davey, I'm a creature of sweetness. I see you crouching there, thinking already you're caught with a straight out sea monster.'

David straightened his back.

'You haven't answered my question, Clyde. Why bring up the subject of death, not only death damn it, but murder?'

'Easy boy. I thought you were a speculative man. We live in a world of mass murder, violence, terror. There's any number of them. In my past maybe I've done wild things, or not so much wild as wilful. Perhaps I had to discover my own limits the hard way, and there's places where grand thoughts have run riot.'

'You asking my blessing on that? It's barbarian, it's old barbarian mayhem, eye for an eye, tooth for a tooth. It's regressive.'

'But I'm on your side. Locate your own *geis*.'

There was a sudden splash in the darkness. The small boat began rocking. Neither of them spoke until it had resettled.

'Look at that bloody dark hulk of the island, it's got its eye on us,' David said, more evenly. 'Clyde, if you've got conscience problems, that's your personal business. To drag me into it, to make me a father confessor, that's just a sort of blackmail. I'd rather not know, I'd rather not become involved.'

'There's more than one way of murder. There's suffocation, there's alienation, emotional starvation, there's indifference, there's brute selfishness.'

'And there's preaching, Clyde. You know something? You'd be the first preacher to land on our island. What's more, a preacher with the burden of a bad conscience.'

'Davey boy, that's a fine rhetoric, and a total misunderstanding in the grand manner. But I'm a patient man. We've got time. Tell you this – it's fine to hear the fire in your anger. A good sermon then? There's a place in the world for that, and what better place than upon the waters? But you might think of your *geis*. Maybe that and not blood mix is what is bedevilling you all these years. Did you know your book was about an inheritance only one people can lay claim to?'

David remained silent. One fish was enough.

'Now you've a taste for it.'

Clyde grabbed the oars and the boat moved out of the deepest shadow. The moon, now high, was past its full, and from the corner of his eye David had the sensation that a thread was connected, lines of light, from the bright dead disc above them to himself, to both of them, to the dipping and struggling dinghy. Why this sudden feeling of hostility? He was a fool; though perhaps Clyde was a greater fool, who knew?

And Clyde that big confident man, with the baby-white pallor and the adolescent tattoos, was he really asking for help, for boost, for confession? Or was it perhaps just some way of control, a netmender's ruse to get David to commit himself in some way?

Clyde, tugging firmly and well, manoeuvred the boat with quietness and skill.

A great boy, a young animal? It was David in one of his neurotic moods who was twisting things. The critic had called his book 'a passionately bad chronicle'. It would take more than Clyde's gibes to rattle him, after that. And, besides, nothing had been negotiated.

VII

David woke late. The immediate feeling was one of a curious refreshment. He felt good. Then the gnawing began. He spent half the day in a struggle of will. No, he was not thirsty. No he did not want to crack open another bottle. No, he had broken the barrier, he had crossed the border and did not want to go back into the swamp. There was too much to think of, to look forward to, he woke feeling so well, he realised, because on going to bed last night he had decided he would start work today on the verandah rails. He would do something. He would get going.

The rails were all there, ready, under the verandah. He had only to cut the supports and spend a half hour chiselling out the connections. By lunchtime, even alone, he could do it, and he knew well the sense of satisfaction which would follow. Perhaps this afternoon he would start the exterior painting too. Wasn't there undercoat in the kids' room?

There were two bottles in the small refrigerator, and another half dozen in a box under the kitchen table.

He would be able to make a start with the undercoat all along the walls facing the verandah. Tomorrow he would ask Jim the ferryman to see if he could hire the ladder again from over in Cleveland.

If he were to put another four bottles in the fridge now they would chill quickly. Warm beer was only for animals, or the desperate.

There was enough undercoat surely to do the entire exterior, though this old timber, so long exposed to the rough sun, soaked it up like a drink. And it was no use being parsimonious, that only meant more work, more undercoats. If he set-to today he would at least be able to calculate how far the cans here could go so if necessary Jim could bring over what extra was needed with the ladder. Perhaps he should start the painting straight away and leave the verandah rails till later?

He went to the kitchen and pulled out the brown carton. He managed to squeeze six bottles into the refrigerator. He took out the two fish. How could he eat that much? They had been scaled and gulleted. Good old Clyde.

What was Clyde really after? He had a way of making even this gutted fish sinister. 'I know you better than you know yourself.'

Ridiculous!

He should save the fish till dinner, ask Clyde over. If he cooked them in beer it might do wonders. In his amateur weekend cooking David went wild with experiment. Should he marinate them?

He opened the first bottle.

He reached for the opener and the second, but then stopped himself. No, he had made his decision, he must act. He went outside and rummaged for timber. He dragged out the long verandah railings from some colonial weatherboard workers' cottage. He measured the length. Not bad. He need saw off only a couple of feet and they'd go perfectly. He began measuring. That one bottle, he explained to himself, was just the drop needed. No more. Just enough to switch the ignition. If you kept in control like that, well drink was the best sort of stimulus, the best sort of sedative; hadn't it always been seen as medicinal?

The tiny gnawing inside was not to do with drink. What was it about Clyde? Was it the talk of murder and mayhem? That fanciful personal life-zone, death-zone bit? Was it the still gnawing pain David felt at having unwittingly let out those confidences about Galina? She, after all, could hardly be threatened by a Clyde. A comparable obsessiveness? David had entered her world and had promised, not doubting its reality.

And because she would understand the urgencies behind Clyde's words David felt both linked and excluded by these two people who had never met, and never would.

Clyde had read David's book.

Clyde would turn up again tonight. Why? Would he appear each night from now on? Would he sit like an incubus on David's shoulders, not to be shrugged off? Why did he assume, damn it, that David would always be here, or would welcome him? So he had read the book – it was as if he had taken something, not been offered it. David could make plans of his own, he could think of many things that might not include Clyde. He could go out tonight, visit some of the others – hadn't Sam offered to set up a game of poker any time, hadn't even Jan the Jenny offered to throw a Pavlova Party if everyone came in fancy dress, hadn't . . . ?

David was quick and accurate, if a bit slapdash, with timber. He enjoyed especially the challenge of doing it unaided. The long verandah rail was not difficult once the supports were firmly in place, it just needed a bit of patience as he fitted the slots and the angle.

The autumn midday sun came slanting through the lower branches of the ironbark trees. Their dappled shadow threw light like bubbles across his verandah. He leaned against the new rail to test it. Then he clambered onto it and sat, straddling. Strong enough, quite steady. He had timber to spare. He played with the idea of adding a series of cross beams.

The fourth bottle decided him. He was hard at work sawing the crossbeams, enjoying the sound of raw energy and the clean smell, still, in old pine. He did not hear the footsteps. He did not even catch the muttered curse as a suitcase thumped softly into the red dust not twenty metres down the track. He was absorbed in a clean final cut through two short beams, measuring the ten, nine, six, four strokes needed to complete the cut.

'Well, aren't you going to say "Welcome"?'

Deirdre stood upright then grabbed her cases again. 'Wonderful! Wonderful! You didn't see me?' She marched towards him. 'With this bloody suitcase? I called out, you know. Back down there. You're not still mad at me, David?'

She dropped the cases on the verandah. Covered with sawdust and grime, he let her snuggle in. She kissed him.

But hugging her in return, he was filled with her smell. He brushed her bleached hair, pecked her forehead again. Surprise? No, this was inevitable. This was Deirdre. It was as if the smell of sawn timber and his energy had summoned her up for him. Who else could share his sense of accomplishment in the task?

'You forgive me?'

He showed her the new work, ignoring that question.

'I'm here for a fortnight,' Deirdre thrust her arm round his waist, her fingers explored his buttock.

'Something insisted. I got time off and the kids are with Mum and Dad.' She walked back down the two steps with him. The new rails made it, for the first time, a squeeze. 'A month's a long time, David, a very long time.'

He slapped at the new railing to prove its solidity. He nodded. He refrained from asking after the kids.

'I'm a brute.'

He found her a chair. He carried her cases inside.

'I think you do look better. Yes, David, you look better.'

Even her agreement had tripwires. He bounced on the balls of his feet, the smell of cut timber still in his nostrils. So he'd been through a couple of bottles while working? It was nothing; truly, it had been nothing. No switch, no floodgates.

'Feel great. Only the last couple of days though. Good you came, Dee. What a surprise. But inevitable, spot-on. Good sign, don't you agree?'

Deirdre bent to unlock her suitcase but paused, summoning his eye.

'Don't ever do that to me again. When you drove off I was dead sure you had it in your mind to smash yourself up.'

He rubbed his thick dark palm along a new-sawn plank. But he was not going to be dragged back to that occasion. 'Don't know how you ever put up with me.'

'Ask myself, sometimes.'

He pulled her down beside him, enclosing her two hands in his own. She sighed, and then smiled, looking up into his face. Touch began its work of knitting, healing. David had always known how to be silent.

Deirdre, after a while, began to draw shapes in the sawdust.

'David. Remember that first night ever? I'd never met anyone who danced with me, talked *to* me. That night. And there was I all set to announce my engagement. The family hated me, and poor bloody Geoff . . . but it was all decided, fate stepped in, I had no part in it, almost. You bastard. You dark, sweet bastard.'

That had been twelve years ago. They had both been ridiculously young. Ridiculous. And young.

'Look what you got yourself into.'

43

'I wouldn't go back, David. You know that. It's been hell. But when I think of Geoff . . .'

'Welcome to the mess.'

Deirdre's belief and loyalty – it was gold. Like gold, though, it could be a hard currency. He reached for a bottle out of the refrigerator. It was the last.

'Pour me one half glass. Is there lemonade?' Was it sharing? Or a gesture of appropriation, a hint at rationing his intake?

'We'll get provisions,' he countered. 'When I'm alone here things revert to base necessities.'

'I see that.' She was already tidying. The fish delighted her.

'There might be someone coming over, thought I'd use the fish for dinner. He brought 'em.'

Deirdre nodded. 'No salt.' She was opening cupboards. 'And no flour.'

'His name's Clyde.' David went on. Was she really angry at him or just finding a space? Always this awkwardness in reknitting connections. The loyalty of a strong woman did not come light. But, damn her, she was compelling! No getting away – how fond the old phrase suddenly seemed. David swept her up and they looped in circles around the room. Then he dropped her onto the table and they gasped.

'Clyde the Carter he calls himself. Did meet you once. Lives in the same place with Jim the Ferry, some sort of cousin. Bit of an odd bod, but I think he's sort of desperate for company.'

'Rings no bells. What's he look like?'

'Big man, orange fair hair. Terribly pale but freckled. Around our age. Hard to tell. Irish, by the accent. The really curious thing, though, he's a night animal. Sleeps all day, goes fishing at night. Think he's some sort of professional fisherman but I don't know about that. Most of the time he seems to go out in a dinghy, except when Jim lets him have his own boat.'

'There was somebody. I went with the kids down near the three creeks. This figure suddenly looms up out of the bladeygrass. Tell the truth, I got quite angry.' But she shrugged and smiled. 'And why call himself Clyde the Carter? Sounds pretentious.'

'He's one of those inveterate game players.'

'Didn't look a game player to me that night. I grabbed the kids and did a quick detour. Thought he might be a drunk.'

'Well, we can't have drunks, can we?'

44

'David. You raised it. I'm not going to question you. So we can expect to see your new drinking mate, can we? My first night here.'

'He's not exactly a drinking mate. In fact since I met him, I've hardly touched a drop.'

'Really?' She was stacking the row of empties back into the brown carton.

'It's true. I swear it. I got thirsty today because I was working. But Clyde the Carter, he's more drunk on words than on booze. I think the coot's desperately lonely. Old Jim's hardly the most talkative company.'

'I like Jim. He came specially over to collect me. He's rock solid. Jim's one of the reasons this place has such appeal. In a funny way he reminds me of my Dad.'

'Well, Jim's a great mate of mine, too, you know. And he can cope with a bit of a wild night with the boys, no worries. Still, you'll meet Clyde later on. He's sure to be over.'

'Oh, I thought this was all arranged. Your little candle-lit dinner.'

'Sorry I didn't bring out the best silver. The crystal and napkins. No, nothing's said. It's just that the last night or so he's turned up. I'm sure he'll be pleased to see you. He mentioned your chance encounter. Know what he noticed: the way you had your hair up in plaits round the top. I think old Clyde's pretty harmless. But he's not above a bit of fine appreciation. I commend his taste.'

David wrapped his arms around his wife's waist and was gratified yet again at the way her hostility softened to compliance, her body fitting into his. It was a claim, a territorial stake, but it was also triggered by some light source in David. Or some dark source.

'And do you commend your wife?'

'She's not for sharing. Except socially.'

And saying it, he knew it made her sound like a chattel.

Late in the afternoon they went out together and stood on the verandah and Deirdre admired, once more, the new rails and the promise of crossbeams. 'Makes it look finished. Divides the house from the antbed,' she said.

'Clyde said the verandah was an in-between space. He liked the thought of it half in half out of the environment.'

'Before the handrails it was like that. Now it's the house, only the house. You've made that distinction.'

'Perhaps we should have it glassed in, with louvres?'

45

'Would you really do that, David?' But she joined in the banter and declared she might plant shrubs just below, now that the entrance was defined and people wouldn't jump on or off along any part of it.

'It's been glorious nights. Full moon.' David said.

She turned to him quizzically. 'Past tense?'

VIII

Let us not underestimate the terror and sheer physical difficulty of the rainforests in the Big Scrub. Those first Europeans were not scientific or trained naturalists, they were a race of mean-spirited survivors, predators, unsocial misfits. The jungle was the only place for them, but they were not really for the jungle. Where they went, they destroyed all.

It was, as John Vader says in his book, Red Cedar: The Tree of Australia's History, 'work for iron men'. 'Imagine,' wrote N. C. Hewitt, 'a lofty cedar 10-foot through, towering high above that living roof with which its trunk is bound and re-bound by scores of vines and roots, some of them stout as a ship's cable. These vines have to be cut before the tree is felled, scrub and rubbish must be cleared away before the trunk can be crosscut into lengths, and a wide lane perhaps some hundreds of yards in length has to be cut through the scrub before the log can be rolled into the nearest river or deep water creek. The men worked naked to the waist. Mosquitoes and stinging flies abounded near the water, trousers and boots are small protection against hordes of blood-thirsty leeches, whilst the danger of snake-bite is ever present, not forgetting millions of ticks. At 4 o'clock the bird voices are hushed, a fast deepening gloom abscures the scanty sunlight, and the sweat-stained men turn homeward . . .'

Or, as another historian wrote, 'Upon everything beneath that living canopy of tangled boughs and leaves there hung a shadow which

47

deepened into the gloom of twilight long before the sun had set. No companionship, no occupation ever seemed to diminish or to dispel the scene of mystery which hovered upon those solemn shades wherein rare and fantastic forms of vegetation grew in rank luxuriance, stinging nettles and stinging trees galore, the devilish tentacles of the "lawyer" and the "barrister" palms, and impervious tangles of noxious shrubs and vines, ever ready with tooth and claw, barred the way. Though the eye might admire and the mind marvel, yet body and mind both rebelled against the diabolical ingenuity of Nature's barbed wire defences . . . the soft wood timbers and innumerable vines fought us foot by foot. Our dog once became hopelessly tangled in a lawyer vine and we had to disentangle him. What hearts men must have had to pioneer a way through such cruel growths!'

And yet, throughout this area, there remain shadows of the aboriginal inhabitants, the natives who often guided those first predators to new valleys of cedar, further groves of fragrant treasure. For their millennia, the aborigines had known this land, and how to move through it and respect it. They were themselves people of the waterways and estuaries. But their lore carried the lines and delineations of countless different valleys, gulleys, plateaux, so that they themselves knew beyond knowing what was their inheritance. There was food. There were medicinal barks and gums and herbs. They had long since prepared themselves against the irritants of insect bites, largely through the use of fish oils, fats and campfire ash. They moved with grace and speed through a landscape where the sullen Europeans crashed and got torn. Their languages had at least eight tenses. And like all true aristocrats, they were destroyed by the lumpen invader.

David Cumberland: *The Big Scrub: A History* (ibid)

*

'The German invasion of Russia began on my birthday, it was my twenty-first birthday. I was the birthday girl!' Galina Darovskaya had said.

It must have been after midnight. David had somehow been able, after a while, to accommodate her thick accent. Her tiny flat, hidden above a row of nondescript shops and along the corridor from the Dental Technician in Mullumbimby, kept its strange world seemingly intact, though here and there were intrusions of outside reality: a tin of Milo glimpsed through the door to the tiny kitchen table, dried banksia seedpods among the decor of shells and grasses on the small glass-topped table; two or three English language books at the end of the bookshelf.

'My birthday had always been special because it was the midsummer solstice. I was not only the birthday girl, I was the midsummer daughter, of the white nights. June 22nd.' Her tiny face concentrated its expressiveness into the bright glittering dark eyes. She smiled, the skin tightening.

'June 21st is the true midsummer. June 21st was the first German bombing of Sevastopol. But June 22nd, that is when midsummer has made its decision. It is committed. I always believed the night and the day of the 22nd was more perfect. And not only because it was special, it was being my birthday. I was romantic.'

She poured David and Vladimir Smolich another tiny brandy each, her back straight, like a schoolgirl, in the dim light of her room.

'It was in the afternoon of the 22nd, as I was preparing for my wonderful party that the radio broadcast the news. We were at war with Germany. It was a terrible surprise, and yet not a surprise at all. Nobody in Leningrad believed the German forces could ever reach Leningrad. Because of our treaty with Germany nobody was allowed to believe the Germans were planning to invade – though their planes were flying, even over Leningrad, all the time. Weather testing, they said. Aerial manoeuvres, they said. Training flights over peaceful neighbours, they told us. Oh, yes, there were many rumours. And there were some people in Leningrad who were secretly hoping for the invasion. Some of my older friends were from Esthonia. They were at the Conservatoire in Leningrad, but I knew they had families passionately dedicated to sabotaging the sovietisation of their country. They admired Hitler, even his racial policies. Of course they did not talk about these things. One was a particular friend, we played duets together, and I knew she was unhappy. It was only, later, many strange things came out.'

'Stalin had a wonderful instinct for plots and subversion,' Vladimir said. 'He was also desperately afraid and jealous of Leningrad and all that Leningrad represented. Leningrad has remained the intellectual centre. Our city suffered Stalin's rages.'

'On my birthday, that morning, it was when the weather at last became perfect. You know we have only thirty-five days of full sunshine? The spring, I remember that spring, though it is now forty years, more than forty years. A wet spring, a slow spring, late coming. And then the perfect weather. I had just had my first poems published. The poems I believe were my first real efforts. Everyone congratulated me on them. Poetry was so important; people sat round in the Café Ice Cream or the Green Frog, and they discussed the new poems seriously – it was important, it was Leningrad. We were all young then, we were all passionately involved. How could we be otherwise? Life was so alive with every possibility. Yes. The alive times.'

'I was not born,' Vladimir said, 'but it is true, still, there is still debate and discussion. To be a true Leningrader is to be passionately involved. Though there is old, dead wood, and the burden of precedent.'

'There was always precedent. But Leningrad is the inexhaustible city. Impossible not to write poems about Leningrad. It is the eternal gem that you rub and some glow shines out of it. It is a city,' she explained, still half smiling, 'built at the edge of everything, it is the city that balances between beauty and horror. I say this truly. You know of Leningrad?' she asked kindly.

'Well, not much, really. At school, in Geography . . .'

'And in history? I think not. History is really a terrible revision of everything we know, of truth, of things that have happened. It is a whore, Shostakovich once said to me, and I was truly shocked. I did not realise, then, what he meant. Shostakovich was my teacher. He only spoke such challenges to those he believed were mature, or understanding. I pretended to be mature, and I had such confidence, people believed me. I had no mature understanding: how might that be so? Well, there are many whores, we all recognise what my master was attempting to define. I have been called a whore in my time.'

She looked old-maidish, virginal. She looked terribly knowing.

'Leningrad was built upon marshes, mud islands. It was Dostoyevsky who first wrote of Leningrad as a double-imaged city, a city of fogs and abyss, the bronze horseman in the marsh, at the edge of Russia, the place where Russia fades into infinity, the boundless sea, the unstable barrier between the edges of Russia and the beginnings of Europe,' explained Vladimir. 'When Peter the Great built it, it is said one hundred thousand serfs died. From the mud and the estuaries of the Neva, arose the new Venice, the perfect city, proud of its symmetry and yet proud, too, of its close way of echoing the contours of nature: canals, open plazas, the bridges and closeness to water. It became the centre of Russian art, music, literature and culture. It is the city of Lenin.'

'My first published poem was due to the encouragement of Olga Berggolts. She was a beacon to me, then and later. It was about the ballroom in the Hotel Astoria. The poet Sergei Yesenin suicided in that hotel. I think it was a silly, young poem, a poem of infatuation. But everyone said to me: it is a song, it is *yours* now, Galina. You see; we believed at that time.'

'Ah, I do not know that one,' Vladimir said. 'Many things have been displaced.'

She recited the poem. David listened, amused and enthralled: to remember word-perfect, and after so many years. It was as if the words still had meaning. Or as if they had become engraved, rigid as ikons.

Vladimir murmured. Quietly they spoke together. Clearly she began reading one of her poems. David might have expected a sound of ball music, or laughter the way Galina's present laughter filled the room. Perhaps it was the convention of recitation. Perhaps the youthful ballroom had become ghostly now with many more dead echoes. Her reciting voice was limpid, burdened.

'We are forgetting you, dear friend,' Galina turned to him. 'But I am grateful, so grateful, you have brought Vladimir Smolich to visit me, to go out of your way to bring Vladimir. But one thing you must promise. I have chosen my own destiny. I have become a recluse. You must promise me to honour my wish for seclusion. Please do not mention this visit to the others. To any others.'

Vladimir nodded agreement. 'Galina will not return to her city. I have tried to persuade her. But I understand and respect her decision. I think, if you were to understand all the consequences, you would willingly agree to her request. It is an honourable one.'

'But we are friends now. If you, alone, would wish to visit me, then I would be honoured. With your dark face, and what Vladimir tells me about your wonderful book on these native forests. You must beware of Vladimir – from what he tells me of your book I believe he already has half the substance of his new major poem. He is ruthless.' She smiled. 'He steals what he needs from everywhere, everyone. I know I will be preserved in the amber of his poem – is that not so?'

Vladimir thrust his hand to his breast in a gesture David might not have believed possible.

Making her point, Galina turned again to David.

'Perhaps we might make contact. My friend Mary, who lives here, who is my only friend, she has stories of the old ways. Strangely, I find some of her stories remind me of the old peasant beliefs – where each hut has its own guarding spirit, that I well remember. Where the forest presences entered into real exchanges with ourselves. Countries with tremendous forests must all witness such ghosts and presences. Don't you agree?'

'You may be wanting to impose preconceptions about what is only there in non European terms,' David began.

'I find they haunt me. Though I am still restrained from attempting to make any commitment. Commitment involves too many inflexibilities, and I am now an old woman.'

'Look, I'm only an amateur myself. A sort of amateur historian. I looked up old newspaper files and pioneer diaries. I got interested in red cedar, it's a lovely timber; polishes up wonderfully and beyond that it's almost free of insect damage, borers and white ants. And light; it is immensely light, not like mahogany, which everyone compares it with. Cedar is a timber made from thousands of years of lighthearted enjoyment of these rainforests. I think of it,' David confessed recklessly, 'as a timber in love with the treefern gullies, the bellbirds, the runnels and waterfalls of rainforest valleys. Polishes up beautifully. Do you believe how you can recognise the look of cedar, once you know?'

'Ah yes. The tone, the conviction.' Her eyes suddenly expressed an alert interest. 'You interest me. I am surprised but your tone of conviction interests me.'

David stood up then, he had to walk around the tiny space of her room. It was almost as if she had asked him to crush it with extraordinary trunks of mythic trees, something her friend Mary may have planted as seeds or shadows across her mind.

'Well, I'm sorry,' he began. Then he reconsidered. It is unusual for an Australian to have to accept an invitation to expand; normally for enthusiasm or knowledge or discovery one has to apologise. 'Bad rhetorics' his reviewer had sneered.

'Do not apologise!' she hissed. 'Never apologise. Australians are always apologising. It disgusts me.'

'Look, I am hooked entirely on the red cedar business. Let's put it this way: there's no use being in anything if you aren't in it to the hilt. Some of the stories of this district! Right here: some of the stories of this area, they would amaze you. It was rough times, a hundred years ago. But they were also people of terrific obsessiveness. That was what got me in. They were not half-hearted, they were flat out and passionate in those days. The cedar getters would spend weeks, months, in the dense scrub around here. They would come out pale as witchetty-grubs. Sorry, Vladimir, that's a plump white insect. This was all immensely dense rainforest. The Big Scrub. Until they set fire to it all. One big blaze, burnt up the lot. That's what they did to our enthusiasm. Only a few pockets and hollows of the old forest remained; after thousands of acres. Hundreds of thousands of acres. It all seemed so simple, and they were simple, just as we are. They wanted the land for the cud-chewers. That's how we do things here, no fine points, no attention to detail, like the really beautiful cedar timber, the red glowing stuff, that takes a thousand years to grow.'

'You do have some longer perspectives then?'

Galina leant her head over, attentive. 'Your voice: it is the voice of someone with a belief in perspectives other than fire. Vladimir, did you ever know another early poem of mine, called "The Believer"? Perhaps it also is forgotten. It was about one such as our friend here, one who pretended diffidence, indifference, but yet whose voice was always full of another story, another commitment. It was about a young man I knew who was brilliant, brilliant. But the late 1930s were not times when that was easy. Too many brilliant people vanished. He was a little older than me. He died, of course. Later. Do you remember that poem?'

'That is your poem which begins . . .' And Vladimir, in a voice suddenly rich and quiet, began quoting. Galina nodded. David noticed the sudden moistening, the blinking.

'So. I am not entirely forgotten.'

'I have memorised all that I can find. It is also a safe way. But there are others like myself, we love best the "Roller Coaster" sequences.'

'You are very brave. Those poems exiled me.'

'They did not understand them then. But we do. When I first read them I was devastated.'

'June 22nd. Did I tell you about my twenty-first birthday? In the morning I got up early, I did not want to stay indoors. There was a friend who was to take me rowing, I thought I was in love then. We all knew the rumours of course, but it was impossible to believe things might be different. I did not want to believe things might become different. In midsummer the lilacs are full of fragrance, so heavy, so pervasive, how can you believe anyone capable of violence, or destruction? And the cherry blossoms. The little alley that had the cherry trees in full blossom was a miracle, a tree in my friend's neighbourhood still flowering on the 22nd . . ."

They had talked long into the night. David was drawn in. He determined to look up what he could about Leningrad, about the siege and the war. With this woman he entered through doors not previously opened, yet they led to a life so well and so passionately invoked that her room unlocked treasuries, it was as if he had been admitted into that world.

They reeled into the cold night air and the street lights of the small township. In the shop below Galina's apartment was a display of dresses, the rigid mannequins spider-like, absurd in mock rapture, rage, aloofness, indignation — arms flowing, necks swan-like, and without faces. The garments themselves in that unlit window hung without conviction, as if no farmer's wife or daughter of Mullumbimby would dare try them. Behind this display, in the island counters, he made out piles of stacked clothing, utilitarian and in all sizes.

David almost tripped over beer cans and rubbish at the Brunswick Valley Real Estate. A dog had torn open garbage bags.

When David and Vladimir had finally left her upstairs retreat in that small village, Galina kissed David on both cheeks. She made him repeat his promise. She reminded him of all his promises and entrusted Vladimir Smolich to him in whatever forest journey they might share together.

Why should it seem like a benediction?

*

A WHITE BALL AT THE ASTORIA

Someone has spoken to the band leader.
'We'll meet again in Lvov, my love',
the singer moans, as if nothing was meant.
There is a revolving multi-faceted mirror.
You must remember that I, too,
believed every image. Otherwise
I would have sobbed endlessly
and the white light of Leningrad
would have seeped, even here, into

54

the unreal world of the Astoria ballroom.
The music, then, would be pitiful,
my white ball gown, your handsome collar,
the gleam, the gleam my dear in your eyes,
so proud, so vulnerable, so beautiful.
We would have believed ourselves eternal
under the glittering multi-faceted mirror.
But the white light has been dismissed.
All the doors are covered in drapes,
there are no mirrors, no windows, only music
and Eddie Roznov and his Metropole Jazz Band
and someone *has* spoken to the band leader.
They are playing our music, our song,
as it is known by everyone.

IX

There were other things that David Cumberland remembered from that first long evening with Galina Darovskaya in Mullumbimby. The fact that she made no real mention, for instance, of the more than forty years since she had left Russia in, David worked out, 1946 or thereabouts.

There was some suggestion that Galina had lived in a shifting flux of places, countries, relationships until the period about twenty years back when it seemed she was blown to this obscure village on the edges of timber country and dairy farms and the pockets of sub-tropical rainforest. It was also twenty years, she said, since she had written poetry.

'I see my daughter, but I do not see my daughter,' she began to explain at one stage and David had to assume that there was a daughter and that the daughter might have been in Mullumbimby, might be accessible, someone Galina could, indeed, see and visit if she wanted to.

She spoke of her daughter in a tone of declaration, finality.

'There was a time when I wrote letters,' she said. 'Many of my friends I wrote back to in those years. Later, when I did not receive replies, time and again, then I began to wonder. Were my letters themselves actually death warrants? One has to ask these questions. One asked these questions in 1952, 1953. Stalin was always deeply suspicious of the world outside his control. A letter from outside to a Soviet citizen: dangerous.'

Later, she had attempted to change the subject back to David's own culture.

'Someone said you have poets. Is it true poetry is universal? I do not yet know the answer. For me poetry was Leningrad, and my country, and the fate and destiny that flowed through us. Someone said, read Henry Kendall, read Henry Lawson. I tried. If these are the poets here, what would I say to them?'

'Vladimir tells me things have changed. I believe him. I am filled with an anguish for my city, yet I know there is no longer my city. Vladimir denies this. He says: look at the Admiralty, look at the Winter Palace. They have restored the old Imperial Palaces: it is an act of defiance, an act against invaders. Did you know Hitler said: "I will raze Leningrad. Let not a stone remain standing"? Restored palaces defy that barbarity. All this I know. To rebuild the monuments of the Czarist excesses into their rococo splendours – parquet halls, silk walls, the Hall of Mirrors – that is what Lenin himself saw as a plan worth enshrining. I always doubted that. But then I was young and romantic, and in the 1930s I was enraptured with the apartment of Olga Berggolts. It was new. It was modern, reflecting the new order. No individual kitchens, no hallway with pegs for coats, no small holes where a family cringed, hidden. No, it was a commune, a shared place, open and flexible. It was called the Communal House of Artists and Engineers.'

'But that place was impossible. No one wanted to live there,' Vladimir exclaimed. 'It worked only when everyone shared equally like a sculling team. Later, it was usually called the House of The Tears of Socialism.'

'All these things are true, yes. But I am speaking of my youth, of things that made deep impressions. But the things that made deep impressions were, for me, not the monuments to particular Czars. The overview, yes. The imposed discipline of line and perspective, the great perspective streets and prospekts. The decree that no building be higher than the road width beyond it. The bridges, the parks, the public places. I never went inside palaces. Well, that is not true, of course, but only palaces turned into public buildings. My Leningrad was the city of art and inhabitants. Of culture that had grown in the serene environment. Of culture that grew in the damp, gloomy environment. It was both things, my city. It was growing. When we coincided, that was the great time. But the bombs destroyed my city. The defence works destroyed it. The deaths and the winters, the streets full of bodies. In the end there was not a wooden house left in Leningrad. The rains in the spring of 1943,' she said, 'after two hard winters, the rains ripped the inside of the Hermitage Museum to shreds, turned everything to mould, to slime, peeled off the designs and the plaster.'

She walked to her own Mullumbimby walls then, stroking them. They became, in that gesture, not some cheap holiday apartment wall, but a symbol of solidity. Even the quaint stencil patterns became, not makeshift, but certain.

'Perhaps it was the wet spring of 1943 when I knew that my Leningrad, that had survived the worst bombs and unbelievable hunger, was being worn away by all the forces combined. We all worked, we all helped, do not misunderstand me. But there are certain things, if you see them fade and decay . . .'

'But the Hermitage has been restored. It is more beautiful than it has ever been!' exclaimed Vladimir.

'Forest regeneration. There are actually pockets of rainforest here that have increased in acreage in recent years . . .' David had added.

Galina smiled. She brought out a photo. 'Photos. The Arabs say they take away the soul. What we take, we take away. I took Leningrad away with me.' She raised her thin fingers. 'No, Vladimir. There is another Leningrad now. Even the Hermitage will be different. It was not perfect, you know. It was not perfect.'

Later, she returned to her twenty-first birthday. 'We were returning from that boat excursion, my friend and I. We were not in a hurry. I had told my mother we would be back by noon so that I could begin preparations for the big celebration that evening. The radio was on in our front room, it was always on. One never knew when there might be an important announcement. So I heard Molotov tell us that Germany had invaded. It was just noon. We had come in wet and laughing. I was actually perspiring. 'We have been bombed from the air at Zhitomir, Kiev, Sevastopol, Kaunay and other sites', Molotov told us. 'The attack has been made despite the fact that there was a non-aggression pact between the Soviet Union and Germany.' I did not know what to do. I could not bear to go on with the idea of the party. And yet the sun outside still shone, the lilacs were unchanged, even children playing in the streets, who had not yet heard, they were the same.

'My mother was suddenly busy with new thoughts. There had been famine during the winter war with Finland. She was not going to be taken by surprise again. She ordered me off to the markets to get what I could find: butter, sugar, lard, matches, sausage. My father went immediately on the streetcar to the edges of the city. He was going to buy a sack of potatoes and onions from one of the outlying villages. My mother went to the bank to withdraw what money she could. I remember later that afternoon: my father came back with only a small bag of onions and a small sack of potatoes that looked as if they might have been set aside for seed. I had spent everything on supplies, but had to push and shove to keep my place and the prices had risen already. My mother had waited two hours in a queue at the bank and then found that all the cash available had been withdrawn. She had bartered her good shawl for roubles, though, down at the haymarkets. She came home with a whole bucket of tinned things. We were horrified. None of us could bear tinned food.

'You will see,' she said to us, and carefully hid them under the loose floorboard in the broom cupboard. 'This will keep.' We had no idea, then, how long the war would be. We had no idea Leningrad would be attacked, or even that it would be reached by the Germans. We could not believe we might be surrounded, cut off, bombed and starved, summer, autumn, winter, summer, autumn, winter, for nearly three years. Who could have believed that?'

X

'David, the lumber jacket, you had it behind the door. Where is it? I'm going to the mudflats, see if I can flush out a mudcrab or two. That's what I feel like, need to get the slush between my toes, clean out the city from behind my ears. You know? Now I'm here, suddenly it's holiday time again and I feel it.'

'I'll come with you. There's that fish of Clyde's, remember?'

'Soon as the sun goes down it'll get chilly, quick as a flash. Where did you put it?'

'What? Oh, the jacket? Should be there. Try the other room. Hardly the thing anyone'd steal.'

'But someone might drop it almost anywhere. Especially someone sloshed to the hilt.'

'No need for that.'

'Well, David, you know yourself without me having to remind you. No, I'm not scolding. It's just that I want that jacket. I only brought the good coat of my own, didn't seem able to see what I'd need on the island. Last time I took everything back to Sydney, all my island gear needed a good wash.'

'I wore it only the other night. It's around.'

But David was nettled. The way Deirdre always skated around the accusation, the pretence of being tolerant. Knives. And when they could not find it, Deirdre did not have to say a thing.

David tried to cling to his new mood and his new resolutions. It was as if Deirdre herself brought her own victimisation with her, as if she were asking him to check with Jim about when he would go over to the pub at Cleveland. Okay, let her spear mudcrabs! Perhaps Clyde had something, with his idea of personal traps and limits. But David relented; the aura of meeting and mating entangled him still in its net; it had been so good he was looking already to the night when they could cuddle up together again, in the best time of year with the chill air there to prove the triumph of warm bodies and locked embraces, right until morning. And in the morning, it would be better than ever.

He ended up offering her the thick army shirt. When she grabbed him, tugged his hair and drew her finger along the bristles, saying, 'Come on. First night, let's go down to the mud together', he needed no more promises.

In his month without sharing he had become disembodied and irrelevant. That David had been another man, a shadow. Not for the first time he recognised the voluptuous contrast that made their skins – fair and dark, but both smooth – so complementary. David recognised, also, her gift of wanting to make the present a point where, like a funnel, a wide circle of things became concentrated. She filtered from the past only its good things. The first riveting moment of attraction – the time of her fated engagement party. *He* raked over the past for curses and portents: the bones beneath pleasures. She refused to call him morbid.

They clambered down the steep track to the mangroves.

A silver glaze had set round everything, a blur that would turn into mist and then fog tonight. They knew the signs. The water of the bay gave away nothing, it was a smeared mirror where no reflection was possible. The colour of trees, leaves, the marram grasses near the sandhill, all had contracted back to basic noncommittal shapes, as if colour were an accessory only for heightened moments. Shadows had been flattened out and discarded. There was light, but it was a no-light; shining but it was only a measure of the hardness of surfaces. They waded out to the mudbanks where the mangrove swamp began. It was low tide. Their bodies became weighed down in the half world between land and water, their voices were overtaken by the squelch and suck of mud and they fell silent. Deirdre's jungle green floppy shirt seemed the colour of their thoughts. David, braving it out, wore only his shorts. His dark shoulders were the colour of the mud and as he moved off in different directions to search for the elusive giant crabs his body blended with things. Deirdre turned round and almost lost sight of him.

For half an hour they moved separately and together around the edges of the mangrove swamp, spears in hand. No success. The elusive crustaceans gave no signs, no shadow or movement. When David rejoined her, he was purposeful, more his old self.

'Come on. We've got the fish anyhow. Tell you what, though, how about I go over to Jim's and see if he's got any spuds. Some chips would go nicely.'

Deirdre caught up with him. They left the spears by the half toppled bull-banksia (no worry about pilfering) and she weaved her arm into his.

'Just to walk around on the mudbank, just to get it back into the system. That was good. I didn't really need to get a prize. David, it's a good place for us, this. Isn't it? I feel it's almost woven us together, you know: you always seem less threatened here. More likely to grin. When you grin and show your teeth, you've no idea how it lights up your face. When you want to you can look pretty grim.' But she plunged on. 'And then, perhaps it's the contrast as well, there comes out the white lights. Lucky me, I think, lucky me to have David. See. Now you're not going to take the hint. Now you'll sulk, just to spite me.'

And he stopped then, and put both arms around her and knew that they were caught up in the deepest flattery, the most important lies, and that it was the one secret of their truthfulness together. Dee's control of him.

He broke off.

'We'll get back just before dark, if we hurry. Perhaps Clyde the Carter will be at Jim's and we can check out if he really is aiming to call round tonight. And if so, what time we should start doing the fish.'

'Sure, he can come, in fact I'm quite curious. So long as you don't keep talking all night and drinking. Or go off fishing and leave me out. Well, you can't do that, I'll come with you.'

But she was smiling too.

'We'll shove him out the door in good time,' he whispered, poking his tongue into her ear. 'But he is sort of fun, or at least genuinely curious, if you can take the blarney and mystery making.' That strange night on the water had receded to harmless moon-echo.

'Sounds all too predictable to me.'

There was nobody at home when they reached Jim's shack. David, not at all abashed, went up the sand track to the next cottage and came back with half a dozen potatoes.

'Said we'll replace them next time Jim goes over.'

The sheen had tightened into twilight flatness. The soft flap of bay water upon sand drew them down to the edge and they dawdled, scuffing the ripples, pretending to look at shells and the line of watergrasses and seaweed near the high tide mark.

They continued to the far end of the beach, then sat down on the grassy edge where three little streams came out of the ti-tree scrub into a low sandy sward.

After a bit David got up and strolled further into the grove, feeling the need to urinate. As he came to the bank of the first stream he unzipped.

At that moment he looked up. In the deep greyish light just ahead someone was crouching, humped. The movement of the shoulders, the body intent on some scrubbing, rubbing motion was what caught his eye. He walked over.

Someone was rinsing out a garment in the pool of the shallow creek, paying no attention – or perhaps David's footsteps were noiseless. As he came close to the crouching figure David saw that below the washing place a dark stain sluiced down through the water. Normally this was a clear trickle. It looked like blood.

The figure stood then and began wringing out the garment. David zipped up and took another six paces.

'Hey! My check jacket . . .' And he realised that it was not some sort of washer woman but was Clyde, his head hooded in an old and particularly dirty-looking duffle coat. He flapped the wash like a towel. Yes, David's lumber jacket.

'Who but David the edgy would turn up at the instant I finish his wash for him? Perceptive friend, see how I look after you. It was covered with blood, it stank to high heaven. You left it on purpose. Lying there the whole day now, out in my dinghy, when I saw it I thought: I owe him this rinse-out. So now, look, all washed. Cleaner than ever.'

Clyde pushed back the hood as if it had fallen forward expressly to irritate him. He handed over the sodden garment. Deirdre came through the clump of wattles. Clyde laughed. 'There's the grand vision!'

63

David made proper introductions. Deirdre at first seemed nettled, as if she had caught her husband in some secret assignation. But she could not dislike Clyde. Nothing more than a great boy, a gawky teenager in his teenage parka and his big bare feet, he seemed too awkward for shoes. There seemed no trace of the big man who loomed, that earlier time, in the dusk when she was already edgy with some sense of the strangeness of isolation too far from their own refuge: the darkness of what was a very strange island. She had laughed, later, at her own fear of the night.

David watched the instant mother. She took the jacket absently, inspected it, nodded and passed it back to David, all the while caught in the net of Clyde's patter.

There was no need for invitations. Clyde lurched and strutted, raced and returned, hands in pockets, as they made their way in the dark back to the cliffside shack in the area already named in Clyde's terms, the Red Antheap.

Only later Deirdre returned puzzled to the gesture of Clyde laundering her husband's jacket. 'That man is playing games of some sort. I'd just watch him,' she said but then regretted it. She did not wish to wake something.

XI

'There's three ways of fasting. And three uses of fasting.' Clyde sat between them at the deal table. His pale cheeks glowed with a fresh sort of warmth, almost with colour. The fish had been wonderful. Their plates were now littered with bones and a light buttery mess of congealing sauce. They were drinking tea.

'The three ways of fasting are these: the first, you close your mouth to all but fluids, then hold tight. The second: you begin by tasting only fruit, grapes perhaps, or oranges. And the third: you begin with a feast. Then you force yourself to void the lot. Stick your thumb down your throat, take an emetic. For days you live on the recollection of that, the vomit.'

Deirdre, unconsciously, smiled at that, her elbow on the table, her chin cupped.

'Secret of fasting isn't the abstinence. It's the purpose. Those who attempt the sudden cut-off, well, they won't last with their faith. You don't go into a sacred place without preliminary prayer and preparation. Otherwise you're just a tourist. If you're strong in your purpose, your body turns into that prayer. Hence the second course: pure fruit. I prefer grapes, they don't cut the throat with flavour. After one day, you can still believe in grapes. Oranges, they throw sunbursts of acid into the stomach. But others may prefer that; it refreshes them.' Clyde the Carter looked towards them at this, challenging them to disagree, or to accept compromise. 'The third course is the most dramatic, but it is also the most sincere. It is life and death combat. The fast is not undertaken lightly, the absent one has become real.' Holding their eyes, he raised his right hand and screwed the little finger into his ear. Absent-mindedly he stared at the evidence of wax.

'The feast and then the fast. Well, it makes good drama. But I don't trust its effectiveness.' David poured his fifth cup of tea, metallic. He looked over to Deirdre. If Clyde were less whimsical he would be sinister. It was as if he had her in thrall.

They would laugh about that later.

'The idea of fasting is no health fad,' Clyde continued, 'It's nothing to do with vanity. All of this talk of teenage girls fasting, becoming anorexic. Most often their parents miss the point. Fasting is the old Celtic ritual to gain recognition for a grievance; those girls are in thrall still to the old powers. They might say, "I want to be thin," but they are really saying, "This is my protest." They are only subconsciously aware of the true power of the old forms. Everywhere they're told they live only for the minute, that the past is old hat. And all the while the little dears have been threaded by genes into very old knots. That's why the old forms always come back.'

'Parents don't miss the point, Clyde. And with *anorexia nervosa* it's more a spiral, a vortex. The stomach contracts.'

David thought of it, though he didn't actually admit it, more as an addiction.

'Grievance, you call it. It's certainly some sort of distress signal, that's recognised. We had friends . . .' he continued.

'Distress? You must understand, grievance is more than distress. It's political.' Clyde's voice had a natural rich cadence. Impassioned, it was resonant. 'Those parents of teenagers think only about their daughters' anti-social behaviour and the embarrassment of neighbours. Fasting is to enter the world of your body, making your body the meeting place of nature and the other than natural – the physical and the not physical. Comfort?? That is like other words of the same ilk: happiness. What is this word, "happiness"? I do not know what it means, it's not a word of naming. It's not a word in the centre; it's irrelevant, a by-product.' Clyde swept his right hand across his face, as if to brush off a cobweb.

'Okay. Three ways of fasting. But you also said there's three *uses* of fasting, Clyde. Well, you've rubbed in the protest bit. That's number one in your books, I've no doubt. And the purging, that's got to be one. What's your third?'

'You know that one, too, Davey boy, you don't need me spelling it out for you. If I were to say, "It's to test yourself," would that make sense to you? Of course it makes sense to you – isn't your whole book such an exercise? Fasting is to move back a pace, to be at one, at least for a while, with the elements and the other spirit outside us – or is it inside us? I don't know, I never question it, except I know fasting has outcomes.'

Clyde pushed his plate forward, and then, resting his elbows on the table, stared at the others in turn, finally cupping his hands then spreading them open with a quizzical shrug.

David stared back. This man teased him.

'So you believe in fasting as a religious exercise too? You're a Catholic?' Deirdre shifted her chair sideways, then pushed it back, stood up and went behind David, rubbing his neck and shoulders, massaging, then her hands fondled the thick tangle of his hair. She reached over and pecked his forehead.

'I think I can say I've done fasting in all its forms.' Clyde smiled suddenly. It intensified his expression. 'And fasting to gain recognition for a grievance. Yes, that too. You may even have read in the papers . . . but these things get forgotten. That's as it should be. Grievance fasting is of its particular moment. I was in prison. I believed in my cause. I prepared myself. I made a contract with my body. We were in this together.'

'You know, Clyde, you intrigue me.' Deirdre leaned over, her forearms resting on David's shoulders. 'I think I should be suspicious of you. But, you know, I can understand you going on a hunger strike. That fits. One thing, though; I don't want us to be dragged into the shit of the politics of old Ireland. You're in Australia now. No ghosts in the luggage, if you please. No ghosts here, you can see that, you can tell that. There's no ghosts here.'

Satisfied, she stretched, then pulled up another chair close to David, who sat almost without moving. She turned hers sideways and positioned herself to rest her hand on him. She pulled his other arm towards herself. He cupped one of her breasts.

'I feel ghosts here,' he murmured.

'You feel me!'

It was as if Clyde remained unaware of their flirtatiousness.

'Water is the first principle,' he mused aloud. 'Once you recognise that, how can you say there are no spirits in this place? You've chosen this place, that in itself has to be a sort of acknowledgment. And of course you must realise that this hill, this red antheap, this is the most sacred site on the island. Right back through aboriginal times, the most sacred. Even I've heard that mentioned, and you who bought it must have set your eyes on it for just such a reason. You, David, isn't that so?'

'We bought it for the elevation,' Deirdre said firmly.

'Was this really a sacred site?' Like a pupil, David had to know more. 'Who told you?'

'And haven't I got friends in the best places?' Clyde the Carter looked at David directly, 'Friends who would know? I asked some of my aboriginal friends over on Stradbroke. They know all these islands. I sought them out moons ago. Moons and moons and moons ago,' he mocked.

David was silent. The red antheap. What was it, could he remember – truly? – the impact behind the impulse that first excited them to buy here? It is special, they had said to each other. It is ours, we knew from the moment we saw it: ours.

Ours. Or, more, his? Deirdre remaining his shadow. Again.

Clyde turned, then, to Deirdre. 'You tell me there are no ghosts here? Do you feel nothing?'

'I can feel something stirring, I can sense. Must be the Rainbow Serpent.' Deirdre tried to hold David's eye. 'Clyde, you know something? I bet you're tricked by my name; laying on the Irish for me. But I've got to advise, Deirdre has no touch of the Gaelic. My mum just took a liking. Our family's pure third generation Aussie.'

Clyde looked through her. No wonder she responded with cheap bravado, though Deirdre was already hating her own performance. And Clyde's possessive reference to her husband's book – how would *he* know? Clyde was playing with power. Why betray herself with cheap rebuttals? Why betray David?

'What time is it?' she snapped.

'I knew this island must have its sacred place, its centre. The moment I arrived, I knew that,' Clyde said. 'At first I believed it must be in the place of the three streams. Such a compelling triad. And it does have a specialness. I keep me dinghy there. And the sweet clean water. And

68

the three colours: each stream different. You've both seen that. Well, have you?'

David looked up, dragging his eyes from Deirdre's, released. He had been listening.

'Yes, I have noticed that. The middle one is clearest. The one beyond that, well it always seems brown, that's the reed patch it comes through at the edge of the swamp does that. And the one on this side, can't remember, it's just sort of ordinary, isn't it, Dee?'

'Rainbow serpent,' she whispered. And again, defiantly, 'Serpent.' For her, Clyde might have been no longer in the room.

'That first stream's clear also, but there's always the taste of salt in it. The middle one's nectar. It flows through the sweet eucalypt grove. It's purified by hidden filters.' Clyde almost whispered now. David was attentive. 'I did meet some sweet men, once, midnight fishers like meself. We lit a fire on the sand and got talking. You know the way it is, and the way talk becomes fanciful, becomes serious out in the night with the stars and the moon trailing their fingers in the water and the sense of time not a thing of any importance, there. They told me.'

'You sure it's this place?' David moved an arm away from Deirdre's embrace. His fingers traced a pattern on the board. 'What sort of sacred, then?'

'I thought you might tell *me*, Davey boy. Because of you living here. Because of your insights, your feeling for big mysteries. Your book.'

'The Rainbow Serpent raises its head right here,' hissed Deirdre, leaning over to lick her husband's ear. 'They say the fertility rites were something special under these ironbarks. So stiff in the moonlight. Yes, there's mysteries. But there's too many ants. We tried it once, out there under the trees. Nearly carried me off.'

'Deirdre's not being serious.'

'What she's saying is serious, under the teasing defences.'

Clyde spoke as if she were not present. David felt impelled to be arbiter, but he was tugged, nevertheless: Deirdre's body, and her alluring mockery; Clyde's offering, his challenges, proposing the past packaged as some reverberating claim, right on this spot. Of course it was all speculation. It was unerring.

'Go on, Clyde.' David looked back, then, towards Deirdre, 'Go on, now that you've been to this bit of hilltop, how do you see its mysteries?'

'Davey, Davey, Davey. Don't be dismissive. Think back, yourself, tell me your own first responses, coming here. These last nights, already things you've said all confirm your own love of this place. The healing place. The circle. The antbed here didn't deter you. And you didn't destroy it, pour poison into it. The climb didn't deter you, though you brought every brick and stick by hand. The end of the island and the stink of mangrove swamp at your feet did not deter you. The great grey ironbarks here, people say they are ugly . . .'

'They are not!' Deirdre called out. Clyde ignored her.

'It was the ironbarks called you? It was their fallen branches littered around that were message-sticks? Is that it? Or was it the view now? The view looking out to the west waters. That's all hard sun and hot summers. You chose the place where the sun nails down hardest, and longest, this little western hill. Nobody else would buy it because of that, cut off from the refreshing eastern sea-breeze. Did your sun-hungry skin seek the endless last lick of the sun?'

'That's a nice point, hadn't seen it that way, but you're right,' David said. 'Like a sort of altar. Hah! More like a sort of Aztec pyramid, perhaps. But I can't really imagine the ripping of living hearts to appease the sun god, not on this site. My sun god's not that blood-thirsty.'

'The aborigines here were gentler, wiser aesthetes.' Clyde smiled. 'They didn't have to appease the withholding gods. They were closer, in their own way, to the Ancestors.'

'What I wrote in that book – about the aborigines. It was half invention. It was a sort of guess.'

'You, David. You dark and golden as the sun hunter himself, now you cannot honestly tell me this place, in your mind, is all innocence? Very well, there's no reason to declare your affinity. None at all. You just retreat here for healing. Ah, my dears, there's the opaque ones, and the clear ones. Clyde must be clear. Claim. Clarity. I get lumped together with decisions. I make them. Once you owe allegiance to your ancestry you can take your life in your hands, decisively. But we've spoken of that. Your husband here.' For the first time since their early flirtatiousness Clyde accosted Deirdre. 'Your husband first came, across sand, and addressed me in the dark like a Guardian. That's the one, I thought then. Even before he shared with me the book of his secret longings and identifications. That one is the man who respects his Red Anthill and the Guardians. But perhaps I was wilful. I tell you this, though. On this island there's not one other speaks to me with the same language and taste for the vulnerable underbelly of living. He knows. But he's caught as a man of this world – hence the bargain with alcohol. And all this time he's not heeding any of the signs, though he's learning them.'

'Come off it, Clyde, you come on too strong!'

'You see? Most of the time your husband protests and protests. I tell you, though, he's one of the clear ones.'

Clyde smiled, smugly, Deirdre thought.

David stood up then. Across the table they stared at each other. Deirdre was the one person who might have moved at that point to recall the eating together, the fish meal and the sharing of speculations. Why was Clyde, in her mind, mocking her as Guardian?

'Now there's words,' she said.

The several offerings and the opportunity to explore together were forgotten, or at least deflected. There was nothing further to say.

They heard Clyde's resonant laughter as he bumped down the new-made steps and into the darkness. The ironbark grove and the antbeds were presences still, but entirely absent. Clyde would deny that, David thought, again filling himself with imprecise grudges.

Deirdre came out to the verandah after him.

'I see what you mean.'

'Do you?'

'How could someone like that stay in hiding for so long? What was it you said: seven years?'

'He says I'm the one who unbottled him.'

They both laughed.

Shortly after, as they lay in bed, Deirdre whispered, 'You still awake?'

David did not reply.

'Look, I'll tell you. It's the way that man keeps on acting so bloody smugly about your book. I know what you think about that book. I know you hold it against me that I couldn't finish reading the thing. Well, I am honest, I have to be honest about such things. It's not that I don't respect your work and all the effort you put into researching and writing it, David, you know how impressed I was by all that, how we all shuffled around in awe at David working on his book, the lot of us. But I've got to be truthful. It wasn't the history part, all those cut-and-paste anecdotes and incidents. It was *you* in that book that, well, was almost embarrassing. I thought you were letting people see things they did not want to see, like watching someone in the toilet or the bathroom when they cannot see you are looking and they do all those little private things that might be universal enough but still make one want to look away. Are you listening, David?'

He had turned on his side, away from her.

'Look, now it's out I've got to tell you this. Especially since that Clyde has clearly been feeding you with wads of ego padding because of the book. Well, that's okay, I'm not questioning his response, or his right. Though I do wonder just what use he is making of the book. To get to you. To get at you. Never believe someone who is too enthusiastic, especially if you yourself have your own reservations. David, I've got to be honest. I do have my reservations about that book. You are not being you, in it. It is as if you are falsifying yourself, taking a dramatic stance. There is a sort of phoniness. No, not phoniness; something, someone there in that book who is not you. A false you, false rhetorics. The David I know is someone else; it's this man here, warts and all, grumps and all. You're the real one, David. It's you, the here and now you, that I am wrapped around, mad about, married to. That's what matters. The physical David, the real you.' She paused. 'I don't know; you're just not *like* the voice of that book. It's as if there were another you. So impassioned, yet so distant. I don't want you out of reach, David. I want you here, now, and for God's sake, sharing with me.'

She knew that she would have to endure his silence. But she knew, also, here, he would return. If the distances seemed longer, the return was always inevitable, and her reward for patience.

XII

It had been quiet for a long time. Silence had become a way of life. There were only twenty in the tribe and the others had been on one of the islands, were probably still there. The goanna had been in one of the upper, hollowed-out branches of the big ironbark all day now. It would come down when the others were about to set out in their dug-out canoes but that might be a long time yet. Time was not the element. Receptivity, patience, absence from within one's own body were the necessary states and he had achieved these states. He had been fasting, he did not know when food had been last eaten.

All his being had become disciplined to this.

Like the string out of his navel that connected with some further dimension, up there, like the long thread that he knew or imagined uniting the sky world with his present moment.

Only silence for a long time achieves such an entry into what music comes from, or may be, one note, one note, one note. The first note, as in music.

The second note. In his focus now he was preparing for the second note. Would it be higher? Lower? Would its vibrations entwine with those of the first note and would they divide, pair off, spin like a gibber across flat water? Or would they be jarring enemies, enough to crack open the sky cover, lead off to thunder, distant and rocking, the hills moving, trees swaying, great and terrible powers that consume even themselves?

Find a point of concentration; that was the secret and he would continue forever. The second note would be harmony, it would be the prism, rainbow. Sounding together: the chord, could that be invented yet? Would he be capable of such mastery? Better perhaps to think of sequence: one note, one note, one note.

Fire is the internalised element. He knew that, it enabled his body to become a husk, a shield, to hold in the warmth and even to radiate it. Think of the focus, then, of the centre from which this heat emanates. Not the head. Not the fingertips or the toes though they burn with strange sensitivity. That is the burning of ice. Not under the ribs, somewhere lower. Not the genitals, the groin that sweats or the too mobile clench and relaxation of the scrotum, heat acts there but does not come from there. The centre then, the navel, the place from which all the original energy entered, that was more possible. The long invisible thread of the sky cord still fed it, giving and returning substances there.

Concentrate.

He could imagine the sleeping mother, the source, in her sleep still providing sustenance, blood, life, death, imagination. Warmth? Does warmth from the mother enter there too? He could not tell.

Somewhere lower. Lower, halfway between the navel and the dish of the groin. Focus there. In the gut, the place where the mystical source arrives and becomes your own. The place where your own body acts upon it, where you having received it now bring your own energy to re-make it, send what it has into all parts of the body, digestion, energy, the acting centre and the core of the heat of one's own body. Heat, radiating, forcing the outer parts to accept the will of energy, the message reinvented through the rainbow cord and the sleeping sky mother. He could accept that.

It was the source, indeed, and food was not necessary, clothing and fire were not necessary, movement was unnecessary.

A snake had come out of the grasses, the black snake with the red belly. He was sending it out from its hole in the soft red earth under the ironbark. It would circle his site, rub through the cold ashes, pass under his immobile bent knee and then move with slow muscular contractions down his almost invisible track until it reached the sand dunes, then it would stop. He would be thinking then of the mangrove area, it would herald a return back into the corporeal being.

But not yet. There was work to do yet.

He would have to face the last ritual. Would it be his own flesh? Would it be the flesh of one of the dead ones? That had not been revealed yet and muscular spasms of the red-bellied black snake were an extension of the way he must take. He must think hard and focus, there was no time allotted for this. It took all time into itself like the rainbow which, if you believed it to be centred within time, you never saw wholly. But the muscular contractions, the belly movements across sand, rocks, sticks, grey leaves and mottled ones, the exertion of the whole body in such ripples of contractions, he did not know if he was there yet, if he must believe it possible. But would he be the one? The black snake sunned itself on a bull-banksia stump now, the rough bark making no dent, no scratch, no abrasion.

Was his commerce with the dead?

Would it be necessary to devour some part of them?

Shaking, his muscles seemed plucked from him and made separate; he was rolling in the ashes now, he could not help it. The long thread had been cut, he had been severed from the great nourishment and his body returned to him now, his own body, real, all too tangible, in this uncontrollable shuddering, shivering, wrenching, jerking, jerking.

His legs buckled up, then jerked downwards, it was not his own doing.

His neck, his head were buckling, unbuckling, and the shivering, the heat source suddenly overturned, water across the fire.

Deirdre was calling to him. It was very distant but it was her voice. Something urgent, called out with anxiety. His fingers had sensation now, he could almost have use of his wrists, elbows, but would his shoulders ever be restored to mobility?

He concentrated thought onto his ankles. He would command his parts again. He could not endure such imprisonment, such absence, such cold terror. He would be in control of his body, he and no other.

'David. David, you all right now? Thank God, the fever's broken. You're all soaking.'

With her calm voice she began, like a nurse, to reassure him while she threw more rough blankets over his body, holding the spirit-thing down, throwing a shroud to keep in the dark.

XIII

It was probably mid afternoon before David rose from the bed. He heard Deirdre in the other room, then on the verandah. She was doing something in the yard at one stage, mattock thumping, thumping. She was beside him with warmed milk.

He hated milk.

She was talking to someone outside, her voice was over-bright. She was laughing. Then back at work, thump, thump. When she came in later he could smell the red dirt on her forearms.

He had stopped sweating. He had been dozing.

Mid afternoon: in the empty house David rose and went to the room where the tap was. He washed himself, standing naked so that every part of his skin claimed for itself the sensation of water, air, movement. He dressed.

Deirdre came in then. She was pleased that he was looking so much better. Colour was back. His check jacket was dry now, a bit stiff and hardly improved so far as cleanliness was concerned, from Clyde's washing, but still it had been thoughtful of Clyde, hadn't it, and at least it did not smell of fish and all the other things. David tried it on.

He sat on the verandah rail and watched Deirdre finish her digging. He offered to go over to Cleveland to buy some seeds, or even go to the nursery. Their voices to each other still seemed, somehow, the voices of other people, far off.

She said if he wanted to they could try to get to Cleveland before the nursery closed but was he yet up to it? He slipped off the rail. He took her mattock from her.

There was a smile.

It was as if he were floating, but his feet did hit ground; if he concentrated he could feel inside the boot the way his toes gripped and thrust, the muscle bunching and moving, the ankle turning, the knot of the calf gripping with sinews, the mechanical complexity of the knee and all its bones and tendons.

At the jetty they came to Jim, just mooring his little ferry. David knew this would be so. He let Deirdre go ahead and sort out arrangements. Jim was happy to go over to the mainland again even though he had just returned from Cleveland. David knew that, before Jim even nodded. He walked up and there was a smile that was an operation of several muscles and the teeth guarding the stretched curve of the lips. He told Deirdre not to worry, he was just fine. He could tell she was dying to reach out her hand and test his forehead for temperature. He placed himself carefully in the boat.

The sensation over water, though, made him realise how fragile his whole body was. He had bones there, he had parts and linkages that had been taken for granted and now claimed tribute. It was almost as if in his fever someone or something had taken out his own bones – the thigh bone, the plate bone of his ribs – and replaced them with something different, more fragile. It was as if his bones had become shell-thin and brittle. He gripped tight.

'Look at this.' Deirdre sat herself beside him; she held up the piece of rock quartz, a small crystal. 'Found it this morning where I was digging. Meant to show you before but just came across it again now when I put my hand into your shirt pocket for a cigarette.'

She held it up to the light. It was white, no, not white: clear, a small shaft with the miraculous natural five-sided walls that you found in all the volcanic cliff rocks around here. She held it up to the light and for an instant it trapped the light's prism. A reflected rainbow was tossed back across her cheek. She pressed it into his hand.

The touch, the pressure: was his skin so sensitive? Or had she meant it. It was as if the small crystal had been pushed right though the skin, right into the hand below the skin. A small veil of sweat broke across his brow. He was a fool to have attempted to get up after the fever. The cold air from across water followed him, dogs with claws, teeth biting the air though they were silent. Was his face showing all this? He dropped the rock crystal.

Deirdre picked it up quickly. As from a distance he could tell that she was struggling within herself: should she take over, should she be the mother? Or was it best to let him have his fit and prove to himself just how unfit he was? She had trained herself to wait, a shadow, she would be ready with aspirin and bandages.

She smiled up at him. Too easy.

It was this water. The trip across water had never seemed so slow, and his own fragility, aching with every bump or lurch: was he actually on the point of being seasick? In this calm bay? What sort of a shadow was he?

They reached land. Rising, he felt stiff, tired, but was determined. Deirdre took his arm but he shoved her off. She thrust her arm through his then and he let her. Her body was solid, warm, substantial and like a pillar. If he gave way for one instant he would sink against that pillar and know it would hold him up.

They were too late for the nursery.

'Come on,' David said, 'Peter will be down at the pub by this time. We can corner him there and get him to give us the keys. He'll let us make our own selection, and we can fix up for the payment no troubles, later.'

But when they reached the pub, someone said Pete was back at the service station, he'd be down later, as per usual. David was on a bar stool by now. The thought of an uphill walk drained his energy. The barman put a pot of Castlemaine in front of him.

He persuaded Deirdre to check up on Pete and come back soon as possible. He'd order a shandy for her.

'And make sure you get things that'll grow in the red soil. The means practically anything. What about hibiscus?'

Deirdre had her own ideas.

As she left he observed her departing figure as from a great distance. It was strange; he could not shake off this sensation of dissociation, as if he were sitting alongside himself, as if he were his own medium. He lurched with his beer to a corner.

'You all right, brother?' Two of the aborigines from the settlement over at Dunwich were standing over him. Their dark faces were large and bent close. He must have dozed off. One of them reached out an arm to help lift him up. David jerked back to consciousness and, without thought, brushed his helper aside.

'Jeezuz, I'm not a cot case.'

'You looked taken away, brother. Like you left us.'

David felt for his wallet.

'Where's me beer?'

But they quickly brought over his glass. He must have slumped back and half-sprawled over the sofa in the pub's window recess. He had to thank the tall one.

They sat beside him. Although there was a sort of quietness in their eyes and manner, David stiffened and was alert, quickly, to threat. What were they after?

But they talked to each other across him in slow rather uninflected voices, taking all the time in the world to explain how the tailor were still over at Bird Island and right across to the bay to the south of Peel Island; they had never seen them in such numbers though the old men said it was like that before, in the old time.

Their voices droned like the buzzing of surf in the distance – not labial, not guttural. It was slow and unhurried, they had all night, it was no worry. He was being included.

Did this mean he would be obliged to shout them a round? Well, why not? he finally decided, and raised himself from between them, excusing himself. He felt wobbly. He knew they were looking at him, mentally with arms under each of his shoulders. He hated that.

When he returned with the three glasses he handed them each one but remained standing himself. They looked down, as if they knew what he was thinking. They would not intrude. That was the part that irked.

His eyes drew up their fire. He gulped the beer down quickly. 'See yuz later!' he said fiercely, gave them a nod, and pushed out into the night air. Dark so quickly.

XIV

The second meeting with Galina Darovskaya had been in Sydney, two weeks before David made his desperate drive up to the island. That was a tense time; the tension had been building for weeks – longer, perhaps, if he were honest.

The night before his encounter with Galina, David and Deirdre went over to Meg and Brian Mackey's. Friday nights had evolved into a habit, one with increasing pressures. Although nothing was spoken, a feeling of vortex seemed to have been engendered, an inward spring that was rapid, exhilarating and irresistible – so long as each one kept with the pressure and pace of it. Terrifying if you attempted to exert individual control – like people in the giant spinner at Luna Park, who count it a feat almost unimaginable if they manage to raise one hand from the spinning wall.

David had raised that one hand. Or had he spun off, over the top, tossed out by the energy machine – merely one of the cast-offs, the victims?

Looking back on it, though, he might have seen easily enough the direction they were caught into. The pace was entirely logical; the result inevitable.

The Friday night before he encountered Galina again they simply played Scrabble at the Mackeys'. The dark bottles were piled up after use in the big wicker clothes-basket under the kitchen bench. Its lid held the count. The woven texture was pleasing and industrious.

The clothes-basket was a thing Meg brought back from Bali, then wondered what use it could be put to. The bottle-bin.

On that following Saturday, David, grumpy and abstracted, took the boys off to the Paddington Markets. It was something to keep them amused and there was some excuse about getting them sandals, or a leather belt hand-crafted, or cast-off jackets (suddenly old vests and waistcoats were irresistible to them, especially if they had silk- or rayon-lined backs). It was stalls with junk jewellery or hand-crafted 'originals', racks and racks of garments, Indian cheesecloth, Chinese formals in theatre colours, wool knitted by thumbs, chain-mail singlets in string, high-priced lace made by slave daughters in bedrooms with 25 watt lamps, Akubra hats from the '40s and black or maroon berets from army surplus, black negligées in their hundreds this week, mirror jewel-boxes, Mickey Mouse alarm clocks, old silver- and bone-handled knives, sheepskin jerkins, drum leather hats, handbags, portfolios.

The crush of marketers and onlookers reflected the mayhem and gregarious style of the mornings – dramatic young, clanking chains and black leather, or punks with their hair and scalps like theatre sets; couples eating ice-cream with the licking tongues of sensualists; gangs of boys herding past without looking; girls dawdling, trying, testing, indecisive.

In the calm sunlight David followed his own and saw that they were fed with spiced seaweed and would be back near the entrance at eleven o'clock. Sharp.

He browsed a while himself among a stall full of kitchen oddments that meant nothing, they were part of his mother's old kitchen; green glass refrigerator storage bowls, an art deco vase, canisters for tea and salt, tins that once held sago and biscuits. He was shocked at the prices being asked for such trivia. Do people have that much to throw away? It was a stall of frivolity, not poverty. The poor would pick up such objects out of garbage bins, or pay ten cents at the St Vincent de Paul depots.

David crossed Oxford Street and headed for New Edition coffee shop.

He was certain it was her. He looked hard, tried to catch her eye. It must be Galina Darovskaya; nobody else had that proud fragile head, so upright and disciplined yet vulnerable, a flowerhead held by a thin neck of such elegance it could be milk porcelain. She was sipping her tea from a glass sheathed in filigree with a silver handle. Was she a regular?

It took him five minutes to make up his mind to approach her. What if she valued her privacy and did not want to be disturbed? What if she did not remember him? And her accent: would it be understandable? He might make a fool of himself with some perfect stranger, the city must be full of old refugees.

He knew it was Galina Darovskaya.

He knew, also, that having seen her he must make contact.

'Yes. I know you. I have so few visitors to my own home.'

She motioned David to sit down. He jammed in.

As with his previous visit he hardly needed to make conversation. It was as if in her long years of silence, without visitors and without appointments, Galina's thoughts had time to become crystalline. It needed only the appearance of the rare visitor, or the chance contact and it all would stream out, her rainbow of interior experience and shrewd observations. Or that part of it she chose to uncover.

'Did you know, I have read your book,' she said. David was startled, almost embarrassed. 'There was a copy in the local newsagent, the very next morning. I said to myself: that is a sign. You will forgive me if I say it is a skimpy and awkward history, and without proper footnotes. But I liked it.'

She reached out her thin hand and smiled, with sudden and marvellous warmth. 'I liked it enormously. I said to my daughter, this is an impassioned man. He is confused and in love with the conflict of his trees and his forests, but he is a poet. And do you know, I found wonders. Here am I staying just off the Parramatta Road, at my one friend's place, in Annandale. And I recalled completely your quotation – in only an English translation, more's the pity – of François Péron, describing the Parramatta Road in, was it 1802? I was trained to memorise. Péron, in your translation, wrote: 'Parramatta Road appears at a distance like an immense avenue of foliage and verdure. A charming freshness and an agreeable shade always prevail in this continuous bower, the silence of which is only interrupted by the singing and chirping of the richly plumed parakeets and other birds which inhabit it.' Did you know that François Péron came from Cérilly, in the middle of France? There is a little monument in the square there which immortalises him. It reads: *Dried up like a young tree that succumbs under the weight of its own fruit.* On the other side of the monument there is a bronze relief showing Péron seated under a mangrove dotted with cockatoos in an Australian landscape peopled with familiar kangaroos. It was in Cérilly that I first decided to come to Australia.'

'Péron, they say, was a French spy, for Napoleon.'

'Péron was a botanist. He was an excellent observer. Dispassionate.'

'You admire that?'

'No. I admire passion, excess, and also temper, control. You see, I am allowed to be contrary. Apollo and Dionysus are both within me. Or were. Now, there is only resignation.'

'You don't strike me as a resigned person.' David smiled.

'My young friend, I see you still believe in the fires. I could be cruel to you; but will not. Your book; did you know it will be taken up by others and made their own? Smile at that; it is a sort of immortality. And you make me believe in your forests, your cedar trees. Truly, you enliven me with a true curiosity.'

'Let me take you there. Sometime. There are some wonderful small stands of cedar still in their wild state not so far from Mullumbimby. Very few people know of them, but I can take you there. Would you be really interested?'

'Not so quickly, young fellow. I am old. You also write passionate descriptions of the difficulties.'

'But these are pretty accessible. A dirt road, gets rough at times, you need a four-wheel drive. But I can take you to within a mile of the stand. Would you be prepared to walk a mile with me into the scrub? There's a sort of path most of the way.'

She looked at him. Her hand stirred the near empty tea glass. Her smile, coming again, was not genial but it was full of a curious verve.

'Come up to my little place again. We must talk further about such projects. You see, I am tempted. When you come I will make you a salad of fresh mushrooms. My daughter gathers fresh mushrooms on her property. And if you do not wish to eat my mushrooms, then you will have to nibble my knuckles instead.'

She held out her hand, as if she would have him kiss it. After a pause, impulsively he did.

'I have been two days in this city,' she said. 'I come here rarely. It is not my place, it is not my city, I wonder is it a city or is it just crowds

83

and more people? I do not know. It will find its own entity. My city, Leningrad, is not much older than this one, but it was a city that began from belief and ambition. St Petersburg. Is that a good thing? It is a good and a bad thing assuredly, because pride builds its beauties upon marshes and silt of bones. Order has the rigid mouth of long sabres, that have neat trenches to allow blood outlet. My city cost dearly. But it forced, also, the fires of true genius. Its very cold and damp made the fires within glow and burn, hold their pressure, flame into unquenchable torches. Forgive me, I was once a poet.'

'You've come down by yourself? You have friends here? There are lots of Russians around this place. You seen the marvellous hand-made chocolates . . . ?'

'Do you know what I see? I cannot explain my thoughts when I see. I see waste, I see wastage and litter. It fills me with horror. I am filled with dread and with horror and the terrible sadness. I would say to these people: do you know what you do? Do you not count the many mouths could be fed? Yet they tramp it into the gutter with their heels, they throw it under the wheels of their cars, they hardly touch it before they toss it out. I have seen food that might sustain many villages cast aside, tossed aside, made into rubbish. Help me. There is a bus stop across this busy road down by the traffic lights. Out of your kindness you will escort me there, please.'

David was pleased to assist. He cleared a path for her through the tiny crowded maze of the café. He felt protective and vulnerable. He found himself hanging onto her words, yet what were they, really? Surely the usual grouch of the elderly, the exiled, the ones who have slipped from the centre and are spinning off, floating, drifting, becoming insubstantial?

She gripped his arm.

'You see?' She pointed with her handbag. A child dropped its expensive ice-cream cone onto the footpath in front of them. Was it deliberate? Galina swept her gesture across to the gutter. A half eaten apple nestled among papers and a crushed meat pie, its white pith already tinged with the brown that would soon shrivel with it. Someone passed in a car and there spun out towards them a can of some soft-drink, a small squirt of fluid making patterns over the asphalt. A cyclist quickly ran over it, lurched and regained balance.

'Last night I watched in the small café downstairs below where I am staying,' she continued. 'Not one plate went back to the kitchen but it was still half uneaten: potato chips, gravy, carrot rings, meat and gristle . . .'

'Those chips are probably deep fried in stale oil, no wonder they're inedible.'

'Even your boot leather is not inedible.'

Then he remembered.

'I have seen your beggars pick and choose out of garbage bins. In the village where I now hide, I have seen small children across in the local school ground throw all their lunch sandwiches into the bins, I have seen them use fruit as toys – balls, targets – in their games. I see them stuff their pet dogs with their own food till they barely leapt after them. I have seen . . .'

'I did all those things. I used to hate cut lunches, always dry by the time you got to them. I used to throw oranges against the school wall till they burst open . . .'

'I did none of those things. I would have died rather than do one of those things. Even as a child, in our prosperous city, I knew the shadow of famine. Waste is the worst crime, the very worst. It is the fat black-marketeer and his plump daughter waddling by, throwing aside the bones of cooked chicken into the faces of the hungry. There is no worse thing than hunger.'

They passed a greengrocer. In the gutter were leaves of cabbage, an abandoned banana skin. Would it be possible to be so hungry that you would really scrabble for those? David knew it was possible.

He looked at Galina Darovskaya. How imagine that lean woman scrabbling in rubbish bins, snarling and baring her teeth over cabbage stalks? And besides: all that was well over forty years back. Think of forty years of good meals. The hunger pangs must have long since been appeased. Or like scars from flesh wounds, do such things remain with you all of your life?

'Now I will thank you.' She let go.

'*Ciao!*' he said, half playfully, half to break the spell of her recollections.

'*Ciao?* Do you know what that means? It is a corruption of the old Venetian phrase, *Schiavo vostro* – your slave. Are you my slave, now, do you think? Well, that we will discover when you make your visit.'

He was the one who was late at the meeting place. He returned to his two truculent children, and bought them hot dogs.

*

85

from THE LONG WINTER

I went out into the street. No,
do not laugh (you see, my dear, I still
imagine muscles and a fine, full mouth) –
I went out into the street today
with snow swirling and hard bodies of snow
under my boots (that were my father's).
Six weeks ago three bodies were piled
just below the entrance door
near the coal merchant's grating.
I walk high, under me a city has frozen
and it is hard, hard, thankfully hard
stuff I walk over.
                              It is wrong of you
(if you were here I would weep at the injustice!)
to accuse me of turning to ice and snow
packed hard also. Just this moment
a woman wearing all her shawls, her furs, her blankets
passed by me on her way to the ration issue.
On a child's yellow sled she pulled her husband,
thin stubble on his small chin, gaunt hollows
to sink his eyes into, his three remnants of scarves
almost debonair, his face engrossed with the skull.
On her thin shoulders, the rope. It was rubbing.
Without the body, no ration card.
The yellow sled squeaked over the snow.
There are now so few children.

*

from THE HUNGER

The morning of our wedding there was a queue
at the end of the square. Rumours
of a special issue of bread and sugar
brought people running and slipping.
It will be a very special day!
They were only rumours,
but people would not move on.

86

Dim husky thud of cannon, the songs of shells
— the orchestra for our wedding
was more expensive than the whole Kirov Theatre.
On the long nights of blackout
we dreamed of the night of our wedding.
I had saved a candle, your warmth
would be fabulous.
Though a shell exploded in the square
the crowd re-formed, hardly noticing
the four bodies that were dragged off
and we looked at each other
not out windows. As if to prove it was special
someone came with a gift of three rats,
strangely plump ones. It was a good omen.
We ate meat on the night
of our wedding, meat.

XV

Nine a.m. and the fog still shrouded everything. A greyness that made the sun some sort of outcast. Some sort of prisoner to the power of water, Deirdre thought, as she moved out onto the verandah. She swept her palm over the new rail: a scatter of drops hit her feet and ankles. She could not even see the trunk of the nearest ironbark.

David was still asleep. It was the best way. She wiped her forehead with the wet hand. Already her hair was netted with a fine web of water. Really thick this morning. She went back inside.

After making herself coffee and reassuring herself that the sleeping form was stable, deep in the healing slumber, she tucked David's blankets closer around him, put on a grey plastic raincoat over her green army shirt and the bulky pullover she had unearthed among David's things, then went outside to the verandah again. The tree trunk loomed like some remote pillar; it could stretch up for miles into that greyness. She walked down and put her hands on its rich, deeply grooved trunk. A spider web was revealed clearly, glistening with moisture. She looked; the whole trunk was scattered with webs, all small, but a positive infestation.

And the boys! Even so young, why was it they regarded her as peripheral? By nine years of age each was absorbed in a world that sought to diminish her. Then she remembered: the spiders, the web-makers, these were mostly female. Their mates hovered under leaves, in crevasses, they were marginal and unstable.

Tiny spiders, she thought.

She looked back to the shack. It loomed, blurred. Inside David would be snug. Last night he had been bright eyed, thoughts random, not really coherent, as if the fever were still fitfully tugging him. She had been stupid to let him go out over water right after that bout of high temperature. She had not been thinking.

Or had she been thinking? Subconsciously wanting revenge for the fright he gave her: take the risk, take the risk? If you want to burn, burn fire over water, let the water stoke fevers again, build them up, let the test be performed, the body fight for its control of things. Had she sought to rekindle his fever?

Sometimes the burden seemed enormous.

Of course none of these things had gone through her mind; how morbid. David, snug back there, like a dark baby, so much in need of mothering though he'd never see that. She had been touched by his offer to share the ceremony of planting the shrubs. It was a new stage in the business of claiming their land. It would be theirs together. Theirs. They had paid for it.

Putting your fingers into the earth, planting and growing things: her old grandmother always said it was the way to keep sane. The old woman got up in the mornings, 5 a.m. and was out digging the rosebeds, tending the beans or the beetroot. Deirdre, in defining the little garden under the newly finished verandah, almost unconsciously had been re-enacting that ancestral logic. And it felt right. How could she not be moved by David's instant proposal and energy at the thought of the garden nursery over on Cleveland? Four weeks' anguish fell off her in that gesture.

She found herself shuffling down the little track to the sand. She grabbed at branches and shrubs to keep her balance, and was showered in sprays of dew-cold water; it was like a baptism. Several spider webs were outlined across the track and she broke off a twig to clear her way. Down on the sand, her foot marks re-christened the smooth dampness. Strange how by evening the sand always looked ruffled, used, covered with traces of movement, yet by morning all had been washed out, a new start prepared. She pushed into the soft sand of the dune and went to the water's edge. Almost nothing visible around her. Fog like padding.

A tern shuffled on the beach behind her, appearing and disappearing out of fog, hunched and disconsolate. Deirdre almost laughed. What would the noise of her laughter be like, here in the mesh of water spun into cloud? It would bounce back at her, shrouded. She knew she had been right to speak out her thoughts at last on his book.

Slowly she followed the shore line until she reached the edge of the mangrove swamp.

For the first week of his absence their house had been calm, the boys pretended not to notice. But the nights bit like tides into her sandbank, eroding that initial complacency. The first ache had been for David: how was he making out? Was he drinking himself to death up there? Would he pull out of the nose-dive? At least she knew that a road accident would be reported quickly. It had all been so sudden. All the earlier signs had been quibbles, the mesh of their lives seemed resilient. There had been trust, even in some of the madder escapades. She had believed in some final core of sharing, of responsibility. She believed in David, the real David. Then this thing, this frightening loss of control. When he lurched into the car and skidded off, it was a gesture like flight; but she had to accept it as therapy.

She had to let him do it. She had to trust him.

Later, the boys grew more boisterous, they took advantage of her preoccupation, to get away with things, raiding the towel cupboard and leaving sodden towels in heaps in the bathroom, in their bed-rooms. Or they sneaked the television set up to their room around midnight to watch late-night horrors. Or they answered her back in the kitchen, well aware that they were now of a size where the physical meant something for them too – power. David would have kept that in check with delight and glee, he had talked often with her about the stages of growth and initiation, the first shave, the first stand against parents (mother first, then the old man). In three weeks they had declared a new territory and she did not like it; she was being used, manipulated in ways that were offensive to her sense of fairness. They were urban terrorists.

In the end she made up her mind. Her parents could still come in handy sometimes – and besides, the boys adored them, they would never try the tricks on them. They knew every weak spot of her own – then went for the kill, unerringly. But with their grandparents there seemed a different space; no need to challenge, no need to claim victory.

The fog had its calming effect. Deirdre appreciated the cocoon of it. And the emergence of trees, shrubs, landmarks came with a new mystery – or a return to original mystery. It was a way of re-entering your own territory. Deirdre had, yes, been apprehensive about coming up, about David's reaction. She had even to face the possibility that he was not on the island. After all, he had not written. For one gulf of a moment she had imagined him off to Darwin or Alice Springs with a new mistress – she had never really checked up on him.

That thought had passed. Unthinkable, really. Deirdre was secure that their centres revolved around each other; it could never be different. The first time she had met him she had recognised this, its inevitability had consumed her, even to the point of embarrassment, so that even his looks – like a boxer whose nose had been flattened, she joked to him once – had meant nothing; they were nothing to do with his reality. His rough energy, and his sullenness, his silences, they played a part, but only a part. She had hoped they would not become too inexorable, too rigid, but if so, there was nothing could be done about it. The bond was made. The ironbark did not choose where its roots moved into the soil; it accepted what was there.

One time David and Deirdre and Meg had gone to bed together, a threesome. Deirdre had long since put it out her mind; but it could recur as a curious disjointed image. Or was it too intense, blurred because of the too-close proximity?

Afterwards, Deirdre and Meg were cautious with each other, but they were still best friends. Yes, perhaps, she deliberately remembered only the good things, the consolidating things.

That game of pool.

Brian and Meg Mackey had a strange old place overlooking Mosman Bay in one of the older North Shore suburbs of Sydney. Cut into the steep hillside, from the street it was just a Federation style timber home. Its outlook was over the scrub and the park that led to the ferry. An ancient terraced garden below the house had been long overgrown, it was a jungle: sprawling banana clumps with rotted cores; a Japanese pool and garden on the third terrace, overrun now with iris gone wild and a vast azalea bush and morning glory entwined in a death embrace. There were one hundred mossy steps cut into the sandstone bluff down to the lower walking path and the Mosman ferry. Brian and Meg never used the steps, they shrugged at their terraces. They bought it in this overgrown state and they left it like that.

The main room of their house went from one end to the other, a ballroom, a presentation chamber, a draughty cold foyer that was seldom used; the family lived in the smaller rooms at the side, in the added-on kitchen and breakfast room. The grand room was only a sort of passage. A passage and a storeroom. At the far end was the full-sized billiard table. Brian and David shared an enthusiam for pool. Above the table an enormous antique Venetian chandelier hung, garish and fantastic, a milky funeral ornament.

The other half of the big room was dominated by fourteen old hanging lamps, Victorian and ornate with a domestic ostentation. They overshadowed the seven dexter rockers and five cedar chiffoniers. Brian had once a sideline in antiques. 'Who else has fourteen hanging lamps in the one room, each in working order?' Brian was proud of his relics. Brian was a good mate, David often declared, not too much up himself. Brian could jolly David out of his moods. Deirdre liked Brian.

David would bend and stroke the smooth polish of these cedar chiffoniers, then laugh – not with envy of his friend, but a sort of shared amazement. Deirdre herself did not feel much for old cedar: so hard to keep polished, so easily dented. She allowed its beauty – but remembered her own mother's constant engagements with beeswax and O'Cedar oil.

That last time at the Mackeys' the game of pool began quietly. David had been drinking at the golf club then at the local; it had been one of those tense weekends. He had forgotten the invitation to the Mackeys. Deirdre, who was no mean dab at pool herself, had gone down to the pub to search him out. She played one game with him, watched by the genial men around the table, beer glasses in their hands, stomachs pouring out above their belts.

One game was sufficient, and when Deirdre reminded David about the Mackeys he gulped down the last of his glass and took out his car keys instantly. It is sometimes dangerous to remind someone of forgotten obligations. Deirdre knew she would receive his silence in the car. She knew to make lighthearted conversation, ignoring the sullenness. It was not really intended for her. It was not really intended to be public.

They played pool till near midnight. Brian had two dozen bottles of a new red wine from up in the Hunter Valley. Even so young it was marvellous, he had declared.

They chatted and sipped, nibbled and listened to old Pink Floyd discs and, like a screw slowly turning, David became separated from the other three. Like an antagonist, he seemed to place himself more and more at some psychic distance.

At some late stage they ended up down in the back terrace, the Japanese garden. Something to do with not waking the kids. Something to do with a dare about spiders and cobwebs, David and Brian each carried two of the wine bottles, the last.

Was it Meg started it? Perhaps it was Meg who first spoke out: why was David so aggressive tonight? Why had he insisted in taking the centre, all through the pool game after supper? Meg complained that he made her feel a stranger, an intruder in her own home and that was ridiculous. Brian hadn't helped much either. He let David take over, even here, down in Brian's own garden, as if other people didn't have a part. It was the bad time of night. It was too late, and they had drunk too much of the acidy red wine, all of them. Why did it have to end up like this, why couldn't they have a good evening together, without drink?

Brian, nettled by his wife's challenge, found himself forced to defend her. It was childish for him to take the schoolyard manner, offering to challenge David with fisticuffs. But something was begun then, and there was no going back. Perhaps that was why Brian turned, after, to verbal taunts, gibes that none of them attempted to stop or to counter – not even Deirdre.

'Learn to be honest,' Brian had said. 'You're the most dishonest bloke I know, Dave, dishonest with me, with Deirdre, with Meg, with everyone. You hide behind every limp excuse and pretext under the sun. You hide behind Deirdre. You hide behind job, games, drink. You hide behind your dark olive skin and your bloody Cornish genetics like they were a curtain. You're not even honest enough to admit you're a drunk, an alcoholic. Everyone knows it. Ask Meg, ask Deirdre. I'll tell you. I'll tell you straight out. You're a drunk, a pisspot, a toper, alcoholic, alcoholic.'

'Bloody drunkard yourself. Who're you kidding? Why all this set on me?' David began with a slow defence but Deirdre somehow had to let him work through by his own means. They knew there was some purge, some cycle set in train that he must go through. In the night

93

garden, overgrown and slushy underfoot, David and Brian circled round each other. They were all caught in the vortex.

It seemed to go on for a very long time. Deirdre felt herself, with the others, part of the action of harrying him, digging at him, urging him: get it out, get it spoken. Something was there, something that had to be uncovered or it would go back underground, as it had so many times.

'Why do you keep terrorising Deirdre, why do you run from her, why don't you accept the real caring she has to offer, why turn it aside and drag in others?' Brian had taunted – or probed.

'Why hurt others, too, what have you got against women, what have you got against people, why hoard the hurt, why bully people with words, why deny your real feelings?'

So that David did begin to crawl deeper, call out, shout and gargle, commencing with incoherent cries and sobs directed at Deirdre. She had at first moved towards him wanting to hold him, to protect.

But she stepped back. Brian motioned her to. Meg put her arm round. Get it out, get it out. The smothering, the loving, the being there always, the turning up, following around, the need to be wanted, the want and the wanting. Deirdre heard all that. Get it out.

No, it was not really Deirdre, he acknowledged that. And not Meg, nothing to do with Meg, and not Brian, Brian did not matter – it was not the source – he could even admire Brian's enjoyment of things, the way he could stop, like the antiques. No, it was further, further back, further.

Get it out, get it out.

Why should it be his mother? Out. Out. He had been cast out. It was his mother, why had she failed him, why had he failed her, why had she kept secrets? He had asked and she denied. He had asked her, she had sworn, oh yes, she had promised, he was unimportant, she had laughed, laughed always.

She did not care, her own skin paler than fish, it did not matter. Why was he darker than the other boys? They said it was boong, was it abo? Laughing at him, holding back, never touching, slapping and cuffing, hearty, laughing, keeping the secret. As if he had not earned the right, as if he had failed and his colour was upon him, him, and nobody other. Not his mum, not his dad, that silent man who was in his toolshed most of the time – how could that man not be his dad? She knew, she knew, only she knew and she laughed at him. Where was his anger then, why had it never exploded at her? Why had she failed him, betrayed him, cast him off, laughing?

Sobs, a dry racking, something never before experienced, his whole frame crumpled, he was down on the grass, wringing, racked. Not sobs, something wrenched beyond sobs; the long denial, the grief unbelievable, the hurt, the anger, the loss, throwing him onto the night damp grass, in the mud where his own feet had churned it, staggering in tight circles. Watched by the three helpless others. None of them had anticipated this.

They say men have howled like dogs. That night he discovered it. Later, when he had recovered and pulled himself together, Deirdre held him and dragged him to the car. The others showed sympathy. They were all shaken.

Deirdre stepped forward onto the first edge of the mudbank, her bare toes sensitive to the different sensation. After the cold welcome of sand with its slight abrasiveness and its gentle parting under her weight, the hard suck of mud and the persistence of its grip was almost seductive.

She splayed out her toes into it, let it slip in between them she carefully trod among the upright bed-of-nails that were the aerial roots of the mangrove system, first advance troops in the strategy of reclaiming land out of the mouth of the sea. The mangrove swamp was a low storage system: compost, detritus, a self-generating world that inched itself upwards with time to make new peninsulas, islands, low lying banks that eventually took grasses, other trees, rose into hillocks. She rejoiced in the physical sensations of this island.

She slipped, then regained balance. Always before she had explored in the huge Wellington boots they had bought specially. There could be oysters with their razor edges, submerged snags and branches, even the poisonous stonefish had been found in these areas, this very bay. Colour of pumice, it lay in such murky shallow waters its spine of poisonous barbs could remain invisible. People had died.

Grabbing up a long stick Deirdre pushed forward, poking around, testing. The fog was now beginning to disperse: the first bank of mature mangroves was clearly visible, they must be twenty paces ahead. The shroud retained its soft shape still; it isolated ridges of mangroves from those behind, silhouetted them. Beautiful, Deirdre thought, the mud covering her ankles: beautiful.

Bubbles of gas were released under her soles; they scrambled up the skin and were set free. Mud smell, decay, something more than decay: chemical, rich. Why do we particularise smells, she thought. It had its rightness.

For such work it was necessary to look downward, pace by pace. Deirdre first realised the fog had dispersed when she became aware of a watery light, an oil of rainbow streaks in the puddles around her. She looked up. The smudged sun would soon reach her.

It was only when she did cut her foot on a rip of oyster shells that she decided to return. She had reached far into the marshy area. Looking back she realised how far.

The cut did not hurt at first, though it bled profusely, colouring the darkness with its stain. Oyster shells cut deeply. She tried to stand on one foot and clean it, wipe the mud with a handkerchief she had pocketed. No use. By the time she reached the sand her wound was beginning to pound and its bleeding distressed her. She ran, using her left heel, and then clambered up the steep track to their hill lookout.

David was up. 'Where'd you get to? Thought you'd cleared out on me.' When he saw she was injured he hopped down and in one sweep picked her up, depositing his trophy on the verandah floor. 'Easy does it!'

He examined the wound and they stooped at the tap of the tank-stand to rinse it.

'Hmm. Pretty deep.'

'We must have acraflavine. Or iodine.'

'Might need stitches.'

'Don't be silly.'

But she let him dress the wound, and then bandage it firmly. She rested her hand on his shoulder as he was labouring, his eyes glittered with concentration. She moved it up to the exposed skin of his neck. They say the neck is the first part to age, she thought to herself. She watched his coarse but sensitive fingers – any part of the skin can become erogenous, yes.

It was only over lunch that David began picking, acting the convalescent.

'All the trouble about getting over to Cleveland so you could buy some new shrubs and what happens? I come out this morning – no Deirdre, no gardener in sight. I come out and the bloody pots are still standing there, as if you'd forgotten them already, didn't care. I can imagine their fate from now on. We were fools to put out money.

Soon as we're gone they'll just curl up and die. Bloody stupid outlay.'

'Don't be defeatist, Dave. I took that into account, that's why I chose sturdy ones, ones that could grow on their own most months of the year. Once they establish a root system.'

'Defeatist? I'm just pointing out the practicalities. Seems we need someone practical around here. Look at the way you wander round, cutting your foot – gashing your foot – in a damned stupid barefoot parade round the mangrove swamp. Even the kids know better. You *told* the kids why they couldn't go barefoot down there. No wonder they laugh at you.'

'I'm the one suffering, Dave, I think I've paid my price. You don't have to rub it in.'

'Wandering round barefoot among oyster beds and stonefish and fish-hooks – think you were a bloody boong!'

'Don't use that word.'

'I'll use what I like. I've got a bloody right. Boongs, lot of them. Boongs.'

It was as if he sought some release by attacking those quiet representatives of the original tribes, there in the hotel last night. She knew better than to mention, again, the 'black Cornish'. What did anyone care? Things are done out of immediate energy. It is nothing: the compost, the mangrove bed rotting and building.

Later that day she said, suddenly, 'David, if you keep persisting in this endless bitch about aborigines I think you'd better face up to the fact of being bigoted. You should go over to Dunwich and speak to them. Try to explore the subject.'

She was surprised when, after a pause, he agreed.

97

XVI

The poet Judith Wright, in a lecture, once described the effect upon the rainforest ecology when one large tree was felled – through cyclone or storm, or by man's hacking. It is like a widening sore, she explained. The weakened infrastructure around the hole in the forest caused by the felling gradually widens as more and more surrounding trees, vines, brushes, are exposed and weakened, their dependency upon the host tree now evidenced. So, over a period of time, the hole grows larger, more trees fall in the next storms, light breaks through and in a short while foreign weeds, wind blown, bird dropped, begin to take a foothold. The old order cannot return. You do not regenerate a rainforest.

In such a delicate balance, is it any wonder that the intruding European found himself outmatched and set upon destroying his own bounty, with such speed that hardly a generation was enough to render his prodigality of energy a prodigality of wastefulness? For those with the will still to search, there are some few and very distant stands of aboriginal cedar in groves that remind us of that former abundance. I will not name the sites. Bulldozers would be there next week. Once whole houses, fences, pigsties and cowsheds were built of the fragrant red cedar. Specialists still comb the dairy farms in search of such treasure, to make rich veneers. Look hard at those veneers, collectors. They are a kind of blood. The very beauty of this timber hits us with a *sting of pain. Perhaps that is the price. For we are all, in the heart, collectors. We are all culpable.*

David Cumberland: *The Big Scrub: A History* (ibid)

*

He had begun with a rush of determination. The long ferry journey to Stradbroke Island quelled his impatience as he must have known it would. The purr and groan of working engines, the sense of purpose and forward movement massaged his muscles into a fellowship with that energy. Now he was on his own.

Hardly so, the bitumen led to the small group of shops in Dunwich. There would be girls behind counters shuffling the display cases, nibbling at chocolate, yarning at entranceways. Two or three cars gleamed in the sunlight. A service station attendant came out and began hosing down the driveway. No one seemed worried that their till was not tinkling. No customers.

It was still a tiny settlement. Fibro and weatherboard, little porches, backyards, green with buffalo grass; the sense of water nearby, the channel. David walked past the shops, watched the mild curiosity from under the awnings.

It was not until he was out among the small houses that he paused. A sign read: FRESH OYSTERS. The yard was flooded with buffalo grass; it had swept up and smothered an old rusty car motor, it was suffocating an abandoned trailer with only one wheel, there were lumps in its expanse beyond that might cover more junk: machinery, furniture, garbage, burial mounds. The three steps at the front were rickety but, following his impulse, David knocked at the door.

An old black woman came out, wiping her hands on an apron. She looked at him enquiringly.

'How much are the oysters? Got any fresh?'

'Only bottles. Big ones are eight dollars, small ones three. Small ones a dozen. Big ones, I'd say mister big ones have lots mebbe fifty, real bargain.'

'That sounds irresistible.'

'You eat 'em with bread, you try brown bread with 'em mister.'

At his smile she burst into a beam, firm white teeth and a sparkle. 'Tell you what, I give you two bottles a tenner. Pretty good that. I think that's a pretty good bargain.'

'You say that to all the fellers,' he joked, leaning back carefully on the shaky rail as he watched her bustle inside, her broad body jovial as

99

a grandmother. 'I'll have to buy a whole loaf to get through that much.'

She returned with the two bottles, nevertheless, from a small fridge on the louvred sleep-out.

'Still, as you say, a pretty good bargain.'

'These real fresh. The boys got them just this morning, right over there, that's our oyster banks.' She nodded across the gully to the glint of water in the passage.

'Perhaps you could tell me,' David said as he riffled through his wallet, 'I met two of your people, over in Cleveland, couple of evenings back. Tommy and Jimmy I think their names were. Know where I'd find them?'

'What you after them for?' The face clouded. 'What you chasing them about? You not one of them Departments?'

'Nothing like that. Truly. I just met 'em. They were kind to me, sort of looked after me. I was pissed out my mind, if you want to know, and they sort of took me in hand. I just wanted to thank them. I don't think I was very . . . was very appreciative at the time. You know?'

She had decided to trust him, though he could tell that she had also consigned him to the hopeless ranks, the drunks and derros even if his casual clothes bespoke difference.

'I don't know what you're after mister, but Tommy and Jim can take care of themselves.'

But she softened; he could see she was still puzzled.

'They weren't pissed. It was me.'

'Where you from, mister? Come on, you tell me.' Her voice was soft now, a melodious timbre like low flute notes. He decided she had been very beautiful, perhaps she still was in her body, inside her body, she still knew it – that quiet confidence, holding her ground.

'Look, if I were to tell you I don't know, would that puzzle you? Perhaps that's what Tommy and Jimmy would be able to tell me,' he blurted out. 'They seemed to know something about me nobody else has clued in with, it was only a sense, something I thought about after . . .'

'That's the booze speaking. Jimmy wouldn't know any of that business, not without Tommy. Tommy's the still one, but. Mebbe it was Tommy saw something. Mebbe it was the booze speaking through all of yuz, Tommy's a great one when he gets rotten and thank goodness that's not often.' She was still holding the two large bottles. She handed them over, wiped her hands again. But she made no attempt to end the silence.

'They around today?' David ventured it hesitantly. He was not sure where the currents were moving. The names were at home, though.

'Where you come from, mister, what's your name? You tell me that, eh?'

Her arms were crossed over her bosom now. It was not a challenge, the tone was too low, almost honeyed. It was a fair enough request. Could it also be a request at another level: what tribe you come from? What ancestry? No telling.

He told his name. He mentioned the other island. He explained about Sydney.

She didn't ask further, she seemed satisfied, as if both of them were exchanging cards, face down. Who would turn up the other side first?

'You go down to the oyster banks. You look round there. You tell Tommy I said, remember that now. You tell him. Davey? That's a nice name, mister. You might come back here later, maybe. Maybe we got more to tell to each other.'

The tall dark man greeted him with a slow smile. He was resting under the shade of a cotton tree, a white enamel mug between his large hands. Old jeans, and a thin cotton shirt. Feet bare, spread wide, absent-mindedly drawing toe lines in the moist orange-tinted sand. David was recognised.

'You all right now, feller? You had bad shakes, remember? Bet you don't remember. That's a lost, a lost man I says to Jimmy. You all right now? Look all right now.'

'Yeah, fine, fine. Getting over some kind of fever, don't know what it was, it hit real sudden.' David felt a twinge to hear his own voice slip into another's cadence, as it he was taken over. 'Look, I came over especially to see you, to say thank you.'

'For what?'

'For, well, thanks for being there, being supportive. You know, just that. I thought about it later and it seemed I must have looked as if I backed away . . ' He was getting entangled. 'As if I . . .'

'That's okay, mister, gubbers usually do that. Or they stare you in the eye, making it a kindness. Either way, no worries. We just go on like we always done.'

He reached out and gently punched David who had hunkered

down beside him. David rocked back on his heels but maintained balance.

'You know they say now us lot been here eighty thousand years. That's the latest number. Eighty thousand years. Maybe that's not the right number, maybe it's seventy-nine thousand years. What you think, mister? Maybe only forty thousand.'

'Yeah, it's a long time. You think your ancestors been here, on this island forty thousand years?'

A sand island like this must be recent geology, David was already thinking, aware he was laying traps, almost unconsciously.

'I been here forty years mister, that's long enough.' The gentle laugh was not telling. 'But my people, they was here a long time, long enough I reckon. My people is Nunuckles, they was part of this island. Jimmy, though, Jimmy's people came from further up the coast, they was brought here. Once, we might have been tribal enemies. The Nunuckles and Noochies was always peaceful but. Not like them fellers up round Noosa. I reckon we was still the clever ones. See, we're still here. Now you go up Noosa all you see is flashy white businessmen and their sheilas. White shoes, white shirts, and them sheilas have all-over beautiful tans. Like us!' He chuckled. 'They got rid of us lot quick enough, but, up Noosa. Except round here – we lasted this far, no one's going to get us off of here now, I reckon.'

'Good for you. You hold on to it.'

David looked around him: a dozen gulls were squabbling over something along the shore line, their neat contours honed into belligerent action; a yacht far across the water looked similarly white and neat; the long shoreline was unpretentious and clean – not the place for Noosa nudists or interstate holiday makers. The bay waters reflected an intense blue from the winter sky, rubbed clean of cloud, and motionless.

'I bought some oysters from an old woman who says she knows you. Like some?'

Tommy laughed. 'How much she ask for 'em? I bet Mary Anne sized you up and asked double. No, matey, only joking, bet she saw you and doubled the bottles for the same money. You pay her plenty?'

'Ten dollars.' David brought out the two bottles from the small shoulder bag where he had shoved a bottle of Bundaberg rum while at Cleveland, as well as bread and some apples added at the last minute from the Dunwich shops. The clink of bottles sounded like stones being clicked together, hard yet musical. Tommy certainly grinned with it.

'You done well. Mary Anne must've liked you. Must've thought you was all right. Some of the blokes, the big cars that zoom over to Lookout, drunk before they get off the ferry, some of them she charges ten dollars a bottle. They can afford it, too, no worries.'

To be admitted into financial confidences consolidates a relationship. David was tempted to ask the question that had still hardly found its correct phraseology in his mind but remained urgent. He unscrewed one bottle, proffered it to the other.

'You got any bread there? Try eatin' them buggers with bread that's the best way if you don't eat them outa the oyster shell.' It was as if Tommy could see through the canvas.

They shared the bottle, spreading out the soft grey molluscs with their fingers, bread balancing on their tightened thighs, salt water dribbling. They did it with separate and complete concentration.

Another round.

The things slipped down like small ghostly remembrances, hardly tangible, simply an echo of salt and pith and something vaguely charnel yet sweet and still living. The earliest stage of a foetus, would it taste as insubstantial? Or even the taste of sperm, would it be something similar, the protein reduced to earliest ancestry? The rough bread crumbled and sopped texture of earth product: grain, sand, fibre.

'Like to see where they come from?' The invitation was another opening. Having shared the small ceremony of the meal – silent, separate, ruminating – this was a step in the direction of hunting, food-gathering. David joggled the shoulder-bag back into place. The tall man loped ahead of him, not looking back.

You are too much a romantic, David thought to himself, not to see his movements as something ancestral. David's own thick dark legs were muscled in tight knots, quite different to the long thin shanks of the other, whose jeans looked loose and ill-fitting. The trousers reached just under the calf, highlighting the long sticks below, and his ankles, the big feet – bird-like, hardly supporting the tall body.

They spent a long day together, first along the ordered professional oyster beds, lines of thin music staves out in the shallows. Tommy then led his new friend in among mangroves, with quick hand rippling off oysters clinging to aerial roots. Pulling a fist-sized oyster knife he skilfully ripped off their lid shells and turned, offering them to David.

'Watch your feet,' he warned, several times. His own feet seemed immune to dangerous shells on rocks or submerged branches.

When he saw that David had eaten enough Tommy smiled back at him and they trudged through the marshy edges and the mangrove fern to the sand line. 'Good tucker.'

'Bloody terrific.'

'Any time you like. Only take what you're going to eat, but. No bringing along bottles. That's our job, that's how we pay for it.' He waved vaguely. David understood.

Later they strolled back to the house where Mary Anne was waiting and all sat round the small kitchen table. Jim turned up within minutes, grinning shyly. David greeted him and again made thanks about the other evening. Jimmy shuffled, looked across at Tommy, shrugged.

'I think you're a bit crazy.'

'What do yuz want, what yuz really want over here? People don't come over here, looking us up. Not even drunks, not even drunken old hatters. There's been lots of those. You got some job you want us to do, hey? Yuz want a coupla strong men to do some liftin' and heavin'?'

'Davey here wants someone to show him the fishing banks more likely. That it, Davey?'

'You boys shut up and stop teasin'. That feller's come off his own bat, no one made him. That feller's stuck with the idea that you two bad buggers was good to him, other night and he's come to say thank you. Strikes me that's a strange thing but there you have it. Isn't that true, Davey?'

It was the moment, with them all smiling and loosening. David produced the rum bottle.

'What'ya know? Well, who'd of thought it? What would y' know?' Mary Anne then went bustling for empty glasses. 'Now isn't it a good thing I went out just this arvo and bought some of that Coca-Cola stuff.' She had to sit down to enjoy her laughter.

'Mary Anne buys that coke stuff just to wash her false teeth in,' Tommy grinned back at her.

'No, she buys it instead of scouring pads,' added Jim.

'I buys it just on the off-chance some kind boy from the mainland will come offering rum to go with it,' Mary giggled, then broke into real laughter.

David began pouring.

It was five o'clock. David reminded himself he must catch the next ferry. They had been telling a series of jokes about the carpet snakes that always turned up around the school yard up the hill. Nothing would keep them away. The kids had no worries, but every now and then a new teacher would come across from the mainland and be terrified.

'Or the goannas,' Tommy reminded them. 'The goannas that get under the house or into the dunnies. Remember the time Miss Mac-farlane pissed her pants cause she damn wouldn't try to get out to the toilets, that big old goanna just staring at her?'

'But the snake that came down off the rafter and curled up on the desk while she was writing on the blackboard. And the kids kept dead silent. Kept dead silent the lot of them, like they were in it together. Then she turns round and even then didn't notice. Not until . . .'

'She was always pissing her pants, that one.' They rumbled together.

'Talk about pissing . . .'

'That way.' The two men said it in unison.

The three of them walked out together. Mary Anne had grasped David's right hand with hers, then placed her left hand on top of both. Her eyes were still playful but the voice was cheerfully sincere, 'Goodbye, Mr David, be good, and take care of yourself until I see you again. God bless you, goodbye.'

'God bless you, Mary Anne,' David smiled in reply, though it was not an expression he would normally think of using.

The others grinned back at him, welcoming.

Down at the jetty David said, 'You've got things to do, don't hang round.' Then he thought. 'Tell me one thing, though. Both of you. The other night. Did you come over to where I was because you thought I was . . . one of you? You know, one of you people?'

Tommy scratched his bare foot round in a half circle, fists in pockets.

'Jimmy was right, mate. You're a bit crazy.'

But he put his arm out and gripped David's shoulder. 'We got this much together. We know you got something on your mind, down there. And it none of it matters. You're a man, just like the rest of us.

What you think? We got an extra thing, extra ball, extra prick? You think we got something extra? Or you think something less? You think you can run away from yourself down with us lot, that why you grease us up with your talk and your bottle? You think you're half black?'

'That's not it at all, Tommy. No one's patronising anyone . . .'

'Tommy's just kidding, mister.' Jim tugged at his friend.

'He's wiped out with that coke. Coca-Cola's not good for him.' Those deep chuckles.

'I don't know if I really have aboriginal blood in me. My parents never said so. Only I . . .'

'You thought there's a magic colouring test, like that stuff, what is it, litmus paper, like the stuff Miss Macfarlane . . .'

'I thought you might have recognised something in me, the other night, over in Cleveland . . .'

'We recognised a sick man.' Tommy let go of his arm. 'What's it matter? You gotta live with you. We're not going to be some sort of tribal witch doctor, cure you with magic. You cut your foot now, like on an oyster, cure that quick smart. Crush the herbs from the swamp there, brush it with feathers of seagull and curlew. That's an old cure, and a pretty good one. That's an accident, that's not sickness. What you got in you, way of your blood, you got in you. Where you go, you take it in you with you. I stay around here, got no need to go anywhere. You're different. You'd go mad living that half, if it's really that half. That half's not the one thing nor the other. You go home now, Mister Whitey, if there's dark in your blood there's as much white in me, none of us's full caste any more. Here's your ferry coming, you might have a tribe and totem but that's other ways now. But don't ask me to look at you and say, like a x-ray, this man's Boong, there in the belly, there in the nose and the hair on his head. You go back now, you do some silly bugger thinking, we got no secrets, we got nothing no more, we got nothing to give, don't you try to take none from us.'

But the gentle wave motion behind the voice was already knitting and sharing, slipping down like soft oysters handed out gently in the palm of the hand. He had accepted that offering.

XVII

'Your loquacious friend again.' Deirdre had wanted to be consoling, supportive, when David returned from his long day. He had not spoken much. When he came in, around 8 p.m., she had made him a coffee; she had the shack swept and clean, the new plants watered, there was a vase of wattle blossom on the table (had he noticed that?), and before busying herself with the meal she had made a point of sharing coffee with him as they leant over the verandah rail and breathed in the scents of eucalyptus, salt air, the vague mangrove whiff. Though David didn't describe in detail his encounter with the Stradbroke Island aborigines Deirdre concluded that it had been salutary. His quietness was not moodiness; rather, it seemed the silence of someone absorbing things.

That review of his book: he had brooded for a bit, but then had shaken it off. One just had to allow him time – and space.

When she began preparing the fish David came in with her; he helped. Every now and then he touched or stroked her, his thick fingers quite gentle. She had smiled. Each time she had smiled. But the sound of someone clambering up the track, just as she was about to serve the meal, although half expected had caught her. Clyde Carter. Her voice could not disguise the threat.

David gave him a shout of welcome, divided the fish so there was enough for three, and became jovial. 'How's that for timing!' It was as if his Stradbroke encounters had blacked out all the nervous tension Clyde repeatedly evoked in him.

'Does the fisherman ever get sick of the taste of fish?' David continued, 'Though these new baby potatoes are great.'

'Cleveland grows some of the most wonderful vegetables I've tasted,' Deirdre coaxed out her own enthusiasm. 'And the avocadoes!'

'Fish, fruit and fine veggies,' Clyde spread out his broad grin for them, 'and you ask why seven years here seems an instant.'

'Well, you've spoiled us,' David said, 'all this fresh fish you keep bringing us. Won't be able to raise a finger in self-defence or in food-gathering if you keep this up. We will end up mere parasites. What a life!'

'Tomorrow we'll go looking for mudcrabs,' Deirdre offered decisively. 'Would you accept one, Clyde, if we offered it?'

'Well, that's generous,' Clyde replied. 'But it's the company, you know, I make the company my payment. Jim now. Jim's family and all that, but he's fixed without shadows; Jim's a man with no shade to him whatever. Now that may be a fine thing, I'm not knocking Jim, he's the salt of the water. But I don't follow football and I don't hanker for horses, and Jim's a great one in boats but in water he's out of his depth.' Clyde laughed at his own joke, splattering pieces of fish over his green shirt. He brushed them off. 'Jim's all right,' he confided theatrically.

'Jim's a person you know where you stand with,' Deirdre said, 'I've got a lot of time.'

So that it was inevitable within ten minutes that Clyde would embark. And he did. 'Let me tell you these witticisms, these three paradoxes of the late twentieth century. You want to hear them?'

'Something topical? Shoot.'

'In our day the Germans talk only of peace. The Jews talk only of war. And the Russians talk of no alcohol.'

'That's surely a Russian joke, I know, because I heard the same joke and it *was* told to me by a Russian – since Gorbachev put a ban on the sale of vodka . . .'

'Aha, so young Davey boy is in with the Russkies, is that it? Now it's not my place to inquire. But if you volunteer this sort of information, that's another thing. And as you've noticed, I am, in my own little way, a man of honest curiosity. What's this young feller David Cumberland up to all this time, here on our island? Davey boy, you've been the hot topic of speculation all over the island, though you do nothing, just doze here and go fishin' or crabstabbin'.'

'Yes, I'm a Russian spy. This is a top priority territory, this island. You know that? Strategic importance: mudcrab breeding grounds; the bite of the mature mudcrab is Australia's new defence weaponry.'

David considered the possibility of bringing out the remaining rum. No.

'I've been sent by the KGB to suss out this place as a new Siberia. What a depot for political exiles. Eh, Clyde?' David winked, but Clyde was having none of it.

'The thought was more that *you* were an exile, Dave, someone in hiding.'

'His Russian bit was when David had to drive a small group of Soviet writers up from Sydney – when was it, Dave, about three months ago?'

'Nearly five.' David put down his knife and fork and carefully surveyed the mess and remains on his plate. 'You're a pretty mysterious bloke yourself, Clyde, for that matter.' He got up from his chair and walked over towards the door, where Clyde hovered half in and half out of the darkness, as if he were smoking a cigarette. 'Now we're talking of mysteries, what are *you* hiding? Really?'

'Me? I hide nothing.'

'But you hint! You hint and you hint, and you love people to be left guessing. Come off it, Clyde. Fishing-net man, come out in the open with us.'

'Now there's someone learning my cadence. I'm just a teacher.'

And Clyde smiled, wearily.

'You're a net mender. Said so yourself. Deirdre and I, we're the ones who are professionals. We're the trained teachers.'

'David's quite brilliant. In front of a class he can be brilliant. That's why they promoted him into administration.'

David caught Deirdre's eye. Clyde must have sensed the collusion between them, the new solidarity.

'I'm not talking school teaching. But, you being trained and paid teachers, with leave and long service accruals, what more do I need to say? You go ahead, leave us poor net menders.'

David would not have it.

'Scuttering off again, Clyde? We've pinned you now and you can't escape so easily. Why did you come to this place? Just answer me that. You some sort of IRA refugee?'

'One of the laws on this island, Davey me boyo, and I thought you as a teacher knew better, is you never ask leading questions – not someone's past, nor their future. This here place remains neutral territory. That's why no cops here, no officials. You never asked Jan the Jenny questions. You never asked Jim. Nor Harry the Jeweller, either, why he hides here so much of the time and him with a good penny and his house full of treasures you'd not see in Government House though it looks like a fisherman's lodgings. You've no right quizzing me, Davey. Let's keep our exchanges to important subjects, abstract and mythical. Let's remain friendly and talk about poetry.'

'Poetry, Clyde?' Deirdre sat down. David veered back in her direction. Clyde was now fully in their room, the light on his pale face.

'I'm from the tradition of Yeats and Synge and of Joyce. And Brendan Behan. In my space the bards won't die out so easily.'

David thought of the rum again. His quizzing had not been intended as vindictive, surely? He would endure Deirdre's silent reproach.

'No. Go on,' she said to Clyde, a voice of practised encouragement, 'you know I once acted Juno, in *Juno and the Paycock*?'

'Ah, Joxer, it's a tirrible thing, a tirrible thing,' Clyde quoted. David produced his bottle. He went for glasses.

'Yes, I think you'd make a good Paycock, Clyde,' Deirdre conceded, 'the poor boy I did it with hadn't a hope with the accent.'

Then she turned and reminded David quietly there was milk in the small refrigerator, it would soften the blow of raw rum. When he poured, she insisted on sharing.

David thought once more: one way to reduce my intake. But he would not be reproved. He had returned with this curious benignity. The shadow had left him. Even this pale visitor no longer challenged and feigned to threaten him. Tonight had been entirely on David's terms, David's.

'I will tell you a story', Clyde sat down to join them. He raised the black liquid in tribute. 'Swear it happened. It was when I was little, but I swear I remember. Every inch. You know a man, by what he remembers.'

'Or by what he invents,' David looked at Deirdre.

She has resigned herself. She was more relaxed now, swishing her milk with its token splash of his rum.

'This was when I was only small. Me Grandma owned a wee hostel, a tavern outside our village. Broadford, County Limerick. It was a cottage, but it was public. Everyone came. Just far enough out of the village for folks to be themselves in, if you know. It was snug, it was warm as your body. Like the church, you were brought there before you understood anything, but while you played there and shat your pants and were cumbersome, you were drinking the blood and the bread of its flavour, the flavours and furies of ritual. It was a lovely place, Grannie made it that. Well, this one night, it was late don't you see, we was all put to bed and the old folks was nodding and yarning around the fire, when Bam! Knocks at the door. Well, who could it be? It was loud enough. I woke up sudden as thunder, and you know how it is when you wake suddenly: where are you? Who are you? What time is it? What's the direction? It's as if the whole room has been twisted around in your sleep, nothing anywhere, not where you expect it.

'Well, the knocking and thumping soon put me right about that. Even me Grandma was scared by it, she whispered to Uncle, they all whispered. Finally Grannie went to the door; by this time she was cursing and getting her temper up. I think she had a stick or a poker. Must have been well after midnight. The time between times, as they say. Only someone needing it knocks at that time. Or someone terrible.'

'No officers of the King's army?'

'Shut up, David.'

'It was no officers. It was three old women, believe it or not. Three old women out in the wee hours. Well, you know what anyone in their right mind thinks of that!'

'That sounds like the witches straight out of Macbeth,' Deirdre said.

'I was only little, remember, but they was as like to witches as you could hope to see. Me Grannie let them in, though. Said she had not seen them since the last village funeral. I think they were three old sisters used to work up in the Lord's house but he'd tossed them out, it was said, because they was so filthy but there was four of them then, and that night it was because the fourth one had died and they could rouse neither priest nor doctor. It was the firelight in our window drew them over to our place. And the fact we was always open.'

'There's a lesson.' David poured out more rum, darkening the white milk further. Deirdre's lips pursed, then she was caught up in Clyde's yarn.

'Well, that was the start. But the funny part was that one of them had a piglet under her arm. Don't know why, can't remember now. Perhaps they thought it could be payment – to priest or undertaker. They was poor as chaff so it was probably the best they had. Well, the pig escaped of course and went diving straight for the cellar, it could smell the apples there and the barley. We were all up and after it, knocking and scrambling, the old ladies shrieking and scratching, as if they thought we would boil it and pickle it. It was all confusion, I can tell you. And I was there in the middle of it, being the youngest. But me Grannie had her wits, she stayed by the fire. She was keeping an eye on her good candlestick, it was all silver. She knew a thing or two.'

'Tactics of diversion, the thief's oldest principle.'

'Yes, Davey boy, she was thinking along lines like that. Trouble was, she was thinking too much on her good silver candlestick and one of the old women comes back cursing and terrible, weepin' and wailing and near hysterical and of course Grannie was water. She swelled up with the pity and the woebegone ways of the poor old neighbour and she brought out the stout and it was all a confusion with the pig not caught yet and me overturning all the neat tubs of apples. And if the truth be known, getting me teeth into them, and the pig squealing and the other two smelly old ones like shrouds trying to beat me to possess it and it all in the darkness down there mind you, and then somewhere the sound of the stout being opened and poured. Well, you'd have thought it was thunderbolts and the others went back out all the while instructing me to catch the piglet and mind I did not get bitten . . .'

'Get the message, general confusion.'

'Confusion! That was only the beginning, because they got drunk up there and I got stuffed because I caught the pig soon enough with others not flapping, but I stuffed it with apples to keep it quiet and began myself searching out tidbits and treasure down there. And I come up and the piglet began shitting. And on top of that before me eyes I saw one of the old ladies quickly slip the silver candlestick into her clothing and I yelled and she tossed all her glass at me, then they all tossed the stout, even the glasses in my direction and Grannie began clawing at the shawl and they screeched out protesting and the worst of it was just happening.'

'Go on – old Grannie got murdered.'

'Not at all. But the pig squeezed out from my tight elbows only this time somehow it got in the fire. Someone kicked out I think. And before any one of us could do anything there was flames slipping up the black clothes of one of the old ladies, and the squeals then of pig, crones and my own terror. It must have been heard for more miles than the church bell. And the worst thing was the panic. Panic kills people. And the flames, soon they was everywhere. I tell you, the next morning, there we were outside, only the old girls had scooted off in the dark, screaming and wailing and we others were left still trying to do what we could with the fire, only nothing you do can be anything once fire takes hold and it was done in ten minutes.'

'Surely there was a fire brigade, even in Ireland . . .'

'Oh, soon enough people were all over us, all the water in Limerick was then offered us. Little good it did then. Grannie's hostel was gutted. I was just ten then. That was the start of me wanderings, you might say. It was the wails of old Grannie. At first I hugged up and tried comforting, but she did not even know I was with her, she was hugging herself and I was not anything. I was invisible. Then I got angry. Angry at her and her drink, angry at the pig and my fault; at the three terrible old people whom I made certainly witches but I see now must have been simply old invalids, a bit dotty with grief . . .'

'Never spoil the story with second thoughts.' David was schoolmasterly.

'Yes you're right. That's the end of it. Here I am. It was only the start. But, another rule is: keep the audiences guessing. But now I've burdened you with this knowledge, you're in bond. The claims go deeper than we dream of. Some claims last forever.'

Clyde got up and strode out of the house. As he left, he turned back a moment and waved, but his smile seemed more a grimace.

'I think he was trying to enlist our sympathy,' Deirdre at last said, as they lay together on the roughly made bed.

David had not spoken. He had made the long drawn-out foreplay more intensely voluptuous because of that trigger-point tension: no, not tension, she had thought, so much as the spring-like control of vast capabilities. His light, slow fingers along the inner sides of her thighs had teased and retreated, then moved with sudden deftness to the weighted softness of her breasts, circling to the nipples, pressing them, gently tugging, extending and straining their elastic connective-points with inner sensual targets. Over and over, closer and closer. She lay back and writhed, then threw herself over and gripped his back – smooth, hairless, well muscled. Her own fingers had too quickly sought him – he had gasped then, and had gently thrust her aside. His pace quickened. His fingers were more assertive. Only when she gasped with a great intake of breath and a long, uncontrollable shudder, did he press himself, then, on top of her, his weight not a suffocation but a covering warmth of pure feeling.

'I can feel it,' she whispered. 'Right in. Right in. Deeper.' And she knew, too, when the release came, it was as if her whole insides were open to the force of the ejaculation. He fell, sobbing, across her. They had lain for a long time. Then, as he moved back to his side of the bed, she had spoken. Could she have been, all this time, subconsciously thinking of him, of Clyde the Carter?

She hastened to explain to David her sense of contentment.

'No, no. Strange, I had been thinking of his yarn-spinning too,' he murmured, his hand again moving to reliven her. 'I don't think it was sympathy he was trying for, though, Dee. More like collusion. I expect next time round he will feel he's softened us up enough for his more sordid accounts of the IRA.'

'You think so?'

'Well, perhaps not. But there's something there he's wanting to prepare us for.'

They were silent again for a while. David's fingers grew more proprietorial. Deirdre knew that this time her own fingers would not be rejected. Suddenly, wilfully, she curved herself over and down, taking him, sticky and half-rigid, into her mouth. Let the night last forever!

This was the David. From this, and this energy, all the good things radiated out: when her mother had finally allowed herself to accept the abrupt and scandalous marriage, Deirdre tried to explain – no, she had not tried, her own eyes told with sparkling fire just how well their conjoining had been. Her mother had smiled a little, and had whispered, 'But it is for so short a time, so short,' and had looked at her own room, all its polish and best Nock & Kirby furniture.

It had become more infrequent. More patchy. But David, when the moon was on him (and it was he who was always the initiator) was still completely engrossed in the act, in the communication. He was taken over. Deirdre was taken over. How explain that? There had been days, days in a row when he had been completely a loving, rutting animal: he had phoned her at lunchtime and they found somewhere. He had once taken her into a public toilet. They had laughed often enough in the mid-afternoon frenzy with the kids somewhere out in the kitchen, buttering sandwiches with Vegemite. Two days, three days, her body had been woken, taken, invoked; it felt itself a sanctuary, she had felt like Diana of Ephesus.

There had been months of great loneliness. But now: it was worth it. Deirdre felt this release was, also, a return for her outspokenness, her honesty towards his book. It had so long come between them. Now it was nothing. A ghost exorcised.

'It's you he wants,' she said again, suddenly, aware that she was no longer threatened.

XVIII

Mr Cumberland

My mother has asked me to reply to your letter. She is standing beside me, telling me what to say but she is aware of her poor grammar. She is a perfectionist (that's my remark, but she has agreed with me). She says she will see you if you come here but please phone beforehand. I suggest from Murwillumbah. Our number is (066) 92 5423. It's under the name Darrow in the book. My mother would be honoured to meet your wife. She remembers your last visit. She also says you were kind to her in Sydney that time she was down there. She has a friend in Sydney who is an artist. This is her only friend. My mother has not been very well since the time of your visit and the visit of Vladimir Smolich. Vladimir Smolich has written to her from Leningrad where he lives. My mother was surprised to receive a letter from Leningrad. She was really shaken up, I can tell you. You would not think she has lived in this country twenty years. It is as if she had never lived here, I tell her.

She wants me to tell you again about those years, those early years and how she still remembers. She says she has dedicated her life to remembering. I believe her, but perhaps I have been too close. The number of times I have said to her, 'Those times are past, Mum,' must be nearly as many as the times she has said to me, 'But I remember the winter of 1941; I learned to value things then . . .'

I make it sound as if we made a regular chorus. I am exaggerating (she asked me to put that). Now I have my own two little girls I do not see her so often. We have a farm just outside the town. My husband is a good man but he is afraid of her. She was very famous once in her country and my husband is from a different background. She is fond of him, and very fond of the children, but she is witty without meaning to hurt. And nobody can compete with the suffering she went through, you haven't a chance. My husband came from a farm near Tsarskoye Selo outside Pushkin, near Leningrad. The German army had their headquarters there, during the long 900 day siege. They lived in the Catherine Palace. The area is very famous, Pushkin was born there. If you have read Pushkin you will also know the long nights of winter, the isolation and the waiting for someone to arrive. My mother knows all of Pushkin I think, but my husband, who was born near there, is not a literary person, he is a farmer. He is older than I am. He was evacuated to Tashkent. After the war he was sent to Libya with a group to study arid condition farming. He met an Australian agronomist with UNESCO and came here, though it was very difficult. There were relatives came out through China earlier in the century, he sought them out.

But I am writing about my family. My mother really was pleased to receive your letter. It has revived her memories of that evening with Vladimir Smolich, an evening she has talked to me about every time I see her. I think she believes her name, truly, may not be forgotten.

The interesting thing, if you don't mind my saying, is that for the first time she talking about attempting to translate her poems into English. I think you made an impression. Do you understand poetry? She believes you understand and are interested. I am sure she is secretly dedicating her translations to you, so I hope you will treasure them. I would say more, Mr Cumberland, I hope you will honour them, even though they are all about events that took place years ago, probably even before you were born (I do not know your age; my mother says you are very young, very energetic, your eyes flash she says, you are *interested*). I write this to warn you.

And, though my mother is reading this, I will add: I believe she has it in her mind to write again, more poems. Not for Leningrad or her old literary friends who are all dead now anyway, or dead to her. But for you, she is talking of writing a poem for you, not an old one translated, but a new one. I think Vladimir Smolich may have tempted her.

She keeps asking me about rainforests and the trees in them. As if I should know, but I have been to the library and my husband has friends who are very familiar with these things, they are apiarists. It is hard to think of them with my mother, though. But she is strange; she has become fast friends with an old woman who comes to my house once a week for washing, Mary. My mother says they understand each other. I cannot describe the contrast between them and I make jokes to my mother about it. Did I tell you she can be very funny and sharp? But she is very fond of Mary, despite my jokes and her wicked laughter that encourages me.

If you want to ask for her in the town, go to the baker's. He is one of her friends.

You must understand: there were many people killed before the war in the purges. There were many people killed after, which is why my mother fled (that is another story). In the war itself there were more people died in Leningrad than in any other city in history and they died without hope of burial for many months; the city was surrounded and bombed daily. Australian people are not political. I am not political. My husband is. My mother pretends not to be but she is very political. Please, when you see her, do not raise matters that are political. There is another Russian poet, from Leningrad, who was older than my mother. She wrote (and my mother quotes it constantly): 'No one is forgotten, and nothing is forgotten.' Her name was Olga Berggolts. In that time, politics was forgetting everything instantly. But that is not politics (my mother tells me): politics is remembering.

Our farm is called 'Glen Vista' and it has the name PETERS. It was once Petrov, but you will probably understand why my husband changed that. No relation.

I cannot explain the nature of my mother's politics, to try to help you. She says: It is Leningrad. Think of the city of Peter built on mud and the bodies of 100,000 serfs. Think of a city built on idealism, and beauty and love and courage and corruption. Everything has been planned, but that still does not mean anything is tolerable. It has been imagined, though (my mother says); it is a city people die for. Are there any cities in Australia, she asks, that you would die for, passionately?

If you wish to bring gifts, I would suggest something sweet. A cake perhaps. Bring it in a box tied with a ribbon. She would like that.

If I have time I will enclose one or two quick translations.

*

from THE HUNGER

I am always thinking of food.
'Galina,' my mother scolds me, 'think
of work, think of paper.'
I think of paper, and ways to eat it.

'You must think of the evening meal,'
she insists, she spends the day
walking the streets, scratching,
just for a pot full of unnamable gruel.
'Think of the planning for it,
think of food as a reward.'

118

I think of food as a punishment
for the way God created us.
'Think, Galina,' she says, 'of others.'

There was the old woman downstairs,
her ration book stolen.
The authorities are inexorable:
she would not live another week.
We helped out the first day, because
she had been kind to us as children.

'Think,' my mother said, 'of another meal,
of the meal we will have later
when this is all over. Think forward
and save your hunger, hoard it with anger
so that the future will not escape
into apathy. Anger and hunger: these
are the great survivors.'

I thought of a meal in the past.
It began with borscht till my chin dribbled;
onions and cucumbers pickled,
a salmon in cream sauce so smooth
you were ladling up parts of your self,
the dream of your own breasts perhaps.
There was meat in my dreams.
I am a carnivore.

*

from THE LONG WINTER

I have been to the very centre of cold.
I searched it out, I hunted it,
I tracked it to its lair.
It hid in the most surprising place:
my own bedroom.
It was not waiting for me, that is a lie,
they tell you lies constantly.
Rations will be again halved, they say,
or rations will soon be doubled.
Or there is a world outside,

a world of warm hearths and soft fires.
Cold comes to other people.
Lying in bed like the old woman downstairs
– it was two days before we asked
after her – I know I am not foolish.
That is why I have searched cold out beforehand.
I want to grab cold with my hands
and strangle it.

There is a secret. In the centre of cold
is a place of heat. Think of the scald
of quick ice on your cheek, the burn
before fingers freeze, or chin.
'Close your ears, do not listen,' a voice said
using familiar, quiet diminutives.
I had thought at the time it was my own voice.
It was Cold, snuggling in to me.
It has nothing more to teach.
I will survive. I am the victor.
There are legends of boys living in the snow
naked, all winter. In the caves
there have been legends of their women.

*

from NOTEBOOKS

There were German messages.
They were dropped from the sky like snowflakes
or like parachutes. I was in Sadovaya Ulitsa
I was going to see my tutor. In the street
women scurried for these sheets of paper
as if they might be bank notes or ration coupons.
The city was full of rumours.
Already I had been held up by sentries at eight posts;
I welcomed their scrutiny – I have seen the deserters,
snails in the dank corners.
I was severe with myself and with others.
In the Komsomol our work
was exhausting but we were passionate about our city.

I understood that through work
all things became possible.
The Germans had power but we had time.
Women seeking bank notes fluttered around me
like pigeons in the days when there were pigeons.
One of them came up: 'The Germans say
that if we go out on May Day in white
then we will be spared. May Day. They will invade then.
But we who wear white kerchiefs will be saved.'
I did not speak.
It was too late for annihilation.
On the first of May
white kerchiefs were an easy target.

*

Mr Cumberland, that last is not a poem. It was something my mother had in the sheaf of notes she sent me to translate and she was angry when I chose that one. But I had done the work then, so I also enclose it.

Maria Peters

XIX

'A friend came to Chekhov once and said, "Anton Pavlovich, what can I do? Reflection is destroying me!" Chekhov replied, "Drink less vodka!".' Galina Darovskaya's laugh was like the primitive bright red and gold of the Byzantine angel trumpeting in the ikon beside her. She had been even more amused when David recounted the joke of the three late twentieth-century paradoxes. She had of course heard of the Gorbachev crackdown on vodka. She did not believe it. 'It simply means hoarding,' she said calmly. 'Vladimir Smolich would certainly have told you, if you asked him of the little old aunt or *babushka*, a teetotaller since birth, but who, as soon as vodka became rationed, began hoarding bottles of it. Fifty or sixty bottles is the usual number necessary to impress that you are a genuine hoarder.'

Her English seemed more fluent, David thought. Or was he just becoming attuned to the accent?

Galina poured David another refill; Deirdre shook her head and put her hand over her glass. She had noted the clutter and the hand-embroidered lace of the antimacassars. Also the large manilla envelope on the table. A present for them? Was their gift of the chocolate sponge sufficient?

The old woman lifted her tiny glass formally towards David's. 'Chin chin.'

He grinned delightedly. In conspiracy, each gulped rapidly to empty their glasses. Galina smacked her lips. Her tongue protruded to savour each last hint of flavour. What is it about alcohol, Deirdre thought, that locks people into its Masonic Order? She had seen David make that quick tongue gesture, many times. It reminded her of reptiles: Lizards, snakes.

'And now you will ask me,' Galina Darovskaya continued, looking up at David sharply, 'why is it I come to live in Mullumbimby? Yes? You will want to know innocent things like that. If you must come to Australia, all this way, you will say, then why not Sydney? Or Melbourne is it?' She sat at last, on the edge as always, but the glint of control was unmistakable. 'Or perhaps you are saying: who ever would think of Mullumbimby? Or of course you have guessed already, Maria lives in Mullumbimby and is married here and I have nobody else, nobody.' She laughed then, as if surrounded by thigh-slapping relatives. 'But then perhaps you ask: do I live here because my daughter is married to a farmer in this area? Or is my daughter married to a farmer in this area because I live here?'

'You like riddles,' Deirdre observed politely. 'That's something the children in my classes are wild about. I am hopeless at riddles.'

'Riddles? No, though it is an old tradition, especially in societies where things cannot be spoken plainly.'

'Russia?' David was too quick.

'I was thinking perhaps of societies where the truth is dangerous to the existing order of preference. Do you ask yourself why your children come home with jokes against peasant minorities? The Irish?'

'Back to the class struggle.' David was determined not to let this evasive woman escape without revealing something of her own reasons for coming to such a remote village in these humid coastal hinterlands.

'The Irish jokes, because it is necessary to establish a lower social order than oneself in capitalist societies, that is true,' Galina smiled, the sudden sweet smile David remembered from the earlier visit. 'For that reason I find such jokes unpleasant, though in Leningrad in my youth we had many similar jokes. The Finns; the Lithuanians. People from Georgia, yes, there was a craze when I was at university for jokes about certain people from Georgia. We thought it clever then, though Stalin was really an Ossetian, not a Georgian.'

'Surely jokes are universal? Nothing to do with the class struggle,' Deirdre put in, unsure where the conversation was leading. The dark blue and green walls were oppressive.

The David who sat opposite her was almost a stranger – some bright-eyed boy, an eager scholar. She was reminded of those times he had come home from the library with the latest discoveries for his rainforest book.

'Everything has to do with the class struggle. You must realise,' Galina reached out and gripped Deirdre's arm, 'when I was a student, in the 1930s, I was an impassioned member of the Young Communist League. What happened in that time, and later, under Stalin, and during the siege, did nothing to dissuade me that our people were moving closer to the new and liberated society. Stalin was a monster, we now know that. But it was a world of monsters. Monsters or weaklings. We were conscious of our part in history, we were going to re-mould the world. In the long years I learned other things, but though I learned the pitiful shallows of the human condition, I also learned the strengths and the fortitude. Though I learned to hate man, I ended loving my own people the more. Do you know, that if we look at the events of history, we can see these things as the expressions of the class struggle. It is foolish to pretend it is all a series of quarrels among monarchies and power mongers. Why did Hitler emerge to power? Why Stalin? Ach, but these are past events and you are young. Maria warns me. Still, even riddles: you do not remember them because you do not want to interpret them.'

As she moved back into her chair, releasing Deirdre from her uncomfortable gaze, Galina inadvertently passed wind.

'Now that! That in Tashkent or the Arab countries would be acclaimed as a sign of successful repast!'

Challenge, her eyes always provoked Deirdre with challenges. 'And here I have eaten only some poor rye bread and this cake you brought me. So it is perhaps less an expression of the internal class struggle of my digestion than a reminder of the aging process. There is an old proverb: God put the smell into farts for those who are hard of hearing.'

Her laughter.

'But I prefer the Greek word for farting, Borborygmus. Though that in this country would be an affectation. My concept of the class struggle is traditional. I lived in the most beautiful city in the world. It was the people's city and it was loved, loved passionately. It was Hitler who wanted to reduce it to rubble. Stalin was envious of Leningrad. But even Stalin would not deface it. The class struggle aimed at a world of equal opportunity, not a universe of hovels.'

'My mother has so few people to talk to, you must forgive her if she lapses into elementary sermons.'

'Ah, my daughter, you see, keeps me in check. She thinks I am an ugly old woman. But I tell her, the ugly may be beautiful; the pretty, never.'

Maria Peters did not return her mother's jibe. Instead, she reached for the manilla envelope on the table beside her.

'Did you know your husband here?'

Deirdre was startled.

'Did you know him to speak of his forest world? When he spoke earlier, to me and to Vladimir, about his forest world I noted instantly the change in him. All his faculties were together. He became as a beacon, an electric beacon. But you, being his wife, you will be all too familiar with that. You will perhaps be wary of that,' she mocked. 'Do you become frightened?'

David hooted with protective amusement. But he glowed.

'Which brings up the real subject,' he said. 'Do you remember when we met in Sydney I suggested a small trip into the rainforest just inland from here? There's a small but wonderful little stand of red cedar,' he turned to Deirdre to explain. 'It's on private property but I met the man in my researches . . .'

'And he's as ardent as you about conservation,' put in Deirdre, with just the hint of tartness.

'So. I see.' Galina was instant. 'The husband has been obsessed and the wife has been dispossessed. My dear, my dear, you do not understand. What takes over the imagination leads to growth, not alienation. Have you been in these forests? Have you gone in there with your husband?'

'Of course. Frequently. Do you remember that time we took the kids to Bruxner National Park near Coff's Harbour? David? The time Marcus got six leeches on his ankle, right underneath the sock?'

'Didn't faze him a bit. A quick dab with the meths.'

'And the Regent Bowerbird playground with all those blue Bic pens.'

'It was Marcus spotted that, too.' David turned back to Galina Darovskaya. 'You'd hardly be surprised that a convinced greenie like me would fail to entice his whole family into every national park going?' he asked.

'We often went camping, for whole weekends,' Deirdre added. 'I can assure you, I have roughed it with the best. Curiously, that all ended when David actually got started on his book. All his time in libraries, then.' She looked across at him.

'So what do you say?' David snapped a finger against thumb. 'We could make it a whole party. Takes just a bit of getting to – not really that hard if the weather's fine. Then I'll show you a little valley straight out of the original Big Scrub. It's magic. It'll make you curse the farmers and the developers,' he added.

'Young man, what are you inviting me to? Do you know, it is your anger and despair which pleases me as much as your enthusiasm. I, too, once loved, and lost, my inheritance. How curious that your Leningrad should be a grove of trees, Ygdrassil. Yet we, too, are ancient nature worshippers.'

'When we bought our land on the island, that was a sort of replacement for David, I think,' Deirdre said. 'I'd almost thought he might get interested in a history of Moreton Bay after that. After all, his first book was an apprenticeship effort. He could have learned from it. But the island seemed, well, complete in itself, I think. A place where you could just go native.'

'The island's different,' David intruded. 'But what we really should be talking about is this special trip I'm proposing. A step into the aboriginal past – a step into the arboreal past.'

'And I am to be cut by leeches?'

'No way!' David laughed. 'I'll look after you. We'll look after you.'

'I once dreamed of the cedar mountains of Lebanon,' Galina whispered.

'Let me show you *real* cedars!' David encouraged.

'Yes.' She looked at him. 'Yes.'

The daughter, who had been standing silently all this time, thrust the manilla envelope into Deirdre's lap.

'I am one of the farmers,' she said dryly. 'I am the wife of a farmer. When my mother knew you were coming, she gave me these papers to translate. I have done this, though I do not know why I do it and perhaps I should just let you know that you have given us both the excuse to attend to something that has been long overdue. I have kept a carbon copy. There are many more papers, but my mother only doles them out to me sparingly. For years she locked her poems and papers away. She exiled them. As if that were ever possible. But, you know,' the rather stiff daughter lowered her voice as if in theatrical company, 'I believe she has begun writing again.'

126

'I would like you to see my poems. There are some journals, some diaries too, that were once precious to me. They may help explain the poems. I had forgotten so much. But then. When I wrote them down, with numb fingers and the knowledge that it was only by writing, writing, writing, that I could survive those terrible days, I wrote down only a few things, only a fragment of those experiences. Reading them again, after all these years, I remember so many other things, things not written down. I am determined to be true to my memory and to those experiences. What I learned in those days gave me strength, as well as horror. I knew I had something to give. That made me powerful.'

'And I have made my contribution,' Maria Peters added, quietly but with strange calm. 'I worked hard on those translations. My English is better than my mother's, there is a lot of myself in those translations.'

She stood now, behind her mother, her stronger, more gaunt body overshadowing the frail creature in the stiff chair, whose laughter came so loudly and overwhelmingly from that small frame.

Later, as they were driving away David let out a long breath.

'Each time I see her, she is a different person. The first time, she was all soul and big eyes and, you know, intense. The second time, in Sydney, everything slapped out like castanets. And now, well, I've no idea what power games go on between those two. I don't even know how I seem to have been dragged into all of this.'

'And the papers. You didn't have to accept these papers. That's a sort of duress, what have the papers to do with you? With either of us?'

But Deirdre could not conceal her resentment at the sense of her own exclusion. 'And the way she kept her eyes on you, David. Like she was sucking out your marrow. I couldn't tell who was egging the other on with all those nips of brandy. I'm not nagging, David, but you know it's a long drive ahead.' Deirdre regretted instantly her outburst. David's jaw tightened. She put her hand on his knee and he looked across. Not defensive, not murderous – there was still elation, he was still charged with the energy of that Russian woman. After a few moments, he put his free hand over hers, gave a squeeze, then returned it to the steering wheel. Energy: Deirdre knew their own secret, shared energy.

'I suspect she's only a poor, sad creature. You know how these things go; it's like at school. Remember Mary Finney's old man who sent his whole book of essays written in pencil on old school pads? If you're a teacher, you're set up as an adjudicator on those sort of creative urges that hit people between 5 a.m. and their fifty-fifth year. Well, not that I expect this to be quite that bad. The subject's too big. But there's the business of translation – didn't you get her sense of absolute frustration? All that torment bound up tight inside her and only her daughter's rusty tools to try to unbolt the manacles . . .'

But he kept the packet proprietorially on his lap until they stopped for a meal at Coff's Harbour.

'And why did she have to look at me as if I didn't exist?' Deirdre blurted out after they had driven for another hour in silence. 'And that idiotic promise to take her into the dense scrub. You want to kill her?'

The next day when he actually opened the folder, bound in pink tape, David discovered Galina's note, in a spidery hand:

> If you understood then that night, may you understand now. The burden is so great I have feared it may never be possible. It is because of your innocence, I know that. But also because of your fervour. The only time you spoke that night with Vladimir Smolich, you spoke of a thing I know nothing. You spoke of the forests here that surround me.
>
> I was not surprised that Vladimir Smolich came. I knew that one would come, at some time. I did not expect such a nice man, so nice I almost trust him. It is because I trust you and for reasons that you will not understand, that I write this and hope for your reply now. In this country, apart from my daughter and through my daughter, you will be the first. There is no other country now but there are ghosts. It is because of the ghosts and for ghosts that I wish you to take me into your forest, the forest you spoke so eloquently about that night.
>
> I was an idealist. Idealism when it is put into practice threatens the whole life of the planet.
>
> You did not say it, but I understand your ties with your own forests, and my friend Mary, who understands many things I do not understand, has tried to tell me some of the legendary events of her people. She is from the coast, though, she does not like the forests. I believe your ardent love of the dense forests is a special understanding. I have always valued absolute ardour, absolute commitment. In

your country of people without ardour, you stand out like a dark pillar.

How long will your forests last? You remind me of one I knew who was determined to be destroyed by his need for passionate conviction. I was cool and ironic then, and a bit wistful. He filled me with fire. I had believed the coals long dead. You will never understand me, but you will never have a need.

XX

The night before David and Deirdre had decided to leave the island
they debated between themselves about how to explain.

'This is ridiculous!' Deirdre had exclaimed. 'Ridiculous that we've
somehow got ourselves so mixed up with that Clyde we find ourselves
having to soften him up, break the news, ask his permission.'

'Not that. Simply, we've begun to know him. You don't just walk
out on friends – on people. Especially not on this island. Got to live and
let live. Got to be able to get on with each other.'

'Since I came up this time, I tell you, David, I've seen nobody but
him. Not a soul. It's as if he took over everything and everyone. Or
scared everyone else off.'

'Ridiculous. You've seen Jim every day nearly. It's the time of year,
not school holidays. The place is quiet, dead quiet, when there are no
kids around, at least not the usual holiday ones.'

'That Clyde is such a night owl! Ridiculous. We spend half our time
mooning over cold fatty plates in the kitchen, while he goes on with his
blarney and his blather.'

'But you get on well together, Dee.'

'Yes, maybe. But when we get to the situation of sitting here and
suddenly working out excuses to make to him, like to the teacher –
well, I'm not going to be put in that position. I know it too well from
the other side. What's happened to our independence?'

'Or our courtesy?'

But she had known not to push too far; the purpose had been achieved. Indeed, Deirdre was still mildly surprised at David's new equanimity. She did not voice her initial apprehensions, knew to adapt quickly.

'You were right about that book. But it was a hard lesson,' he had confided at last the previous night. He understood her reservations about Clyde's excessive enthusiasm. She had put him on his guard. It was for his own good.

His meeting over on Stradbroke had been some sort of break-through. He would speak to her about it sometime. But perhaps Clyde Carter was also someone who had helped David over his hump, in his own curious way. Perhaps David had been able to see himself, in contrast, as a model of equanimity and order.

On that last night they prepared a place at table. Clyde the Carter did not eat with them. He arrived late, nearly midnight, and almost as if he already knew of their decision to drive next morning to Sydney, he gave them a cursory greeting. He exchanged badinage with Deirdre but it was David he was seeking.

'I knew it'd be time to return to your family and your affairs,' he said, 'Though it's been rich, rich times.' As always, his tone carried its sting. 'But you must do one last thing, before you walk out on me. Davey boy, you must come fishing tonight. When you come back here, who knows? I may be almost anywhere and there's still a few things to show you, because I took a care for you and a liking for your battles within yourself and that one night of a major drunken party.'

He gave Deirdre a hug of hurtful warmth.

'But only the one drunken night, and it was more riotous than a wake to announce his arrival with a whole crate full of Russian champagne.'

'Was it nice?' Deirdre turned to David. 'I had a small hankering to try some of that exotic stuff myself.'

'I forgot it was still in the boot, as I was leaving. It was a torrid time.' David explained as if describing a hundred years of archival dust. 'Ask Clyde. I was in a state of indelicate palate. Without sense. I'm sober now, which only goes to prove that we don't deserve what we get, and I still don't really understand why I got that dozen bottles delivered to me. I'm probably being followed by ASIO or the CIA right this minute.'

They both turned to Clyde.

131

'He got the champagne as a thank-you gesture after some visiting writers . . .' Deirdre began to explain. There was nothing further to say. The bottles themselves had become so many things: first tribute, then booty, luggage, reminder, finally penance.

Of all the bottles, casks and containers he brought home in his courtship of alcohol, the Georgian champagne was the only thing that filled Deirdre with interest and curiosity. And she still could not believe the gift was not in some way the trigger to David's sudden crisis, that furious panic and flight. Was this the link with that unknown and powerful woman, Galina? She had become, in his conversation, almost as obsessive a subject as his once-celebrated red cedar.

'So. I caught the taste of meat in your wife's mouth tonight. It is on her breath.' Clyde's voice over the water sounded drumlike, hollow.

'Meat? You're kidding. We had cheese omelette and toast. Using up remainders.'

'Meat shredded into fine strips, marinated in the wine of love for hours, days, years.'

Clyde's voice was mocking, a feast of imagination. David could tell he was revving up.

'Your wife's a delightful cook. She's got patience, a great virtue. She has taste, even better. But she knows some special recipes. She's both cook and patron.'

'What do you mean?'

'Some flesh, boy, is so delicate, it's got to be done perfectly, perhaps with rare herbs. For me, fish has this quality.'

'Don't keep laughing.'

'Your wife, dear friend, has a similar finesse, I recognised it instantly. Her taste, though, is for something more special. She has an advanced taste for the human.'

David, from the rear of the dinghy, was facing the rower. His head jerked up and for a moment their eyes met.

'I'm speaking metaphors, you understand. You, the teacher, the word-man, you of all people should know that.'

'I'm only a cipher, I'm no word-man.'

'Man of words. Even when drunk, I've not seen you a man without words. You haven't submerged yourself entirely, though you keep trying. For one thing, you have the drink. For another, you have anger.'

'You have the blarney. How much farther till we get to this fishing hole?'

Clyde had been rowing. David sat in the back of his dinghy, a passenger.

'There are seven senses, Davey, seven. That's why it's the magic number. Like the seven apertures of the body. Or the seven entrances to the sacred dwelling. Did you know that Apollo, king of the Greek Muses, was a seven? The seventh sense is the sense of knowing.'

'You're crazy.'

'They say that helps. Sight. Touch. Hearing. Taste. Smell. The sixth sense is supposed to be intuition, though it is more probably really the autonomic nervous system – like digestion, intuition happens but we are careless about it, or don't train ourselves. The seventh sense, though: it might be autonomic as well, though I am thinking of time and space and weight and certainty. The seventh sense is the sense of *déjà vu*.

'And that leads you to the right place.'

'The right place. The first time I came here I had that seventh sense, *déjà vu*. Had I been here before? At that time, never. But it was as if I had at some earlier time, in another being – a fish itself, an animal, a man – and I certainly knew what it would yield me: fish. Fish in their dozens. Always trust. That's part of it. We follow our own *geis* or we are bowed by the breaking of it. We're nearly there.'

It was exceedingly dark. The moon, what was left of it, would not emerge for hours. Small plop of water against the sides of the dinghy. Again the echo of their words across the flat surface of water. In the dimness David could see the white mist of his breath. Clyde was a dark shadow only.

For some while they sat in silence with their lines cast. Then Clyde, with a chuckle, felt the first twitch. 'I've got him, Davey. The big one.'

At almost the same moment David felt the sensitive lip of a foraging creature, then the sudden gulping jerk as the bait and hook were taken. In a very short time they had pulled in six sizeable fish. Working largely by hand movement and instinct they had each battled with the panic energy of their victims, and with patience had allowed them almost to suffocate before ripping out the hook, hard boots serving as clubs then weights.

'That's enough,' said Clyde, after pummelling the last victim. He made no attempt to move.

'First catch your fish,' he mused. 'You play with it, you humour it, you get it close to the surface. Then you become determined. There are some who eat the flesh raw. Some who excite the creature so as to get the greater flavour through release of adrenalin. Some who,' he paused and David could sense him looking in his direction, 'some who eat all raw flesh.'

'You really are a morbid person.'

'What I keep trying to tell you, Davey boy,' Clyde's voice was serious now, quieter across water, 'is that there's cannibalism exists. Is that wives cannibalise husbands, husbands cannibalise wives. Once you develop the taste for flesh and the adrenalin, it's addictive. Can't live without it. That's why marriages take so long. Mutual feasting. Munch munch.'

Clyde spat out of the side of the boat.

'Takes a long time to work your way through the system sometimes, munch munch. A little at a time. Sometimes it's all gone in one quick gulp. Now in your case, I'd say the lobes of the ears, the fingertips, the palms of the hand would be first. Little soft parts and I'm not the one to mention secret places . . .'

'Tiberius's minnows! You're just jealous.'

'Yes and I would be if I was in for the flavour but I'm not, I'm the net maker and net mender and the fish have the smell in their flavour. But you, Davey boy, you make a good meal, have you noticed the missing parts yet? Have you seen how the feaster glows, rich as tallow? Or are you benumbed and bewildered, not knowing how much you've lost? Or is it you have a good bite of teeth in there yourself, munch munch, chewing and grumbling? Ah, me boyo, little strips, marinated, soaked and salted, herbs and spices, see if you feel the difference?'

'Look Clyde, with Deirdre and me, you wouldn't have a clue . . .'

But Clyde ignored his friend's remonstrations and in a calm voice he continued: 'I saw the goldfish in my little mate Jan the Jenny's fishpond with the waterlilies – you seen that fishpond, Davey boy? Beautiful plump goldfish. And always hovering above that rocky pool, there are these great blue winged dragonflies. They're beautiful too. But do you know that the beautiful dragonflies lay their eggs in the fish pool and the larvae attach themselves to the underbellies of the biggest and most beautiful of the goldfish? Then they slowly begin eating. They eat and eat, unnoticed by anyone, until they finally gut the living fish. It is only at the last stages that anything is noticed. They feed quietly for a long time on their beautiful living host. Then they change into mature dragonflies themselves and move on to the next feast, leaving the goldfish sometimes still alive, but fatally weakened. Their fellow goldfish finish them off.'

Clyde laughed. 'My handsome friend. Look around. Where are the numbed parts? Are you sure you are not becoming a hollowed-out host for some dragonfly? I do not blame the dragonfly for its own inexorable appetites. It is concerned only with personal survival, after all. These things are ruthless. And I hope I do not surprise you with this sudden suggestion that you, Davey, with your thick arm muscles and your strong chest, are somehow passive, a victim, a host. I tell you this, though, dear friend: you have a heart too generous by half, and too insecure. I think your personal *geis* may be broken by some action that plays tricks on your very generosity.'

David would have protested vehemently, but Clyde's cold eye held him, and for an instant David could not tell if it were genuine madness, or an equally smothering concern.

'Look Clyde, I've been around. I'm no dumb goldfish. I think you're drunk with your manipulative role of the big clever fisherman. Well, don't imagine me your tiddler. If anything's likely, it's me who's the predator. All my life I've been the black bastard – driving my old mum mad with worry and guilt, just about killing Dad with my scorn and disbelief. And then Deirdre. Did you know I deliberately took her from the richest boy in town where we lived? I deliberately set my sights on her, right on the night of their engagement party. How's that for an evil trick? He was a twit. That's not the point. Think how she was chained to me, once she'd committed herself to the black Cornish footballer! Her family has never forgiven her. That's why we moved to Sydney right away.'

'Save me from the guilt flagellation, mate. Can't you see that's a real part of the cannibal's process of eating you? It's called anaesthetising the victim.'

'Or there was the time I dragged Dee into a threesome with Margaret Mackey. Do you really think that was part of Deirdre's nefarious strategy? No, mate, you romanticise. It was me. It was my pure lust – and a bit of curiosity.' David laughed, the hollow sound rattling across water. 'I'd had a bit of an affair with Meg before that – don't you ever tell this to Dee or I'll murder you, I'll hunt you down and murder you! But it was sort of playful: under her librarian's stiffness, Meg's really physical. I'd say "carnal", and good old Brian – whom she adores – is a bit, well, absent-minded. It's not high priority with him.'

'And with you?'

'Actually,' David laughed again, that water-thumping sound, 'it's like the grog. Every now and then it comes over me. I've got to do it, morning, noon and night. It seems to last – well, sometimes it lasts a week, sometimes just a couple of days. Or nights. The shagging fever. A menace to my friends – or my friends' wives. Or the barmaid at the Imperial, the typist downstairs – you'd be surprised just who responds to the beast in rut. Or would you?'

'You've read too much Freud. It isn't you. Don't keep flipping your tail.'

'This is not self-confession, it isn't humiliation, to me. But it is a sort of fixation. A blind binge, like the drink. Margaret Mackey hadn't a chance. The big surprise was to find how deprived she was, how she wanted it, once the barriers were broken. No, not macho stuff. I wasn't just scoring – that's why I had to bring Deirdre into it. Would you believe I wanted to share? I wanted the two of them so deeply. It was a real thirstiness. No,' he tossed the remains of his bait into the water. 'No, it wasn't particularly successful. We were all too self-conscious.'

'You're a fool. It might have worked if you really were a predator.'

'Take me back to the shore now,' David said. He dipped his hands in the water to wash them.

Clyde sat back in his position and said nothing.

'Row me back in now, Clyde,' David repeated. 'We're leaving first thing. Crack of day.'

'Davey boy, let me just tell you something. I'm not the one who's going to save you. I'm not the boy you'll get your excuses from. Don't build me up to be something I'm not. Don't make me an excuse-man. I want no part of that. I'm just, as you say, the mender of nets, an observer, someone who looks from the sidelines. That's okay with me, perhaps it's the natural choice of a night-person; when I do things, they're subtle, not in the spotlight. I can tell you a few home truths, you see. I can see you from different perspectives. Don't be rigid because I see your wife sucking the juice out of you, that's simply part of a long established formula, anyway. Don't forget me, though. Out of the pain of your book that you seem to be disavowing I have read your commitment. Even your clumsiness is an achievement, boy. You have dared to be vulnerable – you, the big black schoolteacher who must be a terror to children – or an inspiration. Don't retreat from that vulnerability, Davie. It's the only thing that'll save you.'

'That book. No. It was just something I had to work through. I can look at it now and hardly believe it was me. I don't think I could open it.'

'It was you indeed opened it. You've gone further, no doubt, but not necessarily better. I'm just saying to you: I have read you. Your heart is open to me.'

'So what does that mean?'

'It means only that I have returned your openness. No one else will ever do that. You heed my prophecy.'

At that moment Clyde leaned on his oars. He looked at David, and waited.

TWO

LENINGRAD

Each province or area had its sacred place that was the
centre of its world; and the name of the place showed the
relationship between earth and sky, the tribe and its
divinity.

John Sharkey: *Celtic Mysteries*

XXI

Notebook

I just can't do more than this; you cannot jump over your forehead, as the saying goes. The radio keeps playing the same song, 'Anyone can become a hero here.' We know the State takes care of us, the Leader takes care of us, there is not room for personal doubts. Why, then, am I so filled with apprehensions? Suddenly and for the first time these will not go away with cool meditation. Is it, as my father says, that I am at last becoming adult? I have always argued against his cynicism. 'There is no room for personal doubts,' and that seemed enough for anyone.

Two years ago my life was without doubts, the mechanism seemed to work wonderfully, I was caught up in the sense of its power and the perfectibility of its impersonal operations. I was Dux of my class. A mechanism needs only screws, I remember myself telling my father (quoting our Leader): each screw in the grand machine has its own responsibility and its own power: it bites, twists, grips to hold the great mechanism together. That sense of gripping – that is what teaches us to feel part of the larger enterprise.

It was that which gave us freedom, I went on. In our own moments, we felt free, I felt free. Just as the screws, gripping to the metal, feel the decision is theirs, the personal exertion is theirs, the voluntary sacrifice is theirs. They hoard that. They are proud. My father, I thought, still treated me as one of the Young Pioneers.

Two years ago. A lifetime.

One year ago my life was without doubts.

And in those years at school I was one of the chosen. It seemed proper and inevitable. I was ardent and full of enthusiasm. People admired my fine bones and my intensity. 'Galya, you are a magnet,' I remember my father saying that. I hoarded his words, only his words mattered, because he refused to give me many words.

I was editor of the school magazine and bullied all my friends, all the class, to write poems, essays, stories to illustrate the new world we would be moving into. We had the sheet of paper, blank, unlined: the future was in our hands and the stylus had been given to us. Our generation would be the first generation born into the new system and the new estate of man and we, the students, had the greatest right of any to set down the words that would define it. We were untainted.

We were filled with the excitement of our mission. We knew the texts by heart that we had to know; our task was to transform the texts into our own words and visions. History was ours.

Two years ago. As Editor I had special status and even the teachers deferred to me. I took it all for granted; I was not proud, but I was very proud. It was pride in my own humility, my own capacity to work, to show the way.

So young; so young, so young! I set it down. I remember one afternoon after school, five years ago, three of us went down to the Haymarkets. We were sticking up posters, posters of poems we had written about the Revolution and the Future and the Future Of The People. In our school these poems had been applauded, we had been acclaimed. We had read them aloud to the assembled students. My teacher had sent copies to the editor of a journal in Moscow. We felt destined for greatness.

Such vivid recollections. I had shown my poem (it was one of the three on that poster) to my father and my mother. My mother had commended my skill with words and the technicalities of rhyme and meter. My father did nod what I understood to be silent approval. He advised me then (I remember well) to consider the real, the concrete, as well as the abstract. 'You can move from the local and concrete into the universal', he said, 'But it is very hard to begin with abstract and universal and ever come back to the local, the thing that ordinary people know and will recognise and hold onto.' I remember his advice. But at that stage, at sixteen, five years ago, I thought him impossible and reactionary, still tainted by his own formalist education. I told him that. He hit a nerve in me.

He knew he had hit a nerve, though I showed only anger and perhaps just a little sullenness. It did not stop me from taking the poem posters to the Haymarkets.

That was the real moment. He came up to us, the old man, we smelt him before we saw him behind us: the smell of damp soil under bridges; odour of open drains and urine, clothes never washed. He came and peered at the poster poems we had proudly affixed to the wall near the stall with black peasant bread. The three of us edged back. 'Thank you, comrades,' he said and we even then knew his irony and hated him for it. It gave us an excuse.

When he read my poem, the first, he laughed. He turned to us showing his brown teeth through a broken lip and dirty knotted beard and he laughed. His breath was sour. 'You wrote that?' he turned to Yuri. 'It is my poem,' I asserted proudly, defiantly. 'I wrote that as an expression of the triumph of all the people and the future we will make.' Yes, those words, I spoke them. I wince at his enjoyment and his scorn. 'Let me take you to some of the people,' he said, then pushed me further into the crowd. My friends were terrified. The Haymarkets have always been dangerous, unregimented, unpoliceable. 'Recite your fine poem to the people,' he jeered, dragging me. I was proud, I would not let him feel the force of his tug, I kept up with him.

I recited my poem: in a crowded cattle stall; among sacks of potatoes; beside fish trays and the mocking courtesy of the slimy-booted women, the men with torn overcoats and rags around their heels; the pickpocket urchins, the jostling housewives and dealers and loiterers. Twenty times I read that poem. My friends had fled. And the bearded man kept hold of my wrist, he held me as an exhibit to his people. His people.

There was applause. There was condescension. There was even pity – and amusement, fear, caution. I was not unaware, even then. But what I started out singing with ringing tones and conviction, I ended tearing in my own mind to shreds. My own words had become self mockery, they had no meaning, no meaning at all in the Haymarkets, in the marketplace, among people; they were words written in the privacy of a comfortable bedroom, repeated in a book-lined study, recited in a hall full of careful mark-counters. Our very magazine where they were first printed, was a self-indulgent protected thing. The

Moscow journal, it also. We had dared to think our words encompassed the universe. Our posters were a glorification of that self-deceit.

After it was all over, my captor turned to me and said: 'Now go home and write.'

I had him traced down later, of course (I knew I was the most important person in my class that year): Dimitri Andorrovich, who once had published a volume of decadent verse and had been a friend of the famous novelist Andrei Bely. He had been thought dead; as my father explained, after 1928 the Futurist and Modernist formalists were no longer encouraged, their books were not available. We all assumed the man, too, had become an enemy of the State.

I went back to school. I was more vehement in class debates, I joined the Komsomol Young Communist League; I was invited. Though in some part of me I recognised that I was now playing games, I also began to be more than ever convinced of my own destiny. I tried to hide any sense of the gulf between the ideal and the actual.

Now, five years later, I begin to rejoice in the hand that first put pressure so that the screw moved back a little, lost its tight grip on the mechanism.

Two years ago. One year ago.

It was all foreseen, though I did not consciously foresee it at all.

*

POEM TO LENINGRAD

I sing of the great industrial city
not the city of Pushkin and Tschaikovsky;
I sing of the five hundred factories
not the five hundred palaces;
I sing of the seven hundred and fifty thousand factory workers
not the million and a half art works
in the Hermitage and Russian Museums.
I sing of the city that is the heart to all Russia
with its engineering works, its metalwork
and the shared labour that makes the Kirov factory
a model for all co-operatives.
I sing of the Baltic shipyards
and the pride of achievement when a new ship is launched.
I sing of the early morning shift workers
and the late night shift workers,

144

their heavy shoes echoing along cobbles
or filling the trams with their white breath.
I sing people working towards a future
that will transfigure the past
and will have forgotten it.
I sing the future built from our ideals
and our foresight. The children of the future
will learn of our efforts but they will
be thinking of their own future
and of the further efforts
leading forward endlessly –
What we think of as perfection
they will remember as primitive.
In that future time they will look at our factories
and call them museums. They will look at our museums
then, at our art works and our poems and music
and will nod, and will smile and wonder
saying: but they did have soul, too, in the olden times.
I sing of the factories and the thoughts of men working together
so that the art works, which are eternal, will count them in.
So that the future will know that we cared, and were counted,
and the white breath of workmen holds its own immortality.
Of the other things, there is no need for me to sing.
I say the name: Leningrad. Within that capsule of sound
all the beauty, the symmetry, the haunted achievement
is already compounded. I add factory dust
I add sweat. I add people.

*

I wrote that poem in my first year at university. It became instantly famous and people recited it everywhere. It was the poem I learned after the lesson with Dimitri Andorrovich in the Haymarkets and the thoughtful advice of my father. I was still a student. My teachers remained respectful, though I began to discover there were sophistications, and ironies, and subtleties possible. I determined to learn. I discovered I had much to learn.

Our leader, Stalin, had signed a treaty with Hitler. We would be left in peace. My father, who had then just become superintendent at the Kirov factory, would sometimes speak quietly with members of his group in the front room. I took things like that for granted, as why not?

He did not trust Hitler; he was always quietly sighing, I remember he once was saying as I passed the front room, how concerned he was that there was no priority to turn factories to weapons manufacture. To say such things too loudly could be dangerous; I began to realise that too. When I asked him, later, he explained to me that the Kirov works had indeed been making a new tank, 60 tons. Those new KV tanks were the most advanced in the world, he said, and I knew he was proud. But production was slow and though he had argued they should be given priority – he followed the news in Germany and said he had a long memory – his recommendations were not followed. He had tried to press for increased production through the committees and the factory organisation but his voice was not being heeded. In one bitter moment he even confided, to my mother in the kitchen, that the orders from higher had declared that any increased activity in military production would be seen by the Germans as provocation. There must be no provocation. The Leader had signed a Treaty.

We knew of the German sympathisers, those who believed Hitler would assist in the overthrow of the Socialist régime and restore the old capitalist order.

There were still many who remember that order, and their own luxurious and idle ways of life. The new system had been in force only a few years, they said; it would not last.

I do remember the German reconnaissance planes that kept flying over our borders and even over Leningrad. I remembered hearing them, and asking, 'Why are planes always flying so low, and with those black crosses?'

And then the German offensive against France, against England. Some people said that this would occupy their military strength forever. I remember some long discussions at university over the terrible bombing and destruction of London; we could hardly believe it. But then others spoke about the street fighting in Barcelona and believed it was possible. Some said it was possible to destroy a whole city like London with bombs and not just fire.

Leningrad: it has always been the first industrial city; it was the centre of the Revolution; it is the jewel of Russia. I thought of Leningrad when I heard these frightening stories of London. And if the Germans should ever turn their terrible new weapons in our direction?

I knew my father was angry, and my mother fearful. I tried to avoid the groups discussing each new German onslaught. I did not want to think about such things. But I was haunted by them. I grew so angry with my father in those discussions last year. I could not keep away from the edges of people talking. Fear is a drink of compulsive fascination.

Then on the 21st of June this year, we were at war after all, after all the statements. Of course we were unprepared. Again and again we had been ordered to remain unprepared and we had obeyed those orders. One does not question the line of command. We did not know what was in Stalin's mind, what tactics, what strategies, what directions. My father insisted on that to me, even though I knew he had his own angers. His face: some things one remembers forever.

I must write down the small details. There was panic, was that surprising? There was also a strange excitement. What could we do? The sun shone down, the white nights were upon us, the season was very beautiful. After the initial rush and clambering for food to hoard, we fell more quiet. Our Komsomol quickly organised defence tactics. Air-raid workers had to be assigned to posts; the city council ordered fire-fighting units everywhere: factories, offices, stores, apartment buildings. Fire was our first concern, and we were right. Attics were cleared of rubbish (later, we would regret disposing of all that burnable stuff) and the fire brigade set up many fire fighting platforms and reservoirs. Camouflage was introduced, especially at the political centre in Smolny, even though the Admiralty spire was doused of its gold with murky paint, and the Peter and Paul Fortress spire was covered in some sort of rigging.

We worked with the energy of immense anger. When the newly assembled troops paraded down Nevsky Prospekt we heard them singing. We wept and cheered. Thousands and thousands of volunteers were mobilised.

Thousands of parents sent their children to summer camps in the south and west. How could we know these were in the direct line of German invasion? I can write these notes now, trying to record such things. Even after a few months I seem to be writing of a distant epoch, an olden time more remote than the sixteenth century.

I have kept notes. At first I did not know what things to set down; I did not value the rarity of the commonplace, the jewels of painfully rich recall in simple things, like that day I took some embroidery out into the park, and sat down on a bench close to the bronze horseman. An old lady came up and admired my stitching. I remember she said: 'I

147

had thought the young people no longer remembered the old designs,'
and she was very cheered by my work.

I do not dare ask myself: where is that old woman now?

In my first notes I tried to be precise and serious. I recorded what
seemed the momentous things:

July 18. Food rationing. 800 grams of bread a day for workers, 600 for
employees, 400 for dependents and children. Cereals, fats and sugar
are available. Meat 2,200 grams a month for workers, but this drops
to 600 for dependents and children. Prices have risen so much! Some
people must be hoarding huge amounts. Father took us for a restaurant meal yesterday and we were expecting the food to be rationed
but no. We discussed this for hours and looked at the other eaters as if
they were all black marketeers but then father said, 'Hush!' and we
talked of my classes. The windows of the big Nevsky shops are all
surrounded with sandbags and the glass has been protected by strips
of adhesive paper. I said they looked fanciful and decorative but the
mood was not right for playfulness. Everyone at the university is
talking of evacuation: who has gone, who will not (I would not dream
of leaving Leningrad). But it is right that many children and their
mothers should be sent into the country. What could they do here? The
Chudovo railway station was bombed. The Volkhov River bridge to
Moscow has been attacked. That is the latest news. Some lucky ones
have been moved to the Urals. I cannot imagine travelling such
distances. If I had gone to our dacha for the summer, what would I be
doing now? Would I even be aware of what is happening?

The news is terrible, terrible. But the thought of no news. That
frightens me more.

*

THE CHILDREN IN YEDROVO AND LYCHKOVO

The German tanks have a terrible hunger.
The German tanks have a taste for very young children.
The German bombs have a malign power.
The German bombs seek out the old, the helpless,
the innocent, the very young children.
Two thousand children were on the train
at Yedrovo, two thousand evacuees
as if it were the summer vacation.

148

Sent out from Leningrad
into the safe rolling countryside
they could smell fields and barns and wide Russia;
they could become at one with their heritage.
Two thousand children were on the train at Yedrovo.

At Lychkovo, also: two thousand children.
The train carried them through fields
and they grew excited to see a hare, a hawk, wildflowers.

The German bombs found a new target.
The German tanks discovered the trainloads
of small children.
The noise of bombing carries their screams.
The silence in the fields, later,
is the shocked silence after bombing
and after the screams have been obliterated.
Tanks crunched through the bones of children
on a fine summer day, with sunshine
and those tanks were guided by men.

*

I did not record the date when I noted that my father came home to tell us it was decided that the KV tank production would be moved to Chelyabinsk in the Urals. And none of us realised on that date, whenever it was, that Leningrad was about to become the very centre of the German attack. These are explanations I can make because the innocent I was has been replaced by someone a hundred years older.

I did not see my father for many days. The plant, here in Smolny, moved onto a 24-hour shift. I remember the triumph in my father's voice when he mentioned that assembly time for the tanks had been cut back to 10 hours.

Finally, I went out to visit my father. People's Volunteer Corps were being formed and I wanted to be a Volunteer. He dissuaded me. I would be needed in Leningrad, he warned. He was worried at the increasing shortage of raw materials. On my return from his factory I was drafted into work on the fortifications of the city. Eight hours a day (shift workers had to work three hours a day on digging trenches and building shelters – even those who were working eleven hours a day on production; my father was one of them, though he was a big, strong man).

I remember I bound my hands because of blisters, that first day. Someone said to urinate on them, that would harden the skin. Someone else advised me that sweat did just as well, it had the same body chemicals as urine. Nothing helped. But of course the skin did harden. After a week my fine pianist's hands were those of a true manual worker. I was proud of them. But I was also proud of my own vocation. In that very last week of June, 1941, I was admitted to the Soviet Writers' Union. At the time I did not understand just what a privilege this would be, when food, and fuel and power disappeared from the city.

To be a member of the Writers' Union meant I was a professional; I was entitled to a writer's pension, and to all the privileges. I still went to the Summer Gardens to dig air-raid shelters. Sometimes a German plane would appear, very high up. At night we would sit on the roof, in the summer half light, to look for planes and prepare with sand pails, water buckets, shovels and axes. We read poetry to each other. The police control points increased. We began to look at anyone who was strange, or a stranger. He could be a spy. I was still at university, so I was paid 9 roubles a day for digging, but when I found that old Natasha Olinsky was paid nothing for her long hours of toil, I shared it with her. In those early days it was still something of an adventure. But my friend Anna Barachevsky was sent to work on the Luga line, out of the city. She went off in great excitement in a car with some others. It was all done in such a rush that she did not even take anything: no towel, no soap, not even a change of clothes. When I saw her leaving I rushed back to my things and gave her a knife, and some bread, and my towel. She returned two days later, her hands torn much worse than mine, and her legs cut and bleeding, black with dirt; her clothes were rags. She was lucky. A German plane had flown over low and bombed them. Three of the others from our class were killed, one outright. She was the lucky one, she felt nothing.

Anna was sent out again the next day. I did not see her again.

July. August. All the things I should have put down but did not. That summer was a time of constant, urgent activity, and then moments of absolute inertia. We listened to the radio when ever we could. Well, I think we needed more and more the comfort and assurances of voices, of songs, of the rallying cries and patriotic slogans. They were like strong coffee, or valerian tea; we could not do without them.

Thousands, hundreds of thousands, hundreds of hundreds of thousands of volunteers with almost no training, we saw them go off to the Luga line. We heard rumours. The city was always seething with rumours.

The Germans were coming closer and closer, that was the only constant rumour. They were hard and ruthless. They were well trained like machinery. They were impregnable. Deserters, we were told, would be shot; but there were still rumours of people who had run off to join the German side. Other rumours said these deserters were all put to the German firing squad. There was grim satisfaction in that thought. I think of it now as being a time of simple but terrible confusion and the memory of constant air-raid sirens seems to echo that feeling of dread. I will not write about that time. Leningrad was still not yet surrounded. That time seems, now, with its late, full summer brightness, a time of idyllic living. We still had food. We still had trams and electricity. We still had the fire of anger to drive us harder. We had not learned endurance.

Luga; Kingisepp – to the trenches. Over a million, yes a million Leningraders worked on trenches, on fortifications all through July and August. I remember going with Ada Vilm, who was at the Hermitage and was a friend of my uncle; we went to Tolmachevo. Tolmachevo: ever since I was a little girl we went to Tolmachevo in August for picnics. Mushrooms – there were always mushrooms and berries for us to gather. The wonderful balmy air and the soft light of those slow summer evenings. We always sang the same songs; they were the songs of that place.

I do not want to remember them.

We came with picks and shovels. Even there the sound of artillery buzzed in the distance, but with a curious calmness, I thought, though memory plays tricks. The whine of shells, a sudden noise of explosions – not so distant – we were nervous enough, and tense. But we grew used to it, that is what happened. We kept digging trenches in the fields where we once had believed in the endless calm of August nights and our fingers had been, once, stained only by berries.

Then the German tanks began to approach in our sector. We were ordered to return to the city. We had to struggle all night through the forest. Luga was burning behind us. We did not know where the enemy was. The shadows played us tricks. It was dawn before we reached a station and we caught the last train back to Leningrad.

Everyone was saying the same thing: Luga is burning, Luga is burning. We were told there would be no more trains on this line until the situation was clear. We were the lucky ones. Through the train windows I saw the last canes and berries.

Here are some notes I did write:

August 16. My father has been speaking to Peter Popkov. He told my father they were told to expect mass air attacks at any moment. The Red Army will not permit the enemy to break into the city, he said; we will surround the city with a belt of forts is what he told my father.

The Germans are broadcasting and they drop leaflets. These boast that Kronstadt is burning; they are preparing to move in to Kronstadt and then Leningrad.

'If you think that Leningrad can be defended, you are mistaken. If you oppose the German troops, you will perish in the rubble of Leningrad under the hurricane of German bombs and shells. We will level Leningrad to the earth and destroy Kronstadt to the water line.'

My father has been teaching me to fire a revolver.

They say the Germans are using gas. They say we have retaken Smolensk and Staraya Russa. They say massive reinforcements are on their way from Moscow . . .

Many mushrooms, many deaths. The old *babushka* who lives on the ground floor has just come back from looking for mushrooms under the linden avenues. It has been so hot this August, but now the lindens are gold and russet, the turn has begun. Kirov Prospekt is full of rubbish in the gutters. All the trenches are dry and dusty; the dust gets in everywhere. Our city has become a dusty earthworks.

I saw a group of 40 or 50 Red Army men drinking water from the Neva, clambering down with buckets. The water was not clean. They were from scattered regiments and did not know where they were going.

*

THE VILLAGE OF MGA

Mga, just beyond the Leningrad freight station,
Mga, out in the country, so small
its name is always being forgotten.

The train moved on with its many passengers.
Evacuees: children, mothers, some military personnel.
It picked up speed across the broad meadows.
It made a great hubbub.
One of the children looked out:
look at those balloons! Look how many!
The Germans landed by parachute.
The train was already on its way to Moscow.
The Germans quickly assembled and overran
the tiny dot that was Mga railway station.
It is the last connection on the line
between Moscow and Leningrad.
No way out after that.
No way in.

*

No, I did not write that poem in Leningrad. How would it have been possible to have such knowledge? I have been reading a group of poems that I did write in that early period. I have burned them all. I am certain that there is no record of their publication, now, in Leningrad, though at one time they were considered my finest. They were read over Leningrad radio, many times. But this poem. No, it fails utterly. I have attempted to recapture the voice and inflection of the girl I was then. I am not that one. I have read the later accounts. At the time I did not really appreciate that the German conquest of Mga station was the beginning of the long siege. My fiancé was a naval officer. He was stationed at Tallinn. The fall of Tallinn, and his silence, that was what occupied all my thoughts in that hot, dusty autumn when even the lindens would not drop their leaves but gripped them stubbornly and hopelessly to their branches.

from
The Diary

Olga Berggolts has given me this diary. She has instructed me to write in it all the things that will be recorded for later. 'And remember,' she said, 'that later generations will not want to be told the theories, the philosophies, the general summaries and conclusions out of our inconclusions. They will want to know things like how we relieved our bladders (they always want to know that), and how and what we ate, whether we still tended and believed in plants, flowers, gardens; what did we talk about, what did we joke about. There will be a need to set down the jokes,' she said. 'They will define us.' She was the first person, ever, to tell me that. She had been three years in prison, in the 1930s, for political reasons; but she still remained loyal to the belief in the Revolution. She was generous to me and I accepted it as my due. Now I have this diary and remember her words, which I set down on the first page. On the second page I will set down what my father said to me, those years ago: 'You can move from the local and concrete into the universal, but it is very hard to begin with the abstract and universal and ever come back to the local, the thing that ordinary people know and will recognise and hold on to.'

It is *September 1*. I have just heard Dimitri Shostakovich on the radio: 'Just an hour ago,' he said, 'I completed the score of the second part of my new large symphonic work. If the 3rd and 4th parts are finished, I will call it my Seventh Symphony. I have been working on it since July. Nothwithstanding war conditions, notwithstanding the dangers threatening Leningrad, I have been able to work quickly and to finish the first two parts. Why do I tell you this? I tell you so that fellow Leningraders will know that the life of our city goes on normally. All of us now carry our military burdens. Soviet musicians, my many and dear colleagues, my friends, remember that our art is threatened with great danger. We will defend our music. We will work with honesty and self-sacrifice that no one may destroy it.'

He spoke to my heart. He told me, in these times when everything seems called into question, of the one thing we must not abandon or question: our purpose and our culture. What we write and compose now is an act of defiance against the barbarians. On these pages I must write, not only the record of what I see, or hear, or encounter, but also the record of what I must offer out of the furnace.

On these autumn days even the goldenrod transfigures the older trenches. Weeds suddenly become poignant; they carry their seed heads as if to promise survival through everything, images of fecundity in our trenches.

It is now late but how can one sleep? Today was the first day of university. So many students gone, so many of our teachers at the front, but there is still a great spirit of belief in our vocation, we will not allow the barbarians to demolish our minds though they may attack our streets, our buildings.

Everyone has been talking of the German panzers at the Izhorsk factory and the resistance from the factory workers. You can see the column of smoke in that direction. In the still, clear air, it hangs like a shroud, or like black washing. There are 2,000 students enrolled.

Last night on the radio I heard Vera Inber, the poet from Moscow, on our radio. She has come here with her husband, Professor Stashun who has been made hospital chief. Her words were full of courage and she reminded us again and again of other times, earlier times, and the great tradition of resistance and endurance of Leningrad. I wished at the time she spoke of attack, of how we could repulse the invaders. My father held me in his arms then. I did not resist him. He has been away so much these last weeks and we listened together, the tears were not my intention.

I am to write about things I observe in the street, in the library, on the steps and bridges. I see only the sandbags protecting Catherine's statue of the bronze horseman; I see only stragglers crouching in the doorways of apartments or lurching from the beer halls – the Brigades are rounding them up, I think many are runaways from the front line – they have that shifty look. But many are from Luga, Pskov, Velikiye Luki, Gatchina, Pushkin, all the villages that have been threatened. It is so easy to make conclusions.

Pushkin. I cannot imagine that village now; there was a boy crouching and shivering under one of the small footbridges. It has been so balmy and hot this first September weather; but this boy had walked all the way from Krasnoye Selo. His family was all killed by a shell, and his pig, he wept, his own pig was killed. I could not understand him and I sent him on to a refuge.

Izhorsk. They have been talking of what's been happening out at the Izhorsk factory, how it is surrounded. I remember the statue in the village square at Izhorsk: a factory worker with a gun in hand, one of the heroes of 1917. Do the factory workers at Izhorsk have guns, can they shoot their way out of the German ambush? No one has answers. No one has any answers.

September 4: at University there is only one subject: Mga. The Germans have taken the railway line and we are cut off from Moscow. Smolny has been hit. Fog. It will clear, sometime; but this fog is mixed with smoke. The Germans are now in Tosno. That is how they were able to train their artillery upon Smolny. I wonder what damage?

155

Today Mother warned me that my pet cat cannot be kept. Already, she says, she sees people looking at it with greed. I cannot bear to be parted from her, in these nights of worry she is my comfort. I will keep her in my room. I will not let others see her. I will show that in this uncaring world someone cares, someone has thought of other creatures. We have a greater and greater need to preserve our civilising virtues. I suspect that old babushka downstairs, though Mother has never mentioned she is the one with hungry eyes.

September 5: shelling. Today the first shell in the centre of the city. An apartment house three blocks away was hit; our fire fighting drills paid off. Nobody was killed, though the top floor and roof were badly damaged. Three families had to be evacuated. How can I concentrate on my studies? At least my shoulders and arms do not ache as they did a fortnight ago. As we do our fortification work a group of us recites aloud: poetry, speeches, even algebraic formulations. Not much learning but good revision. There is a joke going the rounds: 'father, now that vodka is so expensive, will you give up drinking?' 'No, son. We will be eating less.'

September 9: I stare at this open page. How could Olga Berggolts have placed such a burden upon me? I want to record nothing. I want to close the book but cannot. Last night and today have been stretched into infinity, into an infinity of noise, smoke, more noise, fire, flame, stench, smoke, confusion, fear, noise, ache, ache, ache. My stomach still coils and churns. Let me try to set down events, some of the events. Yesterday began normally, or what we now call normally. I walked to the university early, studied in the library and then went to my lecture. There were sirens and a few distant explosions. We had heard that the hydro-electric plant and Dalolin factory had been struck. But the lecture was crowded and we sat through it for two hours – it was if Professor Galischevsky wanted to give us all the notes possible, as if time were shortening – though it seemed lengthening to us, the note-takers and listeners.

Then after a lunch of white bread and cheese which I ate walking back to my volunteer defence group, we set to to build one of the lines of bunkers in our area. It was hard work. But we sang, too, and there was a camaraderie, like summer camps. But just on 7 p.m. we heard the noise of German junkers (someone said later there were nearly 30 of them) and then the bombing started.

It was appalling, and it seemed to go on endlessly, all over the city. They were incendiary bombs; they were made of burning phosphorus, which screamed and whistled – horrible! – then burst, spreading rivers of fire. These streams rolled over roofs, they seemed like liquid from some devil's smelter. Everywhere; thousands, thousands, the air was filled with the stench, and the smoke, and the sound. Then the sound of fire, whooshing up. The noise of buildings crumbling in, or out into the street. There were so many noises they all became one noise. There were so many smells, attacks upon sensation so that there was no sensation any more. I had been given a seat to the Musical Comedy Theatre tonight. *Die Fledermaus* of all things. The Bat. After the terrible swooping bats of the junkers and their endless bombs I could not think of anything. I wanted to stay in my room, locked in like the cat, under the bed. But I also knew that was not possible: what if an incendiary bomb struck our home? Better in the street.

But some of my friends who also had tickets decided they would go. There was nothing else to do and the bombing raid had ended. I said: you are mad. But they replied: no, the Germans, they are mad, but we have made our defences; look, all the fires in our district are controlled, the damage has been in other parts of the city. Already the searchlights were criss-crossing the sky. I agreed.

'Take seats close to the walls, there is no air-raid shelter in here,' the director of the theatre warned us as we went in. The theatre was surprisingly well attended, some people even were in their best clothes. I could not concentrate.

The sound of distant guns – they must be ours – and the pervasive smell of smoke everywhere, like acrid chemicals. Still, we sat through it and I was glad. Yes, we would show them. But when we came outside into the dusk, later, there was a terrible pall of smoke, reddish and heavy. It seemed to be everywhere.

Someone pointed out where it was mainly coming from. You could see sudden fingers of flame high, high, hundreds of feet high: leaping flame, and then black billows. The smell was more terrible now: burning sugar, flesh, oil.

'The Germans have set fire to the food warehouses!' someone behind me called out. The Badayev warehouses have been bombed.

We could not take our eyes from the dull red glow, spreading its huge stain, with its black underside. All the city's main food supplies. They've all been in the big warehouse area, those old wooden lines of buildings near the Vitebsk freight station. Everyone knows that's the biggest warehouse area.

'How much has been saved?' someone else asked.

'How much do we have left?'

We ran home, all the way. I had to tell someone. It was well after ten then. We heard the drone of planes again, heavier, more of them even than in the day. Before we reached our new shelter the bombs began falling. Heavy, low, they rocked the very core of the city, it felt. Have you smelt burning flour? You know the smell of burnt meat, perhaps even burnt sugar – how it catches in your nostrils? We were eaten by the smells of that terrible burning, we were in the stomach of some red creature churning us up, horribly digesting our cries and our panic.

It is nearly 24 hours and the city still crowds and reels and outside the trams are full of people wounded, or people clutching food if they can find it, or people wandering dazed and without purpose. Our Corps has been active all day, that is what has saved me. We have visited partly demolished apartments, we have helped get some of the old people to safer places. Some of us (I was one) patrolled so that thieves and pilferers might not ransack the damaged houses. One old man came back and came back to me screeching, 'You have betrayed me, you have taken my ration card, you have ransacked my kitchen.' He was very violent and we had to call others. 'I will starve,' he cried again and again, as three burly military police dragged him away. We had been guarding that building. Someone had crept in undetected, and then out again. But the worst thing today was also the most weird. At the zoo the old elephant, Betty, had been hit, but not killed. She was on her side, ripped open. Hours and hours she lay dying, no one was able to help her, there was nothing to be done; hours and hours of her trumpeting and crying – like giant human cries, moans, calls for help but there was no help. All afternoon. Along into the afternoon. I once fed her bread and apples.

Tonight I have finally resigned myself to the fact of Yuri's death. I will never mention his name again.

September 11: I write only horrors. All day yesterday it was like the 8th: bombs, incendiaries, bombs, on and on it seemed hours. How does one endure this? I do not know where many of the others are. My father has been gone since the first of this month, I do not know if he is alive. He must be at Autovo or the Kirov works, though Anna told me today that the Kirov metallurgical works were one of the chief targets of the big attack two days ago. My mother looks at me firmly and says we must do what is necessary, and do it well. She has not allowed me to mention father's name. 'We are just people,' she tells me. 'We come, we go; but the city will remain. We must see that the city remains and does not give in to the Germans.' There is no more white bread.

They say the rationing will be tighter now the Badayev warehouses are destroyed. You cannot get pastry or pies or beer or kras. I had an ice cream after waiting in a long queue. They say there will be no more ice cream. Such simple ingredients, yet even they are now treasures.

I went past the Hermitage and the Winter Palace this morning, through the rancid smoky air. I walked the long way round to the university to see the damage and whether any of the great palaces are destroyed (surprisingly little, so far, at least along the great square and Winter Palace), then I looked towards the amusement park. The big roller coaster over there, the one called Amerikanskye Gory has been burned. A twisted charred sculpture crouched and wreathed and writhed in its place. I thought of Laocoon. I thought of great serpents coming out of the sea bed. I thought of the suffering of our city, of its bones and ribs and torment. I thought: this is our monument. Then I looked back at the Hermitage. If they destroy our treasures, I thought then, we will build them again with our bare hands should that be necessary. We shall re-make them defiantly, assertively, triumphantly. I thought of Vera Inber's radio talk. There have been many cities burned: Borodino, Rome, Paris, Moscow. When they are re-built, it is with the inner strength of endurance and self-knowledge. We are strengthened by sackings, not destroyed.

September 17: The headline in this morning's *Leningradskaya Pravda* says: LENINGRAD: TO BE OR NOT TO BE. How can we know what is happening? Rumours everywhere. We have been working all day these last few days, volunteers in Workers' Battalions. In the city I am told there are hundreds of defence areas, they will be defended by reinforced machine-gun posts, anti-tank positions, mortar position. There are 150 protected defence positions. Will the work be accomplished in time? The Germans are just outside the city, everyone says that. Last night everyone said they would break through but so far that has not happened. We were up all night. There have been no heavy raids for almost a week. It is frightening, almost as frightening as the raids when they come. What are they plotting now? Above us each evening there are the big silver balloons that are being flown to protect the city from German planes.

Autumn has really come. Pavelska, my kitten, has been missing for two days. It was not until late today that I noticed. I cannot imagine those nights, night after night, when I used to twist and writhe and pretend my own fingers were the fingers of Yuri. Now I have no dreams.

I have been writing poems in my other notebook. Perhaps I am really mad. I do not understand them. They are as if some other person were dictating them to me but it is not me; it is the voice of the Amerikan-skye Gory, the roller coaster sea serpent. Though it cries in great pain, it will not die, it will not let me be. I am terrified at some of the poems it dictates to me but I am compelled to keep writing. Is this a record? Can one be so private that one is in the end more public and universal than any banner or symphony or military procession?

September 19: Now it is midnight. The last raid surely is done. Four time during the day, and then tonight, two times. Bombs and incendiaries. It is now four hours since there has been any sound of planes. It cannot keep up. There cannot be so many planes in the world or do the same planes return and return? Are they ghost planes, planes that do not have to return to land? I saw three return to land, flaming. No, they are not immortal. But why do they drop their bombs, how can there be so many bombs? Who makes them? Who thinks of their destinations or their damage in some assembly line, who imagines the dust, the stench, the mess, the noise? I think I am deaf now, inured. Yet I know that at the first siren I will be wrenched again, panicking. My father is dead.

The trams rattle through strange canyons like an eroded riverbank after spring rains. No, after dust storms and dry deserts. Yet the maples are burnished with colour. The big hospital in Suvorov Prospekt has been hit. Over 600 patients and staff dead, the radio is saying. I will not go there, I cannot bear to think of the carnage, though bodies all look strangely the same (where will they bury them? Impossible to leave the city). There were women queuing outside a store and a bomb fell in the square; three people at the end of the queue were killed instantly and four others were badly hurt with shrapnel; the others at the front picked themselves up and re-joined their places in the queue. Six passers-by helped the women up; one of them was quite badly injured, her arm hung lifeless and we had to bind her hard to quench the blood, using the lining of her coat (she screamed at us) and we got her into a tram in the next street and then some of the others took her to the hospital. I think the other injured ones rejoined the queue. And now the hospital itself has been hit. But then as we went up Nevsky Prospekt we saw that the big raid earlier must have hit Gostiny Dvor, the big shopping arcade. We saw the smoke was coming from there as soon as we entered the long, straight Prospekt. It swirled low and down into the streets and canals. Yellow dust and then the sooty black smoke, and the smell, burning clothing, I do not know what other.

Many people were killed, mainly women.

There was another raid just after that. We jumped from the tram so did not get close to Gostiny Dvor.

I kept running. It was a long way from my area and I was suddenly very frightened. Someone shouted at me, someone called for my papers but there was an incendiary burst over the end of the lane, I did not really know where I was running, I do not even remember seeing anything. I remember bumping against other people. I remember veering from a crater in the cobbles. I remember the white-washed street signs blanked out by children against identification. I remember thinking: if I can get back to my sector, to our apartment . . . I remember thinking: what if bombs have hit our apartment? For the first time, then, I think, I really thought: what if my mother were killed? I do not think I thought of myself: myself was there, stumbling, running. I remember looking down at one corner and seeing my hands sticky, blood-clogged between my fingers. That old woman. She had been years back. It was only ten minutes.

LENINGRAD: TO BE OR NOT TO BE. That news headline. On the tram someone had been saying that the order had been: 'lay mines throughout the city, in the bridges, in the palaces. Let Leningrad be blown to bits rather than be occupied'.

It is far past midnight. No raids for three hours now. Rumours. Rumours. Someone came in, I heard her speaking to my mother. The

Peterhof Palace has been taken. It is raining outside now. Mud. It will soon be the wet phase of autumn.

September 27: Another day of endless planes and bombs. How can it be that our little street has been spared? Are we being spared to wait for some worse disaster? In the daytime it is not so bad; the Workers' Battalions are charged with keeping up morale. It is true; we know that in our youth and our energy we set a sort of example, we are filled with the power of helping, with the power of doing good, being of service, with the true power of holding together that which will never be destroyed in the city. But alone, later, I hardly talk to my mother. I have nobody. Once, many years ago – two months – I had a lover.

October 1: Early this morning the phone rang in the front room. I had not been in that room since the last time I sat with Father. No one else uses the phone. But my mother was not in, she was in some endless queue for rations or was bartering my father's dead clothes in the Haymarkets. I do not ask. The phone rang and I answered it.

'Until the end of the war, the telephone is being disconnected,' the girl said, then hung up.

Until the end of the war, life has been disconnected. The sea serpent writhes in the pleasure-ground among ashes; its voice has been disconnected.

Is it true the Germans are digging in? Everyone asks the question. Is it true? If they are digging in, does that mean they have abandoned their attempt at conquest? There have been no heavy raids since the 27th. The rain closes in; mud and runnels of water.

My mother has just returned. Her face is thin as my own, her lips have no colour. 'Rations have just been reduced again,' she says without tone. 'One third of a loaf of bread for a day for each of us. For the whole month to come, unless we get supplies in or the Germans retreat, there will be only one pound of meat, one pound for the whole month. A little cereal. If you were under sixteen, my daughter, your share would be half that.'

October 2: I am hungry. Mother sits in the kitchen near the fire. She is listless. I walk about, then feel tired. I am hungry. She warns me not to drink too much water, I will swell and swelling is worse than thinness. Finally she brings out a small stick of chocolate. When I have gulped that she says I have just eaten my father's overcoat. At first I think I will vomit, but I do not. Good, I say, good good good. I am hungry. I begin to wonder what other clothes are in her wardrobe. I begin to wonder about the wardrobe itself. I am very hungry. Wait, my mother says. Have patience. Have a very great deal of patience.

The Germans digging in, she says, means that they also must be prepared to have patience. I think of the potatoes and onions in the rich soil out in the villages. I think of the wheat in bales, of the windblown buckwheat in the lanes and hedgerows. I think of tart autumn fruit, windblown, rotting. I can smell the sharpness, I can savour it.

October 3: A strange quietness everywhere. There have been no more raids. We go about filling in bomb holes with a new lethargy, we have all the time in the world, we have nowhere to go, we have nothing else – though I begin to realise I must have something else. I ran into my music lecturer on the tram today. He chided me for missing classes, he insisted I come back with him and assist in setting up the music stools for a rehearsal, he asked me about the volume of poems I am said to be finishing.

They need me almost more than I need myself, it seems. I have not written in the poem book for weeks and dare not read the sea serpent poems. But I will write some poems to set down the street, this street, in its new quietness. I can write about that. If there is another long raid, another storm of incendiaries I do not think I will write again. I will write again.

October 10: Nothing for days. We are no longer waiting. I think of food all the time, but find I can scarcely keep down the small bread ration. I apportion it out: one third in the morning; one third midday; and this last third now, at night. There has been an urgent decree over the radio (the radio is our lifeline, it is the voice that speaks to us, with us, for us). Every ration card must be re-registered and stamped. If it is not re-registered between the 12th and the 18th it is invalid.

They say the Germans have been dropping not bombs but ration cards, roubles, booby traps. When the plane came over this morning, it dropped down screaming, hooting things, not bombs at all, we thought. The planes have been like dogs on the steppes, herding sheep, biting small bites.

The Germans are digging in. They say they are headquartered in Catherine's Summer Palace at Pushkin. The weather grows chiller, the rain is colder and more persistent. My mother is so silent.

October 14: At 11 a.m. today the first snow fell. I was walking towards the university. The colour of the air was dull, burnished, a sort of bronze low light under the clouds, then it became grey and greyer and tighter. Then after a while, the first flakes. A sudden wind and the flakes ran ahead of me; horizontal lines invisibly vibrating like a violin string, or like ghost notes on a manuscript, the notes rush away from me, searching to recover the original score. First snow, and at least two weeks early; it is still only mid October. It will be a long and a very cold winter.

*

THE ROLLER COASTER AS A SEA MONSTER

We all spent years of childhood laughing,
terrified on the roller coaster.
All those years: the roller coaster
flung us high then clasped us in
tight or terrified: all those years.
These years were long shadows,
they glistened like metal
in our thirty-five days of real sunlight.
The roller coaster in these years
lurched like Betty the elephant,
a tamed monster, playful
and funny. At night, though,
Betty the elephant tramped and trumpeted
and the damp smell of jungles entered my dreams.
Amerikanskye Gory, the roller coaster:
it spun me lurching and terrified
without rails into nightmares.

Tonight I wake rocking, terribly unsafe.
In the darkness there is the wheeze
the thump of underwater monsters. In the darkness
out of the pleasure ground the wrecked roller coaster stretches,
feels its bones, husks of
red paint, green paint, ochre:

the great insect, the snake, this serpent
has twisted itself out of its husk.
It returns for payment. We did not believe
it was other than our own. We spent recklessly.
It turns the night into sea.
It smells blood, and sweat
and it remembers every child, every one.

*

THE ROLLER COASTER AT NOON

Do not be deceived: it is looking upwards
not down. It looks up without fear
it likes the sight of smoke, it remembers fires.
Five German planes fly over.
No, the roller coaster whispers,
not this time.
The roller coaster
has shed wagons, struts, timber
It returns to the shape it had before shape
– iron, rust, veins out of the volcano.
The planes fly over
and metal calls up to metal.
It is dreaming of eggs, of bombs like eggs.
It is dreaming nests;
it will cradle them, nurture them,
make them its own.

It will swim then with them back underwater
into the sea. At night it will lift its long neck
like a serpent, it will pluck the bombers down.

*

NOCTURNE FOR THE ROLLER COASTER

Curfew. The city is dark, no footfalls on the cobbles.
This is the serpent hour.
Because I am asleep I hear the twisted roller coaster
move cautiously, all its muscles of metal
reach tentatively. It has been released
from the old dream, which was beautiful.
It sniffs the new world. Burnt sugar.

Smoke stench. Bomb craters.
It is reminded of primeval swamp and fire.
The roller coaster moves into the city.
It slides down every street, seeking the curse
that sets it free after all these lovely years of form.
'You will seek out the injured places.
There you will nest until you have consumed
all the injuries. Having become the frozen pain
of the entire city you will wait
until the water drips between your girders
and the sea calls you back.
You will remember every shell hole,
every broken wall, every bombed palace.
You will taste bones.
Bring all these things back, harbour them well.
When it is all over, no matter how long, then
you will be allowed to collapse fully.
After midnight, full of your storage
you will be allowed just one hour
to return like a sea serpent back to the sea.'

*

NATASHA

I cup your flame.
My fingers regain colour
and transparency.
The bone hides
in this transparency.
Natalja laughs gravely
at my candle joke,
she believes in life outside
in light
in darkness when it is dark.
Natasha leads me
drags me by the hand
her hand, gripping mine,
eleven-year-old demon on the steps
and delicate angel over ice.
I follow.

THREE

SYDNEY

At night, when the hair grows on your face, and your body grows longer, and dinner is changed to blood, and your nails grow longer, you ought to remember, however empty your sleep, how much is untouched by the *conscious* mind.

Delmore Schwartz: *Journal*

XXII

David and Deirdre walked out, arm in arm, to the flat rock, beyond the old gun emplacements. Banksia bushes, overgrown lantana and weeds, casuarina with its needles that combed the wind, a windy growth of scrub: four hundred feet below them the surf, pushed in through the Heads, crashed and spumed and fanned back with white patterns. The updraught of air tossed Deirdre's long hair. David gripped her more tightly. Middle Head: they not had been here before, the area only recently made into a National Park. Before then it was part of the army defences. A ferry from Manly passed quite close to the rocks below them. Yachts tilted and played in the wind. The two boys were off on some group outing. They had made no fuss about David's return. Their lives had become full of sporting fixtures, homework, television jokes shared with each other and their mates.

'Look. Another gun emplacement down there.' Deirdre pointed and they scrambled down. There was a well carved circle in sandstone but the weapons had long been removed. In low relief was chiselled V.R. 1877.

'They thought the Russians were coming in 1877.'

'Let's picnic here. Out of the direct breeze.'

'Don't you like nature raw?' But David laughed too. Last night he had come home late, quite late.

Within the wide circle David pointed to a low entrance. It was meticulously carved, six foot wide, with gutters. It directed downwards into the cliff.

Someone had scrawled a message near the entrance: 'My dad went in and we've not seen him since.' David grinned and stepped into the darkness. Then quickly he walked all the distance to their parked car for his torch. Deirdre at first was reluctant to enter this tunnel but he insisted, his warm palm surrounding her own.

What they discovered was a whole network of passages, rooms, lower and lower, at many levels. Each one well crafted. There were the remains of electric wires, some blackened remnants of vandals, visits or of parties, but on the whole the network had the appearance of untouched continuity. Following one gradient, David found himself at the top of a sheer drop. He pointed the torchlight down.

'Look. Wooden steps; they've just rotted. All this must have been full of action and importance, back in the war I suppose. The 1940s?'

'The 1870s, you mean.' They agreed it had a life of its own over a long period of time – those electric wires, for instance – and there was certainly something still remaining, some aura or presence. 'Absence, not presence,' David corrected himself. The torch was already losing power.

As they strode out into fresh autumn air, they blinked. The wind from the sea buffeted them. Clambering over flat promontories and through other parts of the headland, they kept coming across further signs.

'I wouldn't go in there alone,' Deirdre confessed.

'We must come back. I'll get a stronger torch. It's a maze, fascinating. I can't wait to see what there is through the whole network of passages.'

'What will you find?'

'Oh, nothing. Everything. I'll find out how far it extends. I'll discover what it all adds up to.'

'I'm sure there are maps in the archives.' But Deirdre knew that was not an answer.

As they pushed back through the thickets they realised that this surface, too, was full of signposts of some abandoned habitation: groups of oleanders among ti-tree, rambling vines of banksia rose, overgrown asparagus fern.

She reached out for David's palm. He kept striding ahead as if he were alone. Absently he grasped her. What was he brooding on this time?

He turned and gave her a sudden grin. 'Let's go down to Obelisk Beach. This time of year it'll be deserted. We'll go skinny dipping.' Only a few miles from the centre of Sydney and they were in the bush. They stepped carefully over the sharp glass of a broken bottle. 'Damn!' he exclaimed. 'Whenever we find some perfect spot, something has to spoil it.' On this headland riddled with tunnels and old military gun emplacements Deirdre looked at the heath-flowers, the harbour below them. Had they ever been more distant?

XXIII

No safety. Deirdre could not explain – she had no reason to demand that explanations might be made. But it was as if everything in their house had moved a centimetre away, as if sunlight were in some conspiracy with poison, or even the back-yard vegetable patch (her favourite retreat in moments of stress, and these had been many, it seemed) was absorbing stained rust out of the good dirt instead of converting all things into wholesome growth: potatoes, broad beans, the much coddled celery.

She phoned her friends.

'Brian? Brian, is Meg there please? No, it's okay, Brian. Damn it, of course David's out . . . no, just if Meg is there, I wanted Meg.'

Yet when Meg came to the phone, what was there to explain? 'Meg, I'm sorry if I hurt Brian, palming him off, I didn't mean . . . I inflict my worries on you I know but I've been all day . . . please, Meg, don't start sympathising, I don't think I can bear sympathy.'

No safety. No safety.

'Meg. One favour? You know I wouldn't, but just for once: you're the only friends we've got who'd understand. Meg, can I ask you? David and me, can you bear to have us come over tonight?'

Perhaps it was years ago that Deirdre had believed she could cope. She could not stop pacing, twisting the short lead of the telephone in its little alcove under the stairs. Her blonde hair had come undone again, it was her own fault for being hasty. She caught herself in the mirror that had been installed to make the cramped space more an illusion of ease. She poked out her tongue at the reflection. She listened as her friend commented on David, and David's drinking and the sudden memory of the time when David had promised to bring over the Russian champagne, was it five months back?

There had been that night in bed, in Meg's bed, the three of them. How could it have been? Unexpected closeness, strange ways of being hostage to him, of being kin and captives: no, like a late night TV film, it may have happened but it did not. Memory can be ruthless, and if unforgiving it can also be like tides washing out the prints on a midnight beach.

Meg, after some phone-muffled dialogue with Brian, agreed. Yes, come over at 9 p.m. The kids would be settled. Was Deirdre all right? They were wonderful friends, both of them.

David had read aloud to Deirdre the bits and pieces of notes, diaries, poems from Leningrad. She heard the intonations of Galina Darovskaya in his voice.

Why had she suddenly felt angry with the daughter? The mother was foxlike, quick, radiant, electric. The mother, on the visit, was everywhere, eyes over Deirdre in the first two minutes so that her sandy hair, unwashed from the island, and her cracked nails from the fishing and mucking about were all quite open and identified. Why did men not see this scrutiny and examination?

David, that time, blundered on and was handed this impossible burden. He did not even realise just the measure of the burden; he said thank you and how delighted. Come and look at my rainforest, he had said.

Even before she read a word, or had a word read aloud to her, Deirdre knew it was a net of claims.

The daughter, she knew that; yes, she knew. The daughter had looked at Deirdre, already aware that the words were to be spread, diffused, leeched out, were being sent on some long treacherous voyage, making demands. She perhaps felt relieved at that, released from some personal burden.

What were they? Both of them were simply migrants, no more so than half of Deirdre's acquaintances from Yugoslavia, Greece, Italy, post-war England. What were they getting at? What was that old woman setting up? What was the daughter trying to escape from?

David, when they returned to Sydney, had been reluctant at first to read any of the material. Since their return, though there had been no outbreak, no explanation – no drunken bender – yet there had been an undefined tension. They both were afraid anything might happen, should this strange calm be shattered. She understood his reluctance to open the package. She would have moved it from the hallway table, except that action itself might well be the trigger. Never had she felt so estranged from her own things, her own home.

Two nights ago, though, he had opened the packet up, flattened out the pages, suggested he would have a peek at what the old girl had written. It was an evening when David had been more relaxed, more companionable. The kids had been almost suspiciously co-operative. On that particular evening the pair of them were glued to television and it seemed admirable, a sort of discretion so that their parents could be together, sharing whatever little chores and house-making procedure were part of the ceremony.

Of course Deirdre had been warmed and delighted by her husband's proposal. 'Please, David, read aloud, remember when you used to read all those books to me? When I was pregnant?' They had once shared so many things.

Maria Peters; that was the daughter's name. Who was Mr Peters?

Why had Deirdre found it disconcerting, hearing all that material?

David, in reading aloud, had paced and grown animated. She was used to his restlessness, caged lion, panther, wildebeest. His voice had a schoolmaster's force and projection but, as he kept reading, something changed in his tone. It was as if he had been taken over.

XXIV

THE ROLLER COASTER SERPENT POEMS

I had a visitor,
water thawed from its scales
the colour of rust.
The turkish carpet with rust colours
greeted my visitor. The vase
with rotting stems of autumn leaves
called to my visitor: welcome.
'Where are you from?' I asked,
not frightened. 'Are you a friend?'
'What is friendship? It is nothing,'
my visitor replied.
'Better to ask what the sea says
as it turns to mist and sprays
on your window.
Better to ask what rust says
as it drags itself back towards the shorelines
among kelp and bodies and old fish heads.'

My visitor turned to me then, bodies
on its breath; my visitor asked me questions.
'What was this place in the old time?

What will it be in the coming time?
Who has made it permanent?'
My guest whispered and I could not escape
the smell of rotting children on its breath.

The book fell out of my hand.
Peter the Great building this city out of mud
and ambition, the hundred thousand serfs, prisoners, labourers
squirming out of the breath of my visitor –
I had an image, maggots on a beached carcass,
each one crying: remember, remember.
My visitor coiled up on my turkish carpet.
My visitor coiled like a cat on my carpet
where outside the rain beat down
the first rain of autumn.

· · · · ·

You think you know this place.
You think promenades, embankments
and on the long white nights
you flirt, or make love, you
chatter like sails flopping.
No, I said.
You think you inhabit the streets of this place?
You think the skeletons do not?
No.
You think it is a place of drinking,
it is green, you think.
You sail in the Neva with friends
and you think that is enough.
It is beautiful, I said.
This place is mountains, hills, full of lakes,
said my visitor.
This place is washed down from the hills
it has mountains in its footprints.
Flat, I said, it is flatness, order, certainty.
This place, my visitor insisted, this place
groans from the birth of mountains,
it opens its mouth and the steam of volcanoes
has to be remembered.

Yes?
So many curves, buckles, so many upheavals:
Only the sea serpent contains turbulences
only the roller coaster jolts experience back
beyond childhood roundabouts to mud
and the shock of ancient ridges and precipices.
The roller coaster dares to declare
what this place must not abandon.
Yes, I said.
Yes.
I was terrified.
'Even your affirmation has the salt taste
of some other habitation.'
I woke. The salt taste was not on my lips.
It was soaking in slow stains on the carpet.

. . . .

Round and round the roller coaster
in and down the alleyways
rondo rondo calls my teacher
music scatters sideways.

. . . . .

The little church that was converted
where we had meetings and songs
it was struck by a bomb.
How strange.
The street where the girl I secretly hated
why should that street be singled out
for destruction?
I think I am tied by invisible threads
to each bomb
to each enemy.

When I utter a word I send directions.
I am the most lively one in the Brigade
yet I feel an instrument
powerful, though, tuned to perfect pitch.

That word is a puppet word
a string word
a word jerking and dangerous. I believe in song
because of its pain and its discipline.
My words are steel scaffolding
rusty, sea dank. They are
wrong. They are right.
Do not believe me.

      . . . .

You will taste flesh
      said the roller coaster
You will chew and swallow.
I know. I have come
     for the children.
It is their taste
     their delicious fear:
     I am privy to that.
I have returned in your dreams
     for that.

No, I said, the taste
     is different.
It is not fear.
The taste is an offering
a gift only to the communicants
like the gift of light
     sunshine
     summer
that must return

And saying that I knew
     the sea serpent
     in the roller coaster
had become, like kelp drying out
merely wreckage, scorned
and abandoned.

      . . . .

Do not believe me. I know the sea serpent
in the roller coaster. We are not friends.
It is terrible; wreckage should be pulled down completely.
Nobody should remember that old playground
and the way we once were.
Who could believe we shared quite ordinary feelings?
Anyone could be deceived into believing
the ordinary is actually happening
among bomb craters of our beautiful city.

*

SONG OF THE ROLLER COASTER SERPENT

It's not enough. We must begin.
Though we grew under the shade of Ygdrassil
the world ash tree, we remained restless,
we sharpened our blades, and dreamed
of sun, of the wheat-tossed plain,
saying: 'It's not enough. We must begin.'

We ate the black snow of burial
we consumed our own city with fire
though we shouted out the names of enemies
and sharpened our angers. We took hostages.
At night their voices bellowed very like our own
imploring: 'It is not enough. We must begin.'

We ended with skeleton hungers
and with all the time in the world.
When we tasted the last flesh we knew
we could never turn back – nor weep again.
Flesh has become but a symbol. Until we recover tears
it is not enough. We must begin.
Though our skeletons become rust, we must begin.

*

NATASHA (2)

Natasha the flame,
it has become her name.
Natasha the light.

In her delight
we invent excuses
to forget losses.
Natasha the wing
she is everything
bones thin as a wing
my flute, my song.
She tugs me along.
*

NATASHA (3)

Last night great wings drew in
they covered my dream. I clung
to the tiny frame of Natasha,
and could not tell
if she felt the same shock
of wings in the dark.
'We are both orphans,' she said
but she is older than I
at eleven years.
'I never learned to cry,' she says
and the dry frozen ice touches me;
it burns.
*

XXV

'Something to be said for pool,' Brian stood back and let Deirdre have her turn. 'Something frivolous!' He laughed. Brian, she thought gratefully, always brings things back to an easy perspective. With perfect precision she cleared the table of targets.

This was her own problem. Only tonight, because she was tense, did she forget to allow Brian the full reward of his generous approval of her playing style. He was the perfect host. Her appetite, if she did not hold it in, could consume everything. 'Sorry, I was on a winning streak,' she explained, 'I was suddenly hitting everything like clock-work.' How shocked Brian would be if she really set out to outpace him!

Brian slapped her shoulder. 'Terrific! Hey Dee, terrific! You should take up the game seriously, become a professional!'

She smiled at him then. Another mistake. A quick fudge, a wry shuffle of the shoulders; all was restored. 'You think I would look good on TV? *Pot Black* and all that English video performance?'

'Don't knock it,' said Brian, shoving up the lost coloured balls from the pockets. Everything he touched, in his messy house, seemed to have charm. Deirdre helped him.

'No, don't knock your talent entirely. Hey Dave, did you realise you have a wife here could be dead set for TV? Her pool playing has picked up no end.'

With a sudden impulse Deirdre moved back to David and put her

arm in his. Two years ago she could have outclassed Brian easily.
'David refuses to watch *Pot Black*.'

The boys were onto their fourth bottle. Brian, catching Meg's eye,
gave his friend a slap. 'Sometimes I wonder, Dave, do you count the
units of debt we owe each other?'

He cleared the table for the match now, between losers. 'After all,
now that Meg has scalped you and Dee did the real clean-up on me, we
are in the same brigade. We have the discernment to have married
brilliant women.' Brian bowed and sent kisses across the room to
where the two others had begun supper preparations.

'Food. Skill. Let the game roll on. We will be waited on by
paragons.'

'Brian, keep that up and the entire dishwashing chore for a week will
be on your head.'

'Heavens!'

Even David laughed at Brian's mock horror.

Not moodiness: something different. An abstraction, as if David
were half somewhere else.

Deirdre felt that old wave of protectiveness, which always subverted
her independence. Then the twinge of anger. Then the concern, the
abiding concern that had welled up from impossible depths. She saw
Meg's glance at David, too.

She stroked the tight knuckles of her husband's hand. He winked
back. There might be no undercurrents, anywhere.

It was that creeping time of autumn, winter round the corner in every
puff through a window, anger if windows were left open, yet the wish
to keep hold of the last tingles of fresh air, holding back against air
conditioning. David had spent much of the evening, when not leaning
over the pool table, with his head half out the window, gazing into the
dark pit of the gully with its distant speckle of lights through trees.

Brian's heartiness: it was as if he were hearing his friend from across
a different field of vision. So warm, so transparent, so very cushioned
with well being. Meg the mattress; no, even Meg was almost translu-
cent, hardly there, hardly a person. So unsuffering. A tickle of night air
seemed to pass along his neck. Outside somewhere, the fishermen
would be riding unstable, sure waves in darkness. And above them,
stars bright as sharp arrows. Frozen as ice splinters.

Deirdre had been following him all night, her eyes big wounds.

Nothing he could do. Nothing he could say that would help her. Some things he could not forgive her. Some things were ordained, beyond will or control. Some things, like Galina Darovskaya, opened new perspectives, opened old wounds – how could Galina understand that she had, quite unconsciously, subverted Deirdre's dismissal of his History?

Later, when they moved to the other room, and Deirdre did remark on the way the harbour sent its chill up through the very floorboards so that she wondered how Meg and Brian endured it, David was provoked to make a passing comparison with Leningrad in the siege and the brute facts of the Russian winter.

Deirdre looked across at him, her raised hand still gripping the slice of quiche. Brian laughed again. 'Go on! You're really hooked.'

Meg urged David to say what was on his mind. Leningrad?

'Deirdre claims I have found a new obsession,' David stated. 'She is secretly convinced that there is a sixty-five-year-old rival, one who can hardly speak the same language.'

'Deirdre,' she said, 'is damned certain you're obsessed, she recognises the signs from way back.' Glint of an edge in her voice – a fire, or a hurt, something too painful for expression.

The others waited, polite and expectant.

'It's the reason I married you, heaven help us both. Well: what were the alternatives? Life's not been dull, dear friend, with you around. But not to give you a swelled head.'

She remained across the room, but Meg's swift glance to Brian was a signal: let it surface, let it surface.

'After all, I also married a bloke as plain as they come, simply a human: man with fingers, thumbs, hands, penis, nose – big nose – eyes – very easily hurt eyes – mouth and teeth. You know you've got very good teeth, David? What else? Toenails, have I ever described to Meg and Brian just how David's toenails curl in? Well, they do.' She was spearing her fork into another slice of quiche on her plate, churning it round and round. 'So, with all these qualities, what's an obsession here and there; now and then?'

She could see her friends' concern but could not stop herself. She could feel David's hurt, possessive silence. She put down her plate with its mussed-up food scraps. 'Well, I think you owe it to us to explain all about Galina Darovskaya to Meg and Brian.'

Meg poured coffee. Her calm voice imposed an order they all must know was surreal. 'Dee's got a point. And we don't have a clue about this mysterious Russian who seems suddenly to be almost in our midst.'

'Well, in the Northern Rivers. Mullumbimby.' David began.

'There's a whole trail of Russian émigrés,' Brian explained to his wife with practical cheerfulness. 'Alexander Kerensky, the bloke who fielded the first Russian government after the death of the Czar; he lived in Brisbane at one time; the 1940s. Married one of the Tritton girls; you know, Tritton's Furniture. She was the wild one, the party one, the poetic one. He just missed out on getting the Chair of Slavic Studies at Melbourne. Nina Christesen beat him to it is the story. He might have been a politician in his day, but he was a lousy lecturer. Still, there are probably stories behind stories. He eventually went on to America.'

'Brian! How amazing!' Deirdre clapped her hands, 'That makes my night. Put my world back into perspective – and what a perspective it puts on sleepy old Brisbane! Or on the dramas of old Russia!' She gave Brian a light kiss on the cheek. His cheerfulness admitted no tripwires. She knew she was right to come over here. David had returned to the chilly knife-edge of air by the window. Sulking, she thought; sulking and still obsessed.

'Any time!' Brian waved. They did not speak further of Galina, then. Deirdre went across to Meg and slipped her arm into hers. For an instant Meg looked exposed and grateful. 'I know there's more coffee.'

But David had the face of one who was inwardly savouring some uncomfortable appetite. He walked down to one of the cedar chiffoniers at the other, darkened, end of the big room. He bent down to examine the woodgrain. The edge he moved along might be whip tight with thorns of lawyer-cane.

*

THE ROLLER COASTER SERPENT APPETITE

The roller coaster wreckage still remembers the children.
It remembers their laughter, high up,
it recalls screams on the sudden dips.
It hungers for the flavour of their hands,
moist gripping palms, sturdy buttocks.
Now it is turned into a sea monster, unstable,

it grows hungry. It grows thin on the booty of water,
having once straddled the land.
It could eat anything.
Six year olds: eyes shining with delight and fear.
Eight year olds: thumping and boisterous.
Twelve year olds bullying their siblings.
Thirteen year olds, fifteeners bleeding with expectations,
sixteen year olds: they fill dreams.

Night. In my own dreams I hear children,
so thin they are listless,
so refined by experience.
The roller coaster monster comes searching
next street and the next street and the next.
The soft breath of starving children
even their fleshless frames –
the monster wants to suck out the marrow.
All the laughter all the crying:
the monster cries in the night for children
with a voice of terrible loneliness,
teeth of rusted metal.
Its teeth make a sound like the crack of ice.

XXVI

Brian ladled out thick soup despite protests from Deirdre. Brian looked across at Meg and was gallant to David who, for his part, had made the effort to return to the cosy circle. He asked a few questions, with genuine curiosity, about Kerensky. The Russian connection.

'Hey Dave, something that might interest you,' Brian clicked his fingers with sudden intrigue. 'I was doing some mucking around last weekend, below the house. You know that big sandstone wedge this place is built on; it goes right along this ridge to the reserve just above the yacht club. Well, since that time we all spooked ourselves out of our minds, down on the old terraces, well, it's been nagging me.'

David looked at him.

'No, not the spooking; the mess. It's a shambles. So you see, you're on our conscience, mate, whether you want it or not. But only as genie of the clean-up.'

'I always said you'd improve the value no end.' David spoke evenly, 'If you got yourself organised.'

Perhaps that was the best way: treat the incident as simply part of the rubble of that tangled backyard?

'Yeah, Meg played her part in getting me activated, too. I was worn down, had to give in to reason. Though I still have a hankering for that gully full of wild runaway vegetation,' Brian said.

'A bit of disorder is good for the soul; especially the soul of a white-collar executive,' Deirdre suggested. Brian nodded happily. 'Anyway.

Went down last weekend, thought I'd better do something about it.'

'Snakes and spiders, just for a start,' Meg said firmly.

'I'd reckon nobody has given it a thought – or a clean-out – since say 1927, or would it be 1926 and a half?'

'Give or take a decade.' David stood up again, then, catching Deirdre's eye, he sat down.

'Well, you've seen the general layout, Dave. Some of the terraces were done as Japanese gardens with little ponds and shrines; the azaleas are now bigger than lantana run wild. The upper terraces are narrower, and someone sensibly planted shrubs to cover everything. It worked. I had to clean out bottles, tins, the junk from every building repair – place was an archive. But that's not the real discovery.'

Brian held up his hand. 'Wait for it. Right under the house – you might have noticed the whole end of this house is supported by that massive stonework wall. Well it suddenly struck me that the lines of the natural rockface, the whole ridge, goes in much further back. Half of the house is resting on the top of that ledge, and the other half sticks out over the ridge until it reaches the big stone wall. Very nice stonework too, I might tell you, beautifully edged. Well, as soon as I realised this, I thought: what a place for a cellar, under there. Or it might even be big enough to make a whole room under there. Then I looked closer. Guess what? At some stage someone must have had a doorway in the wall – there could be a room already underneath us, all blocked up for some reason.'

'What would they close it for, then?'

'Who can tell? But it's intriguing: whoever bricked it up did it very skilfully. Matching stone pieces. I'd never noticed the space before; even the concrete render matches the original. And they used different sizes of stone to draw the eye away from the obvious rectangle of the doorspace. Intriguing, eh?'

'And you re-opened the doorway?'

'Come off it! You seen the size and weight of those stones?'

'I'll come over this weekend. Give you a hand.'

Brian beamed. 'You're on! That's the old Davey-boy.'

'You boys! That place is so inaccessible.' But Meg shared in the general enthusiasm.

'It's like cubby houses,' Deirdre exclaimed tartly.

'Why don't you all come? Bring the kids.' Brian said. 'It's all this bastard's fault anyway, getting me to look seriously at the mess and the workload.'

Deirdre looked at her husband. Yes; it would be good. It would be something different. Yes. Yes, why not? She remembered the underground tunnels at Middle Head. As they had pushed through the walking track on the headland towards Obelisk Beach they kept coming across naked men, sunning themselves, or wandering stealthily through underbrush. This whole place is full of ghosts, she had exclaimed at the time. Then had thought: and so many of them are still alive.

*

THE ROLLER COASTER IN SNOW

I plan to live forever, says the roller coaster.
I plan to survive frost, and wind and snowflakes.
I will test my strength against ice
I will hold coldness in my embrace
until my metal cracks – glee begins from that source.

I will give ice a rusty taste
I will wear ice as an overcoat.
Ice's secret energy I'll hoard;
it is private. Excellent. I will expand.

I believe the roller coaster will not die;
it has become our whole city, our country,
our consciousness.
I dream – the roller coaster prepares sanctions.
I will be secretive – the roller coaster sucks out my secrets
like sherbet.
I will be the dream of the structure, then;
I will be bones defining a skeleton – but the flesh, I still own
the pulpy flesh, too insubstantial for certitudes.
The tyranny of ice is the tyranny of bones, of metal
though it once was limp water.
I have been through many experiences in my flesh
which is still unfrozen.
I have my one counsel. Wait wait wait.
I will wait.

XXVII

Deirdre was ironing and watching a replay of *Casablanca* in a perfunctory way, cursing the rondo of commercials, yet tapping her foot at the catchy ones. The kids were in bed. It was eleven at night.

David was involved in his one teaching job since Administration had swallowed him up: his classes on ecology and the rainforests. They had become popular since the increasing spate of oil spills, die-back, nuclear plant disasters. He had to repeat them this term.

Of course he should be home by eleven but invariably he ended up in some coffee place or bar with a group of students, all clamouring and unable to ease themselves back down from the high he led them to. Charismatic teachers could be more dangerous than good, she thought. Building up excitements and ambitions and a false reliance on adrenalin. But she must be careful of encroaching cynicism: it marked the outset of middle age. There were too many years of possibilities, yet, to allow sourness. David found release in those classes. She must acknowledge that. She acknowledged it.

The commercial break again flashed its quick images of kids at a breakfast table, mum with the carton, dad slouching into the room dishevelled, then suddenly full of vim and cereal. Pure manipulation, but she noticed suddenly that the quick montage of images had a few constants – not only the faces, anxious then smiling, but the colour refrain: a gold vase of daffodils, gold light through the curtains, the mother's golden cardigan. What was the gold motif associated with father? Next time round she would look closer.

A rap at the front door.

It could not be David; he would not forget his door key. Deirdre, puzzled, turned off the power to the iron and placed the iron itself carefully upright on the ironing board. She went into the hallway. They had no security devices, no safety chain. The knock was repeated, louder this time.

Well, she thought, intruders do not knock. They break in.

Rap. Rap. Rap. Rap rap.

'I'm coming,' she called, already obedient to the command of the firm, hard knuckles. She would have to open up now.

*

THE ROLLER COASTER KNOCKS AT MY DOOR AGAIN

Not paper, it is snow in my notebook.
My ink has frozen; my blood is a soft blur.
I will not listen.
I am using my father's last lead pencil.
The letters begin to be curls and hooks
of the twisted roller coaster over in the bombed
pleasure grounds.
A whole page. I have drawn the map
of the roller coaster monster.
Somewhere it has seen my work under snow.
It has shaken off the smothering snow
it has heard the soft shoosh and scratch
of handwriting. Because the night is dark
and snow in darkness creates black around itself
my yellow candle is a beacon.
But it is my pencil, my writing:
the roller coaster hears that. It is coming.
Already it is hunched outside my room
my house my street it is filling my street
with its enormous rusted twisted coils
I remember how long it was how many hills
and gullies how many screams of delight
have been painted along its rails.

They are all there. Nothing is forgotten.
It is not the metal silence
not even the creak and twitch of twisted framework
it is the soft breathing
the soft breathing of all those children
like cobwebs or snowflakes caught up in the frets
and the scaffolding.
The roller coaster is outside my room.
It is waiting. This time it is real.
I am wide awake.

*

'It was your voice, girl, told me the right place. Is David at home? Or is he out on the town carousing, which is perhaps what I should be doing myself in this big wild city. Only this thing in me kept saying: Go and see David, go and see David and his splendid wife Deirdre.'

Clyde straddled the big armchair – David's chair – and he waved aside Deirdre's apologies about the ironing board and the ironing basket. He was at home. Her mouth pursed with politeness.

Deirdre had difficulty connecting this rather gaunt, lumpy person with the net mender and the fabulist of their island. He wore a tie. It knotted under his throat like a sea creature clinging to rock or a seaweed cluster. And his thick rough tweed jacket (which looked correct enough, indeed inevitable). The pallid face beamed out at ease from the green coat and the flannel shirt. His big boots were polished. Deirdre noticed a chunky ring on his finger. She had eyed him coldly, but intensely.

'You are a surprise,' she had said. 'When you knocked I thought, demons. Who could be here at this time of night?' She had turned off the television. 'Well, I knew it wasn't the Mormons.' She had let him in.

'It was me, Clyde the Carter, me, wanting to see both of you. This Sydney is a great sprawling place to hole up in. You could hide an army. You could disappear and nobody give a thought about it. Perhaps,' he laughed, 'perhaps it's Sydney I should have settled in, not my cousin's bare knuckle of an island.'

'Sydney gets in your system; it can be addictive,' Deirdre wavered, 'but just when you think that, you go on holiday. Our little shack on the island has been the saving of both of us.' She resented the way he was sprawled, imperious, in David's chair . . . 'Would you like coffee?'

Habit overcame her. 'David shouldn't be long, though there's always the chance he is laying down the law in some tavern. No, he's pretty good about that now.'

His glint underlined her sense of betrayal. He said nothing. He did not have to. Too falsely she smiled, then excused herself to the kitchen, where Clyde followed her. Like a hound, she thought, on the trail. But they chattered about ferries and smog and the traffic congestion on the Harbour Bridge at peak hour. Then she led the way back to the living room. Clyde was a seductive conversationalist, she realised, making public transport seem high adventure, luring her into a dozen personal opinions and small vehemences.

But David did come in; they both heard the car rev then fall silent. The roller door being closed, pulled shut.

When he saw Clyde in his chair David looked puzzled. Then he nodded. It was as if some catalogue had been raided by vandals, the card system scattered. David walked over firmly. He held out his hand. Clyde was forced to stand up.

'Where you staying?' David questioned and Deirdre instantly understood its implication: there was not room in their spare sleepout. She had, as a matter of courtesy, been thinking, should they offer it?

'Been here long? Uhuh, uhuh. Rents have gone crazy down here I'm told. You might have some luck if you look round Ultimo area, or round Bondi Junction. Though I don't know, you might just as well try Darlinghurst. That's if you're staying. Done your dash with the island?'

'Aah, friend, it's the island is finished. You've not seen the advertisements?' Clyde delved in a back pocket. He brought out a crumpled dodger, printed with cheap colours. 'The whole place has been bought by some new developers, even the mangroves again. See this here? Now you'd think that pretty little paradise with its palm trees and its sandy beaches was some wonderland. Palm trees! That's our island. And you see this? Tropical Paradise Motel and Convention Centre they call it, say it will be built in twelve months, right on the spot of the three little streams. They'll be filled in and the whole lot made concrete.'

He drummed on the paper. 'And all the allotments up to your place, you thought yourselves far away; not any more. When I left they were already bulldozing; all the big scrub down, it's gone already. Nothing but sand. They burned the big trees and scrub almost down to the shoreline. Every time I hear these small helicopters I know some other southern speculator is brought in. Hear they are shown the new sub-division and then sold swamp land; never come here again, just investors. All they want is a title deed with names and numbers. And the savage humour is – this is a replay of the old subdivisions that caught people with swampland, five years ago, and the scandal was even in Parliament that time. Nobody learns. Ah, friend, but it would sicken you, now the trees and the scrub have been bulldozed. That's new. You can see your small hut from my window. Could you believe that? It's true. And it looks naked, a poor tawdry thing up on its pimple and only the trees on your own plot of land are still standing, only those. Wait till the rains come, the whole island will wash into the bay. But you won't see me there. I'm through.'

'Jim, Jim the ferryman – your cousin?'

'Well, he rubs his hands with satisfaction. He thinks of the extra work and the passengers, poor man, it's as if he couldn't understand his small ferry will be the first one to go. They talk of a bridge to the mainland, a series of bridges linking up with Stradbroke Island, hop hop hop across islands. Before I left I said to him, Jim, sell up now. If you stay you'll lose the lot. Of course he's staying. Got an extra job as a real estate salesman, the sign up out front, the suit and the notepad, would you believe it?'

'Impossible.' David scratched his head. 'You've got to be making this up. People don't change like that.' He might have been pleading. Their bushland retreat could not be allowed to change.

'I make up nothing. Things invent themselves, we are just the minders, the messengers, the guardians. That's been my view of life. We make our bargains, and know ourselves better or worse for it. Life invents its own rules. The battle's never our own.'

'Well, what a horrible message this time!' Deirdre, who had returned to her chores, put down the iron. 'I'll make some coffee. You'll have some, Dave?'

'Here, I'll help you,' he said. They went out together. Clyde the Carter settled back into his deep chair. He looked around the room. He closed his eyes. He was smiling.

Later, after he'd gone, David was still restless, he pottered around in his study for hours. Deirdre finally got out of bed and sought him out.

'It's the shack, isn't it?' she said softly. 'Don't think of it. We'll go up in the August vacation, it might not be as bad as it sounds, I don't trust Clyde for accuracy of information. One tree chopped down and he'd say it's a forest, just the first re-grading of the road would be enough to send his imagination round the twist. You could phone up Jim in the morning. Check out the real facts.'

'Jim would take me for a real estate inquiry,' David said, but he laughed after. That long sprawling hillside of ironbark, bloodwood, wattles: no, perhaps he would rather not know.

Deirdre had been the one to shuffle Clyde out. She sensed how deeply David was disturbed about the news of the island, and he was already exhausted from the strain of his classes; he would have come exhilarated and tired. Not the best mood to receive shocks.

In her own home she was ready to shield and protect. Curiously, Clyde began to seem an old ally. She had reluctantly allowed the proposal that Clyde come over again to gain currency. Friday night, that seemed the safest. Friday they had arranged to visit Brian and Meg again for pool. Either they could put that off or, the more Deirdre thought it over, they could drag Clyde along with them; she knew the Mackeys would not mind. Clyde immediately boasted of his own prowess with the cue and ball and that settled it. David had absently agreed. Deirdre began in her mind to explain, describing Clyde. It seemed, curiously, to render him harmless. How could she have felt threatened?

Friday night: pool. Saturday – that was the day finally agreed to by David and Brian to explore the stone wall under the Mackeys' sunroom. They had looked at it by torchlight. It was much older than the rooms it supported, though clearly of a style in keeping with the huge central ballroom-cum-billiard room and antiques showcase. There seemed no reason at all why a large room could not be hidden down there, perhaps part of an original kitchen or servant's hole.

David had flashed his large torch round in that dark valley. The hundred steps down to the parkland were a reminder of the solidity of sandstone, those steps incised like teeth marks gripping though the honey colours. Lucky Brian, lucky Meg. When they bought that house it was a bargain, despite the impractical ballroom. Many decades of later subdivision of what must have been a substantial estate had long since blocked out the original view: Deirdre imagined the crow's-nest outlook across Mosman Bay. Even the trees and scrub on this reserve had tangled and thickened. Still the sense of floating, though, above treetops. In their conversations, sometimes, Deirdre admitted a slight envy of the Mackeys and their good luck; she knew David shared this. Brian had never once acted improperly towards her, though he must have known. Or was it possible he was protected by some simple and generous innocence? Yes, with Brian that might be possible: he was a sweet-natured big boy.

Perhaps what she had most feared from Meg, after that time, was an accession of confession and dependence. How ironic that it should be Deirdre, herself, the strong one, who had turned to Meg in her new distress, who was about to make claims, yet again, with the unpredictable and mysterious Clyde.

*

THE ROLLER COASTER DREAMS OF THE MOON

There is frost on the walls of my room.
In the hallway: white frost. Moonlight,
and the frost wants to recover the moon
it wants to feel the cold windless surface
it dreams very thick ice.
Suddenly I think: that is not frost,
that is the moon itself
and it is very cold, an immensity of cold.
Or is it the roller coaster's breath,
frozen? In my mind
the roller coaster monster grows small,
it is shrinking as we all are.
It is bones, skin, remnants of sinew.
Only its breath, so shallow
creeps under the doorways like frost
its breath is reaching in
closer, closer; old familiar.

*

'Brian, sorry we're a bit late. Meg, want you to meet Clyde Carter.'

David had been taking up all the door space, but now elaborately moved aside, sweeping his arm theatrically. Behind him his bulky guest loomed, wearing a duffle coat that looked straight out of some elderly student rally. Deirdre, on the second step, waved from behind.

Brian Mackey stepped back to let them all in from the chilly porch where their breaths already bespoke a frosty night. He shook Clyde's

195

hand firmly, introduced Meg, who had come out wiping her hands on the apron and also smiling.

'Well, that's some introduction,' Brian grinned at David. 'Sorry, Clyde, but I thought for a moment David was about to unveil a monument. He's not usually quite so theatrical,' he added, taking David's hand then and pumping it with vigorous novelty.

'I'm the monument,' Clyde boomed affably, 'and I thank Davey boy for giving me the opportunity to come to your house. He's been enticing me with talk of your pool table. Not but I'm the most rank amateur, and long out of practice,' he added with transparent modesty.

'Clyde the Carter.' He turned on Meg. 'Clyde the Carter it is, not as Davey introduced me, Clyde Carter: Clyde *the* Carter, being an old form and one long accustomed to, and no amount of census and statistics and passport and customs ever changed it, so why should a single man's voice? Not that David here means any ill to me good name.'

It was true. David had flinched at expressing his friend's name in the descriptive form.

'And do you cart, Clyde?' Meg could not resist, her tone sweet.

'The name has got to mean something. But I've the right to change the occupation.' He laughed boisterously, stepped back a pace and nudged David. 'But Clyde the net mender doesn't have the same ring. And besides, a name's our claim to ancestry, to forebears, to the old roots.'

'To the tribe,' David added. Then he, too, laughed.

They moved through into the big room. When Clyde the Carter saw the chandelier above the full-size pool table he was delighted. He tried out the dexter rockers, all of them. He grabbed up a billiard cue and shouted 'Let's begin!'

*

THE FOOD

The door is closed, I have locked it.
The frost walks through the walls
it is into my room
it is the breath of the roller coaster.
In my darkness and the warmth of my body
I hear its breath. I hear what it is speaking.

I am like the creatures that hibernate
in cold. From far off I hear the voice
but I can do nothing.
Smell, it says, quiet as frost before you touch it.
Smell my gift, it is food.
What food, I ask?
Meat. Meat. Meat.
There is no meat, there is no more meat
even asleep I know that. It is the past
calling this to me, I must live for the future.
Pale, tender, very soft.
it will fill you and sustain you
it will make your skin glow
it will put fat in your fingers
your menses will again believe in life and your body
will again fill you with its monthly seasons.
Eat this now.
I could smell the meat, I could smell it.
Where is this meat from? The frost
spoke then, sharp and splintered:
Do not ask. Ask nothing
and all shall be given.
I woke, and hunger split me open like the sound of bombing.

*

'Now five of us. Five is the balanced number, the pentagram.' Clyde the Carter faced the others, a billiard cue in each hand so that he was framed by them, as in a gateway or between pillars.

'Four of us worked pretty well,' David noted. Clyde beamed at them, from between his magic gates. He was being insufferable. 'Five breaks up the pairs,' David continued, 'it's an instant recipe for challenge and antagonism, if you ask me. Who, for instance, will now have to stand aside in this first game?'

'Shh,' Deirdre reminded.

'I know what you mean,' Meg put in, feeling as hostess obliged to keep the peace. 'Clyde means that numerology thing. Five represents the five extremities of the body – arms, legs, head. Isn't that the pentagram?' She looked round to the others, the perfect librarian. Brian had taken his own special cue and was rubbing the tip with chalk.

'Five is the first number that represents both the female – two – and the male – three. One, being the absolute. So, though David chooses to think of this little group as being divisive, in fact it is capable of the greatest harmony.' Clyde thrust forth the two cues. Deirdre and Meg stepped up. 'Five is the great sign for the force of life, active combined with the passive, the receptive: enlightenment. It's also the sign of the Pope.'

'You out to convert us?'

'No, he's *determined* to convert us,' said David tetchily. 'Enough's enough, Clyde. We still haven't decided who'll play with whom, who plays against whom?'

'Is that your problem? David, you sadden me. Am I the threat? Me who hasn't played the game for decades though it was almost me life blood once? Are you really listening to my boasts and my promises? You think I want to beat you with the stick and balls before your wife and,' here he paused, 'your neighbour's wife?'

David pulled a cue from the rack and began chalking vigorously. 'Careful,' he muttered.

Clyde brushed David aside with a wink. 'If it soothes you at all, this time round, David, I'll be the observer, the one who stands aside and watches. I will be the fifth, the unit that balances the two binaries.' Here he laughed, then cracked his knuckles. 'I get carried away with my love of numbers, sign of the lonely man.' He spread his arms. 'Tell me the newest jokes of the office or the checkout counter in the supermarket?'

Brian took this moment to move into the next phase. He set up the balls and, as he always did, invited Deirdre to have first turn in the game. And, as always in the first game, it was to be boys against girls.

Clyde lounged around, watching. He leaned on the far end of the full-size table. He slouched against the wall. He brought one of the dexter rockers out from its corner, sat in it, and then put it back. He fingered a billiard cue in its rack. He chalked up numbers. The first game was almost finished when he spoke again.

'Strange thing about ball games. You know the original ball game? The beginning of play with a circular toy? Well, it would be no surprise for me to tell you, it being obvious.'

He enjoyed their silence.

'The human skull. The human skull, stripped of its hair and skin and muscle and its glittering soft parts, and perhaps filled with mud to give weight and smooth out the hollows. It makes a good enough globe with the jawbone off as always happens. And the force of the game? The game is always to kick it, to punch it, to pummel and beat it. It will not surprise you that the head was the head of the enemy?' Clyde picked up a ball and polished it. Then he set it down on the baize. 'Ah, if we look further, to the way of the games that developed, then the challenge is obvious. Billiards, games with poles or sticks. There's a male force in that certainly? More little tricks about power.' He moved around to the other side of the table. He took aim. 'Look at the way you all assume the male stance, even the ladies. When you strike, you strike sharp and hard with one eye on opponents. You've been appropriated by the game.' He struck another ball into the pocket, then another. 'You cast down your femininity. It is no great distance to the skull rolling over and over, kicked aside, or into the cave.'

He laughed at their silence. 'In the original days, of course, there would have been the victor's ritual ceremony of eating the brains – and the testicles.'

Brian restored the balls on the table to their previous position. 'I hope your friend won't be disappointed with our supper. Only got prawn curry and a curried egg dish.'

Clyde roared with laughter. 'You must not get me into these moods. Eggs. Prawns. I keep thinking in symbols.'

When it came for his turn, he proved adequate but no real challenge. In the next game he was partnered with Deirdre.

Over supper he pointed out that the upright pentagram was associated with white magic; the inverted pentagram was used in black magic. And that the Pope was only a corruption of the Great Hierophant in Hermetic occultism.

'I myself,' he added, 'hold that the ancient Celts, my ancestors, were the real agents of the mysteries.'

David had found it difficult to rein in his irritation. 'You've been a long time on that island, Clyde. Your game's rusty. You're a real conversation cruncher. You like to lead people a real dance.'

Brian waved across the table cheerfully: no worries, no worries, keep your cool.

'Ah, now dance, that's another thing. It's not always that I'm fixed with the notion of skulls and bones and numbers. Now dance, there's a partnering thing, a thing on the side of life and not conquest. Though conquest's one end of the jig.' Clyde swept up Deirdre and clumped around the room with her, marking the jig with a shrill yet melodious whistle.

David cornered his indignation, was forced to admit his illogic. He offered his arm to Meg and they joined in. Brian clapped in time, once he had satisfied himself that he had cleared the baize.

Meg, in David's arms, fitted herself naturally into his contours. He had once spoken to Clyde, on the water, of those strong fits of sexual hunger. Perhaps in speaking aloud he had exorcised them. Meg was no more than a sister.

No; he knew what it was. There was some underground source directing him to rein in his energies and his hunger. He felt in some state of careful preparedness. And, curiously, the only name that turned a key into this quite physical reality was the least possible sexual initiate: Galina Darovskaya.

He glanced at Clyde and Deirdre together. He was their link, and their bodies somehow confirmed that. Not even they, he had to acknowledge, could have links into that woman's ancient and obsessive energy.

Even alcohol was a drink, only, these days. Take it or leave it. Brian called an end to the dance by bursting a cork of champagne. It was a jeroboam.

XXVIII

Dear Mr Cumberland

This is the last lot I'm doing. My husband has sold the farm and we'll be out of this place soon, not before time. It's not that my mother is difficult but she says we have our own life too and she'll just have to manage. She can come at Christmas. But it's got to stop, it's consuming me, he says, and I know he is right. All those years, I thought it was all settled, I thought I had been through all of that, for years she never gave up. I had thought, when the children came, that would be a new turning, that she would look ahead, and to a certain extent she did, except that you and your friend came and, believe me, nothing had changed at all. It was back quick fast. I am sure you did not know any of that. I have done this lot but no more. I told her. And why do it at all, I kept asking her that. What can this Mr Cumberland do with all that stuff, you're just unloading it on him and what for? He can't publish it, he can't do anything, he's probably burned it already so it's a good thing I do keep a copy. I do look after her interests, I don't think she even realises how much I tidy her things up, put them in order, make them presentable.

When she accused me of changing things, that was enough. Some things have to be changed, that's all. Some things have to be cut out, you can't translate everything, there'd be explanations and too much that just can't be explained anyway. Some things have no words. I know that.

Besides, I said, you have changed it all yourself. That's not the way you told it to me and used to tell it; either it's changed in your own head or you told it to me the wrong way. Then there are the new things. She keeps putting in new things I swear it. It's she herself who is wanting to invent it. Anyway translation has to be a new invention, it's not my fault. I'm not doing any more. She can do it herself. My husband is right, it is too much and what thanks do I get? She says I have got it all wrong, that I have altered things, missed out things, said the wrong things but, if she knows so much, let her do it herself is what I say.

I thought this was all over years ago. She just won't allow it to die.

Don't let her consume you with it: you will never escape. If you want to send it all back, you must send it to her. We will be gone after Sunday week.

She lives in a world of her own. She thinks only of herself. She always has. It's just too much and I've got the children to think of. I curse the day that man came and spoke to her about all that and about Leningrad as if the city still existed. It's dead, I say to her. It's over and nothing more exists. You're out of it and will always be out of it. You know the most terrible thing he did? He said her poems are remembered. Imagine the meaning of that, after all these years. I did not mind doing the poems, even the strange ones. But she had at least got to understand that they were irrelevant, that they did not mean anything any more. And now she not only believes they have meaning, she believes they have taken her over, they have surfaced again and will be immortal.

Immortal! She does not understand the cruel pride of that. I thought my mother had at last come to accept her fate, her present, now, here, where she is. I should have known better of course. But it is too cruel. Nobody believes poetry any more, why should she revive those old wishes? I could speak of the thirty years we were eking out a living, and the long years after the endless travel when we settled in this little place. She has lived in this place longer than her whole life in Leningrad, but do you think that makes any difference? Of course not. You would not believe how selfish. I had to live in the kitchens of friends, I could not bring them home. My husband is not young but I think he is miraculous. We speak the same languages, we have a lot in common though at first it did not seem so. I defied my mother.

Well, I ramble on. But I had to tell you, I had to give you warning. I know it's not your fault.

And I'm not really blaming you.

Yours

Maria Peters

*

1941, October 20: They say stocks of cottonseed cake have been found in the harbour. It had been intended for ship's furnaces but they can remove the poisons by high temperature treatment. The bread made from it is bitter, it tastes of mould and the innards of ships, the rust of ships, the heaviest part. Sometimes I ask them not to tell me, but they say I have an important job, to record and transfigure through poetry. We live in times when wastage can be changed to bread. I wonder did the ancient young man I loved work in the same ship that drowned with cottonseed cake? Nobody has spoken of bodies, only of nourishment possible.

They say Lake Ladoga has begun to freeze over and that supplies will be brought across the frozen lake.

October 31: We used to call this Ski Day, the day that the snow becomes deep enough to toboggan over. My sparkling city of frost. Clear cold sky. We have no heating, none at all. Leningrad may have had such winters in the time of Peter the Great; it has endured many events. People are talking all the time about Napoleon and 1812. I waited in the food queue all day and there was nothing left. My mother did not leave her bed, she has swollen.

And yet I am amazed our building has not yet been hit. Writing this, am I inviting disaster? The fire at the end of the plaza has been burning four days now. There was only one person still living in that entire block.

When I gave my reading at the Writers' Union I was filled with a strange excitement, how can I explain it? I was so weak I had to sit for the reading but afterwards I felt light headed. I devour praise. Am I decadent?

November 5: They say Lake Ladoga will be frozen over shortly. Only six at lecture today. The deep shadows and the great cold hall made us huddle together without thinking. Body warmth has nothing to do with personal feelings; perhaps there are not personal feelings only the impersonal anger and passion: I still can conjure that. They helped me remove my mother's body this morning. I took off her coat and the shawl; they should not accuse me, the dead have no use for them. German leaflets have been dropped warning about the November 7th Anniversary. GO TO THE BATHS. PUT ON YOUR WHITE DRESS. EAT THE FUNERAL DISHES. ON NOVEMBER 7TH THE SKIES WILL BE BLUE WITH THE EXPLOSION OF GERMAN BOMBS.

November 6: Late. All night, all night, flares on parachutes, sudden brightness, daylight being dragged back for whole moments in the darkness. New, heavy bombs, they are saying. Everything shakes in the city, small volcanoes. Finland Station train yard has been completely destroyed, it looks like that to me. All night, all night. It is the delayed bombs that are so terrible. Patrols everywhere, even skeletons like us are restless, we will not give up living, we will not. I found that old embroidery and just for a moment believed I might attempt to finish it. I was strangely struck by the voice of the old lady who once admired it. If we all go, will there be anyone who remembers the design and the stitches? Strange: I had taken such things for granted as if there would always be grandmothers and girls eager to master the stitches.

November 7: No speech from Stalin. I have discovered my mother's lipstick. On the small stove I melted it with the Anniversary food issue: five pickled tomatoes. I made a broth thickened with wallpaper glue. It will last days. Heavy cloud; dark well before 3. The long nights; if only I were not afraid to venture out I would be a more gregarious member of the Writers' Union.

Oh, but the street radios were loud today with confidence and stirring speeches. Mayor Popkov, Lt. General Khozin, I should record them but already they have drifted off like snow. The sound: reassurance. I am greedy for reassurance, perhaps I will always be. Others are here, somewhere, they are alive, they are with me. 'We will tighten our belts; it will be hard; but we will hold out.'

We have no other way. We would dream of no other way.

I have become our city, every stone is part of me now. Wind.

November 9: I hate the rumours. They say the ice on Lake Ladoga is not yet set, not even yet. They say there is no more food in the city at all. They say Leningrad will be compelled to surrender without the blood of German soldiers behind shed. I will not surrender. I have a sharp knife in my bed with me. I have thrown out my father's gun, there was no ammunition. I will not surrender.

November 13: Rations are cut again. 300 grams of bread for factory workers; 150 grams a day for everyone else. One slice of bread. If I live, I will remember this, I will value every crumb.

November 20: I have begun licking ice. Rations cut again: 125 grams a day, sawdust. They say we are being starved so that supplies will be spread for the survivors. I look at other people and wonder are they more determined than I am? If I can hold out, if I can. Then I see other dear friends and am ashamed. And then cunning. The Writers' Union has saved me, though I promise myself I will go there only once a week. We are the lucky ones, and the Young Communist League.

It is when I see those people with no gleam in their eyes, no will, no purpose. Zhdanov said to us, 'The task of tasks is to organise the life of the workers, to give them inspiration, courage, firmness, in the face of all difficulties'. To have a task is to be alive. I believe that. Yet how could it be so simple? How could I not believe that?

Natasha. I think she trusts me but I trust her more.

November 21: 20 degrees below zero. They say by 1st December there will be no more bread at all. They keep saying this, people keep telling me this. Am I the only one to believe the rumours?

November 23: Two days and I have not been out of bed. Natasha seemed close but I was only dreaming it seems. I did not know I was so missed until the others came and nearly knocked down my door, I think it was Natasha roused them, talked to them. My mother's mattress was on top of my own. They scolded me. They even tapped my face and began reciting my own poems at me. You have a task, Galina, Galya, they kept saying, and that task is not sleep it is work, work. Here, one said, here is your pencil. Begin. So I begin.

This is a ghost writing. The words say nothing, nothing at all, they are frost across a window and I am frightened by what else my words may arouse.

You are alive, Galya. Words are the dull thud of distant bombs.

December 1: Crunch of glass underfoot in the snow.

December 9: Trams have ceased. They say that the 4th Army has recaptured Tikhuin. Can this be true?

The bread tastes like bread.

I say the bread tastes like bread again, the rumours must be true: supplies must be coming from across Lake Ladoga, people are calling it the Road of Life. If I am strong again soon I will write whole cycles of poems to celebrate the Road of Life, they will be broadcast on the radio, they will be famous, in my heart I know that. I can believe in my mission. I can believe in this bread. This bread creates in me the most terrible angers, I am afraid of my inner savagery.

December 25: Bread ration increased, one slice for workers, half a slice for others. I am lucky. I was told of this and waited in a queue. When I told the old woman in the apartment above she did not believe me. 'I have been through famine three times,' she said. 'This is the last.'

Yes, I replied. This is the last.

December 26: There was a meeting in the dining room of Writers' House today. Vera Keflinskaya made a speech. Soviet troops have broken two of the three Nazi circles around the city; only Mga has not been recaptured. They say we will regain Mga by New Year's Day. They say there are enormous quantities of supplies only 60 miles from Leningrad.

We all talked, later, of what supplies we would ask for, first. We are creatures of greed. We are holy, all of us, now.

1942, January 2: No one has the strength. Darkness seems to have taken the city, except for the glow of a burning building here and there but the smoke and stench of artillery are a blanket. Long periods of silence in the snow.

They say the English are planning to attack the Germans through Murmansk. I do not believe this.

We are alone. There are no other forces with us.

They say this is the coldest winter this century. Yes, I can believe that much.

Smell of turpentine.

Today I shot someone. I had been assigned supervision of the food queue. They gave me a pistol and said to use it if anyone tries to take more than their share. I did not hesitate, it was only later, tonight, that I said to myself: you have murdered a man. I studied my right hand. I felt the muscles, bent the trigger finger again and again. Then I stopped that game. To have shot a man means you are done with games forever. Or does it mean you are trapped in a perpetual game of denial? Of retribution? I feel nothing, only the skinny bone within my finger.

January 12: The big shopping centre of Gostiny Dvor is burning again.

January 25: There is no power for the bakeries. We were sent to smash fences for kindling. They say there will not be a wooden building in Leningrad by the end of the winter. Natasha and I huddle, in the bed, we build our bridges to islands of driftwood timber, fallen branches, open fireplaces.

January 26: No bread. I had the meat dream again today. I dozed off before noon and I had the dream of pale soft meat. It smelt curiously sweet, like the breath of young children. I did not think my nostrils had the power to smell anything. Of course I did not speak to Natasha.

January 27: No bread. Today I ate rat, with two others in their shared room. It was their wedding. I made them a poem, almost believing it to be my own. Strange, how memory deceives one, makes one always the centre of experience, not the margin.

January 28: I was sent into the Haymarkets, I did not choose to go myself. Three of us went, nobody would go alone. 'Meat pasties, meat pasties,' I kept hearing the whisper. Oily faces, pudgy, in furs.

January 29: I went to the Haymarkets again. I went with my mother's great coat and her casket of jewels. You do not eat jewels.

January 30: I spent twelve hours supervising the ration queues. I have begun burning my papers. Warmth. So quick, but still, echoes.

*

NATASHA PLAYS

Why do we count? she says,
then counts harder.

Why do we sing?
Natasha does not sing
but I hear her breath sometimes
as if the notes might come.

Why do you look at me?
Why do I need this closeness?
She throws her arms around me
as if we might both be absorbed.

Why? she asks
and today I knew
why her questions nailed me down
why she would never be quiet.

. . . .

I went out into the street. No,
do not laugh (you see, my dear, I still
imagine muscles and a fine, full mouth) –
I went out into the street today
with snow swirling and hard bodies of snow
under my boots (that were my father's).
Six weeks ago three bodies were piled
just below the entrance door
near the coal merchant's entry.
I walk high, under me a city has frozen
and it is hard, hard, thankfully hard
stuff I walk over.
                    It is wrong of you
(if you were here I would weep at the injustice!)
to accuse me of turning to ice and snow
packed hard also. Just this moment
a woman wearing all her shawls, her furs, her blankets
passed by me on her way to the ration issue.
On a child's yellow sled she pulled her husband,
thin stubble on his small chin, gaunt hollows
to sink his eyes into, his three remnants of scarves
almost debonair, his face engrossed with the skull.
On her thin shoulders the rope. It was rubbing.
Without the body, no ration card.
The yellow sled squeaked over the snow.
There are now so few children.

*

I have tried. I do not look in the small mirror remaining. There is no
feeling. I think of it as a ritual, I make a ritual of the breaking of bread,
of crumbs of bread. I traded my mother's embroidered smock for four
ounces of sugar: black, fuel of dust, a solid lump of sweetness and
smoke. It has been scraped from the site of the great warehouse fires. I
think of you as I sip lukewarm sweetened water, I remember your
laughter, I do remember that. You brought chocolates, I have counted
them out of their box: twenty-four, very dark, four of them with hard
centres, black toffee. It stuck to my teeth and you kissed me and licked
it off with your tongue. I take another sip. You were very good-looking
in your sailor's uniform with the rolled white collar and your hair
pasted over your broad handsome brow. I have the photograph.

Even then you looked through the lens and beyond where I stood, juggling the camera. I thought you were smiling then, but your eyes had such sadness in them as if you knew but could not tell me. And your mouth, even the smile was sadder than the edges of your lips would allow. We spoke that last time about the future, we insisted on planning and setting targets, our five year plan, our ten year plan, by which time we would both be famous and powerful.

In Leningrad I am famous, in a small way. My poems are published in *Leningradskaya Pravda*. They are broadcast on the days when the public radio has the power. They are poems about resistance and the great battles of the past – Alexander Nevsky – and the long courage and endurance we inherit.

You would not recognise them. Or me.

And you: you were going to be the new Iosef Orbeli, chief director of the Hermitage Museum at least. He is still alive, the Hermitage was struck by bombs last week but there are over two thousand people living in its cellars. Orbeli last month gave his 500th Anniversary Celebration of Alisher Navoi, the Timurid poet, nothing could stop him: not bombs, not fires, not the death of the trams, nor power failures. Vsevolod Rozhdestvensky read a tribute poem. We all huddled and shivered and paid tribute.

I will write a poem to that.

Orbeli is still alive. He is still alive.

*

P.S. Did I send you these two poems? I cannot remember. My mother values them.

M.P.

*

THE MEAL

Natasha remembers food.
Sometimes we play the game of describing food
and the preparation of food
the ceremony of the meal.
'What I like best,' Natasha says,
'is the things that can be saved.'
She means the ceremony.
'I think at night, sometimes,
of all the potato skins we threw out.'

We laugh together
and she holds out her hand to me
like a little old lady waiting to be led.
'And the wine.'
She turns her wrist over, the veins
now pencil lines, 'You will have wine
remember that.' She calculates everything
these days. For the triumphal meal
she would allocate every segment,
each loving part.

*

SONG OF THE ROLLER COASTER SERPENT

It's not enough. We must begin
though we grew under the shade of Ygdrassil
the world ash tree, we remained restless,
we sharpened our blades, and dreamed
of sun, of the wheat-tossed plain,
saying: 'It's not enough. We must begin.'

We ate the black snow of burial
we consumed our own city with fire
though we shouted out the names of enemies
and sharpened our angers. We took hostages.
At night their voices bellowed very like our own
imploring: 'It is not enough. We must begin.'

We ended with skeleton hungers
and with all the time in the world.
When we tasted the last flesh we knew
we could never turn back – nor weep again.
Flesh has become but a symbol. Until we recover tears
it is not enough. We must begin.
Though our skeletons become rust, we must begin.

XXIX

It was a grey Saturday. The cold front from the Antarctic had swept through in the early hours of the morning. After dropping Clyde the Carter at the YMCA David and Deirdre on the drive home encountered the first fall of sleet. Deirdre almost slipped on the thin ice near the garden tap by the carport. Unbelievable. Later, when David got up and shambled out for the Saturday papers, the dog's water dish still had a thin sheet, frozen.

What a morning to go out! But David had promised Brian. He piled all the family into the car. Greg and Marcus were pleased at the diversion and seemed impervious to weather. Deirdre made sure they had good stout shoes on. That back terrace and gully would be certainly messy, slushy.

It was a formidable task. The huge sandstone blocks were tightly mortared; the wall itself was nearly ten feet at its highest part. It began as a natural extension of the sandstone ledge, then angled out to support the straight lines of the house above. Then a right angle back to the natural rockface.

Brian and David admired the masonry work. Yes, David said, you could make out the blocked-in entrance way. It was slightly wider than a normal door frame.

'When I was a kid my friend swore to me there was a secret attic in his house – the gable was high enough. We spent a whole afternoon looking for the one secret button that would reveal the entrance to the hidden stairwell. Pure fantasy, of course,' he added. His boys looked at him with scorn.

No secret buttons. After a careful inspection they decided to start digging out the mortar from the right hand top block of the walled-in door. It had begun to crumble there.

'You probably only have to remove the one stone,' David conjectured. 'Then we can at least shine a torch in and see what's what. Find out if it's worth proceeding.'

'How will you lift it down from up there? That thing will weigh a ton.' Deirdre, also, had been examining the details.

'We'll come to that when we come to that,' Brian declared. 'We might simply be able to swivel it on its base if we're careful enough. And clearly, the first one is hardest.' They set to. But it was a slow job. The stone was at least fifteen inches thick. They began from each end. David spat dust from his tongue. Brian put on his goggles. They each used a file initially, but then Brian began to hammer in a long thin steel rod. Then another one. It was time for lunch break before they had mastered the top side.

Later, with their wives and the assembled children looking on, they managed to clear the masonry filling from the two sides of the large stone, leaving only the base to be tackled.

'We're fools!' David exclaimed. 'We should have done the bottom horizontal fill before the other sides. Now we have to work against the full weight of the thing!'

'Begin from the centre,' suggested Meg.

Mid afternoon. The last edges of support were almost ready to scrape out.

'Try to wedge it out.'

'We need a cradle.'

'Good idea.'

Perhaps it was the cold, bleak day, the cloud overhang. Nobody felt an imperative need to rush forward with the task. It was like a jigsaw puzzle at the point when the last pieces are waiting. Only this was a beginning.

There was a loud rap-rap at the front door, upstairs. Meg went up reluctantly.

Brian slid in several of the long steel rods. The stone was virtually free-standing on them now. Manoeuvre would be difficult, though.

'If there were some way to hook from behind. Even some way to utilise pulleys.'

Clyde the Carter preceded Meg down the narrow stairway and stood, arms akimbo, staring at their efforts.

'Christ!' cried David wiping his dusty forehead against his thick, cement-encrusted pullover sleeve. 'What brings you out of your cave before nightfall!' Then he had to explain Clyde's habits. 'This bloke hates daylight.'

'Sunshine, sunlight, sun-whipping,' explained Clyde, 'long ago I learned to live with me own skin. To live in me own skin. And what's so magic about sunlight, then? Who's to say that the sun is the sole godhead where man is concerned? Why should I be bound by a set of conventions not pertaining to me or the special sensitivities of my skin? Well, and who's to deny me me own sense, then?'

'You stay up *all* night, every night?' young Wayne asked, with too evident excitement.

'We makes our own choice. All of us. But no rule is inflexible. No rule is universal. With the first brisk sting of ice in the air and this blanket of cloud around, I decided the gain is on my side. And besides, with your talk all last night about this secret vault under your house, this cave or this dungeon, who wouldn't be damn curious?' he guffawed.

'Sticky-beak!'

'Oh yes, lad, and indeed the nose twitches. Doesn't yours? Will you be first, me young fellow, to climb into this hole once we've all dislodged this big stone window?'

The boys shrieked and drew back slightly.

'Cobwebs!'

'Spiders!'

'Funnelwebs!'

Clyde laughed good-naturedly and then rolled up his sleeves. He wore no more than his old boiler suit. David, looking sideways at him as he himself carefully began the last attack on the mortar, was reminded of some underwater creature, almost of some body washed on a shore line, so pallid was Clyde the Carter's exposed skin. He remembered the tattoos, the stranger first seen on the edge of the swamp, edge of the water. And yet: was Clyde anything particularly exceptional? Deirdre had a Melbourne friend stay once, who was pale on the beach as an underarm.

213

David's younger boy, Marcus, cried out at the white skin and Clyde unzipped his boiler suit down to the groin to show him he was pale all over.

David called out roughly, with real anger, but Clyde laughed and was jocular: 'What, and you never learned, Davey, what's snuggled down there? It's all skin, and its colour is not your usual Australian colour, that's what the boy's curious over, and rightly.'

Brian laughed too, and asked his boys had *they* ever seen such a pallor?

David's reproof, though, killed their curiosity.

'If you two start swivelling and I pulling we will get a fingerhold at that corner. Then we're in.' Clyde's voice was rough with a certain eagerness. 'Let's get to business.'

The most difficult part of the slow operation was to get the wire cradle in place. Then the stone was wedged out sufficiently far to begin a grip. Clyde took control.

The wire supports were too weak. Before they could use the thin rods as rollers, the first one snapped. A warning. They would have to winch the whole stone out.

The moment its full weight tested the wires, the mechanism collapsed. One wire whipped back and cut Clyde across the fleshy part of his cheek. The stone teetered, then dropped down to the sloping terrace. It split into several fragments.

Clyde's blood began to congeal in small drops among dust and old cobwebs. He laughed it aside, but Meg quickly brought acraflavine and sticking plaster from upstairs. Dark blood. The gash seemed somehow more violent across such pale skin. It was several minutes before anyone thought to peer into the gaping hole.

Finally Brian did so, leaning awkwardly with hands gripping. His body blocked the entrance.

'Well?'

'Nothing much really. There's enough space. Bit hard to tell but I'd reckon it could be a store room, a cellar perhaps.'

'Or a cubby?'

'Bigger than that, boy. We might make you kids your own room.'

'Urk! All the way down here? Damp and cold!'

'Well. Guess the real question is do we plug on?'

David took the torch from his friend. 'Let me look.'

He half wriggled in, head and shoulders. They heard his whistle, a sound hollow as in some well-shaft. He pulled out.

'It's a room there all right. Except for the limestone cliff as a sort of a back wall. That folds back, I'd say it's a cave, really.'

'A cave? Like the one round Cremorne Point?'

'Not quite so deep. But a cave in the sandstone back there, the far end. All these ridges are full of caves and air bubbles.' David brushed his hair, explaining.

Clyde took a look.

'And the signs? What do you make of the signs?'

They all had to take a turn to peer in.

'Only way. You'll have to get in there.' Clyde summed it up.

XXX

It would have been logical to send one of the boys in. They were light and mobile, even if they did dramatise a communal fear of spiders. The natural explorer instinct would have overridden that. Little Marcus, egged on by Clyde, did crane in for a look. Clyde held him firmly as he edged in and began to let curiosity overcome fear. But David did not give him the chance.

'Give us a heave,' he instructed, holding the torch. He began to wriggle through the gap.

The torch fell to the floor inside. David cursed – but at least it did not go out. As he reached for a grip on the stone walls his fingers felt dusty cobwebs and that peculiar friability of sandstone, crumbling almost to the touch.

'Watch it!'

As he somersaulted down into the dark space he felt his trousers rip on something and a long scrape across his thigh. It would begin to nag him in a few minutes, after the deadening first moments of surprise. With gritty fingers he fumbled for the torch. The space of the dislodged stone was blocked by the two others, silhouetted.

The boy in him had sway. David swept the beam of light slowly along the floor area of this hidden room. Beneath the small dust and rubble of many decades of insect life, lizard refuge, water stain and wash, there was an evenness that indicated well designed floorspace. He raised the beam. At the far end, where the wall took its right-hand turn back to the rock face there seemed the remains of a workbench. David walked over. It crumbled as he pressed on it. Dry rot.

His laugh was caught in the hollow spaces, and cuffed back at him.

'Problems of damp,' Brian's voice informed.

'But space, it's enormous,' David called back, almost as if it were his own area.

'And how does it end?' Clyde the Carter was caught in David's sudden beam, leaning in and pointing. The torch had caught a boyish enthusiasm in the face, excitement. David had a sudden realisation: that is a person so vulnerable, so exposed, so lacking in the normal male defences that it's no wonder he hides in the dark most of the time. And he realised the enormity of the gift of confidence and sharing that Clyde had been proffering, even to the point of coming down here (and he was certain Clyde had no other purpose). And Clyde had accepted Brian's world, Meg's world only because of that. His gawky excitements, his gaiety, his bursts of curious knowledge or confused ideas: they were all part of an awkward gift, but a gift indeed. With someone like that it was only possible to offer some equal wholeheartedness – or move right away.

David flashed the light away from the two peering in. It swept the back wall. Rock face.

'A cave all right,' Brian said. 'Something of a marvel.'

'But what can you *do* with it?' David laughed. Yet he, also, felt the excitement.

And then the slow sweeping torch did recover the incised figures on the rock floor, within the bubble of the low cave.

'You know what I think? I think your house has been right on top of some old aboriginal site.'

By sweeping the torch at a low angle David was able to throw shadows around the scratch marks on the flat surface, to pick out a hammerhead shark, clearly outlined. A school of fish.

'You can make out what they are,' he confirmed and ran his finger along the groove of the outlined forms. 'You've got a treasure here.'

He stood up again. His shin felt tight from the graze and he staggered. His mouth was open, like someone hungry, who has been offered food.

The torch caught another group of low-relief carvings. Two human figures, outlines intersecting: male and female, with obvious genitalia, both with arms upraised, legs parted. 'Perhaps not a playroom for the boys,' he quipped, and the torch moved to the back of the cave. Another figure, but this time hermaphroditic: penis, breasts outflung.

Silently he traced the outline with the light, then moved back to the intertwined couple below.

'Do you see it?'

None of them laughed.

'You do see it, don't you? There's a sickle moon there, too,' David pointed it out. 'It's clearly ritual. Notes for performance perhaps? Do you see this merged figure?' His voice was tight with discovery. Under his protective clothing, he felt the body's salute of cold sweat.

'The meaning's as clear as any other form of calligraphy.' Clyde's voice, too, was hoarse with excitement. 'The bisexual character clearly represents union, unity, male and female. A dreamed-for state still in some societies.' Even his laughter was nervously electric. Clyde pushed Brian out of the window space now and struggled to get in. David returned to give him a hand. His skin was clammy, taut as a bowstring or the gut of a musical instrument. Clyde crouched at the cave mouth and when David joined him he took the torch from his hand.

'Look at that now. And this has been here all this time, and us not even dreaming.'

'It's still potent. Not like the Greeks, or the Romans for that matter. This one's stark, an absolute convulsion of union – look at the arms outflung, the breasts tossed in abandon – and all in a few thin lines. No soft androgyny in this state of nature.' Their faces were shadowed by the down-turned light of the torch, but the two crouched bodies were in harmony, springy with eagerness. 'It's the energy. You recognise the energy?' Clyde gripped his friend's arm then, tightly.

'Hey you blokes. Don't crowd the screen,' Brian yelled, 'And give me a hand. Heaven's sake, it's me own property.'

'That's big words, that's very big words,' answered Clyde, moving back in to the dark spaces. David shone up his torch, but could not drag himself from the new-found centre of his attention. He crouched like a protective animal, a guardian quite unconscious of his claim or his possessiveness.

It was decided that Brian should remain outside. They must work from both sides to remove the second stone. As they worked it was impossible to avoid more speculation, further dredged up recollections of the original tribes.

'Well, sex as part of a natural cycle,' David suggested. 'Probably it had to do simply with getting the fish to swarm at the right time of moon.' He stood up. The wound had begun tightening. The sweat had now been absorbed by thick clothing.

'Yes, the moon. Clearly there for a reason – or a purpose. They're all there together in that space, fish, man and woman, moon. The hammerhead shark might be the family totem for the tribe of this area.' Clyde grabbed the torch and made his own inspection. There were no other discoveries.

'Yes, and they're all wiped out. They didn't even get to record their language. It all died with 'em,' David said. 'When we gave them germs and smallpox and syphilis as well as other benefits of our civilisation.' David took back his torch. Carefully he swept it over the images again. 'Amazing,' he said. And again, 'Amazing.'

'Davey boy, who's to say we had any right to their mysteries, or the long past retrospect in their language? The ancient Celts kept their entire culture in their spoken language, and it was sacred, not to be written down. Printing and writing was to them like photographs are to many tribes today – something that takes away your soul.'

'Lot of good it did them when it came to the crunch. They lost everything, or everything meaningful.'

'Who's them, Brian?'

'Them. These aborigines here. Or, for that matter, even the Celtic tribes, if they let their past die with them.'

'Wait a tick. There are signs. Here, under our bloody feet. Or for that matter, Clyde, even I'm familiar with some of the Celtic signs and symbols, all those knotted forms, and those whirlpool circles. They didn't go without scratching down some written signs.'

'You make nice parallels, boyo. But signs like those ones, or like these, they were to show only common principles, or very sacred places. Halfway houses between the living and the other world. They still have potency. And isn't it strange, I can feel there is still potency in these signs in your cave. Brian, I'd have a care about turning this space into a workroom or rumpus room, or what you may call it.'

'Well,' Brian laughed, 'somehow the rumpus room idea just went out the door. Them's big magics,' and he pointed. 'Damned if I know what I'll do with it.'

But they kept working, enlarging the space in the wall.

Clyde the Carter had called for an old paintbrush, and he carefully brushed aside the dust from the narrow troughs of the rock incisions. He did no further work.

'Someone told me some of the aboriginal tribes on the south coast, where they did get to record their language properly, have very complex grammar – eight tenses, for instance,' David said, halfway tugged by the strength of Clyde's concentration, halfway pulled by Brian's urge to finish the job, entirely absorbed in the surprise and discovery.

'That's sophisticated.'

'It's precise about time. And we still think of them as being somehow lost in their Dreaming.'

'Well, I guess you've gone into this, David . . .'

'Oh, yes. Part of the tug. It's okay, Brian, I'm okay. Word legacies from a time of doubt,' he explained, but Clyde the Carter was inattentive, or preoccupied, and David had to make do with explaining to Brian.

'Don't be flippant, mate,' was all Brian said, 'don't knock the unknockable.'

'You know,' said David, 'It's not that I'm battered with the thought of being part Aboriginal. What's it matter? And who wouldn't be proud to have links into a culture like this?' He pointed to the energetic glyphs.

'The Black Cornish Celts were as fabulous,' Clyde reminded him, 'Could even be linkage.' But he would not explain, and David's son Marcus was in like a shot with wonder and incredulity: was his dad a part Abo? Wait till he told all the kids. Why hadn't anyone said so?

Greg, his brother, tried to hush him. He had heard old storms and quarrels. Rather, he had listened, in anguish.

'No, Marcus, we don't know. I'm just saying. For the sake of argument, if you like. You know all about the Black Cornish?' But Marcus was tracing out the signs again, with a fresh curiosity.

*

SUPERSTITION

This morning my lace curtains disappeared.
Their pattern of forest with wind and snowflakes
became part of the flame
so quickly I hardly noticed
though I had intended them as a homage
to dead needlework.

Someone walked by in the street
with two empty buckets: sign of bad luck.
I find, when I walk out of a door
I must put my left foot first.
And this morning I have refused to make my bed;
that is bad luck on important days
and today is an important day.
I will go out in the spring air
as if my hair were rinsed with sweet camomile
I will take the large pickle pot
and will look for flowering branches
of marsh tea.
I will be one with all things.
All week, in the spring sunshine,
everyone is cleaning and sweeping
and the winter corpses are no longer with us.
But I was not prepared for the first hyacinth.
Like the old lace curtains, I am trapped
in old webs of superstition
as if I must melt in the smell of camomile
and marsh tea and hyacinth.

XXXI

Brian remained busy downstairs, working out his excitement on the widening of the doorway. When Deirdre and Meg returned from a drive up to the Spofforth Street shops to get food for the evening meal – it was clearly to be a celebration – Brian took them through the opening and showed the new-found treasure. Meg was delighted and her excitement seemed to become proprietorial; Deirdre did not say much.

While they were still downstairs, David called to Clyde to come for a walk with him: they might go to the pub, or the bottle-shop. He wanted to work the excitement off, he needed to have a stroll to get back on an even keel. Clyde understood.

'We'll be back with beer,' David called downstairs as they trundled up. Deirdre scrambled up the steep steps after them. 'You should have let me know, we would have got whatever you needed when we were up that way,' she began, catching up with the pair.

'It's more the breath of fresh air,' David explained.

'I'll come along, too,' she said, dusting off web and grit from the cave beneath the house. 'It's a raw evening, but a walk would warm me up.'

'No.' David was firm. 'Just Clyde and me. I've got to have a bit of space,' he tried to explain, 'a bit of silence to absorb things in.'

He raised his hand to prevent her speaking. It was an exclusion, yes, but it was necessary. Did she never recognise that her concern, her limpet-clinging was a stranglehold?

She gripped his arm. That look. No, he would not be overpowered. He must not allow himself to be overwhelmed – again – now that so many things seemed to be opening. He could not explain to Deirdre what he was unable to define for himself. Clyde was the only person who might even begin to understand. He needed that contact.

Clyde had walked ahead. David took long strides to catch up. He knew Deirdre was still at the gate, willing herself into his thoughts, determined to hold on to him.

'Not the shops,' Clyde decided, 'I saw water. I want to discover this area. There'd be a lot of strange and interesting nooks, suddenly this area has a further dimension . . .'

'I'll take you to the little cave round the foreshore in Cremorne,' David offered, 'the one the kids spoke of. Bigger than Brian's cave, but if it ever had aboriginal carvings they've gone ages ago. Those things must be very fragile, just a scratch on the surface. The Cremorne cave drips water, they say it was used by tramps in the Depression. Still has a feeling of presence, though. Easy enough to imagine the old ones there, the tribal elders . . .'

'If that was to be imagined or traced, you'd do it, Davey. I saw you before. You don't hide things from me. But those carvings,' he changed his tone, 'they were more than surface cuts. But to keep them alive they'd need to be re-defined over and over. That was the ceremonial part of it, the act of re-definition. Like saying your rosary.'

'They were amazing images. Threw me. And strong, a sort of sophistication that pierces the brain.'

'That's part of the ritual. But not everyone's able to grasp the power. Brian, your rumpus-room builder, he saw only the fish and the phallus . . .'

'He was bowled over.' David thought of his friend's generous eagerness.

'Not the same, Davey, not the same. He's just a new museum curator.'

'Well, he'll take care of them. Won't let the kids cut loose with a screwdriver to add more details.'

'Davey, time's short. And if you keep hiding and harping, how can I say the real burdens on my mind?'

They walked silently down a long set of steps that plunged suddenly into a thicket. Giant trees shoved the darkness into a trough. They crossed a small bridge. A street lamp emphasised the nudging shadows.

Above them were gurglings and scoops of bird sound: pied curra-wongs settling and congregating on branches. Their comment was in a distant language yet one that evoked song and scurry. Noises of disturbance, not reconciliation.

'This track? Or the other?' David offered at an intersection in the narrow path.

'At some stage you will have to decide, I thought you knew that.'

'Meaning?'

'That which is part of you, you must decide if it is of use to you. Or if it is hindrance. Only you.'

David walked behind Clyde for a dozen paces in silence. The other did not look back. He strode along the irregular track as if he had absolute command. The sense of choice seemed to brim with possibility; something to be embraced. How much had Clyde been instructing, how far had he been leading?

It was true. Once you became conscious of certain questions you were committed. Even denial was a stance. David had become, he realised, filled with a sense of coming into possession of himself.

'You're a bit of a magic man, Clyde the Carter. But I guess you know that.'

'I haven't got time to correct your sloppy expressions.' But Clyde did turn around to give him a grin, that boyish change. 'I seem to have this need to tell you this. There's only a few men can be counted. Only a few men I've encountered.' And Clyde broke with laughter at his word play. 'And I counted you among them from the start. Why otherwise engage in speculations in the night air on the high seas? Your book gave you away, Davey. You told me things I suspect you thought still secret – the way you respond to elements in this land form, for instance. The god you have made in the sacred cedar grove. Yes, the god. And the anguish. Man, the pain of anguish you cannot hide. You walk raw wounded. No wonder you carry the big protections – the serving wife, the life as a numb teacher, the shell of rough, tough gutturals. And your skin, Davey boy, o the pelt, the pelt that you draw close. I have seen you naked, in your book, in your very own words. Yes, Davey, I remember them evenings.'

Clyde paused, overlooking a drop onto dark pools of water, oiled with serpent squirmings of light. A ferry cut through the patterns, making animated offspring of light.

'You're a kicking man, you're full of battle within. But when a man's haunted, that shows clear, too. None of your other friends, I don't give tuppence for none of your other friends. And that's not meant to be disparaging, but you understand that. This time I'm serious.'

David was silent. Glinting lights on water, perpetual restlessness. Had his printed words ventured so far? He knew he had attempted communication – with someone unknown, but sharing, out there. He had given up expecting a response. He had believed himself inured. But now he must accept the new terms, and Clyde's authority. He was a novice, still, not an initiate.

'It's like the door opening', Clyde said, after the long pause. They walked now between houses and fences, the water blinking below on their left, boats knocking small bell sounds against metal like disconsolate cage birds. 'It's a door that I knew would be found, though I'd given up hoping. And you were the agent, Davey boy, it was you, and right from the start I sensed you the agent though I would not have guessed something like this.' He grabbed David then, with both firm hands, and pulled him close to his gaunt frame. David could catch the smell of naphthalene, of mothballs in the rough jacket. 'This! Tonight! We've just had wonders.' He slapped David upon the shoulder blade, then, and pushed him back. David's hip caught against the white railing of the small pathway. 'Wonders, we've just had, down in that cavern place. You were the dark horse, turning your light on those symbols. You were the dark messenger. And you, Davey boy,' Clyde stopped and gripped David by both shoulders, 'You understand what I'm saying and what we've both been seeing. You brought me to it. You were a guide to me in this. Untapping the resources. Oho, darkness, we're at one in this.' His grip was tight and David broke free, laughing a little.

Not a guide. No, a discoverer, even a co-discoverer. Each of them, perhaps, had made separate landfall. For a second, a surge of personal claim, of possessiveness, swept over David. But this was a moment for sharing, also.

'I knew you'd see it the same way. Those signs: they were right, *right*.'

'Indeed. Answers.' But Clyde did not expand. Instead, he again took the lead and they clattered down concrete stairways, gripped the white handrail, cut between rock paths and further into pools of dark along the tree-cluttered path until they came out to more open ground, manicured, with gardens and houses neat piled over them, lights glowing in windows and spilling out gold rectangles across their way.

The Cremorne cave, when they reached it, was damp, fire-blackened, and there was a scurf of papers, old wrappings, used tissues. David was quite proprietorial there, and Clyde was instructed. Somehow it was nothing, it was a nothing.

When they returned to the house, everyone had assembled upstairs. The Mackeys' rock cave under their house remained in darkness though, having now been opened, it too was bound into the processes.

On their long returning stroll together, David had meditated on the rock images, the criss-crossed couple with arms upstretched and feet firmly on ground, their sexuality essential yet clearly mystical. And the unified one, the man/woman under the moon – yes, an extraordinary image.

Extraordinary, extraordinary. He must not keep using the clumsy thumbprints of language.

He looked across at Clyde the Carter. Had he been mistaken? Clyde was now jesting with Meg, rough-handling the boys like an uncle.

But when Deirdre came up and asked, 'Where did you get to? Where did the pair of you get off to for such a long time?' David was instantly hostile.

XXXII

Deirdre had watched the two men stride up the hill. No, she told herself, as they turned the corner under an overhanging bottlebrush tree which seemed to finger David's shoulders as he passed under it. No, he must do this on his own.

Yet how could he be so slipshod in his understanding of that man? How could he not see that he was being swept off, being too quickly swept away in the tidal currents of Clyde the Carter's moon circle? Magics? Yes, yes that man played real tricks with power, and surely power was only another word for magic.

David so vulnerable behind that bluff impetuous front, behind that secret shadow that expressed itself in moodiness. Like the long torment he put himself through about his skin and the defensive fear of taint. She had never confessed the secret glamour of his swarthiness, that very hint of different and exotic and unexpected combinations – of colour, of mood, of passion. She was not the first woman to feel her insides buckle at the thought of his tight, drum-like body. No, perhaps part of the allure was his very awkwardness about that part of his being. It remained an unconscious gift. It was still powerful, despite the thickening and broadening of the maturing man. The only thing Meg had ever said that was a giveaway was a later reference to David's burnished dark skin. 'Burnished!' Deirdre had laughed, but the moment was visceral. Meg had later apologised. Strangely, after that, their friendship had blossomed.

Clyde the Carter sought out a different man. Was that the secret of his threat? That he would turn her husband into someone other?

She bit her lip, then carefully moistened it. 'Like buttered toast. Smooth and shining as buttered toast' – that was what she thought that first time he took her to the beach, and had dragged her into the thump of surf, coaxing and bullying her. Its salt flavour came back to her.

Then that other power figure. That woman, Galina. How could David not have recognised, instantly, her voracious half eyes upon him; they never left him, they hovered round his face, stole glances lower, to his strong neck, the broad shoulders half exposed carelessly in that open sports shirt he wore. And as the old woman solicitously draped a napkin across his lap – 'to protect you from crumbs' – Deirdre could swear her thin fingers had lightly stroked his crotch.

Was she becoming paranoid?

Galina Darovskaya was more dangerous than that. Like Clyde, she was somehow seeking to gain possession of David's being, his personality. Deirdre had heard how some people survive and thrive by leeching off the spiritual energies of others. She thought of insects sucking out the juices of leaves and trees. She remembered insects with a proboscis like a drinking straw.

What was it about David that attracted such parasites?

Or were they attracted by something more dynamic in him? Did each of them recognise in him – in each other – some further sign, some hidden imprint which marked them apart? She remembered her young brother, left-handed, who instantly noted every other left-hander with a sort of quiet glee, in banks, at the office, even on the screen. Was there some secret freemasonry of initiates, one to which she had no access?

Or was it herself, Deirdre, who was the insect living off the inner fluids of her victim, her host? David had called her, at times, something very like that. Impossible.

In her heart Deirdre recognised the depth of her self-abnegation, her years of remoulding her own thoughts, her real impulses, to fit in with David's crazy and compulsive ways. No, she was not going to have that. It was the way to horror, self-destruction.

She went inside, hating herself again, and hurt at David's continual caged look. She had given him so much freedom. So much freedom it hurt.

And he was being encircled by a man whose entire being was that of a net maker. Or that woman, Galina, another lost soul with her net of words and the dead world of lost Leningrad, worlds away, lifetimes away from anything to do with David, or Deirdre, or the two boys.

When she had gone inside, Meg wanted to drag her down for another look at the wonderful cave and its rock scratches. Deirdre opted for a camomile tea and then the boys were upon her, Marcus insisting she explain the difference between 'penis' and 'phallus'.

XXXIII

'What are the three dumb creatures that give knowledge to everyone? Go on, that's the easiest riddle.' Clyde the Carter had again won at the pool table. He was drunk and expansive. Was David the only one who sensed in this drunkenness something both exultant yet dangerous? It made David once more the observer. Though he, too, had taken his fair share, he was clear in his mind, glitteringly sober. It was as if his moment were expected. He felt cheated, disappointed in his friend. Something in him wanted Clyde to be invulnerable, beyond criticism.

Though, even in this, there was almost the demonstration of some shared flaw, as if he were seeing a mirror of himself in those drunk moments, but from a different perspective. Even drunk, it seemed, Clyde would remain the teacher.

'Go on; what are the three dumb creatures that give knowledge?'

Brian, from the pool table, guffawed, 'The three dumb creatures? Sure you don't mean us three, Clyde old man, the three of us bruising our hands on the stone to give knowledge all right. Those bloody rude rock carvings!'

'No, I like riddles.' Meg put her hand over her husband's mouth.

'Go on, Clyde, you tell us what are the three dumb creatures?'

'Nobody guess?'

'Here. Let me have a go.' David was looking at his friend Brian with unexpected scorn. 'If they're dumb creatures, as you call them, then they're somehow servants of mankind; right? Dumb: can't speak.

230

Let's say, well, the first could be – have I got it – dumb, did you say? Wait, how's this? It's got to be part of the human body. That's my guess. Three dumb creatures that give us knowledge. Well, the brain. That'd be one. The brain, see, the brain would be dumb by itself, but knowledge has got to be "given". Why not the brain, number one?'

'That's my boyo. The mind, yes friend, the mind, the brain, that's number one. And the rest?'

'Hold on,' Brian was coaxed in. 'This one's my turn. I get the idea now. How about the mouth?'

'Drinks, anyone?'

'Big mouth!' Meg slapped her hand on her head in mock idiocy, 'the mouth is the *non* dumb part. I guess it's the eye.'

'The eye. Right then. I've got the idea. The mind, the eye. My turn this time. It's the ear. There you are, matey, your riddle is solved: the mind, the eye, the ear. All knowledge nicely stacked away in that combination.'

'This is childish.' Deirdre, bored and standing slightly aside near the window, turned to David and handed him a billiard cue.

'Clyde should still be in third grade: that's the age when riddles really get you in.'

'Riddles are older than that.' Clyde smiled gently so that his tolerance hit Deirdre like a cuff. 'But the third part of the riddle still is not answered. What three dumb creatures give knowledge to everyone? Here is the answer: the eye, the mind, and a letter.'

'A letter? That's cheating.'

'A letter? You mean post it in the mailbox letter?'

'Don't be silly, David.' Deirdre turned on her husband. 'He means a letter, the alphabet. Language. Language.'

Clyde bowed.

'As in writing. Or, I guess, as in spoken language – though spoken language existed eons before anyone invented alphabets.'

'True, Dee,' Brian said. 'Before that they had images.' He pointed down toward the floorboards.

'You mean the semioticians were the first?' Meg offered them glasses.

'You dumb creatures haven't got a clue, have you?' Clyde slapped the flat of his hand on an adjacent chiffonier. All the glass decorations of the hanging lamps started to jingle. 'Perhaps I'm impatient. But I'm not impervious. You just don't know what the thing is down there you have discovered.' He corrected himself angrily, '*I* have discovered. Only David and me,' again he slammed the old cedar, 'only we have the eye, and the mind, and the alphabet to even begin to recognise our discoveries.'

'I think your friend, David, is a bit carried away,' Meg said quietly.

'Damned true I'm carried away. Oh, it's all right, I won't break up your nice furniture, I won't take a billiard cue to your footling furniture or the unserious chandelier. You can sleep safe in your bed at night; I'll not strangle you with the lamp cord, though by God, you deserve it! And I'll not deface your front gate with a plague cross. But remember this,' Clyde strode over and grabbed Brian's half filled wine glass. 'When you salute your luck and the signs under your floorboards, just remember how the dumb creatures mourned, how they stamped and were made irrelevant when the first sensate creature – man with understanding – declared himself with such signs in the pride of his nakedness.'

He threw the glass down into a corner. The stem broke.

'Dance with me, girl of the sorrows!' He grabbed Deirdre roughly into a close embrace. 'No, your wife is safe,' he warned. 'But we must dance on the boards over the signs of the first union.' He began stomping.

Deirdre half attempted to disengage herself.

'Kill the life! Kill the living! One two three.'

'Cut it out, man.' David moved forward. Brian still kept his host's expression, prepared to turn it into a romp.

'One two three. One two three. Keep the blood pounding, keep it prisoner. No one's free.' Clyde swept Deirdre off into a spin and grabbed Meg. Deirdre fell, panting and half laughing, into the settee.

'Let it go! Let the demons rip!' Clyde shouted rhythmically, stamping his feet in a jig as he twisted Meg all the way round the pool table. 'How do you bring life to dead souls? Spill your jelly beans? Unbutton your jewels?'

'You're a madman!' Meg gasped, but was caught into the ferocious zest of the stomp. She clung to his shoulder. He bounced her across the room.

'You too. Nobody's spared!' Clyde spun her off to flop beside Deirdre on the settee. He advanced on Brian.

'Dance is the blood-bouncing spirit. All the old sailors knew that.'

He dragged Brian into his thump-footed reel. Brian, laughing, joined in. It was a competition.

David turned away. It was clear none of them understood Clyde's vicious attempt. Or the blade of desperation.

David went over and turned up the record player. It was a slow rigid music, out of time with Clyde's dance. Clyde and Brian separated. Clyde walked over to David – for an instant it seemed he was about to strike.

'You've not been left out, you know. But I'm one of the elemental ones. The element ones. It's in my blood – for the time when there's no words. And you know, Davey, the way there's no words at the best and the worst moments. When there is words, they come later, and grab us from behind. Sometimes they defeat us. Sometimes they lead us out singing. Man of words, without words.' He threw his wide arms around David's shoulders and hugged him ferociously.

Then he laughed. 'There's no words in them signs under your house. But those no-words are still powerful unions!'

'I should report them. National Parks? Aboriginal Heritage? The local council?' Brian began.

'Oh, you will, you will', Clyde boomed. 'That's your nature. But they have escaped already – into my mind; into Davey's mind here. They're convulsing again with the old spiritual possessiveness that it's folly to remember. Folly. Oh dangerous, too, friends – run to your council quickly. Make it a museum.' He laughed.

'Clyde, you're so damned outrageous my twelve-year-old would be jealous.' Deirdre pushed herself from the settee.

'No, he's already observant. He'd be envious.' Clyde slapped his broad hand against cedar. The door of the chiffonier burst open. 'Trouble with you lot, you've got nothing to see with. Eyes but no eyes. Mind but no perceptions. Atrophy of the magic bone, seizure of the surreal system. Comfort!' He came back to the baize table. 'Trouble with all of you – you, too, Davey – is you let the sun spoil your senses. You're all, all of you, indistinguishable in the dark.'

'Have a strong coffee,' Deirdre said dryly, 'and shut up. You're getting boring, Clyde.'

'Not to mention transparent.'

'Please. Don't gang up on him.' Meg reached for the percolator. 'After this exciting sort of day, we're all a bit strange with the strangeness of it.'

'Meg's right. We're all sort of skirting the subject,' added Brian.

'Oh, dancing it away!' David could not resist. He caught Clyde's wide stare. Could the man be on the verge of a crack-up? Some deep panic neither words nor jig could contain? The awful part was that David could understand exactly what that panic was, what Clyde was seeking to grasp. Once, when he was twelve he had crept into St Andrew's Cathedral, hiding. He had been stopped in his tracks by the extraordinary high sound of a choir in the gallery, practising. It was unlike any sound he had heard before – remote yet passionate, as much a part of the dim resonance of the vault as it was sound of itself. The scratchings underneath this house caught with a similar surprise and inevitability. Their silence brought in every sound out of the bush into this night, tugging his rainforest memories.

Brian had gone over to the chiffonier. He gently shut the lurching door and examined the hinges.

'You want to be a bit more careful of this cedar, Clyde old man. This is an antique. This really old cedar is fragile stuff.'

'Oho. So this is the cedar? This is the magic timber!' Clyde was in behind Brian, straining and then fingering. He lifted the entire chiffonier up and carried it easily into the centre of the room, under the over-vivid light of the great Venetian chandelier, that incongruous celebrant.

'It's a matchstick. Light as a feather. This is hardly timber, me lad, hardly wood at all. Now what do you make of it?'

David came over. 'Brian was right when he said handle it carefully,' he said. 'But lightness isn't all of it. Just look at that grain. Look at the whole size of the door there – all from one solid piece of timber – how many hundred years? Look at the smoothness of it. Go on, you can touch.'

'I think Clyde's at last made speechless,' said Deirdre.

'No, not speechless. At a loss. It's just wood. Simply wood.'

'What did you expect? Plastic? Veneers? Something tricky, like a roll-top desk?' David was scornful.

'It's a very simple piece. Domestic. But look, hardly a join. It's red gold. Just the beauty of the timber itself is all you need, no fancy dowelling, no inlays, no Victorian messiness,' Brian added. Meg, behind him, reached out her hand to stroke.

Clyde stood back.

'It's the darkness,' he said. 'Dense as the dark.' He turned to David.

'Well, I've seen it. It's yours, though. It's yours, David, not my own, I'm not a competitor, not in that world of wonders. I'd not have known. I'd not have looked at it. I can begin to understand, now that you've taught me, I believe I can begin to understand.' He lifted up the piece again, this time more decorously. 'A feather, it's that lightweight. Now me, I was brought up on timber weighty as oak. Something like that I'd not own. Ah, you're a gentle man, David, under that beetling brow and that frown. Well, it's magic, but a toy.'

'I knew he wouldn't understand,' said Deirdre protectively.

'Look at you. Just look at you all, lining up as if I'd scratch your pretty furniture with a will. That's hardly necessary. You're all so protective of it, just look at you. I'm surprised, Davey, at you entering this, this kept world of furniture, this genteel parlour where the first fingerprint would be sacrilege, where a hard slap could kill.'

He thumped the top of the chiffonier. Then again.

Meg pushed herself between Clyde and the chiffonier.

'Not in our home, if you please. You're the guest here, and if you've any sense of that you'll save your bad graces till you are somewhere else.'

Brian loomed behind her, taking Clyde's shoulder with his mild but strong grip.

'You've shared our wine and our hospitality, mate. Even our downstairs adventure. A bit of the old commonsense, a bit of the old common courtesy . . .'

Clyde shook himself free and took a pace backward. Only David noticed the puzzlement, the slight sense of confusion. He did not budge.

Clyde had not understood. He had not understood.

Clyde swung then, back to the pool table and grabbed up a cue.

'No more snooker, I think,' Brian said gently, as if he were already thinking of his baize and a sudden desperate tear with Clyde's erratic plunge.

Clyde seemed caught again in their crossfire of eyes. He placed the cue down with a terrible gentleness.

'Come on Davey, I'm a bit impatient with all this.' Clyde strode across to pick up his parka. He paused in the silence, looking back to David.

Then Clyde walked out of the house. The front door shut after him.

They heard the front gate slap to. His boot steps were lost in the grey humming traffic noise, usually disregarded.

'What's with him?' Brian said, after the long pause. Meg looked guilt-stricken.

'I'm sorry I invited him,' David shrugged.

'No. It was my original suggestion.' Deirdre put a hand on David's arm, either in restraint, or support. David allowed her. Too much had been left unsaid, unfinished. After a minute he realised all eyes were on him. He shrugged again, this time consciously. He picked up Clyde's abandoned cue.

XXXIV

In their car, on the way home, Deirdre looked back at the sleeping boys, and then to her husband.

'The way he tried to summon you over to follow him out! There's something quite wrong about that man. He's not just odd, there's something wrong about him. If I were old-fashioned I think I would use the word "evil".'

David drove more slowly. 'Why use such a word, then? I think you're over-reacting. After all, you're not in any way threatened.'

'But you are.'

'Thank you, Dee. Thanks for the vote of confidence, just what a bloke needs. You think I'm somehow in the thrall of our mad Irishman, then? Come off it.'

'I'm actually not being funny, David. I meant it. That man, Clyde the Carter, he's trying to get some sort of hold over you. I don't like him. I don't want to see him again.'

'What's he done? Forget that drunk outburst. What's he done to you?'

'Not me, oh no, not me. Can't you see what a change he makes come over you whenever he turns up? You stand off a bit, you try to joke around things, but he's filling you with all sorts of – of ideas, I don't know, of silly chains and coincidences. He keeps trying to prove the here and now doesn't matter; he's got his head stuffed with magics and myths and I don't know what other nonsense. You're not a teenager now, David. Don't let him drag you in.'

'You've still got a real set against him.'

'Why, for instance, did he try to drag you out with him when he left?'

'Well, he was my guest, my charge. I was the one first brought him over. And the discovery under the house. I can understand why he went overboard. But I realise his behaviour was quite unforgivable. I was as embarrassed as anyone. Perhaps more so.'

'And why did you wander off for hours, the pair of you, just when it got dark?'

'Dee. You're not jealous?'

'I'm threatened. I find him threatening. Why do we have to let him keep coming over. We've got nothing to do with him. He's grotesque. He's a fish out of water.'

'That's better. Not so threatening after all.'

But how could David explain the silences and the shared excitement of that rock-carving discovery: how it gathered up in one strange image everything they had ever talked about, on those balmy nights on the little island, making sense beyond sense, meaning that did not have to decipher meaning?

It had never happened before. Now it had happened twice. Perhaps this was the outcome, the sign, that seemed to hover over him – this, and not the Russian poet's collusions.

In a sense, Clyde's failure of understanding about the cedar actually strengthened the bond. David retained his own secrets. The power of this shared discovery under the Mackeys' house was expanded. Common ground, and their own.

'And as for the big fuss over the rock carvings. It was on the tip of my tongue several times to point out to you gaggle of boy scouts that exactly similar rock carvings are there and available for all to see up at the Kuring-gai Chase National Park, just up the end of the peninsula. I would have thought you were quite familiar with them. I know I've been there with the kids several times. So what's so special about the fact that there are some others closer in Mosman?'

'You're sure of that? How come I've not seen them? We were up there only at Easter. I swear I saw no rock carvings remotely resembling Brian's.'

'Even more distinct, and more of them. Lots of big dangling pricks.

238

Though it's true, I've only seen one of the sex merger, or whatever you like to call it. But it's there.'

'There's a man with some sort of belt and a weapon, up near the picnic area. And lots of fish, and some animals, and I remember one of a female figure.'

'The big set are at the signpost No. 12, if you walk in half a mile along the sand road . . .'

David negotiated the last intersection. They had lapsed to silence. As they drew up to their house he asked, 'And this Kuring-gai rock carving, did it have any sort of effect on you, any sort of power?'

'What a curious question! As I recall, the time I went there with the boys the place was full of visitors, a party of teenage girls. They were all tittering and embarrassed. All that male genitalia. I had to say to them, "Well, they'd look funny *without* them", and I tried to be serious and point out to the boys that their meaning was probably religious. They laughed at that, too, like the girls. But I'm not without sensitivity, you know, David.'

They drove though several intersections. David remembered how Clyde had once suggested a *geis* that gave him immunity from any drink-drive test.

No, not immunity. But perhaps that man had suggested even more intriguing things? Correspondences?

'I wish you had mentioned these things, Dee.'

'Why?'

'Stop us going overboard. Stop me.'

'What difference does it make?'

'In the long term, none. But somehow it seems as if you were hoarding this information, to deflate us. To deflate me.'

'David, I want to protect you. Against yourself, against this wave of enthusiasm, this romantic belief. Do you understand me? I was trying to find a way back to us, to the real.'

'Look, I know I *am* swept up in this, but what a discovery! I'm not excluding anyone. Not you, not anyone. I'm merely rushing as far forward as my mind and senses can carry me.' He reached out a hand, but it seemed heavy with accusation. 'It's as if you really want to hold back something essential, some part of my ancestry.'

'Rot! I will not answer that.' Deirdre sat rigid beside him in her car seat, a seat designed to curve the spine to passive alignment.

'Sorry,' she added, after a pause. She stared straight ahead.

'You're not sorry. You're being truthful at last.'

'David, you're forcing me to say what I don't want to say. You're making me an accomplice where I was only wanting to be, dear David, simply your wife.'

'That again!'

How could they have recognised that their shared anger in fact defined their conjunction? That neither could be alone again, ever? That to be alone would be to defer to either one or the other's challenge, in a relationship where neither owned the game?

'Let's count the parts of ourselves that matter.' Deirdre put her arm on his leg. After two or three minutes in silence David allowed himself to be warmed. He accepted the offer, as if it would be forthcoming always.

Not true. He could not express the sort of disturbance troubling him. It was as if he had been torn apart by two forces, and the worst of it was that he did not understand either of them. The admission was not even a relief, it was a betrayal.

'Why the hell didn't you ever tell me about those other rock carvings, Deirdre? I can't understand that, I can't begin to understand that.' But the accusation did not fit what he had been intending.

Would it have been easier if Deirdre had been with him at the moment of illuminating the aboriginal carvings under the house? He glanced across at her, stiff beside him. Her anguish. Her desolation. Was he the cause of all this?

He reached the last few streets and cut corners mercilessly. Deirdre refrained from comment so pointedly that her silence was a further cry of pain.

Why him? Why this claim, this hurt? All of it, smothering the real claim, the real discovery, the sudden and surprising revelation. How could he submerge that?

The light of the car swung into the driveway. There was a figure on the front porch. 'Oh, my God!' Deirdre exclaimed.

'Look. I'll get rid of him. I'll keep him away. You just put the boys in bed. If you really feel so set against Clyde, let me do the talk. I'll drive him somewhere, get him away from you.'

'I just cannot face the man.'

'It's okay.' David gave her a quick hug. 'You don't have to get mixed up in this.' But already his mind was racing, even as he tried to be consoling. 'I'll take him up to bloody Kuring-gai Chase. There's an excuse. We'll confront the whole business, strike while the iron's steaming.'

Deirdre threw her arm round his neck. He could feel her wet skin. 'David, dear David,' she whispered, 'I'm not playing rivals, I am not trying to be difficult or intrusive. But I am terrified. He uses you like fuel. He burns other people up. He's a destroyer.'

But already his stiffening muscles closed her off.

'Take him to some crowded pub, David, some Irish party, some ocker community.' She gave a last desperate squeeze, then let go.

David understood the depth of trust behind that statement. He did not have to explain to her that, in this new context whatever it was, the crucial thing was alertness – insight, not the oblivion of drunkenness.

David pulled up in the light of the night driveway beacon. He gave her a brief peck, then slid out, calling over to Clyde.

Deirdre clambered from her seat and the groggy boys followed her, shaken from sleep only after she had poked at them several times. With a guilty wave in the direction of the two men, she headed for the door. Once inside, she locked it. In the dim cluttered rooms she moved swiftly. No, there was no guilt. Also no sanctuary. She wondered only at absence, and how absence actually knitted itself into long distances and periods. It was a very abstract conjecture.

It was very terrifying. She had failed utterly.

XXXV

A full moon now. The low cloud and the rain had been swept away by a cold southern breeze. Light from the moon seemed to increase the stillness that had fallen over the edges of the city. They had driven to the wild forested area deep in the National Park.

It was 3 a.m. The moon hung low. No gleam of light from any car or building. This cold, distorting light seemed to wrap itself around the two figures straggling down the sandy track. They had left the car at the bitumen road, officially closed from dusk to dawn, that wound through the Kuring-gai Chase National Park out to West Head. David had driven slowly so as not to miss the wooden signpost marked No. 12. The Basin Track.

Clyde the Carter beside him in the front seat, had said only one thing: 'You didn't come.'

David had filled the gulf by describing the new aboriginal rock carvings. As they had driven along the quiet northern suburbs he became silent, too. Clyde's stillness was as of someone or something poised, hair-trigger.

In the end David had to admit to himself that he was the one curious to explore this site, the moonlight drenching the whole landscape around them. What an extraordinary moment to do this! He could feel his own scalp tingle as he had closed the car door and moved out into the water-cold air.

Shallow marks on an ancient volcanic platform, a table top raised above the thin scratchy scrub: yes, he remembered the general area. How could he not have come across these particular designs before? The park was full of numbered walking tracks, many of them with almost identical flat terraces and carvings upon them. A country quite familiar, yet suddenly full of surprises.

The scrub twisted itself into flowers like red spiders, tangled webs and knots of blooms, stars and purple trumpets and white tipped heath serrations, clasps and brooches and pins. In the moonlight these flowers had become bleached of their colour, but in the night air their nectar was potent. In moonlight the two men's shadows were cast onto the pale sand. A few hundred yards over the low ridge they reached a curve in the track.

David stopped, pointing to a sign. They reached the outcrop of cold rock. He placed his hand on it. It was like the feel of reptiles: frog, snake, lizard.

'Clamber up,' he instructed and sprang lightly himself over the flat ledge. A few straggly bushes and grasses had rooted, even here, to grow among cracks and clefts.

'Start looking.'

Clyde moved cautiously behind him, pale skin held by moonlight. Almost underfoot, just a few yards in, David suddenly knelt, then pointed. The slant of moonlight revealed shallow markings, indentations of lines that caught the images of man-recorded creatures. A large fish. Another animal. A humanoid figure with outstretched arms, each finger delineated. It had a round body, penis and curiously outflung legs, as if floating. The head was simply another shrouded protrusion.

'I think that might be some sort of animal, perhaps a platypus,' David said, peering slowly. Beyond was another male figure, quite certainly human. Again, outstretched arms as if welcoming the sun, or the moon. In this light the angle of the figure appeared to be reaching directly for the blue pale orb that was above them, low to the hills.

'The legs, not a stick figure at all, look at the curve and the muscle in those legs.'

Clyde was silent.

Beyond, they discovered a female figure, but strangely bloated: the head was merely a drape, the hands too broad, the legs almost

243

club-footed. The genitalia had been scrubbed out by someone, European.

Clyde's silence seemed to hunch up into his body. David took more paces and came across several other figures. A female, whose immobility was mocked by the strange energy of her hand and arm posture, caught in some ecstatic movement and then frozen. The male figure beside her had a strange crown, or was it a series of flames, rising from the head?

'It looks like an aura?'

He stood up, looked over his shoulder and around. The place contained an undoubted aura, he felt, though only that night out on the water – again with Clyde – came to his mind.

Clyde was a thousand miles or years away, though his closeness was electric. David could almost feel Clyde's fingers, gripping each other, binding into tight knots.

They discovered a line of escaping wallabies, a whole tribe of them, leaping and startled by hunters centuries ago, pinned down in accurate line, quick, observant, recreating the quarry with hunger and extraordinary deliberation. There were fish, also.

'This has to have been the place of ritual preparation and invocation for the hunt.' Then his eyes caught the figures beyond. Male and female, in the now familiar attitudes of upflung arms, outturned breasts. A sickle moon.

'And then this.'

The single figure, with huge flaccid penis, the two female breasts outflung, and the arms pushed out. The outreach of this image, though, was horizontal, not upwards. It seemed to be seeking to encompass the flat wide rock platform, not the carved image, above, of the moon. It had no discernible head.

Clyde the Carter, close behind now and craning to make out the images, gripped David's shoulders tightly, then as suddenly let go.

'They knew something.'

'All gone. All gone now.' David felt his own throat twist and gulp. He also felt a pang of something like betrayal. It was wrong to have brought Clyde here.

As he stood aside to allow Clyde to crouch in the moonshadow, casting darkness across the lower, male and female figures, David looked down at the other. He could feel the power of his absorbing eyes. Yes, it was wrong to have come here with him.

Was it no more than a sense of appropriation? Could David not admit that he was in some way jealous of the other's intensity? Clyde was appropriating this knowledge to himself, translating it to some chain of progression that would enhance his own sense of whatever mysteries might be intuited or carried forward.

David had made these images his own.

He strode off, leaving Clyde still crouched and fingering the rock patterns. Clyde had begun a low humming. It was unnerving.

David walked to the very edge of the rock platform, then followed a clearly defined walking path, through broken piles of smaller granite outcrops and hard sand flattened by many footsteps. Clyde caught up with him.

'Can you imagine what this place was, back then?' His voice was thick, husky again. 'I'll tell you.'

David paused, impatient yet held still by the certainty in Clyde's tone.

'This was near the water, there were inlets of water, I can hear the sound of it. I know it. There was a fresh spring, perhaps. There was a meeting: fresh water and salt water. I can feel the bubbling conjunction, froth at the edges. But the fresh water – imagine that. Imagine that clear as moonwater. I have been there. I know this place, I do truly. When I was at the beginning of things I was the fish in that water, then the wallabies, I tell you, David, I can feel it, quite precisely. I am the figure with the halo. I have inherited it, or have been there in whatever form. And I tell you this. That halo, that aura, it is not the sun. It is a moon halo. I am that one. And you, unknowing or perhaps knowing, you brought me here in the moonlight, you do not know your own inheritance. Or what you have done.'

'Clyde? Don't over-react, mate.' But David knew the words stumbled, fell far too short.

He pushed onward, brushing the springy branches of heath and melaleuca aside. Hoping they would slap back, wishing them to caution Clyde against following.

But Clyde's hand gripped his shoulder again, spinning him round with its force.

'In the old legends, the messenger knows too much. He becomes a sacrifice once his task is done.'

'You're mad!' David tried to wrench himself free of the manic grip. 'The moon's got you.'

'You don't understand. At the end, you don't understand.'

Clyde tried to drag him back to the area of carvings. David punched out.

In the scuffle that followed, the blood pumping through his own head defended David from the deep howling noise of the other, at least for the first moments.

They became gripped in a savage embrace and David tried again to free his arms. He had not realised the strength of the other.

They stumbled and he was again able to jerk his knee up, jarring into the soft vulnerable groin. Clyde hissed and buckled, thumping heavily into a clump of branches.

'You all right?' David was instantly solicitous and ashamed, the guarding and over-protective host. Clyde still lay crouched up, gasping. In the pallid light his face looked torn, the mouth a black hole.

'You were crushing me,' David said, after a pause. Indignation was seeping back, like the sense of the pulse after a shock.

'Just give yourself a few minutes. You'll be okay. I can't have done that much damage.'

The other did not respond.

'I'll be just over there.'

With a callous shrug David stood up from his crouching position. It had, after all, been war. It had been also, clearly, an ending. How would he endure the long drive back, the resumption of formality?

Still seething with an anger grown comfortably secure, he pushed between thorn bushes and came to a lumpier, larger rock outcrop. He knew this overlooked the entire valley. In the far distance he noted one small light. Otherwise, it was a dark bumpy sea of darkness, treetops shining in places, deflecting the light.

David jumped from rock to rock. Quiet deep crevasses. Some of the rocks looked to have caves, like broken-toothed mouths. Hollows and bubbles. What was Clyde's image of fresh water, salt water?

It was Clyde's appropriation of everything – that was the real chafe. No, he did not want to be part of Clyde or what Clyde was absorbing. Let Clyde make of it what he could; it had nothing to do with David.

He required aloneness.

But standing rigid and tensed on this outcrop, David could not deny that this vast aloneness was something quite different. He stood for a long time. It was a communication. It was part of him, the part that was him was almost indistinguishable. It was as if he linked back, linked in to this place and was no longer a stranger.

Take it slowly. Close your eyes. Breathe. Breathe again. Now open. David put both hands out, flat, on the curving rock. Coldness, yet there was some hidden memory of sun warmth as well.

He stood close to the edge. Immediately below in the black shadow, the pale trunk of a eucalyptus seemed like a white arm sinuously reaching towards him, calling him over the edge. David clambered down to a lower level, another shelf jutting out.

He heard a small noise, scrabble of pebbles, and looked backwards, but could discern only the cliff edge, reaching five or six feet up to the plateau in awkward steps.

'No anger, Davey, you don't understand. So I have to do this. You're not to return from my sanctuary. You've got to be the one.'

A large boulder bumped over the edge. It struck the rock near David's head with a jarring noise. He twisted and slipped sideways. He fell, reaching for a handhold, over the smooth rock edge, then bumped onto another outcrop, and into a springy grove of melaleuca bushes below that. The large rock cracked into pieces which spattered close to him. The main body of it bumped and rumbled lower, chipping off rocks and tearing through bushes.

He yelled angrily. Then another rock cracked the silence. He clambered under the overhang. As quietly as possible he shifted crabwise as far as he could, then realised there was a small bush track at this level that must be leading somewhere back to the sand road.

Clyde was far beyond drunkenness.

David knew he was shaking. And the worst thing was that he also knew what was driving that man.

'It's not yours, Clyde. It is not yours!' he called up, into the moon-darkness.

He had given his position away. A shower of rocks – was Clyde clambering down after him?

David had the car keys in his pocket. He knew he would have to make a break for it.

XXXVI

Dear friend

It is true that I died. As a poet I died. I think my creative spark died in 1943 although I did not admit it to myself until almost the last days of the Great Patriotic war in 1945. So we deceive ourselves.

I will not describe the subterfuges I adopted to keep that spark alive; and I was busy. I was always busy. To be in demand, also, is to mean you must keep producing more poems – to be read and broadcast, to be repeated in factories and schools and among friends. I believed I had many friends.

But the spark was dead. What snuffed it out? It was an eleven-year-old girl snuffed it out. She had died. She was as it were my ward, we were both fatherless, motherless. But she was greater than I, and I made the mistake of believing in her wish to impart something of her courage and endurance and calm to me. These things are impossible.

In Leningrad Dr Pavlov is famous at the university, he was very famous. Some things can be artificially sustained, but not the small pure flame of poetry. It was as if I, myself, doused that flame with fatty thumbs.

My friends believed, of course, that it was the Roller Coaster poems. 'You will pay for those,' they said, even then. I paid *with* those. It is an irony that they were to become a sort of tribute, even, it might be said, to a kind of survival. But I did not survive.

I will not answer your questions.

But I will come sometime, the shell, the husk of me that remains, *that* will come. There is something I had in mind to talk to you about. Although I am dead, I am not yet at rest. There are some things that we share.

Forgive my handwriting, it loops like an erratic beast, almost beyond my control. When I was young my handwriting was so firm, so well curved and elegant. I think I am still proud, and I know myself. What I have done, I have done. My daughter is a fool; she believes I crave immortality. When I received my gift, I did not understand that the body must pay interest.

We have made an agreement. I will not let you escape without taking up some part of your offer.

Galina Darovskaya

*

The sale of the island property was something David did not discuss with Deirdre. He simply made two phone calls to Brisbane and had a brief conversation with his bank manager. When he remarked, two weeks later, that Deirdre had better come in with him to sign some forms he confided to her what he had done. A contract had already been signed.

Deirdre did not protest at all. She was surprised at how much they had been offered. It was an 'as is' offer. Somehow neither of them, as David allowed the words to sink in, could really contemplate a trip up there to retrieve the few beach-shack belongings. There would be six whole cartons of unused white bathroom tiles; some army surplus blankets and the one really good fishing line, as well as the crab-pots and the boys' surfboards and flippers. They could be replaced. There would be two copies of David's history. Let them read it with fascination! he thought to himself.

Later, after signing, they had coffee in a cheap, glitzy restaurant. 'You must trade-in that car, David,' Deirdre suggested. 'Mine will last me years,' she added. 'We should put the rest on term deposit; at least for the meantime. There will be the boys' secondary school education.'

'This is real money, Dee. The thing is, not to fritter it. I was actually thinking a shack in the Blue Mountains.'

'No,' she said decisively. 'No, I think not. They get those terrible bushfires and, well, David, let's not bind ourselves too quickly into hideaways this time.'

He knew what she meant.

'Well, we've got time,' he conceded. His mind was already turning to the Northern Rivers district – Byron Bay, Coff's Harbour, they might even pick up an acreage with rainforest back of Murwillumbah. Or Mullimbimby.

After their last sip of the overpriced bitter brew they went into the street and began to look in the window of the Honda Agency.

'You are not surprised that I should phone? I wanted to make sure, but you know and I know that it is time we made our preparations together. We are both at a stage of preparedness, we are both ready now.'

At the first rasp of the phone David had reached out his hand. He had not time even to whisper 'Hello?' before her voice cornered him. Deirdre, thank goodness, had not stirred from her sleep.

'I confess I was reluctant for a long time. I will not go into that now; when the present you live in is unreal, then the past of your own years makes special and particular claims. If that past, like mine, was turned into wreckage and twisted monuments – or playground toys – and its dream of a restored future turned to imprisonment and persecution then should it be unremarkable that all things, later, revolved from that? I was reborn in that experience. It was a terrible birth but, being accomplished, it became inevitable and real.

'Your wife is sleeping. Let her sleep. She does not understand what brings us together in this project. I call it a project, that is the cool, clear word to make it seem objective, a work of curiosity and research. It is a venture into unknown territory.'

David was about to interrupt, several times, but now he realised that his actual speaking voice, pinched and tightened through the phone with the constraints of his sleeping partner, might disrupt Galina's flow. She might almost not be requiring his response – only some implied complicity.

'That first meeting, I knew it would be you. You were not ready then. Neither was I. I consciously avoided it. Why else do you think I sent you my papers, some of my papers? With my own hands I translated much of it, my daughter is clumsy and spiteful. Do not believe her when she claims authority in these matters. As a translator she is pedestrian, no flair, no inspiration. Even with my English I have a great sensitivity. I always did have. Never mind. That is not the challenge. I wanted you to read my old words so that you would be forced to accept our joint purpose. I wanted to trap you, too, into the amber of my past and my past life, its experiences and suffering. Suffering is excellent currency.'

Deirdre stirred, shifted her weight. David's free arm moved to rest itself on her hip. She re-settled.

'It was a test. You for your part have been making your own test, upon me. Do not think I did not appreciate this, even that first evening. Your innocent talk of rainforest and National Parks and small anecdotes of timber cutters and explorers: neither of us was deceived. I still remember the sudden passion of your tone. You had offered me your secrets.

'I spoke at that time, of my aboriginal friend. That also was a ruse, a testing. We are allowed to make these moves, it is part of the chess game – though to call it that is to suggest competition, one victor, one vanquished. That is not what I mean. But you must be prepared.

'Our second meeting. That was the surprise, your recognition of me. I was astounded and instantly terrified. I have kept my secrecy, my privacy I have kept inviolate. Or at least I have been in control.

'There is no reason why you should not have recognised me in the coffee house; the best disguise, I had thought, is to be without disguise. When you came to my table I knew you and I must have further business together.'

David coughed quietly. There had to be some reassurance that Galina was not talking into a long, hollow tube.

'You are not ill?' She said, with a sudden change of tone.

'No,' he replied hoarsely.

There was a pause. Then she continued.

'That was why I was not surprised when you contacted me again, and then called in. Your wife was hardly an intrusion, just as my daughter added nothing to our negotiation. What was important then was that we began to understand the terms and the degree of our . . . of our exchange.

'It is very strange, but not strange. What we are offering each other is a way forward. We are, both of us, blind and like children in this. I find that charming and, I confess, very frightening. I am accustomed to a very subtle way of response, I read signals before they are present, I attune myself to the twenty layers of possibility in every question, the politics within a smile or a jest.

'You make abominable jokes. That is why I began to trust you from the beginning. I also knew you were not entirely innocent. Those who are haunted can never be.'

Another pause. The luminous numbers of the bedside clock shuffled their card-like characters: 3:26 3:27.

'That it should be such a daemon, such a curious project, surprises me. I was prepared to be amused: that is why my aboriginal friend, a woman of pure charm and experience, seemed such a useful cipher. I did not realise she would be a key to this purpose, not at all. Or at least, not then. If you like, this is all a pretext.'

David moved himself further upright in the bed. He rearranged the blankets to protect Deirdre's back. Their bodies were now separate. He waited for Galina to continue.

'Nothing can be otherwise. We operate in patterns because it is necessary that there should be patterns, even as we are in the very course of changing them or subsuming them or destroying them. Patterns are amoeba. The energy is only evidenced through them, not explicated.

'Am I preaching again? My daughter always accuses me, but then she has no other real comparisons to draw upon. I would not dream of confiding in her the implications of our project. And your wife? No, let her sleep. If she is drawn into this she will be, at the least, resentful; she will see it expressed as rivalry, which is of course even more amusing than my daughter's rage and frustration. I cannot force my daughter to be more intelligent, more sensitive to nuance. You cannot force your wife to move into this dimension we have struck, you yourself hardly understand it and I am not at all sure that I do. I can theorise, but that is not the same.'

Deirdre's face was turned from him. In sleep she seemed to be impossibly remote, inviolable.

'I appreciate also that it can be a matter of degree, and training. Training as in all things expands the quality of humanness and possibility in us all. I think that it is by the discipline of training and persistence that we only approach that quality, what do you call it: God? No, that is such a bourgeois term. Perfectibility I once called it, but I was young and idealistic. Not now. We are, however, protagonists, we are included in the larger energy tug of our project.'

Why him? A slow resentment had been building in David. How dare she barge into his sanctuary to invade him with her booklike talk? He was fully awake now. He was compelled to listen.

'I have been reading your anthropologists on Australian aboriginal lore and society. If we are to explore this thing together, it is necessary I should prepare myself. It was after your second visit that I knew I must do this. The first book I consulted was by one A. P. Elkin. It is called *Aboriginal Men of High Degree*, an interesting and strange book. Strange because it quite unexpectedly suggested to me some necessary links and bridges. Let me quote you the passage I memorised. After you have rejected it, consider it again, as I did:

> *Some of the Tibetan occultists are also believed to practise ritual cannibalism, but in esoteric teaching this is associated with a doctrine of transubstantiation. Some human beings 'have attained such high degree of spiritual perfection that the original material substance of their bodies has been transmuted into a more subtle one which possesses special qualities. A morsel of their transformed flesh, when eaten, will produce a special kind of ecstasy and bestow knowledge and supernatural powers upon the person partaking of it'. So it is with the Aboriginal postulant in some regions. He partakes of the corpse and in mystic way sees the dead or visits the sky, thus deriving power and knowledge.*

'Let me tell you of a certain experience of mine. It is time. I have never discussed it, I have never spoken of it to anyone. It was crucial.'

No, he would have said. But her tone had changed. She, he felt, was now genuinely talking to him, David, not her imagined *other*.

'You have read my notes and diaries, my poems. They represent me as I was, but before the moment of change, before the transformation. It is hard to speak of difficult things, but you have called me into declaring just that.'

In this quick intensification of concentration David was jarred when Deirdre heaved her body again. He moved his leg to thrust some warmth and weight against her buttocks. What if she wakened now?

'Do you believe there are some persons who quite unconsciously become spiritually chosen? I am thinking of a young child, perhaps; or someone young, young enough to have compressed a life experience into something as concentrated as a few months, a year of constant trial and intensity. This has happened in prisons, in concentration camps, in Siberia. While most people become animals, or lose the superficial habits of civilised behaviour, or become apathetic, some, some few special ones, increase in intensity and insight, becoming burning torches of clarity and purity. This is true, from my own experience I tell you this is true; you must not grow impatient with me. I can vouch for it.'

'I believe you,' he whispered. It was almost not himself speaking.

'No, I do not speak of myself, though I did believe myself one chosen, I always believed myself one chosen, and that belief sustained me for very many months. Later, I was sustained so that I not only survived the terrible nine hundred days of Leningrad but I was seen as one of the young leaders. Burning torch, yes, I was called that, and not only once, many times.

'Let me confess to you the source of that burning fuel, that energy. You must not be horrified.

'Some things are a necessary sacrifice, I could not believe in my own later strength and dedication otherwise.'

There was another pause. Again, David was about to appeal: *Why me?* But by now they were both too far in. A few minutes earlier his eyes had been straining to redefine the ikons of his bedroom – quilt pattern, curtain fold, his shirt over the stiff little chair. The prodigious mirror.

'And do not say the word *cannibalism* at me. What I experienced is not contained in the pretext of such a word.'

'What are you saying to me?' He was suddenly jolted.

'Galina?' It was the first time he had ever addressed her directly by that name. In the silence the minute whirr of the bedroom clock was a hovering insect, a dragonfly.

'Natasha was not twelve years old. She lived in the apartment above ours, with her mother and grandmother. Two brothers and her father were volunteered to the front at the very beginning of the invasion. They would have died. Her grandmother died too; she swelled up, and then would not move. Natasha had been devoted to her. After the old lady's death, Natasha began to change. At first she went into convulsions, into screaming and choking. That was when I became closely involved. I was always said to be a calming influence on her. I was bright and energetic, obsessed with order and organisation, but I could also be smiling and quiet, very still. They said it was the calm within the combustion stove, the drive inside the peaceful moon of my face that characterised me as a young woman: they may have been right. I tell you this only to explain.

'Natasha became devoted to me. Because she was a child and

therefore received only the smallest allocation of bread or of broth, as the first autumn and then winter wore on, and rations were reduced and then again reduced, she became one of the cruellest victims. It is curious, I hardly recall her mother. Olga, that was her name. She became one of the huddled ones, forever in queues. Natasha became my mascot and even in the Writers' Union, where I became a member, Natasha was a favourite, for those few months.

'She became one of those strange wise children, who speak with the voice of old wisdom and startle you. In a street full of burning wreckage, constant incendiary bombs, the shock of impact, slouching refugees or soldiers or derelicts or groups of police or the Youth League keeping order, Natasha would speak of time, or of the way the sun seemed only to be a mirror reflecting some greater energy, like the magnifying glass on a sheet of white paper. I remember that. I remember her saying that. Or she would talk about the snow and the bodies under the snow and the way the earth under the bodies and the snow was not a cold place, a grave, but simply a means by which we could learn, if we were still enough, how much we merged into each other, how much the many different and fighting people were expressions of each other. She made me angry, she saddened me. She instructed me; I even began to use her thoughts in my own poems. "But of course," she said, when she read the poems, "that is what I mean."

'Twelve years of age. It was a heightened time, it was a time when so many things were flattened, torn up, not heightened. I tell you this about Natasha because, of course, she died. I am not memorialising her. I am speaking of transubstantiation.'

His fingers were clenched round the receiver. He became aware of their tightness.

'That, at least, is the word that can attempt our range of discourse. She ran, then walked, then seemed almost to glide beside me for those months, the first winter of the siege. My own family were all gone, my lover whom I slept with only once, one time to touch his young body and to embrace his laughter and his sobs and his too quick urgency. Her mother died, I do not know when – it hardly mattered at that time. Natasha moved into my bed. Body warmth was the great urgency. We were both very pure, we were both filled with loneliness and cold. We both had begun this other exchange. Exchange, yes that is the word, though it was hardly exchange at all: nothing said, no embrace more than the cuddle against the cold.

'Cuddle: that is a curious word, I have learned it here.

'We were entirely concerned with the candle, the candle flame. Is that a curious way to put it, a more curious way?

'I am growing sentimental and dissipate the experience. Natasha died. In the last week before she died we talked together; rather, she talked to me. I listened, I listened and looked at her, I wanted to soak up everything and hold it as if it might hold her soul, her being, her energy or her spirit – we are all parts of words, none of them tell us even that little essence of us. She was calm, knowing she would die, she grew very rational, she began planning.

'"First," she said, "in the time that is to come you must not remember me but you must use me." You understand what she said?'

The weight that was Deirdre had become vulnerable. David's free hand was stroking above the bed clothes. To reassure, but not to disturb.

'My shattered window was stuffed with rags to keep the ice out though there was frost on the window sill. The rags were my mother's summer under-garments, I did not believe summer would ever return. Natasha spoke to me out of a shared knowledge and a shared horror, though for her there was never horror, only a purifying flame, a knowledge a certainty. I am told children who have been through death-approximating fevers have evidenced something of the same calm purity. It is not calm. With Natasha it was not calm, it was intense, it was inevitable, it was stoic, aware, positive yet implacable. She could be frightening and I was often frightened by that quality in her, during those last weeks.

'Perhaps I am self-justifying. We all try to defend ourselves. But I must insist on this: Natasha was quite certain and quite ruthless in her instructions, in her knowledge of what had to be done. "I will tell you," she could say.

'"I will tell you," as if from her proximity to ultimates she had not time any more to be childish or playful or timid or tentative. "I will tell you exactly what you must do. You must get the big knife and cut off the parts of my flesh that can be used – my buttocks, they still have some lump and some gristle," she said. "Do not use my brain, though," she asked me. "You do not need it, and somehow it is the one part that I still hold to be private. I am not rational," she said, "but even you, dearest Galya, even you do not have access to that part of me and I reserve it for the earth through which I re-enter the abode of the ancestors and the inheritors. When you eat my other parts, I will know you are sharing their energies with me and I will be glad, and also grateful. You will not consume my brain because you do not really wish to overpower my own soul; but you will have need of whatever other parts of me you can cut up and not vomit."

'Let me tell you this now: I cut the parts and I did not vomit. She was right. It was a sacred eating of the flesh, it was sacramental. You will find this curious, but I did not even think of the Christian ritual of partaking of the flesh of the Christ; nothing like that. And yet the parallels were evident, or have become evident.

'In that long and intense winter the flesh did not spoil. Each day for many weeks I remembered my friend, and I paid homage.'

His hand clutching the receiver: unendurable. The angle of his spine against the pillows: unendurable. The false twist of his knee and leg against Deirdre's skin and the persistent slow breathing: it was all beyond endurance. David was a man of free will. He could simply put the phone down. It was as if Galina understood the end of endurance, too.

'Now we are ready for our shared endeavours.'

He heard her connecting line click off.

XXXVII

David held the receiver in his hand and Deirdre curved her body close to his, as if unconsciously relocating the necessary warmth. Very gently he placed the receiver down. There was an instant ringing. Again he grabbed up the phone with an adrenalin jolt. The STD dot dot dot warned him. Distance. With a sweep of her covers Deirdre wrenched herself from the bed. 'Damn it. Be firm with her, David, you let her bully you day and night. I'm going to sleep in the spare room!'

Before he could exclaim or protest, Deirdre was striding towards the door, still tugging on her dressing gown. The voice at the other end began again. David had no choice; he was too far in. Deirdre was right to be angry, but even that anger seemed, in this context, simply another claim. He murmured his recognition into the receiver. Galina's voice held on to all the world she could not abandon.

'So. We are ready. My initiation was more than forty years ago, but I was not truly ready. I was not able to use this other awareness. You invite me into that. Do you understand?'

'Look, this is madness. What are you asking of me?'

'Not to draw back. We will begin our real journey soon. It will be dawn shortly and your wife, sleeping, she has many questions and worries, some of them serious. Have patience.'

'What you've just told me . . . Look, Galina. I understand. I'm deeply moved by that. But it's nearly 4 a.m. . . .' David could not betray Deirdre's decision. The tousled bed seemed even more vast.

'Have patience. We are curiously united now that the direction becomes clear. It will be interesting to see you again, though I must steel myself against the gaucheries and the awkward physicality of things. I would not have chosen something as entirely remote as jungle, leeches, whiplash vines, spiders. I have a horror of spiders. Yet I tell myself: interesting, interesting.

'If you fail me, I will not forgive you. I will not forgive myself.'

It was as if this disembodied voice were more urgent, more pertinent, than what his own eyes were reading to his almost panicky scrutiny: combs with dead hair clinging, his wallet bulging with credit cards, a Kleenex tissue clenched up and discarded, a wrinkled knot of pantyhose.

'Do you remember that time of our first meeting? You were telling me about your forest and about the tree that so obsessed you, the native red cedar? You said: "In the spring the cedar getters used to get to some hill or cliff or outlook. They would then look over the valleys where the red cedar grew. They would be able to pick out the cedar trees instantly from among the jungle of many species, because at that season they put out red new foliage, moist and fragile and fabulous. It was their great beauty at the this time which betrayed them. They were marked for felling."

'I remembered your little talk. Those trees that survived the massacre, you said, are the more precious because of that. I know, I replied: I know that too.

'The trees and the forest you have created for me are your own, but as we all learn, the need for telling is both a blessing and a curse. Where there has been this witness, and this need, then we must believe there will be someone, sometime, who will receive the message behind the symbol, the impersonal that is what we share in even our most personal discoveries. We will be conspirators, you and I.'

David, though, was thinking of the cold space in the double bed and Deirdre humped in anger and resentment in the other room. He had placed the large sea shell, once given to him by Galina Darovskaya, in that spare room. Deirdre had admired its nautilus shape.

*

Yet one has to admire individual grit and determination among the first settlers. The pit-sawers worked long, tedious hours in the most impossible conditions. Tommy Chilcott, who relieved the tedium of his pit by visiting the Sawyers Arms at Ballina often enough, worked alone on the sawpit at Emigrant Creek where he 'by brute strength levered a cumbersome log onto the platform, attached heavy iron wedges to the lower end of the saw and effectively worked the saw from the top' (Richmond River Historical Society). Tommy Chilcott featured, also, in one of the most notorious fist-fights on the Richmond. Hundreds of pitsawn logs had piled up and were being prepared to be rafted down the river to Ballina. On the eve of the task a large consignment of rum had been brought into the fledgling settlement at Emigrant Creek. As one of the Irish cedarmen Paddy Mace had said, prophetically, that night: 'What! Ten gallons of rum dhrunk, and not a blow struck — 'twill never do!'

At eight o'clock the next morning an argument broke out between a man called Fighting Sandy and Tommy Chilcott over who owned certain of the piled logs. 'If it's not mine I'll burn the lot and nobody'll get it!' Sandy had vowed. Thrusting his axe aggressively, he now set fire to the valuable pile. But Tommy Chilcott took him on. For eight solid hours they battled it out, neither giving an inch. It was not until 4 o'clock in the afternoon that Chilcott finally forced his maddened opponent to the ground. The entire battle was watched in silence by the settlement. Chilcott walked away, then, surrounded by admiring cronies. Fighting Sandy crept off into the scrub. But later that night, clearly rum-sodden, Fighting Sandy suddenly broke into an isolated settler's hut. 'What are you frightened of?' he shouted. But a shot rang out and that was that. Nothing was said around the traps.

We cannot say there was no law. There was the law of strength. There was the law of possession, and of survival. There was the law of taking. It was the very paradigm of European settlement on this continent. It was the law of the battlefield, all but universal.

But there is a deeper element here. It touches some instinctive sense in us all, which asks: In the same place, in the same time, would we not have done the same? Only the shadowy aboriginal tribes, endlessly tolerant and even accommodating seem to have watched these cruel, clumsy sports with something like amazement and incomprehension. How many millennia before we learn what it was they lived by, and for, that made our efforts so irrelevant?

David Cumberland: *The Big Scrub: A History* (ibid)

XXXVIII

In the morning David tried to explain to Deirdre, but all he could manage was that Galina still urgently wanted him to take her into the rainforest so she could see the red cedars in their native stands. Deirdre was not impressed. She had not been able to sleep in the spare bed.

The thought of that rainforest trek aroused her scorn at first, but as she simmered down she expressed her pity and her irony.

'Imagine Galina Darovskaya hiking with you through some slippery path; I can't conceive of her dressed for it, I can't see her in army boots and something waterproof. Imagine leeches, just imagine leeches and scrub ticks on that white skin?'

'What she's been through, leeches would be the least of her worries.'

'And if you wanted to get to any real cedar stands, that would mean really rough work. I remember that time you dragged me up that damned creekbank and I got an awful cut on my cheek from a lawyer cane or wait-awhile or whatever. It didn't heal for weeks.'

'But when we got there . . .'

'Trees. Simply trees, with leaves and bark and the sort of girth and buttresses you'd expect in a rainforest.'

'But that very night you told me you'd had that forest dream . . .'

'You would remember that. Why am I the one always forced to be so pragmatic? One of us has to be.'

It was breakfast and she was busy with toast. She made coffee for them both. She brought in the marmalade. David laughed in a puzzled way, and then shrugged. Everything in the room seemed so normal, so everyday, and Deirdre concealing her passions might be straight from a prime-time commercial. She sat down and gripped her cup.

'But we'll go into that forest, David, won't we? We'll show her something of the real Australia.'

And he knew she would not be excluded.

The boys had been pestering so David agreed to take them out to Middle Head, to the old army fortifications. It was early spring.

They went armed with torches though at the last minute Deirdre pulled back. Some balance had been restored, it was true: without talking they seemed to be talking again. There had been difficulties: David had endured a seemingly endless month of impotence.

His boyish delight with the new car was so ebullient that the kids now sought him out in the mornings. It got him out of himself. They began going to the heated pool at North Sydney for training. The blockage had eased so naturally David now found it hard to understand how and why things had got into that knot, coiled and conquered him. Deirdre's banter: how could that once have seemed threatening, mocking him?

The animal hungers and needs were so natural, so good, so very simple. Now they were restored, they seemed even more valuable. He had begun driving over to her school at lunch time. It was near the Lane Cove National Park, where there were lots of secluded gulleys. The spice of discovery *in flagrante* added to their breathless, hasty couplings. He had begun entering from behind, animal fashion, half-clothed.

Up on the high ridge, with its one hundred and twenty degree view of the harbour David watched the two youngsters tear in and out of the surface fortifications: circular gun emplacements, the magazine chambers, little connecting tunnels with light shining in from both ends. They used their torches to explore inner rooms where they imagined officers sitting to stare at maps and give dramatic orders, as in the TV films. David went along with them. Later, they came to the deeper passageways underground, so meticulously carved into the rock and so immobilised in their forty or hundred year darknesses.

David instructed the boys to turn off their lights. In the blanket suddenly thrown over them the two boys made loud noise. It struck back at them from the remembered corners of walls. David felt Greg grip his arm. He reached out for Marcus, an instinctive gesture of protection. His hand groped outward. A splash and scrape to his right forced his senses into a clearly defined direction. Greg switched on his torch.

'Let's go back, Daddy,' Marcus the younger said, two paces ahead of them already. They huddled close as they scrambled over the small litter of old wires, boards, debris.

'That water's cold,' Marcus said, sliding his Adidas as if to dry the one new-sodden shoe.

The boys raced ahead as soon as they saw the blur of light that defined a corner. There were two rooms to his left as he followed them, David discovered. Two black holes of immense darkness. He poked his head in one – charred remains of a fire, smoke-darkened walls. No one would know who hid in here, nights. Night-lovers, cannibals of darkness, madmen, derelicts.

Out in the fresh air David realised the sweetness of salt wind, wildflower and heath breezes, sparkling water gusts.

He found Greg, but where had Marcus raced off to? David swore to himself. They searched down steps cut into the outside cliff face that led to a small watch-tower, then up again and around through the underbrush to another wrecked gun emplacement. Why did vandals have to scrawl obscenities everywhere?

No other soul around. The abandonment of it all was pervasive. LETS FUCK AND SUCK. It was a place rotted with hidden angers, lusts, disciplines, perversions. In those underground corridors – so well crafted – madnesses had been ritualised: army madness, drills, pickets, rote penalties. Or plans with telephones, moves and counter moves. No, it was a wasp's nest, a termite citadel, the corridors of trapdoor-spiders. Vandals. Before vandals, there were other, earlier forces. Enemies of the first jawbone. Abel and Cain.

'You keep close,' David ordered Greg. He called too loudly. Greg yelled too, 'Marcus! Marcus?'

A small honeyeater whistled and chirruped, dancing ahead of them along twigs and branches of the heath. The Manly hydrofoil sped under them, splitting the blue waters with its white power.

'Marcus! Mark!'

David reached the flat grassy place that was once, clearly, the parade ground. Nobody in sight, the whole area was deserted.

'Marcus!'

So many submerged pits and passageways, so many entrances. David had been scornful when Marcus had said they reminded him of public toilets. Now he wondered: where did Marcus get that knowledge?

'Where the hell is he?'

Greg shrugged, and raced with great energy as if his younger brother had the edge on him. At the far end some painted arrows had been daubed on a flat rock, directing to another waste of scrubby bush. After calling again, and looking round for any last hiding place in this arena, David decided to follow the painted arrows. The old knot in his stomach had returned, a sick tightness. There were more sunken shafts and gun emplacements, deep in the overgrown tangle. More layers, even more tunnels. David pushed down into them all. Anybody could hide here. He grew angry at the thought of allowing these hideouts to be left unguarded, anyone could get in, any freak could be hiding. Drug-crazed teenagers with party bottles and broken glass; covens of pederasts goading each other into brutalised acts – that eight-year-old boy abducted and murdered, last year the papers were full of it, every stinking detail! David broke the branches of overhanging wattles. He increased his pace.

Marcus had always been so trusting with strangers, so eager to talk to people. David remembered that incident when Clyde brazenly exposed himself before the boys. Why hadn't he been more forceful at the time? He burned with protectiveness now. The thought of Clyde the Carter in this place of tunnels and darkness. David could not remember what Clyde had said to Marcus; he had never really noticed. Now, there was only an appalled recollection of those newspaper stories: the attacker is usually someone known and trusted by the young victim.

In one of the underground tunnels there was a torn magazine: a naked pin-up of a girl holding her breasts, with legs wide apart to reveal in meticulous detail the folds and moist privacies of her vagina. David screwed it up, though he knew Greg had seen. In the next tunnel a pair of underpants had been thrown. Quite recently.

He kicked at the rags, viciously.

As they came to the surface of the latest tunnel David began running. The rough track led to yet another outpost, a small lookout right on the cliff edge. It overlooked more tranquil waters, the ferries, white swooping yachts far below. A fresh breeze ruffled the thin leaves of the casuarina and melaleuca scrub. Someone was inside that lookout.

'You wait here,' he ordered Greg. He picked up a large broken branch. The person inside was naked. David had, in the one glance, seen further: the person was masturbating – a glimpse of pale belly and shanks, rhythmic pattern of pump motion. No, even a glimpse revealed it could not be Clyde the Carter.

Visions of some ritual, with small Marcus being initiated by one of the pale elderly grubs he and Deirdre had encountered that last time, filled him with rage, a murderous wrath equal to that which now surrounded the image of the net mender. This was the search; this was the desecration. Not the carnal, but the affront: David's white fury itself burst out of the twisted corridors and tunnels of his mounting anxiety; it would not be stopped. He raised the thick branch and advanced shaking with fury. He whipped the branch across a leafy shrub, stripping it noisily. Again, then again.

Inside the gun emplacement, the thin fourteen-year-old saw him and ducked away, scrambling and laughing into the undergrowth. He had been alone in the small shelter. David whipped the filthy walls till his branch shattered. The sexual graffiti were not obliterated.

David realised the extent of his fury. He would have killed that person. He would have murdered him surely: he was out of control. And if he had indeed found him with Marcus? David could not contemplate the consequences. He was shaking. But it was a kid. What he felt was not righteousness; it was blood anger.

'That boy had nothing on. Did you see him go!' Greg chortled. He had seen nothing ominous. All the way back to the car Greg giggled and wondered. Both the boys had been otters on the island; they loved skinny-dipping.

When they got back, Marcus was waiting impatiently in the car.

'Thought you'd never come,' he complained and was envious when his brother told him about the further tunnels and hideaways. By this stage the big boy was hardly even an afterthought in Greg's imagination. David drove silently back to their house, still coming to terms with his own anger, his murderousness.

*

Dear Galina Darovskaya

I still find myself confused by all this. I think you are wanting something that cannot happen. I woke this morning thinking of your

265

phone call. Let me put it this way: you want me to take you into the rainforest to seek out the cedar. But even if we found you the cedars, they would not be enough. In my own mind I've made them enough, for me they'll do. But not you.

What are you asking for, then? I knew someone once who believed we all worked according to some predetermined code, not a general predestination but what he called a *geis*. A personal set of choices. You would be right if you called it simply *hubris*. But there's some truth. You've made me realise the cedars have served some need in me. Perhaps if I were to go again up there to the rainforests they would be simply trees. I had not really asked them to be more than that before, so the rest was a bonus, I think I took it for granted. No, I sort of expected that others would see them as I saw them and even Deirdre seemed to endorse this, though she didn't talk much about it. Still, she did come with me, once or twice, and we were both silent when we found the trees.

I'll be blunt. I don't want you to see them. I think I would be as much afraid of your silence as of your speaking. I've learned once or twice lately that if you expect too much of a thing you'll always be let down. More than that, it can release a terrible sort of danger, or frustration, or destructiveness. Am I making sense?

It's suddenly occurred to me that you might really be asking me for something else. When we first met I remember you talked about there being no Australian poets. You mentioned only Lawson and Kendall I think. I should have thought at the time, why not send you the work of some of our more recent poets; after all, I taught English for years. So I have just been to my bookshelf to look up the collected poems of Judith Wright, one of our famous modern writers and I came across a poem that hit a nerve. Curiously, it is also about the rainforest area. It is called 'The Precipice'. I will copy out only part of the poem:

> There was no moon but she had brought her torch
> and the dark of the mountain forest opened like flesh
> before her purpose; possessed and intent as any lover
> she fled along the path, the children with her.
>
> She reached the edge at last and no less certain
> she took the children in her arms because she loved them
> and jumped, parting the leaves and the night's curtain.

Now, and for years to come, that path is seared
by the blazing headlock torrent of their direction;
and we must hold our weathercock minds from turning
into its downward gale, towards destruction.

I tell you this: I would never have any intention of jumping. Perhaps
that is my *geis*. I've looked over, though. I've looked right over. Now
I'm content to stay just where I am. I don't think I can help you. Write
to me if you still feel nothing has changed.
    Sincerely
    David Cumberland

*

His letter was returned. NO LONGER AT THIS ADDRESS. He phoned.
He tried to contact the daughter but remembered that the Peters had
sold up.

They talked about dropping in, making a weekend of it, giving the
new car its first real run in. David had never spoken to Deirdre about
Middle Head. When he finally did, she held him in a close embrace and
said nothing. She understood. 'It's okay, it's okay,' she whispered
finally. 'You got home okay, no harm done,' she added, feeling his
need for reassurance, expanding to fill the gap in him.

Nothing had happened, she whispered. In David's mind, everything
had. But the overbalance; that, too, had to be seen in the light of his
sustained sobriety. Life was flatter – but he could live with that. When
things did overbalance – Middle Head – the vertigo was like panic.
How could he ever have seen life as some drunken roller coaster?

One weekend he drove all the way up to Mullimbimby by himself. He
would phone home to explain, stay overnight in some motel.

He nosed around the village. No one could help in his search. Most
of the people he spoke to had not heard of the Russian woman, though
the name Peters rang some bells.

He drove out to the secluded valley where the last stand of cedar had
been left. All the way he thought of her, of how she would have asked
questions, endlessly. How she would have responded. He thought of
her handling the deep timber of Brian's old chiffonier. She would have
looked intensely, and have understood, old connoisseur that she was.

He reached the end of the dirt road. He slammed the door and began
the steep track, a cattle line, down the long side of the gully into the
groin of the two cleared hills. The rainforest edges were already close

below him: pencil-cedars, groves of cabbage-tree palm, acacias and some fine mature specimens of crow's ash, half covered in creamy sweet flower.

She would at this stage have asked to pause. He would understand that. He would name the trees, the species, pointing out the variety and the uniqueness. She would smile at his enthusiasm as she always did.

When he came into the shade the track virtually disappeared, but he knew which direction to take, and the real rainforest had hardly begun. Lawyer cane and wait-awhile vines grew quickly in these moist valleys. He had brought a machete, just in case.

Galina was, as it were, still beside him, her eyes quick with enquiry, testing him out, taking him in. What would she ask of him now? But he did not really have to put it into words: she would be moving at his pace, breathing with the same inhalation of fragrant compost-breath, the undeniable muskiness of self-regenerating cycles. At this point – watch your step! – he would offer his hand. Her twiglike brittleness, that would be a surprise. And her firmness, so tight he must wait for her to let go.

Half a mile into the scrub David realised something had changed. Recent treefall, indicated by a sudden widening in the overhead canopy of leaves, torn branches. Could there have been a storm? A large staghorn fern had thumped onto the leaf-littered ground. At least it wasn't fern robbers, who brazenly sold these things along the highway, with tree orchids and other rainforest plunder, usually from the National Parks.

The first great cedar had been chopped down.

He looked slowly skywards. There had been a moment he had been hoarding in his mind. He would position her so she was in just the right place, then he would point upward, through layer above layer of the outspreading branches, the eye kept close to the soaring vertical of tree trunk. Right up, to the gauzy aureole where the giant tree pushed above the surrounding forest canopy. A few last top lateral branches in full sunlight, then the rediscovered sky, perhaps even sun. He had planned to say nothing at all. He had anticipated the strong and intense grip of her hand.

A huge gash of raw sun. Absence stomped into this space like invading hordes without discipline. Thank God she was not here, how could he have explained to her, had she come? David dropped to his haunches. He paused for several minutes, as if dizzy.

Had he been guilty of *hubris*? Was this some form of answer to pride? Galina Darovskaya was an implant in his mind, nothing more. The rainforest sprawled all around him taking up space as if it were forever inviolate, even in the very midst of this plunder. It defined him, it exceeded his imagination, even here.

Nothing for it. He pushed further in. Four large specimens of the *Toona australis* were still standing, forming a sort of square. There were red paint marks on each of them.

David looked round. He pushed towards the nearest thick tree. He laid his hands upon it. He looked upwards, right along the straight line of the trunk, into the light-dazzled upper foliage. He found himself thumping his fists against the bark. The tears stung his eyes. He allowed them to flow, and the thing in his body to heave and take possession of him, then to move outwards, into the moist shade of his surroundings. He wiped away the evidence with a grimy shirt sleeve. He tried to memorise the grove as it now stood. There was only one person, only one who would understand. He had forbidden her to come. He knew that decision was right, but for the wrong reason.

*

Before breaching the brown envelope which announced on the package that it was the magazine *Soviet Literature*, he flicked through the pile of typescript and the letters, already thumbed-through and growing shabby. He turned up two of the last batch of poems received. He lifted them out of the pile and set his glass down. He screwed the cap on the bottle.

*

THE MEAL

Natasha remembers food.
Sometimes we play the game of describing food
and the preparation of food
the ceremony of the meal.
'What I like best,' Natasha says,
'is the things that can be saved.'
She means the ceremony.
'I think at night, sometimes,
of all the potato skins we threw out.'
We laugh together
and she holds out her hand to me

269

like a little old lady waiting to be led.
'And the wine.'
She turns her wrist over, the veins
now pencil lines, 'You will have wine
remember that.' She calculates everything
these days. For the triumphal meal
she would allocate every segment,
each loving part.

*

Had Galina been a little old lady, waiting to be led? Assuredly not! And yet: it was a trick, this sense of the possible still. David knew her sharp intake of breath, there in the fern and foliage drenched gully, her answering voice. And the tears, their ridiculous authenticity had been a private confession, a sharing. Galina, Galina: they had entered each other's confessions. He turned to the other poem.

*

SONG OF THE ROLLER COASTER SERPENT

It's not enough. We must begin.
Though we grew under the shade of Ygdrassil
the world ash tree, we remained restless,
we sharpened our blades, and dreamed
of sun, of the wheat-tossed plain,
saying: 'It's not enough. We must begin.'

We ate the black snow of burial
we consumed our own city with fire
though we shouted out the names of enemies
and sharpened our angers. We took hostages.
At night their voices bellowed very like our own
imploring: 'It is not enough. We must begin.'

We ended with skeleton hungers
and with all the time in the world.
When we tasted the last flesh we knew
we could never turn back – nor weep again.
Flesh has become but a symbol. Until we recover tears
it is not enough. We must begin.
Though our skeletons become rust, we must begin.

POSTSCRIPT:

Soviet Literature

GALINA DAROVSKAYA: REASSESSMENT OF A MAJOR POET by Vladimir Smolich

It is many years since the work of Galina Darovskaya has been widely available in the Soviet Union – or for that matter, in the English-speaking world. Her poems were not translated into other languages as was the work of her slightly older Leningrad contemporaries, Anna Akhmatova or Olga Berggolts. Her poetic career covered a very short time-span. Apart from student pieces in the late 1930s, she enjoyed a brief, and some thought inflated, reputation during the Siege of 1941–44. Only a few poems were published between 1944 and 1946, when she was publicly accused of Formalism and an attempt to revive Decadent Experimentalism. She died, it is generally accepted, in 1947, near Vladivostok.

Although some of the later complaints against her work are not altogether incorrect, and the superficial impression produced by her works can suggest self-indulgence and self-dramatisation, yet there is a case to be made for her obvious strengths and even universality. These qualities were much admired in those courageous and tragic years. It is time that a reassessment of her positive contribution to Soviet culture be undertaken, small as that may be.

It is obvious even to the most cursory observer that Darovskaya's art belongs to the twentieth century and no other, that such a poet could have emerged only in Soviet Russia after the October Revolution and that her life and creative endeavour are inseparably linked with the history of her native land and the reality of her time. It was not obvious only to the

271

vulgar sociologists of the immediate post-war Soviet period who labelled Darovskaya a Formalist.

Galina Darovskaya could turn wide-ranging contemporary themes and images into a concentrated and impassioned expression of her personal emotions. In her best works (and we must admit that there were numerous failures) this deep and genuine humanism erases the self-absorbed narcissism of her art. The crux of the matter is not modernness as such, but what the poet extracts from it and how she lends it an undying significance.

The true poet acquires immortality and produces a lasting impact on the minds of future generations by absorbing and condensing, as it were, the loftiest, the most significant thoughts, feelings and spiritual searchings of her time, its truly progressive and creative ideas, and by an ability to discern and express apparently inexpressible nuances in the most moral and physical make-up of their contemporaries, their gestures and movements, the revealing individuality as well as the universality of their thoughts and emotions. All this can obviously be accomplished by realist art only, an art that does not simply mimic the practices of the past, though it must of necessity draw on the accumulated experience of the past.

We can forget the early poems. Their brittle, even playful wit and tenderness, seemed to acquire a much greater emotional portent at the time. In the siege years some of them became almost universal currency, like old folk songs. It is easy to see why their blend of simple, direct speech and haunting lyrical cadence so appealed. But their moment has passed. Not so the later poems, or at least those ones worthy of our mature assessment.

The later poems were indeed celebrated in their time and their place. Leningrad has produced many great and famous creative spirits. There is in Leningrad, however, also a tendency to inwardness and self-obsession. In the immediate post-war years Galina Darovskaya encouraged this interpretation of her oeuvre almost wilfully. There were some attempts at epic poems. They were not successful. The nearest to achievement (and it has moments of great beauty and feeling) was the Alexander Nevsky cycle. It falls far short of the wartime sequences on 'Hunger' and 'The Long Winter'. These have undeservedly fallen into neglect.

If we are to understand the courage that led to survival and eventual victory, the spirit of Soviet heroism on a grand and terrible scale, it is salutary that we should recognise it, too, in this frail girl (she was just twenty-one at the beginning of the Siege), whose personal survival and spirit of aspiration for a future of Revolutionary progress became in those long years a password for the unquenchable human spirit. The few self-pitying poems underline how much more remarkable was her strength and endurance. She herself has said that it was the fraternity of the Young Communist League and her friends who worked with her that enabled her to find within herself the courage and spirit to survive and keep striving. If we forget these aspects of her work, it is because the ambivalent and later notorious 'Roller Coaster' sequence of poems became the subject of much publicity and scandal. It is now time we stood back to examine them more objectively, and in doing so, to examine the flawed achievement which I believe to be still undimmed in the best poems of Galina Darovskaya.

Let us look at her first, major poem, written at the time of the sustained isolation and bombing of Leningrad. Its initial popularity, as I say, was enormous. In 1946 it became the basis of the first sustained attack on her work, largely because it was affirmed that the poem dwelt too indulgently on the perfection of both the future and the past but with almost derisory support of the present – the 'present' being at that time the much troubled industrial areas of Leningrad. It was seen as a criticism of lack of forward planning against the unexpected German invasion. I think we can take for granted the political sensitivities of the post war years. Later history has revealed Stalin's unjustified belief that Hitler would continue to honour the Nazi–Soviet Pact of August 1939. This poem (and this poet) were unfortunate victims in a larger crisis of conscience. Here is the poem. With the passing of years, its affirmation of a truly realist awareness of the time reflects the artist's progressive and active world outlook, a faithful echo of human values in the true sense of the word.

*

POEM TO LENINGRAD

I sing of the great city of industry
not the city of Pushkin and Tschaikovsky;
I sing of the five hundred workers' factories
not the five hundred cold palaces;
I sing of the many thousand workers marching home –
not all the art works in the Hermitage Museum.
I sing of the city of the Revolution
I sing of engineering, metal, iron
and the Kirov Factory, that model of all
co-operatives social and industrial.
I sing of the Baltic Shipyards, of each new ship
– I sing with pride of Soviet leadership.

I sing of early morning workers on shift
and late night shift workers – their boots lift
across cobbles like the beat a drummer welcomes you with.
I sing of workers in trams with their white breath.
I sing of people whose work leads to the future.
The past will be changed, it will be changed forever.

I sing of the future and our great ideals.
The future's children will hear us, but their wills
will turn ever onward in their turn.
They will call us 'primitive', they may even spurn
our factories as fit for museums.
They will be filled with their own advanced dreams.
They will see our art works, our music, our poems.
They will nod, then, they will hear our intention.
'They did have soul, too, in the first days of the Revolution'.

I sing of the factories and of strong working men.
The future will know – it will remember our gain.
I do not sing of our treasures, our jewels, our Palaces.
My song adds factory dust, and the sweat of workers.

*

It was after the charges of Formalism in this poem that the 'Roller Coaster' verses were suddenly rocketed into the limelight. Their existence until then was scarcely known, except perhaps to a few friends, who tended to see them as an aberration, at best as a safety valve for private thoughts and insecurities during a time of sustained fear, privation and terror. After the siege was ended she had been urged to destroy them. Curiously, Galina Darovskaya chose to do the opposite. She read them aloud on every possible occasion. It was seen as an act of defiance against the authorities, and can scarcely have assisted her case.

The notoriety has long since faded. I believe it is time these poems in particular were re-examined. They are uneven and sometimes turgid and defeatist; yet they contain a basic image that is sustained and persists in the end. Indeed, given the course of history, the twisted wreckage of the playground roller coaster, named at the time *Amerikanskye Gory*, has an almost prophetic quality – it becomes not only the childhood past of many Leningraders, but a symbol of a 1930s' dream of America joining in a Soviet future, a dream already being twisted by the progress of the war. The roller coaster, in these poems, becomes a sea monster, a vengeful ancestor spirit, a crippled heroic Laocoon, a spirit of something unquenchable in the Russian spirit as well as the more obvious images of pain and destruction and defeat. It is in the very range of these associations that the 'Roller Coaster' poems, though confused, retain their power and their haunting resonance. They are twisted and personal; but they are also uniquely expressive. In their brevity and emotional force they should be seen, in my view, as a poignant testimony to a tragic and heroic era. In translating them into English I am aware that their lyric melodiousness must be lost. It was said early on of Galina Darovskaya that the lyric quality of her poetry was akin to the gayest laughter, but that in listening to the rhyme and playful metre you did not know whether to smile, or to weep. The 'Roller Coaster' poems retain the sound of laughter, but sometimes it mocks, sometimes it weeps openly. Sometimes it calls to us from the very chill of those terrible winters.

*

THE ROLLER COASTER AS A SEA SERPENT

All these childhood years, these years
of growing up and laughing always
on the roller coaster, close to tears.
Up and down, so many ways –
It gripped us tightly all those days.
I remember all those years:
the changes, dreams and new ideals
as sharp and real as metal shears
or sunlight on the coaster's wheels
that heard our laughter and our squeals.

The roller coaster was our friend,
safe as the circus elephant
something we laughed at; we'd pretend
at night we heard her wheezy pant
along our street, that elephant.

Tonight I wake and it is dark.
I hear the roller coaster creak
and now it sounds as though awake
with noises from beneath the lake.
Insect, snake, or serpent: Look!
Someone has killed this childhood game,
the roller coaster's not the same,
I hear it wheeze, it feels its bones;
night turns to ocean, oceans to dreams.
The monster hears our cries and groans
and then remembers long dead gleams

of children playing, sliding, glad
on the roller coaster that they had.
It comes at night and calls our names.
We spent, we spent: it was a gift
or so we thought, but now it claims
each child; not one is left.

*

If, in conclusion we can add the spark of Galina Darovskaya's oeuvre to the great legacy of Soviet poetry, we should do so with a final caution: there was an undoubted element of self-destructive self-indulgence that flawed her work and her final vision. Perhaps, in the end, she serves as a warning to us all, of how, in the soul of our people, we can also be seduced by the narcissistic indulgences that have characterised the so-called 'modernism' (and the even more sterile 'post-modernism') of the West. All the more wonder, then, that out of this flawed vessel the pure flame of true universality so poignantly flutters and shines. Had she lived, one shudders to imagine what wallowings of false martyrdom and indulgence she may have reverted to, the lyric voice turned strident and the humanity curled in upon itself.

Out of the horrors of the siege came the pure gold of her best poetry. We can afford, now, to be appreciative and generous. Let Galina Darovskaya take her place among the poets of Leningrad.